Leon A. Wortman

To Catch a Shadow

A Wartime Tale of Espionage and Intrigue from Africa to North Russia

By

Leon A. Wortman

ISBN: 0-7596-7801-4

Library of Congress Control Number: 2002091494

This book is printed on acid free paper.

Printed in the United States of America
Bloomington, IN

1stBooks - rev. 04/04/02

Introduction

by

Alan T. Wortman

Human memory is a mixture of experience, fantasy, repression, hopes and dreams. We recall and talk about our good experiences—and try to forget the bad.

My father never liked to talk about his life before he met my mother. He did not like to talk about World War II. We knew he had gone overseas with the U.S. Merchant Marine. We knew he had worked with the O.S.S., the Office of Strategic Services that preceded the C.I.A., the Central Intelligence Agency. In what capacity? We did not know much more.

Dad rarely talked about his youth in Brooklyn in the 1920s and '30s. His parents were Ukrainian immigrants. His father died when Dad was barely out of diapers. His mother worked as a seamstress in a sweat-shop while raising her four children. Other than the poverty, we knew little about Dad's childhood. Despite these difficult introductions to life, Dad never exhibited any self-pity. He could be tough with those who opposed him. But, he claimed, "I'm probably the only man who cries real tears while watching a low-budget western movie."

In his early 60s, Dad operated his own, successful, management consultancy. To help one of his favorite clients, he personally acted as CEO of a Silicon Valley electronics firm fighting a hostile takeover. He worked hard, late into the evening, every night. We didn't usually see much of him until the weekend.

One afternoon the front door opened and I saw my father leaning against the doorway. His face was filled with anxiety and pain. He could barely walk. His speech was slurred. He was very groggy and disoriented. Mom and I helped him into the house and called the doctor. He had suffered a stroke during a client's staff meeting, made his way out of the building and driven himself home. In one heart-beat, Dad made the irreversible change from unstoppable corporate tiger to mortal human being.

Skilled doctors, medication, expert physical therapy, Dad's strong will and powerful instinct for survival, plus Mom's strict dietary discipline and an exceptionally rigorous regimen of learning to relax—all these things enabled Dad to completely recover his strength in a few months. The stroke had left no apparent damage. Nonetheless, it became clear Dad would never be the same.

Dad started to talk. He didn't just talk about mortality, fate, family values and other things people typically prattle about after a serious accident or illness. He recited from memory folk sayings, stories and poems in English, Yiddish, Russian, Ukrainian, French and Spanish. We even heard a few words in Italian, Arabic and German. He told stories we'd never heard before about his childhood—and about World War II. The stroke had unlocked many of Dad's hidden memories. Or, perhaps, reflecting on his life and the meaning of his life, the incident had released the flow.

We learned his impecunious childhood had been rich in culture. His mother took in boarders to help make ends meet. Her "guest list" of friends was long. It included legal and illegal immigrants, government agents, law officers, gangsters, artists, linguists, musicians, scientists, drinkers, prostitutes, drug addicts, successful businessmen and the destitute. Grandma's house was neutral ground, "safe territory." The good guys and the bad guys all respected the inviolability of her home.

Grandma spoke at least a half-dozen languages fluently, as did many of the people who gathered around her. Dad, too, had become multilingual. She and her international house guests taught my father a love of languages and encouraged his natural flair for accents and mimicry.

Dad went on to study languages in college. He augmented his semi-native understanding of European languages by learning to speak French like a Parisian, Spanish like a Castilian and Latin like a priest. People would often ask if he was French, Spanish, Russian, Polish, British, or an Italian Catholic. His natural accent became a mixture of these early influences. Although he was born and educated in Brooklyn, New York, it is not uncommon for people to ask him what country he came from.

He had another passion: radio. Radio was high technology in the 1930s. Television, jets and rockets were science fiction. Radio was so new there were less than 3,000 people in the whole country licensed to work as engineers in commercial radio stations. At the age of 17, Dad became one of those people. At 20, one of the country's biggest and most powerful commercial radio stations, WHN, hired him as a studio and transmitter-engineer. Then, Pearl Harbor. Everyone's priorities changed. Dad was and still is fiercely patriotic. He took military leave from his job.

His World War II stories are far more interesting than any of the other stories he told. Amazing! Enthralling! During Operation Torch, the invasion of North Africa, a U.S. Navy Destroyer put him on the beach at Casablanca, French Morocco, where he posed as a Belgian, although he had never been to Belgium. In Casablanca he fought a shoot-out with a notorious Nazi agent. Overtly, during part of the war, he served as a civilian Chief Radio Officer on a U.S. Merchant Marine freighter carrying supplies and munitions to North Russia. Dad was actually an undercover O.S.S. agent, a spy—a word he very much dislikes. He sailed aboard a crippled freighter chased by U-boats and the Luftwaffe in the Arctic Sea north of Russia.

He saw men die and he saw men survive. He wintered in the ice of the Russian Arctic. Betrayed by a double agent, Russian intelligence officers arrested and tried him in a military court in Archangel, North Russia. And he did all this by the time he was twenty-three!

As Dad recovered from the stroke, we heard more anecdotes about his youth. Each time he retold a story it became more detailed. Dad remembered things he had forgotten; events, places, faces, beaches and battles. In time, he became less reluctant or unwilling to talk about his amazing, always heroic adventures.

Although Dad would sometimes tell parts of his stories to a few close family members and friends, he still wasn't ready to tell them to the world. After all, World War II happened a long time ago.

Two presidents of the Federation of Russian States, Mikhail Gorbachev in 1992 and Boris Yeltsin in 1993, awarded my father medals for his contributions to their efforts in defeating the Nazis during the "Great Patriotic War." Newspapers, radio and TV stations photographed and interviewed Dad. Now, he felt ready to tell others about his adventures. Mom, my brother and I encouraged Dad to write this book.

There are some gaps in the memories he repressed for decades. Now, more than 55 years since the end of World War II, some of the identities are forgotten. Governments and places changed names. Military records have been lost or destroyed. Covert intelligence records are permanently sealed—or "can't be found." Many of those who might confirm or deny these events have passed away. Some, or family members may continue to be active in intelligence agencies and, therefore, Dad prefers to allow them to remain nameless. In some cases, he identifies them through pseudonyms. He feels strongly they and their descendants have the absolute right to guard or reveal their own families' secrets.

Who cares if there is a crate of dusty old papers in a Pentagon or CIA vault to confirm any of Dad's stories? Who cares if we do not find one or a thousand aging veterans willing and able to testify to the validity of the events? You will discover this book contains some of the most exciting real-life war-time espionage and adventure stories you will ever read.

And that is what really matters.

Acknowledgment

I've tried to forget those unreal times when both World War II and I were young. However, my experiences as a "shadow catcher," a nicer word than "spy" required a more deliberate effort to forget than one might imagine. The mere struggle of trying seemed only to strengthen those memories.

When the war ended President Harry S. Truman dissolved the O.S.S. and created the C.I.A. I don't think he realized the core people of his new C.I.A. were former members and agents of the O.S.S. I was asked to "come back in."

Most, if not all, of the people with whom I have worked have probably gone to O.S.S. heaven. Or, for personal and professional reasons, they don't want to be acknowledged. I respect their needs and their families' rights to privacy. Therefore, I've given fictitious names to many of the real people who appear in my story. In the interest of security I have taken some liberties with places and events.

Reviving the memories of my years as a shadow catcher hasn't been easy. On the other hand, some of the memories are happy ones. It wasn't all bad.

I acknowledge with pleasure the most recent and important support of several people whose affection, constant friendship and encouragement led to the completion of this book. These include: Dorothy, my wife and best friend and Alan and Chris, our two sons.

I also acknowledge the fact, during the war, I couldn't unerringly tell the difference between friends and foes. By the same token, my opponents couldn't always tell whether I was a friend or an enemy.

Yes, shadow catching was and I suppose still is a fascinating game. The stakes are the highest possible. You either win or lose. But you can't do both. You can win many times, but you only lose once. I salute those who lost and am grateful to be among the winners.

Leon A. Wortman
Los Altos, California

Prologue

Alone…very much alone. Just as I had insisted. But on a deserted beach in French Morocco, a mile north of Casablanca? I had not insisted on that.

Too late to turn back. The drop-off ship has already pulled away, silently vanished in the darkness of the Atlantic night. My heart pounds. My breathing is shallow but quiet.

I take a quick look around for signs of life and race across the beach to the relative safety of the sand dunes where I can sit, tame my pulse and regroup my thoughts. I lean back and press as tightly as I can against the base of the dune to make the smallest possible silhouette. Carefully studying the area around me, I hold my breath and concentrate—listening for people-type sounds.

Only the rhythmic break of the surf and the thump of my heart come through.

I begin to wonder what a guy from Brooklyn is doing way out here, all alone on the west coast of Africa. What's more, my Chief hasn't told me specifically how to get *out* of here...*if I complete my task.* Maybe he doesn't expect me to make it back from this assignment. Possibly, he would prefer me to disappear...forever.

I have devoted many hours to training for survival against other men. They tell me my skills with knives and handguns are extraordinary. I have been taught to kill. However, purposefully, this time, I carry no weapons of any kind.

I wear a beat up, dirty, ill fitting, green, pinstriped civilian suit and a soiled, very tired Tyrolean hat with the brim turned down. My clothes have no labels. I have no papers, no identification cards of any kind. And I am cold!

I have almost forgotten my real name; my first or last name. No one has called me by my "real" name in months. Instead of Leon Wortman, I became *Jiraud Brevier.* For security, my name had to be changed again. Now I am *Dejacques; Léon Dejacques.* For this mission, my appearance has been slightly modified. I have grown one of those thin mustaches and a short closely-cropped goatee considered quite dashing and gallant by young French men and women.

Young? Me? Yes, 21. French? No. My Russian-American mother introduced me to the world in a hospital in Brooklyn. Most of my young summers had been spent on an isolated farm high up in the Catskill Mountains, operated by a trio of émigré Russian-Cossack soldiers. The only beaches I have known are Brighton Beach, Coney Island and Far Rockaway in south Brooklyn, and the cold mountain streams of upstate New York.

What am I doing on this remote waterfront in the middle of a cold night disguised as a Frenchman? Why am I here?

For more than 50 years I have kept details of the story to myself. Now, for some reason I feel an urgent need to tell you about the series of bizarre circumstances that have brightened, challenged and added unexpected excitement to my life...even though they often threatened and endangered my survival.

You see, my friend, for many years I had been a key player in a secretive, deadly game. I was referred to as a *Shadow Catcher*.

And this is how it all began.

Chapter One

I'd completely lost track of time.

At 7:30 a.m., Frank called me down from the hut at the top of the City's Fire-Training Building. I was completely confounded to discover I had been in that five-by-ten brick shack for two days and nights. My task of setting up the special two-way radio equipment for the fire department's trials of a new, highly advanced communications system was proceding perfectly. After just one more work session my solo concentration could be relaxed and field tests initiated.

Frank Borsody, my chief and supervisor of New York City's Fire Department Communications was delighted with my oral report of the system's status. He offered to drive me home to Brooklyn in his fire-red station wagon but I was too exhausted for the long drive. Frank decided to take me to the Fire Department Dispatch building on the 79th Street Transverse Road in Central Park where I can get a hot meal and a cot. With siren screaming, we headed down Fifth Avenue and onto the Transverse Road.

When I spotted the ancient, castle-like turrets of the edifice, I heaved a deep sigh and physically slumped down on the station-wagon's seat. Frank half carried, half-dragged me into the building. I am told he and the Chief Dispatcher fed me some hot soup and put me to bed. I was happily unconscious, deeply, soundly, dreamlessly asleep.

"Hey Leon! Leon! Wake up!" The Chief Dispatcher shakes me vigorously, shouting, "Time to get up! Up, Leon!"

Groggy, disoriented and alarmed, I leap to my feet. Had I missed or somehow slept through important fire alarms, emergency calls, fireboats, rescues, catastrophes? The room quickly stopped spinning as I came to and my senses returned. "Wha...what happened, Chief.?"

"Pearl Harbor's been bombed! The Japs have attacked us!"

Confused, I asked the same question millions of Americans must be asking this Sunday morning, December 7, 1941. "What's Pearl Harbor?"

The Chief's quick lesson in Pacific geography clears this for me. I immediately head for my emergency post at the controls of the Fire Department's radio station, WNYF. This provides reliable two-way communications with all the department's units as well as the specially-equipped automobile of that famous fire buff, Mayor Fiorello H. LaGuardia. The equipment allows our high-energy Mayor to keep in touch with his office and all fire department activities. He especially thrills at the sight and sounds of the fireboats when they are called into action on the Hudson River. Nothing can keep him away from this activity.

The next days are filled with fiery action, not just inside the department, but throughout the world. Congress declares war on Japan and Germany. The pace of the Selective Service, the draft, accelerates. Posters with their exciting patriotic messages and slogans appear everywhere. Their illustrations seem to point directly at me.

I had just received a letter from a colonel in the Signal Corps offering an immediate commission as a captain. Tempting. But, I do not find the offer at all appealing. I don't like the idea of a regimented lifestyle. I have been a loner all of my 21 years. I'm not ready to become one of the crowd. Not just yet. No. I decide to hold off a while until I have a better idea of how I can best serve my country. Decision time has come. A telephone call to the colonel abruptly and rudely (on his part) ends the Army's interest in me.

A short time later, over the protests of several friendly and well-meaning officials of the fire department, I join the technical staff of commercial radio station WHN. The station's publicity bills itself as "America's most powerful independent radio station." I like that. (Four years previously, in a feverish burst of activity, I had voluntarily taken and passed all the Federal Communications Commission's examinations and earned licenses as an Amateur Radio Operator, Commercial Radio-Telegraph, and Radio-Telephone Operator.)

I do lack hands-on experience in broadcast communications and WHN has just installed a state-of-the-art transmitter. Becoming a member of that station's elite technical staff is an exceptionally attractive opportunity to enhance my sophistication and my status in the communications industry.

I am especially delighted with my companion, Bill Brady, with whom I regularly stand transmitter watches, monitoring the equipment-filled building, studying and memorizing the complex diagrams and learning to instantly identify problems and correct them. Bill and I make a fine team. He is ten years my senior and I learn much from him. We separate the transmitter's elements into manageable entities and agree on our individual responsibilities. With Bill as my tutor and my own self-assurance in a technical environment, we never panic in any of the frequent emergencies and quickly develop an enviable reputation for competence. I confess I am disappointed when Bill takes a military furlough to join the tehnical staff of the U.S. State Department. However, shortly after Bill leaves, I receive a telephone call from him.

"Hey, Leon. This is a very interesting activity I've gotten involved with." He goes on to describe some of the new things he is learning, such as radio-photo transmission and reception. And, "I'm getting ready to begin a series of fascinating tests with military bases in Alaska and Latin America."

Bill knew he had me hooked. He paused. "I'm sure you'd like it a lot, Leon."

"Are you recruiting me, Bill?"

He ignores my question. "We need more guys like you. If you are interested, I can put your name in the hat...at the top of the pile."

"Well, Bill, I am interested but...the way the government moves...I'll probably be drafted before they can investigate me and make an offer."

Bill's tone becomes more serious. "How interested are you?"

"Very...but..."

"How soon can you meet me at the Metropole Café in Manhattan?"

"In an hour. Okay? But, Bill, how long will the investigation take?"

"Not to worry, Leon. It's been completed. See you in an hour at the Metropole."

The last bit, "It's been completed," seems odd. However, I do not pursue the point. Bill knows this is the kind of challenge I cannot walk away from. Two weeks after my request for military leave is approved, I report for work, not in Washington, D.C., but in a sparsely furnished office at 57th Street and Broadway in Manhattan. According to my "employment papers," I am classified as *Field Represenitive, Outpost Division, U.S. State Department.*

"Bill. Where's the equipment? The workbench?"

"Just sit tight. You'll see it soon enough."

The whole thing seems very odd, irregular and unfamiliar to me. Bill recognizes my need to know and assures me this is a legitimate "military leave." In fact a new draft card is hand-delivered to me in a few days. It reclassifies me from 1A, fit for military duty, to 3B, a civilian in an essential occupation. Clearly, somebody has good connections with the authorities, with the Draft Board anyway.

The "office" has no identification on the door. Only a number. Inside are several tiny, closet-size private and windowless rooms. Not a poster nor a picture on the walls. Just a desk and two chairs in each room. My desk has a stack of technical manuals on radio-photo equipment with "CLASSIFIED" stamped on every page. No pencil. No scratch pad. This obviously means *do not attempt to copy or remove any of the data or diagrams.*

The only persons I meet in the office that first day are my friend and recruiter Bill Brady and Joe Humbel, introduced as The Chief. My universe always seems to have a Chief.

The Chief is always referred to as "Chief." Everyone addresses him as "Chief," never as "Joe." He rarely shares a coffee break or socializes with his subordinates. Is he a snob? Or just too busy? He rarely smiles or engages in small talk. If he had a sense of humor, it's been laid to rest. Perhaps only for the duration. He is not tall. In fact he is short, about 5'5". Heavy set. Salt and pepper hair. I estimate he is in his late forties, early fifties. What did he do before the war? He never gives a hint. Obviously, mysteriously, he wants me and all the others to avoid any attempts at developing a personal relationship with him. Okay. If that's the way you want it, Chief.

The Chief is the only one in the office who has a secretary, Mary. She's nicknamed "First Aide." Descriptive of her importance in the organization. Mary appears to be in her thirties. Moderately attractive. A model of competence. She enjoys small talk. It's her way of avoiding questions about the organization: The

Office and The Chief. Mary has an assistant, Barbara. She could have been Mary's twin sister. The Chief never addresses Barbara directly but speaks to her through Mary. Our nickname for Barbara is, naturally: Second Aide.

I didn't know then I would be spending very, very little time in my private, windowless closet—or in The "Office." On the second and third days, I meet a few of the occupants of the other rooms-without-windows. All of them are older than I and equally new to their jobs, whatever the "jobs" really are. All have been recruited by a friend or former work associate. Each of us had been thoroughly investigated and screened by the FBI—and who knows what other organizations—before the job offer had been made. Each of us has been advised to exchange first names only. Although things were moving slowly, they were becoming more and more interesting...to say the least.

The fourth day on the job, Joe, The Chief hands me a sealed envelope and a door key. He instructs me to go to an address in Times Square at a very specific time today. After I locate the door the key fits, I should open the envelope. I would get further directions over an intercom. Following my instructions to the letter, I arrive precisely on time, quickly find the door the key fits, enter and lock the door securely behind me. The only furnishings are a desk and a chair. On the desk are a pencil and pad, an intercom and a manual telegraph key.

As instructed, I may now open the envelope. It contains several pages of alphanumeric characters in groups of five, a coded message for somebody. Things happen sequentially, like a well-oiled machine, smoothly, noiselessly, almost spookily.

A no-nonsense voice on the intercom instructs me to "Stand by to start sending the characters at a Morse Code speed of approximately 15 words per minute. Start immediately after the five-second tone you will hear on this intercom. When you have completed sending the groups, add the end-of-message signal: *dit-dit-dit-dah-dit-dah.* Wait for a possible return message that might come through on the intercom."

I complete the transmission and, sure enough, a reply comes back immediately in plain-English Morse Code: "*Get me the hell out of here! Get me the hell out of here!*"

Who is he? Where is he? What is he doing there? No one could or would tell me. Eight years later, through a remarkable set of coincidences, I do meet him and learn the complete story behind the extraordinary Morse-code cry for help.

Chapter Two

Instead of becoming clear, the situation becomes more confusing. After two weeks on the job, I am told I am no longer with the State Department. I am now with OWI, the Office of War Information located in a ramshackle building in very-far away, downtown Manhattan. Bill Brady reassures me. "No, you haven't done anything wrong. We've both been transferred. No. I don't really know what's going on. We'll just have to wait and see what happens."

Once more I have a new Chief. Name's Bill Elliott and all he can say is, "There's a lot of reorganization going on. How do we figure in it? We'll have to just wait it out for a while longer. Hang in there, Leon."

He tells me I have to take a phyiscal exam. "No, your job isn't dependant on this. Just regulations, that's all." We walk down a long arcade with many doors on either side of the narrow passageway. Neither The Chief nor I comment. No questions from me. No explanations from him. At the end of the long corridor is a door. The Chief opens it and motions for me to enter.

We are in a brightly lit, relatively large room; about 40 by 50 feet. Three men in open, white lab-coats are at the far end of the room. The stethoscopes around their necks trademark them as doctors. Their shirt-collar tabs display the caduceus insignia and their military ranks. All second lieutenants. They smile and watch closely as we approach. The thought occurs to me they are actually observing the way I walk—automatically making mental notes about possible physical defects. Well, nobody's perfect.

Bill Elliott makes brief introductions. "Mister Wortman is here for a complete physical. Look him over and give me a copy of your report—physical and mental conditions and—you know the routine."

He turns to me. "These docs will let me know as soon as they finish with you, Leon. He looks at his wrist watch. "About three hours I'd guess. Right, gentlemen?"

The three lieutenants nod agreement. Elliott quickly touches his forefinger to his temple—an abbreviated salute—turns and leaves.

For the next two and a half hours I am stripped, punctured by needles and probed by fingers. After each flurry of activity, the doctors make notes on a large yellow pad and on long white forms. They give me no clues to their observations of my physical condition.

Finally, "You can dress now."

They pull up four chairs to form a group. One of the doctors starts to chat about all sorts of things. This must be the mental test and, probably, this doctor is the psychologist or psychiatrist. They continue to take notes.

An hour later, my three examiners seem to run out of "chat" material. They smile at each other and simultaneously turn to me. More smiles. Impossible for me to tell what all this means. Do they consider me unfit? Insane? Are they humoring me? Laughing at me? They give no hints or statements of *pass* or *fail*, *accept* or *reject*.

One of the doctors goes to a telephone on the wall. Calling for a straight jacket or for the cops to come get me? No, he's calling Elliott, The Chief.

"Yes, sir. All done here. Fine, sir."

The Chief joins us in a couple of minutes. The yellow sheets of notes and the white forms are placed in a large envelope and handed to him. Handshakes and thank-yous are exchanged all around.

"Welcome to our team, Leon. You've some interesting assignments ahead of you." He frowns, drops his voice a register and adds, "To say the least."

I don't attach special significance to his words. I think I have just become a radio-communications something or other. However, The Chief quickly disabuses me of any such notion as he introduces me to the mysterious gallery of doors with no markings. Without a word, we enter that corridor. The Chief opens one of the unmarked doors, steps through and motions.

I follow him into my future.

Chapter Three

The room on the other side of the door is windowless and small—no more than eight feet by ten. A ceiling-mounted fixture provides some lighting. The pale green walls are bare; no pictures, not even a calendar. The only furnishings are a diminutive wooden desk, three chairs, a telephone and a chalkboard. *Is this a holding pen or is it really an office?*

The Chief supplies the answer. "Use this as a temporary office until we find more suitable quarters for you." He hands me a small packet. "Read the information in this envelope. It includes a reservation at a small, nearby hotel."

He notices my puzzled expression at the mention of the "small, nearby hotel."

"You'll be working all sorts of crazy hours. We all do in this office. In fact the Government practically owns this particular hotel...so you don't have to worry about the rate or the charges. Rooms are clean. Food's pretty good in the dining room. I know you'll like it."

In view of the fact no option is offered, I am sure I will like it.

I feel edgy. "Tell me Chief, when do I get a specific assignment?"

"Eager to get started? That's good. Good." An evasive response.

I shrug my shoulders and smile. "You did say the war effort needs me. Well, here I am. Let's both make the best of it, Chief."

"Right. First thing you have to do is go to the basement of this building with this envelope. It's an equipment requisition. Because it is convenient as well as useful to your work, you will be credentialed and outfitted as a captain in the U.S. Signal Corps. Should prevent problems with the local police. Also, we maintain a small, reasonably complete quartermaster's warehouse down in the basement. Introduce yourself to Sergeant Apple. Show him the requisition and he'll fit you as though you were at Brooks Brothers. Then check in at the hotel listed inside the envelope. They're expecting you. If you need any personal supplies, razor, toothbrush and other such stuff, be sure to get them from the sergeant before you leave."

The Chief wears a broad smile as he firmly shakes my hand. "No, you are not in the Army. The uniform and rank will keep you out of trouble with the New York Police. Better get used to being called 'captain.' We're pretty big on titles around here. Call me 'colonel.' When we get to know each other better, we'll switch to first names...unless the general is visiting us. Get me? Go 'head. Get fitted. Come back here in exactly one week for your IDs and assignment. Oh, and bring some of your civilian clothing, suits, shirts and so on."

"I'm with you, Chief." Then, as I've seen it done in the movies, I salute and head for the basement.

The quartermaster's warehouse bears no resemblance to Brooks Brothers, but it seems to be well-equipped to serve its clientele—men and women of the khaki cloth. Sergeant Apple knows his business. In short order he takes my measurements and expertly outfits me with two uniforms, shirts, ties, trousers, hat, collar and lapel bars, brown shoes, socks, handkerchiefs and, to my surprise, a dark-brown leather travel-suitcase.

"How come a suitcase? No duffel bag?"

He points to the paper. "Right here, sir. It says on the req: 'leather suitcase'."

I admire myself in the full-length mirror. "You do good work, Sergeant. Just like made-to-order. Custom fit."

"Thank you, sir. I was a men's tailor before I enlisted, sir. Please call me 'Apple.' Everyone does, sir." Tenderly folding the garments, he packs my new wardrobe, including my now-obsolete civilian clothes and a fresh set of toiletries into the suitcase, carefully snaps it shut, hands it to me and salutes. Out of lack of experience, I forget to return the salute until I notice Apple is standing at attention, his eyes looking up at the ceiling. I return his salute and extend my hand to shake his. He's all smiles.

I leave Apple's "haberdashery" and make for the hotel. Didn't Elliott say "nearby?" The address is in the Bowery Section of Manhattan. Too close for a cab ride, too far to walk in the refrigerated air of the New York winter. In the interest of time, I opt for a cab. Certainly, by the time I check in and unpack at the hotel I will be ready to check out its cuisine.

Dinner turns out to be okay. Breakfast is even better. Huge, hot portions of everything. The waiters are in military uniform. Come to think of it, everybody here wears khaki or olive drab. Clearly, the U.S. Army is the proprietor as well as the occupant.

Bill Elliott is in a colonel's uniform and having breakfast alone at a corner table. He waves at me to join him. "I see Apple did his usual outstanding job of customizing a uniform for you."

"Yes, sir. He seems to know what he's doing."

The Chief gulps some coffee, takes a deep breath and looks directly at me. "Bet you have lots of questions. Let's finish our coffee and get to The Office. I'll do my best to bring you up to speed." As seems to be his habit when he is being serious, he frowns, leans close to my face, looks me straight in the eye, drops his voice a register and slowly adds, "I'll tell you as much as I am allowed to."

Unlike the hot and muggy summer weather, New York City's winter sun and relatively low humidity can make the air feel thin,. The warm sidewalks, once fabled to be paved with gold, are heated by a system of underground steam pipes that makes the air at eye-level seem to shimmer as last night's dampness escapes upward from the pavement. Today's climate is invigorating, brisk.

Automatically, left-right left-right, we stride in unison. Occasionally, there are attempts at conversation. The Chief seems distracted by private thoughts.

At this moment I have few thoughts of any value. I respect the need for temporary withdrawal. If he speaks, I will respond. I glance at him and try to visualize the man in action.

The Chief's bearing is precise, military, straight posture but not stiff. As he walks, he swings his arms vigorously—more British or European than American. He looks directly ahead as we stride at a brisk pace.

His hair is light brown. Though I can't see them now, I recall his eyes are grayish. His skin-tone has the color and cragginess of a man who must have spent large amounts of time outdoors, either at sea or in the mountains where the sun is strong. He is an inch or two taller than I am—perhaps six feet one or two. A robust physique matches the ruggedly masculine complexion. I doubt he grew up as a city boy. This handsome man certainly is one to be imitated.

We make a winning impression as we march in spirited unison, eyes straight ahead. Heads turn. Men smile and women lift their eyes. *Oh, what a spectacle we must be. Here's a good place for a fanfare of trumpets. Presenting Colonel Bill and Captain Leon!*

We enter the small building where our offices are located. The elevator operator, in civilian clothing, apparently knows or recognizes the colonel. She stops the elevator at the correct floor. The colonel automatically salutes her as we exit the elevator. I salute, too. Why not? Without breaking his fast pace, the colonel enters The Office, returns the salutes of the privates, sergeants, lieutenants, captains and majors in the crowded space one must pass through to reach the door to the colonel's sealed-in-opaque-glass private office; the sanctum sanctorum.

I follow closely on his heels and imitate his saluting. My assumption is this is his intention. He hasn't indicated otherwise. After all, I wore civilian cloth until yesterday. I haven't had any basic-training. No one has yet told me how to behave. No doubt, when I am wrong, Colonel Elliott will be the first to tell me so. Okay with me...for the time being. It may take a while for me to completely resign my civlian independence.

Colonel Elliott puts his hat on a hook on the wall. With silent thanks to all the grade-B movies I've seen about the Army, I remove my hat, put it under my left arm and stand at attention. The colonel sits behind his desk, looks up at me and, with no change in facial expression, motions for me to sit.

I impetuously test the environment. "Thank you, Chief. Now, if you'll just point me in the direction of the communications equipment, I'll get out of your way, sir."

"Plenty of time for 'equipment' Leon. We have other priorities for now."

"Fine, sir. But, at the moment I have no perspective on my specific duties. Do I go to a basic training camp to learn how to be a soldier and an officer?"

"In time...in due time, Leon. Right now I have a special, unsupervised task for you."

I don't really know what he's talking about. In the very brief time, a little more than 24 hours, I have been one of The Chief's captains, I have had the feeling his group has been put together for some very special purpose...as yet unspecified as far as I am concerned. This has the aura of melodrama with new things to come and different things to do...all very much to my liking.

"You have my undivided attention, Chief."

"And an open mind I trust, Leon. I have one more document, a memorandum, for you to read. Assuming you accept its conditions, you will officially become a special member of my unique team of uncommon men and women." He hands me the document, a single sheet of paper with printing on one side. "Read it carefully, mister. We mean every word of it."

My name is typed in at the top of the page:

AGREEMENT BETWEEN *Leon A. Wortman* AND THE U.S. Signal Corps

> I, ________________, recognize the assignments given to me during my tour of duty as an employee of the U.S. Army must be treated with the greatest of confidentiality and I agree not to disclose them in part or in whole to any person or persons of any nationality whether or not they are in fact or claim to be members of the U.S. Army or of any other organization, military or civilian, foreign or domestic. I understand any breach of the spirit of this memorandum shall be treated as a willful violation of national security and shall be dealt with accordingly.
>
> The term of this Agreement shall endure for 15 years from the date of termination of service with any other branch of military, government service or agency to which I may be transferred.
>
> I have read and fully understand the contents of this memorandum.
>
> Signature________________Date_______

I start to ask questions. The Chief holds up his hand to stop me.

"No questions. No answers, Leon, until you sign and date this memorandum. Of course you don't have to accept. You don't have to sign. You did volunteer to join us." He anticipates my next question. "What happens if you don't sign? You'll just be drafted and transferred for five...maybe six months of basic training...as a buck private. After that? You will probably be reassigned to this unit.

"Chief. Despite the detailed dossier you have on my background, you haven't known me very long. You don't know what kind of guy I really am."

"And you know even less about me. I...we are not kidding. We mean every word you've read." His face slowly breaks into a friendly smile. "Leon, I think you underestimate me. Do you imagine I would have brought you into this group if I didn't know with reasonable accuracy how you'd react to this memorandum?" He hands me a fountain pen. "Sign in two places, please."

I hesitate for a millisecond, take the pen, sign and date the memorandum. My nerve endings are tingling. The adrenaline is pumping. I am absolutely flooded with excitement and curiosity, waiting for Colonel Elliott's next move.

Colonel Elliott presses a button on the intercom and talks to it. "Madeleine. Come in here, please."

The box talks back with an obviously French accent. "Yes, sir."

The door to The Chief's office opens. I don't turn around to see Madeleine. However, as she gets closer to The Chief's desk and comes within my view, my breathing halts and I silently gasp for air. This woman, Madeleine, has to be one of the most gorgeous brunettes I have ever seen. She is petite...in height...but the rest of her is...I am having trouble finding the right words...large, voluptuous, *delicieuse, ravissante*...a distracting fantasy of a woman!

"You're staring, Leon. Close your mouth and say hello to Madeleine Brouillard, my secretary."

I stand up awkwardly. My voice croaks a weak "Hi."

Madeleine's face lights up and I think I hear her say, "*Bon jour, capitaine.*"

Colonel Elliott motions for her to pull up a chair and join us. He cannot hide his amusement at my self-conscious reaction to Madeleine. My expertise at nonsense-talk, which is even less than small-talk, has fled. Gone! Pfft! In an instant I have become a shy, bashful, speechless kid. But, really, one doesn't expect to meet people such as Madeleine anywhere in the vicinity of an Army Chief's office. *I need a little more time to adapt to this lifestyle.*

To take my eyes and mind off this awe inspiring creature, I force myself to concentrate on The Office's decor. I am a bit discomfited by its harsh environment. No rug on the floor. A beat-up metal desk and unmatched chairs, probably rejected by the Salvation Army and, out of pity, donated to the U.S. Army. The linoleum on the floor is badly scuffed, stained and indelibly discolored. The walls are bare. No maps, pictures, diplomas or certificates of any kind. The dirty-gray plasterboard is badly in need of a cosmetic paint job. A grotesquely large, black-metal safe, complete with combination lock, stands ominously in the corner to the left of The Chief's desk. Several four-drawer file cabinets with padlocks are along the wall to the right of The Chief's desk...

"Leon. Leon! Hello! LEON! Where the hell did you go? Are you still with us?"

"OOPS! Sorry, sir. I'd just noticed how naked...er...bare your office walls are."

Madeleine brings her hands to her face to hide her amusement.

The Chief taps his right index-finger on the top of the desk. He's annoyed at my attention to such trivia. "We took over this building just a couple of weeks ago and we've been too damned busy to pay attention to such items!"

I feel chastised.

"I did especially want you to meet Madeleine." Pause. "You do wonder why, don't you?"

Of course I "wonder why". But I try to avoid sending any signals. No eye or body movements. I am no expert on such matters, but today's events do not match my expectations of the military. Evidently, the work is not exclusively in signal-corps radio-communications. Maybe Colonel Elliott is going to give me some hints.

The Chief is what I call a "strong" man. I've met some of the best, but he is *the* best. The man is an expert practitioner of the art of mastering others—a brilliant power-player. When he talks, he makes and tightly holds eye-contact. He leans forward and lowers his voice, drops it a register. No doubt this is a thoroughly practiced and deliberate technique. It can establish leverage, dominance over the person to whom he is speaking. He may do this deliberately to intimidate, put subordinates on the defensive. *Bet he doesn't play this kind of game with his general or his peers.*

As though stalling the conversation or collecting his thoughts, The Chief turns slowly, once around, clockwise in his swivel chair. He stops, leans forward, elbows on the desk. His eyes are fixed on me. "Mr. Wortman, I have a special assignment for you."

This really brings me to full attention. "Great, sir! What...?"

He glances in Madeleine's direction. *This could indicate she knows the assignment. I am also aware, while I am watching The Chief, Madeleine is watching me.*

Without signaling any messages, elbows still on the desk, hands clasped tightly together, Colonel Elliott frowns and again holds eye-contact with me. "Leon, as I started to say, I have a special but unofficial assignment for you. Your first one."

"Do you mean my 'first' assignment or my first 'unofficial' assignment?"

He completely ignores my question. "On your own, I want you to find the answer to a simple-sounding...but important...question. Don't...do not underestimate its significance."

"Sir?"

"You must tell me...what is the primary task of this office?"

I resist doing a double-take.

"And I expect you to have the answer within the next 24 hours—or less."

Primary task? I am right. It is not radio communications. "Any suggestions, Chief, leads or clues on how I might get started?"

Madeleine interrupts. "*Bien sûr, Capitaine Léon.* You can begin by having dinner with me tonight."

Still dead serious, Colonel Elliott points a finger directly at me. "Don't get any wrong impressions, captain. For security reasons, Madeleine also stays at our hotel. You'll have dinner together in the dining room. A business dinner. It's up to you to get as much information from her as she will allow you. I warn you, Leon, Madeleine's mind is exceptionally keen. She is very perceptive. A 48-hour time limit is her idea. I think 24-hours are actually enough."

This soldiering business becomes more interesting by the minute. Madeleine suggests we move to her office and discuss details for our date tonight—I mean our "business dinner."

Madeleine rises. I rise. The Chief remains seated.

I salute smartly. He salutes casually.

Madeleine and I turn and leave.

Chapter Four

My head floats several feet above, behind or alongside the rest of my body. My ears feel stuffed with cotton. My throat is dry and my lips are parched as I follow Madeleine to her office. She's, oh, perhaps five-feet-two in low-heel shoes. Her waist is narrow and the roundness of her hips is emphasized by the snug, form-fitting dark brown skirt. I can't see, but I can very well imagine, the front of her tight-fit tan sweater. Walking behind Madeleine is not easy for me.

C'mon Leon. Pull yourself together. You've seen gorgeous women before. Haven't you? You've even dated one or two as sexy looking as Madeleine. Haven't you?

Just as I am about to respond to my soliloquy, Madeleine opens the door of the office next to Colonel Elliott's. With a soft smile and a flirtatious tilt of her head, she whispers, "*Entrez, Capitaine Wortman.*" Her left arm is crossed over her breasts as she holds the door open for me. She quietly closes the door and isolates us from the rest of the U.S. Army and the world. I am ready to die for my country...and Madeleine!

She is seated now on the other side of her desk, leans forward, arms crossed in front of her. "*Quel âge*...?" She breaks off her French and, frowning at me, continues in English. "How old are you, Leon?"

This question wakes me up, makes me realize how silly I must look to her. "*J'ai à peu près vingt et un ans.*" I admit to approximately 21.

Politely, very politely she puts me in my place. "You are still a boy, Leon."

No doubt, Madeleine has read my mind. Her message to me is quite clear. I humbly apologize. "*Je vous en prie...pardon...s'il vous plait, Madeleine. J'en suis gêné...embarrassed.*"

Madeleine jumps up wide eyed with excitement. "Leon. I didn't know you speak French! *Je suis entièrement enchanté! Vraiment, c'est merveilleux*!" Apparently, she is starved for conversation in her native tongue.

When she rises so suddenly from her chair, I can't help but notice her breasts are lusciously full. Not only is she amply endowed, but the jiggle betrays the absence of a brassiere or any other man-made support-structure. However, I must remain calm and in full self-control. Is this the Army? If so, it is one helluvan Army!

Well...I tell you...the next ten or so minutes are devoted to an extraordinarily lively exchange of questions and answers.

"Where did you learn to speak French, Leon?"

"*À l'école supérieur et...*" I explain I studied languages in high school and college and had tutors for many years. Madeleine oohs and aahs. Her eyes dance and her arms wave, gesticulating as native French women do to illustrate their reactions and punctuate sentences.

Now it's my turn. "*Dites moi, Madeleine.* Tell me something of yourself. May I ask how old are you? What part of France are you from? Why are you in the United States? When did you come here?"

She haltingly gives me a brief autobiography: Twenty-eight years old. Born in Paris. Educated at the Sorbonne. Married her boyfriend, Edouard when they were both only 22. He had been conscripted into the French Army...Immediately sent to Maginot. It was supposed to be impregnable. But in 1940...Tears begin to well up. Madeleine exhales a long sigh and changes the subject. In London she learned to speak English. Soon after, she came to the United States as a civilian secretary for Colonel Elliott. "*Je me sens trés seule.* Life has been very lonely for me." The tears roll slowly from her eyes.

Filled with protective compassion, I go to Madeleine, offer my handkerchief and struggle for words to express my feelings of tenderness mixed with sadness.

After several moments of silence to regain her composure, she stands and rewards me with a long, tight hug and soft kisses on both my cheeks. In control again, she draws away from me, moves to her desk, sits down and says with a half-smile, "*C'est la guerre, non?*"

Studying the front of her tight sweater, I shrug. "So they say."

Following The Chief's instructions, we agree to meet for dinner at 1900 hours. We shake hands and I leave her office to return to mine.

On the desk is a folder with no identifying tabs. It holds two manila envelopes. The smaller one contains a handwritten, unsigned note:

You have already used some of your 24 hours. I suggest you try for 12!

Obviously, Colonel Elliott feels no signature is necessary. It appears The Chief is deliberately giving me clues to "*...figure out for yourself...the primary function of this office...simple sounding...but important...*" Although my deadline is 24 hours, he now tells me, "Try for 12!"

The larger envelope has a sealed-flap. I carefully break the seal and withdraw a one-page document. The message is typewritten:

CONFIDENTIAL
TO: SIGCORPS iDIV-NY OFFICERS
FROM: Lt. Col. W. C. Elliott
DATE: January 6, 1942
TIME: 1500
SUBJECT: SPECIAL FIELD-TRAINING PROGRAM

Prepare for deployment and temporary reassignment to a new location for 12-days field training. Take no documents other than SIGCORPS ID-cards. Wear civilian clothing; no weapons, military gear or uniforms of any kind. Transportation will be provided. Detailed instructions will be given to you verbally at 1130 01/07/42 in my office. Be there.

Lt. Col. W. C. Elliott

I begin to understand why he told me to bring my civvies to the hotel. He's not actually playing a game with me. Its plain he is doing everything he can to make it easy for me to identify the game plan. I don't know exactly why, but I do believe he wants me to succeed.

And this is the first time I have seen the letters "*iDiv.*" Of course they are an acronym or a contraction; a particular passion of the military. I am very much aware of the fact I have not been introduced to any other members of The Chief's group. If I have interpreted the significance correctly, it could explain the lack of social courtesies, coupled with privacy and isolation.

Maybe at dinner with Madeleine I can get more information, hints, tips, clues or even a direct explanation. Tonight...at 1900.

Chapter Five

The hotel's dining room is definitely not a "chow hall." Probably, the elegance has always been there. I don't think the Army would dare build something like it right here in Manhattan, especially while the nation is in an economic depression. Still, it's nice to be able to serve my country in such a splendid environment. Enjoy it while it's available.

I hadn't really noticed before...there are no more than two or three people to a table. Some of the "guests" are in civilian clothes. Those who are in uniform are officers; 1st and 2nd lieutenants and a captain or two. There's no maître d'. It seems you pick out any empty table and seat yourself, which I do; a small table at the back of the dining room against the wall so I can see everyone and everything.

The room is dimly lit. I doubt it is a concession to romance. It probably just makes lip-reading difficult.

Aah, there's Madeleine. She sees me and is moving toward our, er, this table. Everyone seems to know her and she knows everyone, too. She waves to some, stops briefly to chat with others. The way she walks, tilts her head, moves her hands and arms—the woman is a fascinating model of femininity. As she approaches me, I have a valid excuse for examining the details without appearing to gape.

She's wearing a neatly tailored dark gray skirt. Around her waist she wears a wide belt. It's tight. Makes her waist appear to be very tiny. The freshly-ironed long-sleeve blouse is simply styled in a very suitable lighter gray. A frilly, blue-flowered kerchief neatly tied in a symmetrical bow perfectly dresses up the blouse's collar. The trailing ends of the kerchief drape themselves in a downward slope over her...

"Have you bgen waiting long?"

She's nine minutes and forty seconds late but I won't tell her it seems like hours. "Not long." As any gentleman does when a lady joins his table, I help her into a chair and offer my sincere compliments on how absolutely lovely she looks.

"*Très gentil, cher Leon.*"

Madeleine is talking to me, but I'm not hearing. The woman's dramatically simple beauty fascinates and almost paralyzes me.

"Leon. You are not listening to a word I say."

"I am listening. *Entièrement aux yeux*!"

Her delightfully unrestrained laughter makes me realize I had said "I'm all eyes!" This might more accurately describe where my attention is focused but I did mean to say, "All ears!" I try to apologize for my faux pas. But she puts a finger to my lips, smiles and insists my attention is most flattering and, with an amused tilt of her head, "Leon, are you sure you are as young as you say you are?"

Her eyes are a very light shade of blue. Or are they light gray? Or green? They seem to absorb the color and hue of the environment. The color almost blends into the whites of her eyes. Magnetizing! Spellbinding! I slowly heave an exaggerated sigh and notice one of the waiters standing at the table, pencil poised over his pad. He clears his throat and asks if we are ready to order.

"Ladies first. Madeleine?"

She looks at me. "If the hotel has a special dinner tonight, I am ready."

Before the waiter can answer the implied question, I add, "Make it the special dinner for two, please."

"Leon. You didn't let him announce the 'special dinner.' Who knows what he will bring?"

"Madeleine." I sigh again and feign the expression of a man lost in love and with no appetite for the food of mortals. "I don't care what he will bring."

She laughs throatily at my humor and takes my hand in hers. "*Assez. Assez. Léon. Il nous faut parler sérieusement.* Enough, Léon. We must have a serious conversation. Colonel Elliott expects to hear from you in the morning. You must remember your task."

"No, Madeleine. I haven't forgotten."

"Shall we begin by you asking questions of me? Or shall I ask questions of you?"

"Neither, if you don't mind. Let's just talk and see how much we can learn from each other without playing question and answer games. Eh?" I have just spoken a question and, thus, passed the ball to her.

"Excellent, Leon. What shall we talk about?"

She has just returned the ball to my court. I pick it up. "I'm fascinated by your adventures in escaping from France to England. May I...can you tell me more about them?"

"There is no more to tell or that I can reveal without endangering those still in France who helped me. However, I can tell you I succeeded in escaping...obviously...and went to an address in London with which I had been supplied. This led me to the British Intelligence Office, MI5 who needed me for French interpretation and translation. While working there, I was able to improve on my English which I had learned and studied at the Sorbonne."

"Did you have...were you given a *Secret* or *Confidential Clearance*?"

"Yes. For both MI5 and MI6."

"And you were all alone in England?"

"Not completely alone. Oh, I had no family at all in England. But the Free French Forces were training there, under General DeGaulle, of course. I also worked as one of their contact-liaisons with the new anti-German underground activities in France. Certainly you have heard of the Maquis?"

"Yes, I did read something about them in the newspapers. As 'contact-liaison', did you have to make any trips back into France?"

"I did."

"Oh, you poor woman. How rough it must have been for you." I muster all the sympathetic expressions I can think of.

But, why is she so readily telling me all this? I have the same disturbing feelings I had when I first met Madeleine earlier in Colonel Elliott's office. She is well rehearsed. Is this a game being elaborately played? I think it is and I don't like it. Not one bit, I don't. Je me garde de ces jeux! Careful of these games, Leon.

I believe I have learned all Madeleine and The Chief want me to know at this time. Despite the ego-flattery of being seen with a woman as beautiful as Madeleine, it's best not to get too close to her. Well, not until I know her better. This is going to take all my willpower...after all I am young...and healthy. Instinctively, I feel I must avoid questions from her.

I deliberately look at my wrist watch and put my ear to it as though to make sure it is running. "Madeleine." I pretend to be agitated. "I hope you won't think me rude, *impoli*. I must contact The Chief right away—before the deadline of my 'task'. Do you suppose he is still in his office?"

"No doubt Colonel Elliott is at his office. He always works late into the night. But, Leon, you haven't had your dinner. You are so compulsive. Are you always like this?"

"Sorry, Madeleine. It's my nature. You have no idea how difficult it is for me not to be able to spend more time with you tonight! *Au 'voir*!"

Madeleine smiles, stands up as I push back from the table and kisses me on both cheeks. "*Au 'voir, cher Léon. À bientôt.*"

"Taxi! Taxi!" Luck is with me. Ten minutes later, without knocking, I dash into The Chief's office and start to raise my hand in a salute.

The startled Colonel Elliott jumps up. "Okay. Okay, Leon. What's the hurry?"

"I've completed my task, sir. So, why wait to make my report? Unless you want me to wait."

He sits back in his chair. "Okay. In 25 words or less, tell me now what is the primary function of our organization?"

"First, colonel, if I am correct, I do hope...for its own good...the rest of this organization is less transparent." This extracts no reaction so I continue. "As members of the Signal Corps, we are very much involved with communications. But not in the usual sense. Start counting my words, sir. This is an Army intelligence group. We are a bunch of goddam spies! At least we are trying to be. There you are, sir, in 20 words. I didn't need 25."

Colonel Elliott leans back in his chair and smiles. "Now, that wasn't difficult for you. Was it?"

"Of course not. You couldn't have made it easier. *iDIV* is obviously a short form, a contraction, an acronym of Intelligence DIVision. But why are we playing games?"

Characteristically, with elbows on his desk, hands clasped and eyes fixed firmly on mine, Colonel Elliott leans forward. "Would you have accepted volunteered to join us if I had disclosed everything? Don't answer. National security prevented me from revealing our true function to an unauthorized civilian, which you were at the time I invited you to join us."

He holds up his hand as though shushing me. However, while he is in this tell-all mode, I am not going to interrupt.

"So, Leon. Before I tell you anything more, I ask you: knowing what you do, do you want to be one of us? I need your direct response right now. This is a 100 percent volunteer activity."

"Do I have an option?"

"Certainly. You can refuse."

"And, if I do refuse?"

"Remember, Mister Wortman, you signed up. Your 'option'?" He leans back in his chair. "As I once told you before, you can resign and be drafted into the SigCorp as a buck private. You'll go into six months of basic training and then..."

"And then?"

"You'll be assigned to this group."

"As a buck private?"

"You will probably have earned a stripe by then. No doubt you'd be a private, first class."

"Either way—I'm to be a spy?"

He bristles, "We prefer to refer to ourselves as 'intelligence officers'."

"Where do we go from here, Chief?"

"Tell me, Mister Wortman. Are you with us? Or shall I call you Private Wortman?"

"Yes, sir. No, sir. I prefer the relative freedom and lifestyle you offer a captain."

"It won't always be so comfortable. I have several special assignments for you and your skills. You are here by design. Not by accident."

"And when will you tell me about my 'special assignments'?"

"You start preparing for them in the morning." He leans forward again. "We have to learn more about your reactions to stress—under life-threatening conditions. You will be under continuous observation during your training period. When we are confident you can handle the load, we will discuss your assignments." He sits back in his chair. "Until then you will just have to be patient, attentive and—etcetera—etcetera—and more et-cet-eras."

Things can't be more clear to me. He cannot or will not tell me anything else at this moment. Colonel Elliott rises. I stand, too. We share a strong handshake. We exchange salutes.

"As my memorandum said, be in this office—ready to travel—at 1130."

"Oh, one more thing, Chief. I feel like an intruder. When do I get to meet some of the guys in this group?"

"Okay. Except for Madeleine and myself, every one of us goes by an assumed name. We guard ourselves and our identities as thoroughly as we can. Choose a new name for yourself, one that bears no hint or resemblance to Leon Wortman. Let me have it first thing in the morning and I'll have a second ID card cut for you before we leave here."

"Sir. May I borrow a pen and paper. I've always wanted to be known as Jiraud." Writing as I speak, "*J-i-r-a-u-d.* And I have always liked the sound of—*Brevier.*"

The Chief looks at the new name. "Okay, Jiraud, citizen Brevier, you've just been converted. From now on, that is how this office will know you. Tomorrow morning you will be introduced and addressed as *Captain Jiraud Brevier.*"

Chapter Six

Five of us "civilians" are crowded into Colonel Elliott's less-than-spacious office. No one, including me, seems to know anyone else. Two of the men have their hands in their pants pockets. One has his arms wrapped tightly across his chest as though he wishes he were somewhere else. The fourth holds his arms and hands down at his sides in a relaxed at-attention posture. I clasp my hands behind my back as in "at ease, men." However, my hands are tightly clenched together. I am not at ease. We all scuffle our feet and self-consciously avoid each other's glances.

Colonel Elliott looks up from his desktop, which is covered with sheets of paper and manila folders. He turns his head to study each of us slowly, in a heads-to-toes inspection. Without comments to indicate approval or disapproval of what he sees, he clears his throat. His expression is, as usual, authoritarian. He puts down his fountain pen and leans back in his swivel chair. "If you are not wondering why you are here, you don't belong here." He waits for reactions and continues to stare from one to the other of this group of five intimidated men who stand uncomfortably in front of his desk.

Other than a brief shuffling of pairs of feet, none of us reacts visibly.

"Okay, now. Let's have introductions. State your first and last names only. No ranks. Do not volunteer any other information. Get it? Start with the first man on my left."

That happens to be me. I look directly at The Chief. "Jiraud Brevier."

The Chief hands me my new ID card and looks at the fellow on my left.

"Ray Wolcott, sir."

The Chief reacts instantly with annoyance. "Didn't I say 'do not volunteer any other information'? Drop the 'sir'. At my orders, you are all civilians...temporarily."

The Chief is being quite literal. He looks at the next guy who announces, "William Short."

Next in line reports, "Harry Sonenfeld."

The last one identifies himself. "John Winston."

"Well, at least you remember your names; your assumed names. From now on, while you are part of this *iDIV* group, that is, all you will know about each other's identities." He focuses on no one as he adds, "You can try to pry personal details from each other. In fact, I urge you to try, try hard to get the others to open up and reveal more facts about themselves." Again he pauses to give emphasis to his next statement. "However, if you do give accurate responses, gentlemen, you fail the first critical test of privacy—your ability to keep confidential information strictly to yourself. Any questions?"

He is instructing us that lying is okay. Lie like hell, if you have to. Don't trust your buddies. Not a very warm beginning. There has to be more to this whole event. He has my undivided attention.

The Chief looks at his wrist watch. "In 10 minutes you leave this office as a group, go down to the basement and exit the back door to the alley. A car and a driver will be there waiting. You will be taken to an airport operated by the Army Air Corps. You will board a C-3 and be flown to another airport located near Albany, New York. Another car will be waiting to take you to your training location." Pause. "We call it 'The Farm'."

Ray Wolcott starts to raise his hand to ask a question. The move is quickly stopped by The Chief. "I'm sure you all have questions. I'm also sure there are answers. So hold the questions for now, please." With command restored, The Chief goes on. "You will leave here as you are. No, you may not return to your rooms. Lunch? Do without. It's part of your training. You will be fed when you get to the The Farm. Clothes? There is a large supply of everything you need; including razors and toothbrushes. Do I make myself clear?"

A nervous shifting from one foot to the other is the only response. This is not the time to say anything. Why risk The Chief's disapproval?

After a long silence and a prolonged visual inspection, The Chief continues his monologue. "A couple of more things, gentlemen. You'll be at The Farm for as long as six weeks. Except for a radio link to this office, you will be incommunicado. No one beside me and, of course, Madeleine, will know where you are, who you are or what you are doing there. Who is running The Farm? An elderly man you will refer to as 'Pop.' No one else. He is your housekeeper, chambermaid and cook. He will ask no questions."

The five of us loosen up a bit. We look at one another. Exchange quick smiles and nods.

"Now for the final news of the day. I will not make the trip with you and I will not visit The Farm. Therefore, I am appointing a group leader—Jiraud Brevier.

"Jiraud will use the radio link to give me a progress report at the end of every day. From this moment until you return to my office in six weeks, he is in direct charge. He is the guy to whom you present your daily gripes, problems, needs and, I hope, praise." He looks at me without changing his expression. "Is that clear, Jiraud? Mister Brevier?"

I am surprised and a bit nervous about saying anything more than, "Very." I hope for an immediate description of the extent of the authority of a "group leader," but it is not offered and I am intimidated enough to avoid asking any questions.

The Chief looks at his wrist watch and stands up. "Time. Gentlemen, please wait outside my office for Jiraud. Won't be but a minute."

The Chief and I are alone. Perhaps now I'll get more instructions.

"Jiraud, don't ask me why I appointed you group leader. Sometimes, as you will learn, we act on instinct rather than facts."

"Thank you, Chief. I am flattered."

"If I am wrong, we both pay a price."

Now I dare ask the question. "But what do you expect of me as the group leader?"

"When five men live and operate in close quarters, as you and your group will be doing, stress—sometimes very severe stress is inevitable. I want you to watch the other men closely. If you see any indication, even the slightest suggestion of a bad reaction to the pressure, you will confidentially report his name to me and the specific reasons for your negative report. This is for his own protection—as well as to safeguard the others." Chief Elliott lets this sink in.

Privately, this disturbs me. Am I to be Jiraud, the official rat, the appointed fink, the designated tattler? Well, on the other hand, as The Chief said, 'for his protection as well as others'.

"Two veteran marine sergeants, training specialists, have just returned from Europe where they spent a lot of time observing and training with the British Commandos. They are assigned to The Farm for the next six weeks. Their credentials and expertise are genuine."

I continue to listen intently.

"You and your group will receive special instruction in survival. You will be taught self defense and attack techniques. This includes learning to disable or kill your enemy so you will be the survivor in a close engagement. They, the marine sergeants, will teach all of you knife combat. How to improvise weapons. You'll learn weapon safety and concealment. How to use a handgun. How to shoot—shoot to kill. You'll become proficient in hand-to-hand close fighting—with and without weapons. Yes. You are going to be taught to kill—or be killed. To win! To never lose!" His voice drops and, to emphasize the importance of the statements, he looks intensely into my eyes. "You can only lose once."

When I was a kid in Brooklyn I had many street fights, but they ended as soon as you or your opponent called out, "Uncle! Uncle!" I have never visualized myself as a killer.

"This Farm is very large, about a thousand acres. You'll go out into the acreage alone and as a group and learn to survive on what you can scrounge from nature. You'll go out on short, night patrols and find your way back in the dark. And whatever else the sergeants can think of and offer you—for your own survival."

I try to be sincere. "Looking forward to a very valuable six weeks, Chief." *Maybe this is the real reason why, from the time I was seven until 16, I spent every summer on Yacov Timoschuck's 780-acre farm high up in the Catskill Mountains of New York State.*

Colonel Elliott waves his hand to punctuate and end his speech. "Now, Leon or Jiraud, join your group and head for your transportation."

"Right, Chief. And thank you for your vote of confidence."

Is this military leadership? Wonder if he has given the same instructions privately to the other four guys.

The Chief may not be the most admirable man I have ever worked with. However, when he talks, everybody does listen. I must say he does have excellent organizing skills. So far, everything has gone exactly as he ordered; from the car that transports us to the airport, the C-3 to Albany, a second car to take us to The Farm.

I recall the long hours of travel, sitting on the painfully hard deck of the unheated C-3 that normally carries Army cargo, not Army humans. And the terrible air turbulence! I certainly do not want to be reminded of the humiliating airsickness from which none had been exempted. What a mess! All the way from the airport to The Farm we made no, literally no, conversation. And, sure enough, there is a "Pop." He is an apron-wearing kindly old gentleman with an inexhaustible supply of steaming hot coffee, platters of hot stew and fresh-baked bread for his five exhausted visitors. But now, we are all refreshed, relaxed, refurbished and reconditioned. After Pop leaves the kitchen, we sit back in our chairs at the table, bring out our cigarettes, light up, quietly inhale and noisily exhale the comforting, blue smoke.

I look around at the group of men and become acutely aware they are all looking directly at me, their temporary leader. Obviously, they expect me to speak to them, perhaps deliver an inspirational talk about—*je ne sais quoi!* A wise friend told me, "When all else fails, try the truth." Why not right now? Within limits, of course.

"Fellows, if you were surprised by Colonel Elliott's announcement 'Jiraud is your group leader'—or words to that effect—I had the same reaction. At any rate, official Army stuff aside, if any of you has an objection to me—personally or as the so-called 'ad-hoc leader' of this group now is the time to let me know it. Perhaps it might even be best for me to step out of the room so you can have a private, uninhibited discussion. Maybe, take a vote?"

I wear my friendliest smile, rise from the chair, turn and start to leave the kitchen. One of the fellows calls out my name. "Jiraud!" Ray Wolcott raises his right hand and laughs. "Hell, friend, you don't have to leave the room. We just voted. Nobody likes or dislikes you. You're okay with us—until we hear from The Chief again."

The three other men smile as they chorus their acceptance. "No problem, Jiraud. We're all in this, whatever 'this' is, we're in it together."

John Winston moves my chair to the head of the table and steps back. "That's your place, buddy."

William Short lives up to his last name. "Yo-oh!"

I thank them for their vote of trust, and Harry Sonenfeld comments "This must be the egalitarian section of *iDIV*. Who ever heard of democratic choices or voting in the Army?"

I catch the hint. "Okay. I get it. Best not to mention this special voting procedure to The Chief."

Heads nod in agreement. Smiles slowly fade. Eyes are on me.

Time for me to demonstrate leadership. I tell my four companions everything Colonel Elliott had said to me in private, after they had been told to leave me alone with him. I tell all. All except my direct orders to report their abilities to handle stress. It is not prudent to reveal my role as a possible rat-fink—or my guilty feelings about it.

William Short asks to be called "Bill" and, no doubt speaking for the others as well as for himself, asks, "When do the marines land? Any idea, Jiraud?"

"Honestly, I don't know. But it's not likely The Chief sent us up here just to kill time. So, to be ready for them, let's anticipate their arrival, oh...tomorrow morning or midday. For now, lets get a good night's sleep. I have a feeling the marines may not allow much time for even that."

We stand up and move our chairs away from the table. The men shake my hand as they leave the kitchen for their quarters upstairs.

Pop had assigned us two-to-a-room but to me he said, "You are an exception to that, Jiraud. Colonel Elliott told me 'Jiraud is to be quartered separately, in a private room'."

Privileges of rank? Or a special reward for the confidential reporter? Right now, what I need more than logic is a night of solid sleep. As I start for my room, Pop returns to the kitchen. This likable, obviously discreet, gentle old man and I are alone. He opens a cupboard and shows me the two-way radio equipment linking us to The Chief's office in New York.

"Pop. When do you expect the two marine sergeants to arrive?"

"Oh, they'll be here in time to have lunch with all of you at about one o'clock."

I extend my hand in friendship. "Don't you mean 1300 hours?"

He chuckles, "You bet I do."

Pop probably knows quite a bit about *iDIV*. He answered my questions and volunteered nothing more.

Eagerness or anticipation—one or the other, maybe both—keep me awake. All I know is I have powerfully jumbled thoughts as I toss and turn. At 5:30 in the morning, I decide it's a lost cause, get dressed and go downstairs in search of hot coffee.

"Yoh, Jiraud! We didn't get much sleep either."

All four fellows are at the kitchen table, drinking steaming hot coffee and trying, without much success, to look and sound wide awake. Pop in his khaki-colored apron stands at the cooking range, spatula in one hand and a giant skillet in the other. The hearty smells of bacon and eggs and freshly baked bread saturate the air. You can't beat the unique aromas and warmth of a country kitchen.

Pop, very wide awake, turns and smiles. "G'mornin' Jiraud. You're just in time for breakfast. Pour yourself some coffee. Breakfast's about ready."

Except for Pop, we all wear the same clothes in which we arrived. Pop apologizes for not outfitting us before we turned in. "You fellas sure looked worn out so I skipped those details."

Pajamas and toothbrushes would have been nice. But, for now, those items seem to take a low priority.

"Right after you fellas fill up, we'll go to the storeroom and fit you out properly. Ok?"

Half-awake yesses, moans and assorted groans are all we can muster.

The storeroom is in an unpainted concrete building adjoining the one where we slept last night and are now having our breakfast. With some cynicism, we refer to The Farm as *GHQ-2*. We reserve *GHQ-1* for our office in New York City.

We nickname the storeroom "Pop's haberdashery." The room is about 25 feet square. Floor-to-ceiling shelves are filled with neatly folded and stacked items: pants, shirts, socks, shoes, sweaters, ponchos, underwear and all the toiletries we need. Everything, but everything is khaki, or olive drab and shades of brown. Someone declares, "I hope the toothpaste isn't khaki, too."

Pop advises, "Take whatever you need, fellas. Sizes for everyone. Take a week's worth and whenever you need more, just let me know. Incidentally, there's a hamper in every room. Just put your things in it and I'll see they get cleaned and ironed and returned to you within a day or two."

I try not to sound officious. "I suggest we go to our rooms, change and take care of other morning things. Let's meet in the kitchen in half an hour."

Pop invites us to explore the other buildings on our own, which we do. One, also unpainted concrete, holds a well equipped radio laboratory and a machine shop. The adjoining supply room has everything one could possibly need to construct and service just about any type of communications equipment. I feel like a kid in a toy store.

Another similarly colorless building houses a small conference room. A door is at the far end of the room. I cautiously open it and reach into the dark space to find the light switch. I gasp involuntarily. Glass-fronted wooden cabinets line the walls of the 30 by 30 room. They are filled with varieties of small and large pistols, revolvers, rifles and shotguns. Most of the guns are flat black. One cabinet, standing off by itself, displays an astonishing assortment of knives. Canes, short and long sticks lean against the cabinet's side.

Oh, if Mayor LaGuardia were to see me now. He'd probably look up at me and screech, "Leon! Just what do you think you are doing? Get your butt back here in New York City where things are beautiful and peaceful!"

As we walk from cabinet to cabinet, the five of us repeatedly exclaim "Whew!" and "Wow!" A singularly tall, heavy-looking metal cabinet reveals an assortment of ammunition in quantities sufficient to sustain an armed revolution.

Pop, out of breath with excitement, comes into the room. "Just had a call from the airport. The two marines should be here in 40 or 50 minutes. They have limited time to spend with us so they want to start the training sessions as soon as they drop their bags and have a cup of coffee. Say! Why don't you fellas have coffee with them, in the kitchen. Friendly and...well, it gets things off right. Don't you think?"

Obviously Pop has met or housed the two marines at The Farm before. They greet one another like old friends. My impression is Pop might have been a training expert in the service before age took direct charge of his body.

"Jiraud, Captain Brevier, meet my old buddies, two of my oldest and best friends, Sergeants Frank Murphy and Joe Bofort."

Pop is observing protocol by introducing the sergeants to me first. After Frank and Joe and I shake hands, Pop makes no effort to introduce the others. He leaves that up to me. Thus, after a flurry of name-repeatings and hand-shakings, Pop asks us to pick up mugs and fill them with coffee, sugar and milk and help ourselves to freshly made cookies. We emulate the marines and gulp the coffee. Clearly, we are all eager to get started.

Frank appears to be slightly older than Joe. I put their ages in the mid 50s, about 10 years younger than Pop. They may have been called out of retirement to serve once again as trainers. Their rugged, deeply furrowed faces and brows can only be the result of years of working in the outdoors. The broad, barrel-chests probably came from continuous, heavy-duty physical exercise of the kind one would encounter in roughing it up with young recruits. Of course, the crew-cuts, almost to the skin of their skulls shout "I am a member of the U.S. Marine Corps and damn proud of it!"

The marines tell us—it sounds more like an order—to meet them at the conference room in a couple of minutes. Evidently, they need no tutoring on where the "conference room" is located. We rush to the building and are followed within seconds by the two sergeants. When they say "minutes" they mean "seconds."

Before we sit down at the conference table, Joe makes a statement. "Okay you guys. First, while we're here you all rank below Frank and me! Forget your bars. They don't mean shit to us—not while we're in charge of the training. You listen and follow orders. You don't give any orders here. Get it? Am I making myself clear?"

Frank says a simple but forceful, "You guys don't want to argue the point, now do you?"

He is not putting a question to us. Not at all. As though we five had one set of vocal chords, we meekly reply, "No, sir. No argument."

Frank sounds angry. "And save the 'sir' for your Chief. We, Joe and me, are to be called 'sergeant'. Clear? Understood?"

A bit intimidated, nobody says a word.

The next three hours are dedicated to lectures from the sergeants about always winning and never losing a fight; about being tough and resourceful when our lives are in the balance. This is followed by a lecture on weapons, formal and makeshift. The sergeants are a great team, passing the subjects and thoughts as though they had rehearsed every line. *Rehearsed? No. Just thoroughly experienced. They must have given this type of training session together many times.*

The discussion continues in the conference room until Pop comes in to announce "Supper's on the table, men." We hadn't realized the passage of time and had gone right through lunch into late afternoon.

Looking at his wrist-watch, Joe tells us "Let's grab a quick bite and start again here in about 40 minutes. Today and tonight you start with disassembling, cleaning and reassembling pistols and revolvers."

"We are sure moving fast, sergeant, aren't we? Must be a good reason."

Frank frowns and takes me on. "Our orders are to make every minute count because none of us knows when you are going over. Could be tomorrow. Even tonight. We are on alert, under orders to move on to another training site as soon as we can get away from here. Sorry, guys. Too bad you have to get shortcut training. Hope, when you get out there, your luck is good. You may need it."

Without further chatter, we head for the kitchen where the two marines continue their dissertation. They have our exclusive and intense attention. We don't make light of the importance of the advice of the two veterans. Our desire and need to learn about weapons and survival are genuine.

After dinner we return for specific handgun instructions. "Before you fire a single round, you guys will learn how to care for your sidearm. Your life could depend on its condition. It's gotta work when you need it most."

The rest of the evening is devoted to disassembling, stripping all kinds of revolvers and pistols, cleaning them thoroughly and reassembling them. Our conference room is filled with the sounds of clicking hammers, triggers and slide-actions. To some of us, the strong stench of lubricants and solvents is very familiar. Others will soon find it difficult to get rid of the persistent odor.

"Tomorrow morning we go to our firing range. For safety, it is in a deep gully 520 feet northwest of this building. You'll load and test-fire all the guns you fellas worked on tonight. You'll continue daily workouts at the range until the safe handling and firing of your sidearm is second nature. We'll teach you the difference between defensive and combat shooting."

Harry asks, "What is the difference."

"A matter of judgment on your part. Do you shoot first and study the situation later? Or do you take the time...it might be no more than a split second...to figure things out, decide if it is necessary for you to shoot at all."

"Hey! This is great stuff!"

"Yeah, it's 'great' if your gun fires every time you pull the trigger." Words of warning from Sergeant Joe. Humorless echoes from Sergeant Frank. "You'll all learn to draw and shoot without hitting yourself in the ass...or your buddy's back...by accident, of course."

Their warnings reverberate in our ears and minds as we leave for the kitchen and some of Pop's goodnight coffee and cookies.

Chapter Seven

"G'morning, Leon. Trust you had a pleasant trip?"

"Dammit, yes, Chief. Excuse my language, sir...but...well...your sudden call for me to rush back to your office...after only one day at The Farm. There's so much for me to learn."

"Couldn't be helped. Everything is moving quickly. We do what we can to keep up with change." The Chief leans forward with elbows on his desk, his usual posture when very serious. His eyes fixed on mine demand total attention.

I listen closely for what comes next.

He writes briefly on a slip of paper and hands it to me. "Get down to this address before 1700 today. It's a private doctor's office. His nurse will be expecting you."

"What's this about, Chief?"

"It's about you starting a series of 13 shots."

"Okay. But why now?"

"I'm ordering you overseas as soon as you finish the series."

My jaw drops. I cannot hide my surprise, confusion and pleasure. I am speechless. I wait for The Chief to tell me more.

The Chief tries to interpret my mixed, visible reactions. "What do you say to that?"

I take a deep breath. "Where? When? What do I say? I say let's go. But there must be more to tell!"

"You'll learn more...as soon as they tell me more. However, I can guess."

"Please, Chief."

"I'm guessing you'll go to the UK for briefing sessions with your counterparts in British Intelligence, MI5 or MI6. When? Pretty soon. Probably soon as you finish the series of shots."

Exciting news to me. "How long for the shots?"

"Two to three weeks. In the meantime, in between visits to the doctor's office, you'll continue your weapons training at The Farm. I'll set up a schedule for transportation with the Air Corps to and from The Farm."

My senses are calming down. I relax, stand up, salute and turn to leave.

The Chief stops me. "One thing more, Leon." He holds up an envelope and points it at me. "One of our guys has been...well, I want you to visit his widow, and tell her. There's a formal letter from Washington in this envelope. Give it to her, please."

"Where is she, Chief? What's her name? Can you give me some advice on how to do this? It's my first time."

"She's at the Lafayette Hotel in Greenwich Village registered as Mrs. Michael Endras. Don't worry about how to do this. She and Mike didn't get along well. By the way, you should change into your uniform first."

A short ride to my quarters at the hotel, a quick change into uniform and I am ready to go deliver the message to the widow, Mrs. Michael Endras at the Lafayette Hotel.

My palms sweat and my heart pounds as Mrs. Endras opens the door and invites me into her room. She is about 21 years old, short, with sand-blond hair. I take off my hat and, with feelings of embarrassment, accept her invitation to sit down. I'm embarrassed because she's wearing nothing more than a see-through negligee and a seductive smile. I try to keep my mind on business by looking only at her eyes. *How can one make small talk at a time like this*? I go right to the reason for my visit. "Mrs. Endras, I am afraid I have bad news...very bad news about your husband."

She doesn't flinch or lose her smile. "What news?"

I try to avoid making the announcement. "It's in this formal letter from Washington." But she doesn't let me off the hook.

"You tell me, captain. What's the news?"

I take a very deep breath and haltingly begin. "Well...I didn't know Mike at all...but I am unhappy to have to be the one to tell you..."

"You mean he's missing?" She is a cool one.

I look down at my feet then up and try to avoid her eyes.

"You mean he's dead."

I nod yes. But I didn't expect an ice-cold reaction.

"Well, the damn fool had to rush off to war. Serves him right."

I stand and hand her the envelope. Now that I have done my job, I can use a cigarette and a hot cup of coffee. Hesitantly, I invite Mrs. Endras to join me downstairs in the coffee shop.

She smiles and slowly opens her negligee exposing her well-formed personal non-military secrets to me. "Why thank you, captain. But why not have some coffee sent up here where we can relax and drink it in...comfort?"

Egad! What kind of woman is this? I've just delivered the message that her husband has been killed and all she wants to do is lay the messenger! No. This is not for me. Under the circumstances I'm not sure I can even get it up.

I hear myself stammer. "Er...ah no. Thank you, ma'am. But The Chief ordered me to return right away to his office."

She drops her negligee to the floor.

Sometimes I am a coward. The most courage I can muster right now is to quickly open the door and retreat to the safety of the hotel's lobby.

In a cab on the way to report to The Chief, I practice describing the Endras incident without a smile. I shall, I will keep a straight face.

"So help me, Chief. That's exactly what happened."

This is the first time I have ever seen Colonel Elliott's face break into a grin which quickly expands into a loud, roaring laugh. The no-smile practice on the way back to The Office is forgotten. My self control vanishes. Slapping my thighs and gasping for air, I collapse with unrepressed laughter into a chair. The Chief and I wipe our tears.

A knock on the door to The Chief's office forces us to straighten up. Colonel Elliott is coughing uncontrollably. He tries to sound official as he manages a hoarse "Come!"

It's Madeleine. "I heard loud noises through the walls of your office. I couldn't imagine what..."

Colonel Elliott wipes at his eyes with his handkerchief. "Jiraud...Leon, tell Madeleine. She will get a kick out of it."

Instead of two, there are now three of us falling out of our chairs with laughter.

"Okay, captain." The Chief regains his unsmiling self-control. "You and Madeleine get out of here now. And don't forget about your shot...by 1700."

"No, sir. I won't forget. What time tomorrow do I return to The Farm?"

"I'll leave a message for you at the hotel. Plan on departure from the hotel at 0800."

Madeleine and I go to her office. She softly suggests dinner tonight away from the hotel, after I get my shot. *I do not understand what suddenly makes me so attractive to women. First Mrs. Endras tries to seduce me. And now, Madeleine.*

"I'd like that, Madeleine. Where shall we have dinner?"

She gives an "I don't know" shrug.

"I know a delightfully romantic, tiny out-of-the-way Spanish restaurant on Macdougal Street in Greenwich Village. It's called 'Granados Cafe.' Rosendo Lorenzo, Larry, the owner is an old friend. I think you, he and I will get along famously. We three are very much alike, *gentil, amicaux et très...romantique.* Shall we meet there at about 1800?"

A hard hug and a soft kiss eloquently express, "Yes. *Bien sûr*!"

I arrive at the doctor's office just before 1700. The short, very overweight nurse ushers me quickly down the hall and into a windowless room about 15 feet long and seven feet wide. It has a small wooden desk, a swivel chair, an examining table, several wall-mounted white, metal cabinets, and a refrigerator.

"We close promptly at 5:00 P.M., captain. Please come earlier next time." She's not smiling.

"Yes ma'am. I'll come as early as I can." I shed my overcoat and jacket and roll up my sleeve.

"A few minutes more and you'd be too late for today's shots!" the nurse grunts.

Needles, shots are one of the few things that scare the hell out of me. I don't know why, but they do. I suggest, "Maybe I'd better come back tomorrow?"

"You're here now. So let's do it." She turns to the refrigerator and withdraws a small vial, fills the syringe and holds it high. Straight up. A drop of the vaccine squirts. She swabs my upper arm and aims that awesome needle at me.

I turn my head and brace myself.

Suddenly, I hear voices calling to me. "Hello! Hello! Do you know where you are? What's your name? What's today's date?" It is a man in a white coat, a doctor speaking. I open my eyes and look up. Both the doctor and the nurse are looking down at me. I'm on my back. On the floor. "Wh'...Wha'...What happened?"

"You fainted. Think you can get up?"

With help from the doctor and the nurse, I stagger to my feet.

"You've got a little nose-bleed. You hit your nose pretty hard on the end of the table as you went down. We'd better have a look at it in X-ray."

The nurse adds, "You went down so fast I couldn't catch you."

My head clears quickly. I apologize.

"Oh, don't give it another thought. It happens all the time, even to men bigger and tougher-looking than you."

X-ray shows the bridge of my nose has been fractured. The doctor manipulates my nose and places a large adhesive bandage across it. "Just to hold it together for a week or so. When you remove the bandage the nose will be good as new. No more shots for you today. Come back in five days and we'll continue the series."

"How many shots do I get?"

"A total of 13. Next time you come visit us you'll get five. Then five days later, five more. And finally, in another five days, two more will complete the series. However, be aware that if you miss any of the five day intervals, we have to start over. So, don't be late!"

As he leaves the room, the doctor stops at the doorway and points toward my wounded nose. "Incidentally, captain. The areas around your eyes and nose will quickly begin to look severely bruised...slight internal bleeding." He illustrates his advice by rubbing below his eyes and across his nose. "You may be black-and-blue in these areas. Oh, one more thing. You can expect a doozy of a headache. Take some aspirin for it. You should be fully recovered by your next visit."

"Thank you, doctor." What else is there to say?

Better get to The Office right away. Maybe Madeleine is still there. In the taxi, I struggle with my thoughts. *Hell! What timing, dammit! But, I don't feel romantic. And I am sure I look weird with this bandage across my nose. The headache's starting. The bruises are probably showing. Damn! I'll have to tell Madeleine the truth. Embarrassing. What will she think of me? What will The Chief think? The sooner I get back to The Farm, the better. Frankly, I'd just as soon hide in my room until tomorrow morning.*

Madeleine is sympathetic. "*Ah, mon pauvre Léon.* You do not look as handsome as you did when last I saw you."

All I can do is stand there and wish some magic power would make me vanish. "Is The Chief in?" I dread the thought of telling him.

Madeleine is wise. "*Non. Il est sorti.* He has gone out. Léon, I think we should postpone our rendezvous for tonight until your next trip from The Farm. How far away is it? Only five days? Can you wait?"

"Guess I'll have to, Madeleine. Only five days? Right now five days seem like forever."

Madeleine comes close to me. She looks compassionately at my eyes and hugs me tightly, pressing her breasts against my chest. I can feel their firmness through my jacket. Her head tilts up, inviting a kiss. I accept the invitation and make it a long kiss. When we end the kiss, Madeleine puts her head on my chest and sighs mightily. "*Bien entendu, Cher Léon.* I, too, am disappointed. However, it does make the anticipation even more *passionant.* Very exciting to me."

Alone in my room at the hotel, I undress, take a long shower, reexamine the day's events and drift off toward sleep.

The stinging ring of the telephone abruptly awakens me.

"Good evening, captain. You're doing the wise thing. Get a good night's sleep and be sure to meet the car at the basement entrance at 0800. All set?"

"All set, Chief."

"Good for you. Sleep well. And...don't blow your nose too hard."

How the hell does he know it's been broken?

Chapter Eight

"G'morning, Pop. Or is it afternoon?"

"Whatever it is, you're just in time for lunch. Mike, Frank and the other fellas should be here in a bit."

"Good. How'd training go yesterday? Any problems you're aware of?"

He looks down at the floor and speaks with noticeable hesitation. "Things went okay...I guess."

Although I have not known Pop very long, I sense this hesitancy is not typical. He has something to tell me. He turns to the wall cabinet, removes two mugs and slowly fills them from his perpetually brewing coffee pot. As though the mugs weigh a ton, he slowly brings them with a pair of spoons to the table and carefully sets them down. He pulls up a chair, sits and waves for me to do the same. Silently, we stir our coffee, each waiting for the other to speak first.

Pop heaves a deep sigh, glances at me...looks down at his coffee mug and takes a long, slow drink. He looks directly at me. "Jiraud. I'm a little concerned about one of your men." He takes another, shorter drink and looks down, waiting for me to react.

In a gesture of friendship and confidence, I grip his left forearm with my right hand. "I've only been gone for one day and a night. What happened? Please, tell me what your concern is."

"Okay. Mind you, I'm probably only going on instinct. I could be very wrong. But..."

"Pop, my friend. I may be going on instinct, too. I will have a lifetime of good, powerful experience in working with men and, when my instincts swing into motion, I try to listen and follow them. Tell me."

He reminisces. "You're right about my lifetime of working with men. I retired from the Army, did a stint with the marines...a 30-year career as a DI, training special-services troops for combat."

"So that's how you know our two marine sergeants."

"Yup. Trained them myself when they joined up." Pop smiles and sighs as he recollects the past. "That was a long time back."

"You've had a great life, Pop. We're lucky to have you with us."

He turns to face me and smiles broadly as though in gratitude for the recognition. I accept the offer of his right hand. We grasp our hands and wrists in a tight, warmly felt grip. He looks down for a moment and then up at me. I think I see his eyes filling with tears. In an emotion-packed moment, he leans over toward me and we hug one another. I pat him on the back and we break apart. Life is far from over for Pop.

"Sorry about that, Jiraud. But I don't often meet someone who makes me feel I haven't been forgotten. You...you make a big difference...important to me"

I am a bit embarrassed. "No, Pop. We are the ones who should be grateful. It isn't often I, we, get to meet someone like you. And we better learn all we can from you while we have the opportunity." In this I am sincere.

He puts his hands together in a praying posture and looks down at the table. "About my instincts. One of your guys doesn't fit. No. He's a bad fit. I for one would not want to go on a mission with him on my team."

"What has he done or not done, Pop."

"Well." Pop hesitates again.

"Please tell me what your instincts tell you."

"Okay, Jiraud. I'll try. He's a loner, for one thing."

"Pop, they call me a 'loner', too."

"Being a loner isn't all bad, especially in the kind of work you are headed for. But, combined with an inborn ability to make your buddies dislike you...then you have a seriously bad, a dangerous mix under combat conditions."

"Tell me his name, please."

"Remember, I'm going on my instincts."

I cannot hide my feelings. "Who? Which one? Please, Pop."

Our conversation is interrupted as the guys noisily come into the kitchen. It's lunchtime. At the sight of my gauze-covered nose, I am greeted with loud laughs, grins and wisecracks.

"Her husband came home too soon!"

"Next time pick on a woman smaller than you!"

"Put your nose where it didn't belong?"

And so on. I join in the laughter. "Every one of you has it right. Oh boy. I sure learned a lesson!" I don't want to tell them how I broke my nose while getting a shot. It is unwise to tip anyone to the fact I'm getting ready to go overseas. That information leads into a bunch of unanswerable security questions. Beside which, I don't really know exactly where "overseas" is going to be. Best to change the subject.

"You fellows are getting way ahead of me. I'm eager to get back in the swing and play catch up. Mike. Frank. What are you working on today?"

Mike answers my question with another. "Ever heard of 'instinct shooting'?"

I glance around the room for responses. None of us has heard the phrase.

Mike puts down his fork, takes a drink of water and wipes his mouth. "If you consider the kinds of conditions you guys are likely to run into, in the field that is, you rarely have time to take careful aim on your target. Also, for your own safety, you have to keep both eyes open to maintain as wide a field of vision as possible. You shouldn't close one eye to focus on your gunsights. And, suppose you have to shoot from the hip at a moving target? Suppose you have to suddenly whirl on your target and fire at it and you don't have time to aim?"

Nobody is eating his lunch. We are all listening closely.

"That's when your instincts go into action. You have to shoot accurately from whatever position your arm is in." Mike takes another swallow of water. "That, my friends, is what's called 'instinct shooting'. It works with handguns as well as with rifles." He returns to his lunch while all of us look around the table and grunt our complete comprehension.

Frank adds, "Okay. Fill 'er up, you men, and let's get back to work."

Mike's logic, briefly and clearly spoken, has made a deep impression on me. Silently, I promise I will turn myself into one of the best instinct shooters the military has ever known. Oh, well. Once in a while I do allow myself a dream of glory.

Pop and I exchange brief, subtle shrugs. Our interrupted conversation will have to be continued later. But, the sooner, the better.

Suppertime is very late tonight. The seven of us would-be-warriors, well, five of us if you don't include the two marine instructors, are absolutely beat, bushed, worn out. Mike and Frank are indefatigable, indestructible, two heavy-duty guys. If our instincts hadn't obviously started to become too careless for safety, they could have skipped the evening meal and continued the shoot-from-the-hip exercises throughout the night.

Personally, I didn't think it wise for five exhausted neophytes to continue practicing in the darkness with live ammunition. Mike and Frank became convinced when I sprawled out on the ground and begged for mercy. Mike thought it very funny and conceded a short supper break. "Then, maybe, if we all feel up to it, we'll return to our shooting site for more instruction."

I am more interested in continuing the dialog, in private, with Pop.

We aren't making much conversation this evening at the dinner table. Between bites and swallows, yawning is rampant and genuine. Pop and I avoid looking at each other as he goes about filling our plates and mugs. My four guys are nodding off in their chairs. I pretend, with little effort, to be falling asleep. I try to be convincing as I speak out through a large yawn. "My fork gets heavier each time I try to lift it to my mouth. I'm ready to hit the hay. What about you fellows?"

Ray, John, Bill and Harry echo my sentiment.

Mike and Frank look at our exhaustion with obvious disgust. "Okay, you sissies. Let's call it quits. But we start again at 0530." Frank turns in his chair. "Pop, may we have breakfast at 0500?"

"Not a problem, Frank."

We take this to be a signal to leave the table and head for our beds. I go to my room and wait for the sounds of bedtime brushings and flushings to stop. I add ten more minutes and noiselessly go down to Pop's kitchen. He's sitting at the table reading a book of some kind which he closes and puts down when he sees me enter and whispers, "Figured you'd be back as soon as things got quiet upstairs."

I sit across the table from him. "You are right. How can I sleep without hearing the rest? Now, please. Before we are interrupted again...tell me his name."

"First let me tell you what stirred up my instincts. While you were away I noticed the fellas didn't have much to say to one another at the dinner table. I'm sure Mike and Frank gave them a lot to think about."

"They do that all right."

"But, I've seen many groups of young fellas...like yourself...come through this Farm for their initial training. Most of them go through their tough two, three or more weeks of training with Mike and Frank without any problems. However, this time...one...maybe two of the fellas could mean big trouble. And...because Colonel Elliott has enough confidence in you to make you the group leader...you'd best be aware of what I see is going on here."

"Pop. I value and appreciate your observations. But..." Although I feel somewhat impatient, I try to keep it from showing. That's not easy for me tonight.

"Okay, Jiraud. Late at night, when things quieted down in the house, I heard voices arguing. I identified them as Bill Short and John Winston."

"Did you hear what the 'arguing' was about?"

"Not all of it. But I heard enough to know John was criticizing Bill. Said he thought Bill is a wise guy who shouldn't be allowed around guns. Bill laughed and called John...sounded like a 'scaredy cat,' and John said, 'You bet I'm a scaredy cat when guys like you start playing cowboys and Indians with a loaded gun!' Frankly, Jiraud. When I was a DI, that kind of behavior, Bill's, would have been enough to earn a discharge for mental instability or, at least, a desk job with no access to firearms."

"This is serious. Are you sure of what you heard? And are you sure it was between John and Bill?"

"Yup. Dead sure."

"What do you suggest I do?"

"Watch Bill's behavior. I think he disturbs the other fellas, too. Then, if Bill is a problem, you decide how to handle it. You should discuss the situation with The Chief."

"Of course, Pop. I'd better move in on this quickly." I stop to think and unconsciously rub my eyes with both hands. "I'll keep a sharp eye on the men, all of them, form my conclusions and be ready to make a specific report and recommendations to Chief Elliott...ASAP."

Elbows on the table, I clasp my hands tightly together, shrug my shoulders, take a deep breath and look up at Pop for approval.

"You have no other choice. It's your only choice. As long as you are in the service you are going to have to make many tough decisions...some on the basis of even less information than you have on this situation. Lives...could even be your own life…will depend on your ability to make the right decision in quick time."

Lots of luck Leon or Jiraud.

Chapter Nine

What a week this has been.

I did make it abundantly clear when I volunteered for service with the Signal Corps: I work best when I work solo. The Chief seemed to comprehend at the time but he either forgot or ignored my preference for action as a single.

It would be unwise to make him aware that my first crisis as group leader has made me edgy. After all, he is my boss. He might be rankled by any suggestion, reminder or implication that my understanding was our understanding.

I try not to fidget while I wait for him to conclude a lengthy phone call and give me his undivided attention.

Finally. "Hello, captain. Have a good flight down from The Farm?"

"The best, sir."

He wastes no time, gets right to the reason for my sudden trip to his office. "Immediately following your call and report on the behavior of the two men in your group, I requested a special-priority check of personnel records by both the FBI and G-2."

I lean forward as he opens a folder on his desk and holds up several sheets of paper.

"They moved right on it. They redid some of their investigations of both Short and Winston—with special concern for any personality problems."

I move my chair closer to the front of his desk.

"Very interesting, Leon. Some data that had escaped the initial and the secondary inquiries showed up on this update."

I frown and grunt to indicate my deep concern.

Colonel Elliott looks up from the papers. "Big surprise—I don't know how it slipped through. Our trouble maker is Bill Short."

"What about Winston?"

"He checked out 100-percent clean." Reading from the papers, "Stable. Responsible. Not a popularity-contest winner, but well liked by employers, coworkers, friends and neighbors. Not at all antagonistic but, when challenged, defends himself calmly and intelligently. Avoids confrontation. Totally non-violent. And so on."

"And Short?"

The Chief shuffles the papers and reads silently. "Aaah. He's different—the exact opposite of Winston. Bad news, very bad news there." He puts the papers down and looks up at me. "You did the correct thing reporting this to me right away."

"Thanks to Pop for bringing it to my attention."

He looks away and meditatively rubs his chin. "I don't know why the FBI and G-2 didn't uncover these facts before I offered Short a commission." He shakes his head and in a half-whisper. "A very serious oversight. A major—a senior screwup."

"Chief. It isn't the first time. I have a story about the FBI's checkup on me. This actually happened—before you invited me into this group. I have never told anyone about it."

He sits back in his chair and, as usual, makes steady eye-contact.

"I was visiting my friends at radio station WHN. On my way to master control, I went into one of the control rooms. You know…where the engineer sits at the audio console, riding gain…and there's a sloping glass window through which he is able to watch the performers and announcers in the studio. One of my engineer-friends was inside the studio talking with a man I didn't recognize and who appeared to be taking notes. My friend saw me and pointed in my direction. I switched on the studio microphone and heard him say: "Why not ask that fellow on the other side of the glass? He probably knows Leon Wortman better than anyone else I can think of."

The Chief, senses what's coming. He sits up straight. "You're kidding…aren't you?"

"No, Chief. This is real. It does sound absurd. The man picks up his brief case, shakes my friend's hand and leaves the studio. My friend broadly displays a cat-that-ate-the-canary smile and waves hello to me.

"The stranger comes into the control room and introduces himself. He says he is 'From the FBI Office.' He's been told I know Wortman. I acknowledge this, of course. His information is accurate. In fact I tell him 'We are very well acquainted'."

"How long have you known him?"

"All my life."

"How long is that?"

"Oh, 21 years, give or take."

Colonel Elliott's eyes are wide open, staring at me in disbelief. His jaw is slowly dropping lower and lower. "Tell me, Wortman. Tell me. Did you identify yourself?"

"Well, the guy doesn't ask me my name until we are several minutes into our friendly chat. He looks up from his questionnaire and note pad and, finally, asks what he should have asked at the very beginning.

"Sorry, I forgot to ask. Your name is...?"

"With as friendly a smile and as straight a face as I can manage without busting out in laughter, I tell him the truth: 'My name is Leon Wortman. Call me Wortman. Everyone else does'.

"He drops his fountain pen. Fumbles his papers. And, with as red a face as you've ever seen and as tight a throat as I've ever heard he mumbles, 'Boy, did I screw things up!"

The Chief is enjoying the tale. "Serves the bastard right!"

"He confesses he's been with the FBI only a couple of months. I promised not to tell anyone about this. We can all slip up."

The Chief glances up at the ceiling and nods affirmatively.

"So, this FBI guy gathers his papers, stuffs them into his brief case, shakes my hand and apologizes. Obviously, he wants to be anyplace but here with me. He almost breaks his neck as he stumbles down the control room's steps and hurries away."

"Well, captain. I've heard of investigators, so-called 'intelligence men,' making mistakes like that...and worse. This is the first time I've had a first-hand account." His smile stretches from ear to ear. The smile disappears, he turns to me and we are back in our official roles. "You are scheduled for several shots today, aren't you?"

"Yes, sir. I believe five."

"I'm sure you'll do fine. I think you deserve a weekend's leave. Any social plans?"

"There is a certain young lady I've been eager to date. If she's available, she's an important part of my social plan. For this weekend, that is."

The Chief stands up, smiles, returns my salute and offers a handshake. "Excellent. Your leave begins right after you get your shot. Be back on The Farm by Monday morning."

Standing outside his office, I contemplate my approach to Madeleine. Oh, hell! No games. I'll just ask her. But not in The Office. I'll call her from an outside telephone.

"*Enchanté*! Delighted! Léon, I have a suggestion. I hope you understand. It is best we are not seen dating. A good friend of mine is going out of town for a week. *En vacances pour une semaine.* She loaned to me her keys. Let's go to her place. *C'est un petit appartement in Greenwich Village. C'est okay*?"

Could I have asked for better?

We arrange to meet at Granados Café, just minutes away from the proposed scene of our mischief. I call my good friend, Larry, the restaurateur and owner of the cafe. He's an incorrigible romantic.

Larry understands and insists, "Leave all arrangements and the menu *en mis manos.* You and your lady shall have a night to remember!"

When I show up for the shots, my mind is far from the doctor's office. The nurse's voice sounds far away. The room seems to be filled with indistinct, distant echoes. No. I haven't passed out. But my head and feet feel unusually light, detached from my body. Please, nurse. "Give me the shots. I'll take them sitting down...and let me get out of here!" She does—five of them this time. And I do get the hell of there!

I arrive at Granados' 20 minutes early and, sure enough, Larry has done himself proud. He has actually closed the cafe for the evening. The tables and chairs are out of sight...except for one, small, round table and two chairs in the center of the dining room. He has changed the lighting. Instead of the usual soft white, everything is bathed in muted, pastel colors. Larry has done romantic things for me and my lady guests before. Nonetheless, I never expected this much romance! This is some first date for Madeleine and me.

Larry says, "For you, my dear friend, *mi compadre*, there's more to come. After you and your lady are seated, had your first drink of wine...and I want you to know it is the finest Spanish wine in my cellar...you will share my special broiled-camarones appetizer to be followed by my incomparable *lomo*. Then you will share and enjoy a portion of the sliced Spanish Ham I have just received from my father in Valencia. You approve?"

"Larry, this is *maravilloso. Hermoso. MUY HERMOSO*! But, do you realize the lady and I are on a date? Not a honeymoon. Aren't you getting carried away?"

"*Pero no*! You are serving our country. Now I shall serve you!"

I am uncomfortable. "Larry...this is too expensive for me. I make much less money now than I did as a civilian."

Larry stands up straight. Crosses his arms, puts his nose close to mine and abruptly lets me know how he feels. "I am too old for war. But I think maybe you are too young for love. Did I ask you, did I tell you how much this will cost?"

"No, Larry. But after all. You can't just close the restaurant on a Friday night. Isn't that expensive?"

Larry dramatically pretends to be offended. He waves his arms and whirls round and round. "So now you are telling me how to run my business! Please. Either enjoy being my guest tonight...or go elsewhere!"

I apologize and vow there is no better place for me to take my lady.

Larry signals and, within seconds, he and I are seated and enjoying good Spanish brandy while we await the arrival of Madeleine, my date for either the evening or the weekend.

Whichever she chooses, I know she's in for an extraordinary, unforgettable evening. Superbly exotic, fragrant, delicious, authentic Spanish food, fine wine and, because I have been through these events with Larry before, an evening of classic, sensual Spanish poetry recited in a whisper across the table by Larry himself accompanied by a real, live, Spanish guitarist.

Only one thing bothers me. I don't have the nerve to tell Larry that Madeleine Brouillard is very, very undeniably French, not at all Spanish.

Chapter Ten

I feel like a smug teenager every time I recollect the delicious joys of this past weekend. I would have halted the intrusive ticking of the clock, suspended time forever, at least until I experienced total physical exhaustion or Madeleine begged for mercy...whichever happened first. Either way, I could not lose.

From the moment Madeleine entered the café Larry had been especially attentive to her. With grand gestures, he declared that she did Granados and the Lorenzos great honor by having dinner in his "humble café." He made frequent *salidas*, visits to his kitchen to oversee personally the preparation of each dish. He opened and sampled every new bottle of wine he had selected specifically to accompany each course. And a toast, softly spoken in the purest Castilian, accompanied every raising of our freshly filled wine glasses.

At one point in his uniquely romantic recital of Spanish poetry with his adopted son Andres providing guitar accompaniment, Madeleine turned to me, squeezed my hand tightly and whispered, "*Léon...c'est presque trop fort pour moi*. This is almost more than I can bear. *On doit sortir. Quand*...when can we leave...go to the apartment?"

I reassured her. "*Oui, calmes toi, mon amour*. Be calm, my love. We will go there soon." I was eager to be alone with Madeleine, but how could I interrupt Larry while he was delivering one of his finest performances? It would have been unkind.

Larry rose from his chair, held his brandy snifter high, gazed tenderly at Madeleine and softly, slowly offered his favorite toast: "*Salud, pesetas y amor...y tiempo para gustarlas*. Health, wealth and love...and time to enjoy them."

I leaned toward Madeleine and softly kissed her ear as I whispered: "*Santé, la richesse et l'amour...et le temps pour y trouver du plaisir*."

Larry gently kissed Madeleine's hand and bowed deeply as though to royalty.

I don't think she fully understood his Castilian Spanish. His tone of voice and facial expressions, however, spoke eloquently for his inner emotions and transcended all cultural and language differences.

And Larry? He was so charmed by Madeleine's uncommon loveliness and gentle disposition, I don't think he ever became fully aware she was not Spanish. He accepted Madeleine completely.

A tap on my shoulder wakens me from my paradisaical reverie. Lt. Johnstone, the aircraft's co-pilot, looks down at me. "Pardon me, captain. We're approaching Albany airport. Heavy turbulence just ahead. Mind fastening your seat belt? Thank you, sir."

With a deep sigh, I fasten my seat belt, sink back into the seat, tip my cap forward to shut out the light, pull up the collar of my topcoat, close my eyes and try to recapture the thread of my memory.

Madeleine proved to be practical as well as romantic. She had arrived at Granados late for a good reason. She had carefully shopped for supplies to sustain us through the weekend in the *petit appartement*. Breakfast foods, varieties of fruits, breads, salad ingredients, cheeses, crackers and, of course, the French red wines with which she is most familiar. It was obvious she expected me to stay for the weekend. And, in matching expectations, I had made no other plans.

We made love. Oh, did we ever! Under Madeleine's guidance, tenderness and burning need for love, I demonstrated an outstanding fitness and endurance as a love partner.

She hugged me tightly and laughed lightly, "*Cher Léon*. You are one *très bon praticien d'amour*. You have learned well the art of love."

"It is not I, it is you, *mon partenaire d'amour* who deserves the honors."

I remembered how she had once confessed that, since her Edouard had been taken prisoner by the Nazis at Maginot, she often felt very lonely. Did she still feel lonely?

"*Non, Léon. Pas du tout*. I am no longer lonely. Not tonight."

And so we filled our two days and three nights together. Madeleine, the beautiful, passionate and insatiable one, and I, the partner who rescued her from loneliness.

The turbulent, real world snaps me out of my placid daydreams. The aircraft begins to roll and yaw violently. I tell myself I will not get airsick. Officers are not supposed to get airsick. Besides, as the ranking officer on this airplane…although I am probably the one with the least military and flight experience of all on board…to need a "bag" would be extremely humiliating.

I convince myself the first thing is to relax. The second thing is to take my mind off the turbulence and think only of balmy weather on a smooth sailing ship. Calling on my limited experience, I imagine myself on a warm, breezeless day in a rowboat on a lake in New York's Central Park. The queasiness disappears.

As usual, an unmarked car meets the aircraft and, half an hour, later Pop and I are enjoying mugs of hot coffee drawn from his perpetually-brewing pot. Pop quickly fills me in on everything that has happened since last Friday morning.

"Bill Short received a call from Colonel Elliott on Friday afternoon. Within an hour, a car came for Short. He took all his things—didn't even say 'Good-bye'." Pop looks directly at me. "Guess The Chief checked up on him and didn't like what he found."

He stops, waiting for me to comment or fill in some missing information. However, I feel it is inappropriate for me to offer any details. If and when The Chief wants Pop to know, The Chief should be the messenger.

"I'm going up for a shower and shave, Pop. Then I want to catch up on my training with Sergeants Mike and Frank. They're still here?"

"Sure are. They've completed the shooting sessions and, this afternoon, they begin knife combat. You might like to know they think you are one of the best instinct shots they've trained in hip shooting. The way they tell it, within a few hours of the start of the lessons, you were letting off five shots in less than four seconds at five different paper targets and each shot scored a perfect kill! Mike and Frank said they rarely ever have a student achieve that in a lifetime of training."

Everybody is enjoying lunch. The group seems more relaxed than they were last week. No one hints at or wonders out loud about Bill Short. He's gone. Although we are silent, all are happy with the change. That's enough.

By the end of the week and to my surprise, I have developed skills in knife throwing. I can repeatedly hit a target, a playing card mounted on a pine board 30 feet away. The sergeants are pleased, but point out I may not always have access to a well-balanced 14-ounce knife made for the military by the famous Harry McEvoy, specialist in the design and manufacture of professional-grade throwing knives.

In the meantime I enjoy showing off my newly acquired skill. I discover I can throw and dependably hit a target holding the knife by either the handle or the blade, in either my right or left hand. The sergeants proudly make a point of telling all of us this is unusual for a beginner.

Beware you Nazis! Sometimes I wonder what I am really about. What makes me tick?_All through my growing up years I have avoided violence. Now I no longer really know what is, who is the real Leon. Learning to turn violent behavior on and off at will is, I suppose, one of the objectives of this sort of training. We have been shooting and throwing knives at paper targets. But...how will we...how will I react when the target is a real, live human being? I try not to think about that.

Thursday night. Tomorrow I return to New York for five more medical shots in the series. That makes 11 with two more to go. The communication system signals an incoming call from Colonel Elliott. He tells me to take all my things with me this time. "You probably won't be coming back to The Farm."

"What's up, Chief?" Friday evening, immediately after my shots, he and I will fly to Washington D.C. for a weekend conference with *iDIV* senior officers. "What does this signify?"

"Probably an overseas assignment. Where to? We'll learn that from *iDIV* in DC."

"Without completing the shots, sir?"

"You can complete the series when we get back to New York."

The Chief already has the tickets for our commercial-airline flight to Washington. We race to our hotel in the Bowery, quickly pack a few of our personal necessities, grab a cab to the airport and make it just in time to board the airplane. Military passengers outnumber civilians. Not surprising, I suppose. We are at war and trying hard to get everything up to full speed.

At the moment, things look bleak. Great Britain, depending on the United States and Canada for supplies, is barely holding on. Hitler's Navy knows this and is amassing wolfpacks of U-Boats in the Atlantic to sink merchant ships headed for the United Kingdom. The Germans can apparently build their attack submarines faster than we can build our Merchant Marine. Not good.

Where do I fit into the scheme of things. This visit to iDIV's HQ may provide some enlightenment. So far, all I have done is achieve high marks in instinct shooting, knife throwing and making love to Madeleine. In my private moments of honesty and self-evaluation, I do not feel useful to the Allied war efforts.

A khaki-colored car and its khaki-uniformed driver meet us at the airport. We are whisked away to a suburb of Washington and deposited at an unmarked, decrepit building—a warehouse or some other industrial structure. Colonel Elliott and I show our IDs to the MPs outside and again inside the entrance to the building. After consulting a folder, we are cleared and provided with a two-man armed escort down a flight of stairs. Once more, an MP asks for our IDs. The contents of a folder are consulted. Apparently we are expected.

Our escort opens a door and, at last, we are at our destination...an impressive, well lit, high-ceilinged room, about 30 feet wide and 40 feet long. Huge maps of the United Kingdom, the Atlantic Ocean, and Europe hang against the far wall. The long conference-table is surrounded by large, swivel chairs. The room is very quiet, apparently soundproofed.

Doors suddenly burst open and a river of uniformed men enters. Colonel Elliott knows everyone. He salutes and greets each person by rank and name. I have never seen this many high-ranking officers in one place. The lowest rank I see is major. The highest is a one-star general. We are invited to take seats at the conference table across from a full colonel, apparently the leader of the conference.

After a brief review of the state of affairs in England, very dismal and even more so in France, the general takes over and looks directly at Colonel Elliott. He describes a small band of resistance people in France who call themselves "Maquis".

I know the word, *maquis*. It translates as "underbrush" or "scrub growth."

The general points out it means underground. "And these Maquisards desperately need our help in getting organized and equipped so they can become effective in screwing up the Nazis in France!"

"May we hear from you, colonel?" The general means Lt. Colonel Elliott. "I understand you have some interesting ideas and have volunteered to help." He waits for Colonel Elliott to speak.

"Thank you, gentlemen, for giving me the opportunity to expand on the subject of the Maquis. We are fortunate to have two members of my group who are ideally suited to the task of initiating direct contact with the Maquis." He turns toward me. "I'd like to introduce one of them: Captain L. Wortman."

All heads and eyes turn toward me. For a moment, I am startled. I have not been briefed at all on the specific objective of this Washington visit. I nod in the affirmative and slowly turn my head in acknowledgment of the men at the conference table.

"Captain Wortman is a native-born American. He's fluent in French and one of the smartest strategists in my group. The other is an exceptionally bright Frenchwoman, Madeleine Brouillard, who has been working for and with me for the past year. She comes to us directly from a background of work with England's MI5 and MI6 operations."

The general sounds very interested. "Continue, please."

"I propose to send Captain Wortman and Miss Brouillard into southern France to meet with the leaders of the Maquis, get first-hand knowledge and information about their strengths and objectives, assist in the development of plans of action and bring back to *iDIV* as much information they can acquire. We will then have a significantly stronger base of knowledge and know exactly what we can do to implement the Maquis' action plan.

"It might work. I leave it up to you and my staff to fill in the details and get this going. When do you propose to start, colonel?"

"Captain Wortman and Miss Brouillard can leave for England within the next few days, if air transport can be arranged, general."

"Good as done." He turns to a major seated at the table. "Major Hall will make all the arrangements for transportation to UK."

"Thank you, general."

"Thank you, colonel. And..." He turns to me with a smile. "Captain Wortman. Tell me. How long have you been in the service?"

I muster a semblance of self-confidence. "Several months, sir."

Scattered coughing breaks out among the officers, followed by an eloquent silence.

An hour later, Colonel Elliott and I are flying back to New York City. We are deeply involved with our own private thoughts. No conversation.

I have some difficulty absorbing the nuances of the day's events. I am trying to understand the uneasiness, the discomfort I feel about the colonel. In many ways he is admirable. Yet, why do I not completely trust the man? And Madeleine—is she actually what or who she appears to be? Technically, the colonel does have total control over me. And I am quite aware of the dangers inherent in any emotional attachment to Madeleine. My instincts and intuitions have usually been dependable. En garde, Jiraud!

In the cab returning to the city, I break the silence. “I can still make it to the doctor’s office in time for my medical shots, colonel.”

“Okay. I’ll drop you off. But come to my office directly from the doctor’s.” The colonel hesitates and stares out the cab’s side window. “We have a lot to talk about...you, Wortman or Jiraud, Madeleine and I.”

I detect a inexplicable smirk on the colonel’s face.

Chapter Eleven

Cabs in New York City are never plentiful at this time of day. I run along the street frantically waving arms and whistling at every passing taxi. People must think, "He's mad!" or "The City is under attack!" By the time I manage to flag down an empty cab I have almost closed the distance between the doctor's and the colonel's offices.

The colonel greets me without a smile. "Okay, okay. Catch your breath. Relax. You're here now." He points to a chair; a brusque message that means unambiguously: SIT DOWN! He presses the button on the square intercom box and tells Madeleine to "join us right away!"

Madeleine comes in and, without prompting from the colonel, sits in the chair next to me, her legs close together, feet firmly planted on the floor and hands clasped tightly in her lap. Despite all my resolve, she continues to charm me. The woman is beautiful. Dammit! This is not easy for me.

The colonel leans forward, hands locked together. I have seen this posture dozens of times before. His head turns and his eyes fix on Madeleine and then on me, back and forth, back and forth. He continues to do this until he is absolutely certain of our complete attention. One of his personal power-plays. Not only suspenseful, it is intimidating—and deliberate. He is the only one allowed to interrupt this *petit jeux*, this little game. He invented it and he sets up the unwritten rules. Other than the ticking of the clock on the wall, not a sound is heard. One cannot help but be slightly startled when he speaks.

"Let's clarify why the three of us are here." He unlocks his hands. "Wortman, you already know the operation as it was described at our *iDIV* conference. Stick with me while I explain it to Madeleine. The two of you will be flown to England or Scotland for a briefing with U.S., British Intelligence and, possibly, Free-French Intelligence Officers. Major Hall, *iDIV HQ*, is setting up your itinerary from here to the U.K. Your objective is to make physical contact with the Maquis in Southern France, collect data and return to the U.K. for a debriefing. Then back to the U.S. for your next assignment...to be determined later.

"How much time do you spend in France? Your entry and exit dates will be determined before you leave England. Air Corps will take care of getting you to England. The British and our own people in England will work out the specifics of getting you into France and getting you out of there when your mission is complete.

"When do you leave? You are on standby alert right now. Go directly to the hotel from this office. Behave normally, casually. Do not leave the hotel's premises until you are advised, by me, that a car is waiting for you at the hotel's back-door. Tell no one, neither family nor friends, where you are going. In fact you will not tell anyone you are going anywhere. Each of you will pack a small duffel bag with minimal supplies: one complete change of clothing and necessary toilet articles. If you need anything else that is not already in your room, request the items when you arrive in England. Do not make new purchases at our hotel's commissary."

He leans back in his chair and again looks from Madeleine to me, back and forth. "No fuss. No change in behavior. All normal. Nothing to give yourselves away. Do I make myself clear? Now, any questions?"

Madeleine and I look at each other for a long moment. I respond, "No, sir."

Madeleine echoes, "None, sir."

This strikes me as odd. I learned our objective at the Washington conference this morning. Madeleine was not there...yet she has no questions. Has she learned the details from_someone, possibly someone who had attended the conference? From the colonel? Or does she have other, secret sources? My instincts are waving a warning flag. Stick close to Madeleine. Do not let her out of your sight.

Colonel Elliott looks directly at Madeleine. "Tomorrow morning I will have new IDs and dog tags for you. During this operation, you will be identified temporarily as Second Lieutenant M. Brouillard."

Although I think I know the answer, the question must be asked. "Colonel. Why is Madeleine being given a temporary rank and IDs?"

He answers without hesitation. "While you are in enemy territory, France in this case, if you are not in military uniform with a serialized ID—and if you should be captured, taken prisoner—you can be declared a 'spy' and executed. And there is not a damn thing we can do about it."

Madeleine stands up and declares, "But, Colonel Elliott. I am a French National. If I am in a foreign country's uniform, such as the U.S. Signal Corps, I can be considered by the Nazis to be a spy. *N'est ce pas?*"

The colonel frowns. "Possibly. But we believe you are better off wearing an American Military Uniform. You decide whether to wear it or go civilian. Nazi reaction to such situations has been unpredictable. You will have to make the decision on that. Wortman is your superior officer. After the briefings in England you and he decide what you think is best."

As if reading my thoughts, Colonel Elliott looks directly at me. "Madeleine knows the risk. I think she can handle the situation." He shifts his attention to Madeleine. "In the morning, go to Sergeant Apple, our quartermaster in the hotel's basement. Hand him this envelope. It contains a requisition for two sets of uniforms for yourself to be ready no later than noon, tomorrow. He will ask no questions. The requisition is stamped 'SECRET' and he will keep it exactly that way, SECRET. Any questions now, either of you?"

"I have one, colonel. Shall I carry my Captain Wortman ID or am I Captain Brevier?"

The colonel sits back in his chair and rubs his chin while staring at me. “You were introduced at the *iDIV* conference as ‘Captain Wortman’. Major Hall will probably refer to ‘Captain L. Wortman’ in all coded dispatches and conferences related to this operation. So, what do you think?”

“Wortman I am, sir. Don’t know anybody called ‘Brevier’—for now.”

Chapter Twelve

When a General of the Army issues orders, the lumbering, gigantic, military bureaucracy moves with surprising energy and speed.

Madeleine and I stay in our separate rooms at the hotel standing by for Colonel Elliott's order to start the operation now labeled "Operation New Ark." I haven't the foggiest idea who determines these code names. This one might have been created by a student of the Bible.

In less than 19 hours, Colonel Elliott calls and issues a one-word command: "GO!"

From now on, Madeleine and I are the principal figures in this unwritten scenario. Only Act One has been plotted for us—the flight on a military air transport to Scotland. There we meet with several men in British Army uniforms and identified only by first names. No further descriptions are offered. I assume they are with one of two British Intelligence Agencies, MI5 or MI6.

They are smug about the fact that British Military Intelligence has been in operation for years and, without question, knows all about the game of espionage. They refer to our Yankee intelligence group as "a diapered infant," "a spoiled, overfed, under-trained bunch of nitwits!"

Their overbearing attitude annoys me, but a heated reaction could easily escalate into something approaching an international incident. Fortunately, Madeleine changes the subject and diplomatically steers us back onto the right track and the reason why we have flown here on short notice under "direct orders from Brigadier General Leblanc of the U.S. Signal Corps." Name dropper! *But...how does she know the General's name? I have never heard it mentioned.*

The arrival of Colonel James, U.S. Signal Corps, accompanied by his British counterpart, Colonel Fort-Blaine, is very welcome. Colonel James, now stationed in the U.K., makes a big point of talking about how closely U.S. personnel work with the British. He sounds more like a public relations representative than a communications officer. *I never have been good at the acrobatics of diplomacy and politics. Certainly, I am totally inexperienced at the international level. I will have to work on changing this. That is a personal promise.*

We become absorbed in a discussion of the objectives of "Operation New Ark." Colonel James has apparently been thoroughly briefed and speaks plainly about our need for secure transportation into southern France, preferably Marseilles. We will remain there for ten days and then be picked up and transported back to the U.K. Each time he says "our" or "we" he waves toward Madeleine and me. The group answers all questions promptly and concisely.

Col. Fort-Blaine asks "What supplies—clothing, weapons, food—Captain Wortman and Lieutenant Brouillard will need?"

"The U.S. Quarter Master will attend to all that."

"They will travel light, of course."

"Only what they can wear and stuff into small hand-sacks."

A flight to Gibraltar is the first leg of the route into France, then probably by coastal fishing boat into the waters off Marseilles and a smaller boat onto a beach outside the city.

Many details are omitted from our conversation. Safer for all concerned—especially for Madeleine and me. Colonel Fort-Blaine agrees to communicate with Colonel James, who will then advise us when and where we board our transportation to Gibraltar. Colonel Fort-Blaine advises us to be ready to "go" at any moment.

As they leave, the Brits shake hands with us. "Bully! Good game! On with the chase!" Colonel James suggests Madeleine and I go with him to his quarters where we can shower and have a light dinner with him while we wait for Colonel Fort-Blaine's call. Also, if we make a quick list of basic supplies, he will have it filled within an hour. Madeleine elects to stay in uniform all during the operation inside France.

At his modest quarters, Colonel James hands me a wide-web belt, a holstered British Walther pistol and several clips of ammunition. He winks at me. "You never know when a little back talk might come in handy. And this little puppy has a very mature vocabulary."

I check the pistol's trigger and slide-action, emptying, inserting, removing and reloading all the clips until I feel sure of myself in handling the gun.

Colonel James suggests we do not retire. He feels certain that Colonel Fort-Blaine will have us on our way at any moment. The mission is being coordinated by British Military Intelligence. Colonel James tells us Madeleine and I will be flown in two separate RAF fighter-planes to a base on Gibraltar.

"What about the Luftwaffe spotting us?"

"Intelligence has a plan for that condition. As a diversion, a flight of six RAF fighter-bombers will take off from here a quarter of an hour before you depart and will cruise at a low altitude just off the coast of Spain. This should draw Nazi attention away from a flight of two fighter planes, not bombers, flying alone—which will be your planes. This simple ruse should work. The Nazis never seem to grasp strategies as silly as this one."

"What happens after we land on Gibraltar?"

"Damned if they told me. Security, of course. All I can tell you is that the two of you will be met in Gibraltar by a British agent who will fill in the rest of the details and give you the route into Marseilles and your rendezvous with the Maquis. He should also have exact info on the signals you will use to identify yourselves to the Maquisards and, of course, their confirming signals to you."

As we try to enjoy a second cup of coffee, we hear a series of knocks on the door—three, then two, then one. Colonel James rises. "You transportation is here. Ready?"

The colonel's quarters are no more than a mile or two from the airbase. Inside the communications shack, Madeleine and I are handed wool scarves, fleece-lined flight jackets and boots. "You'll need these. The planes have no interior heating and it gets cold up there."

Quickly we are led to two Spitfires. Their engines are running, warming up. Madeleine and I are separated. I am directed to the lead plane, Madeleine to the one directly behind mine. Just before I enter the cockpit, I look back at Madeleine. She waves, briskly climbs up and her tiny figure disappears into the cockpit area behind the pilot. I force myself into a very small space directly behind my pilot. The canopy is lowered and I am encased in a cocoon. I can only see the back of my pilot's head as he turns right and left, leaning sideways for a visual check of the exterior of the Spitfire.

He waves his right arm. The plane lurches forward as the restraining wheel-chocks are pulled free. The engine racgs loudly. The plane vibrates fiercely. I feel it moving, rapidly picking up speed. I have a sensation the Spitfire is slowly pitching forward. Must be the tail rising off the ground. Within seconds we are airborne and climbing into the dark blue-black sky.

Chapter Thirteen

My sense of direction has been overwhelmed. I have no impression of our altitude. No lights in here. I can barely see the pilot tapping the top and side of his head. Does he want me to put on the helmet clipped to the back of his seat? As soon as I do so, I hear his heavily, British-accented voice. "G'evenin', sir. Name's Minster, Flight-Lieutenant Minster. We can talk to each other through the microphone and earphones built into our helmets."

"Loud and clear, Minster. Are we transmitting over the radio, I mean the wireless?"

"No, sir. Strict silence all the way to Gibraltar. And, except for our sidearms, we have no guns or ammunition. Had to reduce the Spitfire's weight, you know."

He is feeling talkative and I am in a listening mood.

"If we're lucky, Jerry won't spot us. Our pals in the diversionary flight will do a bang-up job distracting them and deceiving their—whatever those Nasties use these days to see in the dark."

"Is our partner plane in view?" I am thinking about Madeleine.

"Maybe not in 'view', sir. But we are both flying at a planned altitude, same speed and compass bearing. We will be over the Atlantic most of the way. I dare say we won't have a visual sighting of any landmarks until we are on approach to the strip at Gibraltar."

I confidently pat the pistol strapped on my right side, and try for a nap. Nothing else for me to do.

The sudden roar, a change in pitch of the plane's engine and a steeply-angled left banking sensation awaken me. "What's up, Minster?"

"We should be just west of Gibraltar, sir. No sign of Jerry. I will briefly blink our landing lights as an identifying signal to the guys on the landing strip. I must watch for a confirming string of lights down below, on our starboard. They should be bright enough barely bright enough for us to see in the night. They will indicate the boundaries of the landing strip as soon as our identity is confirmed."

From my deep-down crouched position I can see nothing beyond the inside of the cockpit. I feel the Spitfire's steeply banked turns to port and starboard. My stomach tells me we are descending. Then the bounce of the touchdown. The engine emits an angry roar and we roll to a full stop. Madeleine's plane lands 200 feet behind us. Following Minster, I climb down from the cockpit. Madeleine runs over to me with arms outstretched and moves to hug me. Minster clears his throat loudly and Madeleine restrains herself. Military decorum, of course.

A vehicle pulls up and the driver motions for us to climb in. Before I can thank my pilot, we are whisked off in the darkness. In no more than ten seconds time, we pull up to a sudden stop at...I can barely see its outline...a small structure, a shack. The driver of our transportation jumps out and salutes smartly. "This way, please."

We follow him as he opens the shack's door, closes it quickly behind us, pulls aside a blackout curtain and motions for us to continue on through. For a moment, the sudden light from the room on the other side of the curtain blinds me. Madeleine and I are introduced namelessly to an equally nameless British Officer and a short, unshaven man in rumpled black clothing and a knit seaman's cap.

The officer speaks up immediately. "Beg pardon my friends, but there's no time for unessential conversation." He introduces the rumpled man. His name is Raoul. Appears to be in his mid-fifties. Dark clothing, jet black hair, unshaven face and dark eyes give him the appearance of being in a state of natural blackout. Raoul strikes me as an open, friendly sort of man. His powerful handshake, strong eye contact, husky voice and easy laugh make me feel instinctively he is the kind of man one can trust.

Raoul operates his own small, fishing trawler, a *chalutier*. He tells us his boat is well known to the German coastal-patrols and U-Boats in the Mediterranean and should provide us with reasonably secure passage to our rendezvous "with his friends." He is our transportation and guide to Marseilles, our direct link to the Maquis.

The British officer points out, "At the moment, the Nazis control the Mediterranean, the air as well as the sea, and Raoul's boat offers the best way for us to avoid detection."

To take maximum advantage of the darkness, we must leave at once. The trawler is docked nearby. The over-size fuel tanks have been refilled and, after a hurried bit of food and hot cocoa, we are ready to go. Raoul suggests we continue to wear the heavy flight clothing, boots, jackets and scarves. It can be very cold at night on his *petit chalutier*. We can change to lighter clothing—he will provide it—when we reach our destination. The plan is to appear to trawl for fish as we sail two or three kilometers off the southern coasts of Spain and France. This is least likely to arouse the suspicions of the lookouts on the German patrol-boats.

The Germans know Raoul always works with his brother, Barduc. U-Boat periscopes sometimes observe and follow their trawler. German scouting planes will sometimes fly low over the boat. To be safe during the day, Madeleine and I must remain inside the boat's modest cabin. He apologizes for the boat's interior. It consists only of a single bunk, a small cooking stove and, of course, the hold for the fish, the engine compartment and the two very large petrol tanks.

"You will have very little freedom of movement." With a suggestive twinkle and a husky laugh, "I suggest you use the bunk to lie down and refresh yourselves." A friendly but bawdy innuendo. Madeleine and I exchange glances. We are much too tired for anything but quiet and rest.

"The voyage to our meeting place will take approximately 40 hours, more or less, depending on the weather and the curiosity of the Nazi patrols. However, fortunately, the weather has been fine lately and the Nazis rarely board and inspect my boat." With a gutteral scowl and an imitation of spitting, Raoul demonstrates his hatred every time he says "Nazi."

Raoul is amused by the game he plays. "They seek much bigger fish than I can pull out of the sea. But, to satisfy their inspectors, we must return with some cargo of fish to sell at the market. So, as we enter the *Golfe du Lion* in the Marseilles area, I will slow my *chalutier* to throw our nets overboard and drag them for a while."

When we board the trawler, Raoul introduces his brother. Barduc is about the same height as Raoul, but about five years younger. Unlike extroverted Raoul, Barduc is quiet. He does not offer many opportunities for small talk or conversation. As though in imitation of Raoul, Barduc wears dark clothing, rumpled, of course. He has a weatherbeaten complexion and, like his brother, is unshaven. He does not wear a hat. His black hair is as rumpled as his clothing. His hands are large, rough and strong. For many years, the brothers Raoul and Barduc have worked together as a team.

During the long trip to our destination, Raoul and Barduc take turns at the ship's wheel. They alternately catch naps on the bare deck of the boat. Their last names are not revealed to us. As Raoul puts it with a wide grin and his hoarse laugh, "Better for all to not know this. *Mes amis en terre et nous, moi et Barduc*...my friends ashore...we always use and offer only first names or nicknames. *Ça vaut mieux*. It is best. What one does not know, one cannot confess to the enemy. *C'est vrai. Non*?"

Raoul reveals the identification signals. "We must arrive at night in the *Golfe du Lion*, approximately 100 kilometers west of Marseilles. An hour after we reach our destination, we must flash a light, briefly, just once toward shore. Then we watch most intently for a small answering light from the shore. If it shows one long and two short blinks, we are able to come ashore. If there are no blinks, we must move away, continue to trawl and return the next night."

Exhausted, Madeleine and I sleep deeply. As far as we know, our sea voyage is uneventful. We are totally surprised when Raoul tells us we were approached twice by Nazi patrol-boats and several times by airplanes. His eyes open wide and his usual smile twists with anger. "Oh, they recognized me and Barduc and my boat all right and did nothing more than wave hello, *salut! Mon dieu*! Those *bâtards* can appear to be so nice. I think they probably smile even as they *découper en filets leurs victimes*, cut their victims into fillets." He shakes his fist and pounds the boat's bulkhead as he curses. "I despise them! *Merde alors! Merde alors!*

Barduc ehoes Raoul. "*Merde alors!*"

Raoul slowly removes his knit cap. Our two fishermen-guides humbly apologize to Madeleine for using such language. Madeleine reassures the two men she has heard those words spoken at other times, and not always in anger. "*Après tout, j'ai grandit avec deux frères de bonne santé*." She graciously tells them, "After all, I grew up with two healthy brothers."

Raoul and Barduc, our two robust fisherman, repeatedly and warmly say, "*Merci, Lieutenant Brouillard. Merci. Merci.*"

Timing of our voyage brings us into the *Golfe du Lion* on a starlit, moonless night. Raoul whispers, "There." He points to our port side. "That direction. The small communities of *Les Arles* and *Ville-Fonette*." Barduc slows the trawler's engine almost to a full stop. "In one hour we will make our signal. As soon as *nos amis* are certain they have identified my boat, and the *Golfe* and the shore are clear of the Nazis, they will signal to us. We must all wait. Barduc and I will keep the lookout for the lights. As soon as we see the signal, you two and I must immediately jump into the *youyou*, the dinghy trailing behind us, and row strongly in the direction from which the signal lights have come."

Time drags. The slow, staccato *sicsh-sutsh* of the engine and the gentle, legato sounds of the sea swishing and slapping against the trawler's side seem unusually loud. Suddenly, appearing to float in the air above the two villages—a speck of light—a bit larger and brighter than the stars, flashes once. Then two short blinks. Okay! Come ashore!

Raoul and Barduc spring into action. They bring the engine to a full stop, quickly pull the *youyou* to the stern of the *chalutier*. Raoul jumps in and beckons for me to follow him. I can hardly see the small boat as it bounces and rocks in the rolling sea. I do see Raoul's hand signals. I jump. He clamps me in his arms to keep me from falling into the Mediterranean. Together we catch Madeleine. Raoul thrusts an oar at me. He motions. I must sit on the board next to him. Madeleine at the stern.

Raoul frees the *youyou's* towline, then he and I pull hard for shore.

Chapter Fourteen

Raoul continuously turns his head from left to right, nervously watching for patrol boats. Like keeping an eye out for your executioner. If we are intercepted by the Nazis or by French *collaborateurs*, there is no escape. Prison. Interrogation. Possibly worse. Raoul would probably be executed. Barduc would be on his own but, without a doubt, he, too, would be trapped. I silently sing the Marseillaise. *Why should I be concerned? I'm rowing in the Mediterranean Sea with a goddamm French hero! Yet, the distance between the trawler and the beach seems to be the longest of all straight lines.*

Every few seconds, without breaking his stroke, Raoul looks up at the sky and backward over his shoulder to make certain we are still rowing toward the shore. He doesn't need a compass. A lifetime as a fisherman must have sharpened his hearing. Familiar sounds of the sea tell him the general direction of his travel. He corrects the bearing of the dinghy by pulling harder and faster or by holding his oar out of the water.

Every minute or so, Raoul signals for me to stop rowing and puts his index finger to his lips. Shh! Shh! He slowly turns his head to the right and then to the left, listening for sounds of the enemy on the sea around us and on the beach.

Sea spray slaps at us and makes the air feel cold. Madeleine buries her head in the protective collar of her heavy flight jacket. Continuous rowing keeps my body temperature comfortably high. My thoughts are on the next steps as soon as we are at the beach.

Obviously, the first thing we must do is drag the dinghy ashore and somehow conceal it. Then Madeleine and I will follow Raoul closely as he guides us past the Nazi patrols to the Maquis' *cachette*, the hideout. A forest? A cave? A house? I don't know which or where. As Raoul said, "What one does not know, one cannot confess." So, I do not ask for details. I am certain only that Madeleine and I will be taken to the cachette as quickly as possible. Maybe, at last, I will be able to pay off all those hours of defensive training and shooting with the two Marine Sergeants, Frank and Joe. Bless 'em.

Like a mechanical rowing machine, I have been concentrating intensely on getting to the beach. Raoul suddenly signals me to stop just as the dinghy's bow heaves upward and slides onto the beach. We must move immediately. In one continuous motion, we carefully lay the oars down inside the dinghy and jump out.

Following Raoul's unambiguous hand signals, we pull the dinghy onto the beach as far as we can. Fortunately, we find a patch of heavy, dry shrubs in which to hide the little boat. Raoul expertly uses his fish-skewering knife to cut down some branches and cover the dinghy more completely. He signals us as he drops flat onto the beach and listens for sounds of activity. Madeleine presses close to my left side. I draw my pistol. A voice inside me whispers, "Wortman, this is not a training exercise."

Okay. If the Nazis capture us, it won't be because I didn't fight. I have often wondered how I would react under the pressure of the real thing. Right now my heart is pounding. My breathing is deep but steady and quiet. I am very much alert. All my senses are sharp. Bet I can hear a twig snap a mile away. Or detect the soft kiss of two young, French lovers. I can smell the putrid, fishy, salt air and the dry, stinking sand close to my nose.

Part in fright, part in wonder, Madeleine stares at me. Our eyes meet and she smiles. I gently take her right hand in my left and reassuringly squeeze. *What a crazy thing to think about right now. Maybe later, Wortman.*

We remain motionless a quarter of an hour. Raoul again signals us to be quiet as he slowly rises to his feet. He crouches, moves forward and waves his arm, "Follow me." Imitating Raoul, Madeleine and I get into crouching positions. Raoul points toward the hills in front of us and moves forward, still in a crouch. I signal Madeleine to follow him. I follow closely, protectively placing Madeleine more safely between Raoul and me. We maintain a separation of about 12 feet as we follow Raoul. Never saw a man run so fast while crouching and still make no noise. As an American boy, I thought only Indians knew how to do it.

Raoul is lightly dressed while Madeleine and I are still in our heavy, bulky flight jackets and boots. I am aware we are going uphill in a forest. Again and again we change direction by as much as 90-degrees left and right, reverse and resume our ascent. Every time the sky becomes visible through the overhead branches of the trees, Raoul stops, quickly examines the stars, assures himself we are moving in the correct direction. As his own ship's navigator, he has learned to steer by the stars. For him, the same stars serve the identical purpose on land.

Hard as we try, we cannot avoid making some noise. Each time we do, Raoul stops abruptly and listens for new sounds. Have we been overheard? Spotted? We hold our breath for a moment and then move on. This stop-and-go continues for several hours. The eastern sky becomes brighter as dawn approaches. I have the feeling Raoul has been leading us in circles.

Am I becoming paranoid? Distrusting every one? Wortman, put yourself in Raoul's place. I am just one American. Sure I've got credentials—but the Maquis have an entire population to care for and protect. I'd probably do the same, at least as much, if this were my country, my people.

For a moment I have doubts. But my brief meditation plus the pistol near my hand and nobody at my back—give me added confidence. *Besides, Wortman, at this moment you have no_other option. Right?* I almost shout, "Right!"

Raoul quietly drops onto his belly and waves to Madeleine and me to come alongside him. Madeleine looks back at me. I nod, "yes" and crawl to her. Together, we scramble to Raoul's side. Raoul, in a hoarse whisper, cautions us. "*Quinze minutes d'attente ici.*" We shall wait here 15 minutes. He puts his head on his left arm and falls asleep at once. I test my exercises in autohypnosis to quickly put myself to sleep.

I am being shaken. Raoul stands above me. Madeleine lies on the ground. In the half light I see a group of armed men looking down at me and Madeleine. I reach for my pistol.

Chapter Fifteen

Raoul holds out his hands and shakes his head vigorously. "*Non! Non! Ce n'est pas nécessaire.* No! No! That's not necessary." He waves his arms in a circle. "*Voici nos amis. Maquisards tous!* These are our friends. All Maquisards." Madeleine awakens with a start and I repeat Raoul's statement as we both stand up and share vigorous handshakes, tight hugs and cheek-to-cheek greetings.

Is this the French underground? Eleven men? We are cautioned about noise and loud talk as Raoul and the 11 Maquisards escort us further up the hillside through more forested areas. The sheltering tree-line ends abruptly about 50 feet below the hilltop. From this clearing one has a panoramic view of the surrounding countryside and the Mediterranean. Whatever the strategic advantage this spot may have, Raoul points out we can also be seen by others down below. One never stands upright in the clearing.

The Maquis campsite is about 30 feet inside the edge of the forest. They have dug a pit approximately five feet wide, four feet deep and 15 feet long and covered it with tree branches. In this hand-made below-ground trench, they store their weapons, ammunition and supplies, all of which are...well, it would be an overstatement to describe them as "meager." Their guns are typical civilian sporting weapons, rifles and shotguns in assorted calibers and antiquities. The supply of ammunition is virtually non-existent. Just a few small, wooden boxes. No wonder they have been crying out for help, for support in the form of ordnance. They can recruit and train the men, but warriors without armament are not effective. They can neither attack nor defend. Impotent against the heavily armed Nazi forces. Powerless to aid their own people.

"*Quel dommage! Quel dommage*!" Madeleine repeats over and over. "What a pity!"

Raoul and his friends talk quietly among themselves and then turn toward Madeleine and me. "We have much work to do. First, you must eat and rest here for a while." Madeleine pats her stomach, smiles and nods agreement. Neither of us has had sufficient food or liquid in the past 24 hours.

With proud smiles, two of the Maquis produce several bottles of red wine. Loaves of bread and small wheels of cheese appear. Madeleine and I shed our flight jackets, and thirteen men and one woman squat at the makeshift banquet table, a blanket spread on the ground.

I am not a connoisseur of wine and cheese. However, at this moment, if it were in my power to do so, I would award this *vin ordinaire* and the delicious *pain et fromage* the grandest, most golden of medals.

Even in her hastily converted man-soldier uniform, Madeleine's shapely, sensuous form is apparent. I have become increasingly aware of one Maquisard, a relatively older man, staring at her while we refill our stomachs. He bites into his bread, chews slowly and takes small swallows of wine as he studies her. It is not her body that holds his attention, he focuses on her face. His expression is serious, intense, as though he is trying to recall something, wondering, "Where...where have I seen this woman before? Where?"

Raoul, too, must have noticed. He moves over and squats in front of the man. They are talking to each other so quietly I cannot hear a word of what is being said. I look at Madeleine. She, too, notices the man's stares. They make her very nervous. I move over and sit next to her. "*Dis. Madeleine. A quoi penses?* What are you thinking about?"

She turns her head in my direction and, although she replies, "*Rien. Rien du tout.* Nothing. Nothing at all." I can see anxiety in her eyes, a degree of distress I have never seen before. She looks back at the man and attempts a self-confident smile, but it falls short of the mark. I do not know exactly what is going on. But something bizarre is in the works.

The toughest part of my job. I think, is identifying people I can trust without reservation. So far, in this damned war I doubt I can name a half dozen of them. What about Raoul? On a scale of one to ten, I thought he was a tenner. But...right now I have some doubt. On the other hand, the Brits back on Gibraltar give him the highest marks. So, give Raoul more time before you give up on him. But, still...keep your pistol close by...just in case. At the first sign of treachery, Wortman, shoot accurately...and be ready to run like hell! Looks like you're still in this thing practically all alone.

"Amusing game we play, isn't it Madeleine?" I try to sound concerned but not anxious.

She whispers to me. "*Je ne m'amuse pas. Je vois que c'est un jeux bizarre.* I am not amused. I see a bizarre game. *Très bizarre.*"

With artificial compassion, I put my arm around her shoulders and add, "*Oui. Très étrange.* Very strange."

The fear leaves her eyes and she becomes, once again, the self-assured, unafraid woman who escaped from France, joined British Intelligence and came to the United States under the protection of "my colonel, Bill Elliott."

That's one helluva résumé. Opens the door to lots of questions. Maybe, from among these Maquisards, I can learn more about her complex background. At least, they might be able to put to rest the concerns, doubts and suspicions I have been closely guarding ever since I became part of Colonel Elliott's strange bunch of iDIV mavericks and misfits.

Raoul and the older man end their whispered conference. Raoul stands up, waves and smiles at me. He motions to the others to gather around him, except the older man. They walk off into the forest about 50 feet from where Madeleine and I sit on the blanket. The man continues to chew his bread and cheese slowly and sips his wine. Never, not for an instant, does he take his eyes off Madeleine and me.

My body is tense. I feel a strong pressure at my temples. My legs and arms are like tightly coiled springs ready to snap. It won't take much to trip the latch and turn me into a fighting demon.

Chapter Sixteen

Raoul and the others return. Raoul glances at the older man who has been watching us and says, "*Tout d'accord.* Everything's okay." The older man relaxes and smiles at me. Madeleine and I stand up and the men gather around us. Raoul confirms he is this group's leader, Capitaine Raoul. To protect their families, no last names are exchanged. We all relax and move around comfortably—except Madeleine. She seems troubled.

Raoul must return to the dinghy and his trawler tonight after dark. He introduces one of the men as Lieutenant Baptiste. A little older than I, perhaps in his mid to late twenties, Baptiste is neither handsome nor homely. Very ordinary. Plain. He holds his slightly built body straight. His posture is impressive, almost but not quite soldierly. Dark brown hair and brown eyes offset a fair complexion; definitely not that of an outdoorsman. However, his manner personifies drama, determination and dedication. No doubt what he lacks in military weapons is more than compensated by the firepower of his spirit.

At Raoul's signal we gather round. He advises us Baptiste is in charge when he, Raoul, is away. I am to remain with Baptiste's group and discuss the ordnance they need to wage their kind of underground warfare against the Nazis. "*À peu prés trente-sept kilomètres au nord de l'est*, approximately 37 kilometers to the northeast, one of our other groups is planning counter-actions against a relatively large force of Nazis—as soon as they get proper weapons—guns, grenades, ammunition, explosives. In a couple of days Madeleine will be led to their hideout by Paul." He points to the older man. "Three of our *confrères* will also go with them. We need the same kind of information about the other group's ordnance and communications requirements."

Colonel Elliott had made me responsible for Madeleine. I am her senior officer and I don't like the idea of not being able to supervise her. However, with some reluctance, I agree. What else am I to do? Temporarily, I am a Maquisard. I cannot refuse to allow her to leave when Capitaine Raoul orders the action.

Night is coming on fast. After hand shakes and embraces, Raoul leaves and promises he will return for Madeleine and me in exactly eight nights. He will meet us on the beach. Use the same signals. We will return to Gibraltar on his boat.

Under the leadership of Lieutenant Baptiste, the discussions begin. Writing as fast as we can, Madeleine and I list the arms and communications needs of the Maquisards. Two days later, Paul and the men prepare to head northeast with Madeleine. She is nervous and clings to me tightly. Her behavior seems unusual, but I cannot modify Raoul's orders. The four men and Madeleine leave.

Less than 72 hours later, Paul stumbles into our campsite and falls to the ground. He is alone, winded, disheveled, weak, thirsty and hungry. His group had been ambushed by a Nazi patrol less than 50 kilomètres away. Our puny weapons were no match for those *satané chiens*! The other three Maquisards were killed. And, *quoi de* Madeleine? Paul looks up at me as he tells us she was taken prisoner. No, she did not appear to be harmed. In fact the Nazis were very polite, almost courteous to her.

Paul had often seen other women taken prisoner. None, not one had ever been treated so nicely. Always...always they were roughed up, beaten...or worse. Paul quickly recovers his strength, sits up and stares straight at me. There is anger in his eyes. He rises to his feet and, with clenched fists and hunched shoulders, walks slowly toward me.

I stand up. "*Qu'as tu*? What's the matter?"

Paul is breathing hard. I see frustration, anger, hatred...and tears in his eyes. "I tell you what is the matter!" He swallows hard as he tries to catch his breath.. He thought he recognized Madeleine as a woman he had often seen in the city of Villeneuve, outside Paris. His anger increases as he continues. "She was always in the company of Nazi officers. A *collaborateuse*? When you arrived...I did not press the matter...she was in the uniform of an American officer...accompanied by you...who is supposed to be an American Captain!"

I am trying to deal with my own anger and, at the same time, cope with Paul's severe distress. I feel damn tight, tense and furious. But I cannot strike out at any one. Paul would like to beat me, that's plain to see. No doubt he feels I am to blame. Didn't I bring her into this secret Maquis shelter? Baptiste and most of his men recognize my own distressed feelings and regrets for this dreadful turn of events.

Baptiste takes control. "It is Madeleine toward whom we'd best turn our hatred, anger and, yes, our fears; not toward one another. If we quarrel among ourselves this Maquis group could collapse. This only serves the Nazis' purposes."

Why didn't I pay attention to my instincts and doubts about Madeleine? Was it because I wanted to make love to her? Well, I did make love to her. And the doubts remained. Was it because I also wondered about Colonel Elliott's loyalties and his protection of her? Hell! Who am I to question a colonel or for that matter anyone else on the basis of instinct. Intuition is not tangible support for official accusations or condemnations. Instinct and intuition are all I have had to go on—not one single solitary fact, not one bit of hard evidence—not until now.

I had automatically placed my hand on the butt of my pistol. Ridiculous. Who do I intend to shoot? Paul? If so, I might as well shoot myself and save the Maquisards the trouble. I slowly, sensibly move my hand away from my hip and clasp my hands behind me.

Baptiste, although younger than Paul, demonstrates his own maturity. He motions for me and Paul to sit down. "We must be more careful than ever now.

We cannot stay at this campsite but must change our location every night. We cannot afford to lose any more men." Baptiste displays his humanity. He allows a moment of release...brings his hands to his face and chokes back the tears. "Men with courage are very hard to replace. And we lost three of them escorting that...that Madeleine...to a rendezvous up north. *Nos trois frères...nos amis courageux...*" Baptiste's voice trails off, muffled with emotion.

The men stand with their arms tightly folded across their chests. As though by a common design, they cover their eyes with one hand. Some, with a slow, deliberate movement, make the sign of the cross. I believe they are silently praying for the souls of their friends. A major loss for this small ill-equipped cadre of French warriors.

I, too, keenly feel the pain. I move to where Paul sits, staring at the ground. I offer my right hand in friendship. Paul slowly looks up, rises, presses my right hand in his and, without exchanging words, we embrace each other. We have grief in common.

After a moment of silence, Baptiste gives instructions. "There is very little time to spare for mourning. We will conceal ourselves near here and wait to see if Madeleine comes back. If Madeleine does return she had better have a very credible explanation. How did she escape from the Nazis? If Madeleine does return, will she have disclosed our location to the enemy? Setting a trap for us? On the other hand, if she does not return is it because she has been imprisoned or tortured and killed? If she is dead, did she confess our numbers and location to the Nazis?"

I, too, wonder. *Has she jeopardized Raoul and Barduc, his brother...and my return to Gibraltar? According to Paul, she had been "politely, almost courteously captured." Did Paul accurately recognize Madeleine as a collaborator?*

For the remainder of my stay with these Maquisards, I will be closely watched. After all, I did bring Madeleine to the hideout. Perhaps, therefore, they cannot be sure I am who I claim to be. As long I make no suspicious actions, do not try to get away from the group, I doubt they will harm me. Though they may not trust me completely, the underground fighters need the supplies I might actually obtain for them.

However, they will not deliberately introduce me to any other group of Maquisards. This I know.

We change our location several times each day and post lookouts for Madeleine...or the Nazis. I continue to take notes as quickly as I can. At night we all sleep badly. On the eighth night since Raoul's departure, I carefully fold, compress and wrap my field notes in a waterproof oilskin pouch provided by Baptiste. We lie close to the ground at the top of the hill to watch for Raoul's boat. Clouds conceal the moon. The Mediterranean is dark.

Soon there is an exchange of signals. After quick handshakes and traditional hugs, Paul leads me directly to the beach. Raoul is on the shore with the dinghy. We row back to the trawler, start the engine and quickly get under weigh.

I tell Raoul all that happened. Clearly he is disturbed by the bad news. "My Maquisards will abandon the pit and prepare another campsite. Perhaps, too, they will find a farmhouse where we can conceal the armaments you have promised to send us."

I tell him I will request an American radio operator be sent in at once to establish two-way communications with Gibraltar or England. Then, before the supplies are dropped, the radio operator can send the identifying code-signals and the locations for delivery by air or sea.

Raoul avoids a discussion of the loss of his three men in the Nazi ambush. He makes it clear he does not want to hear Madeleine's name. We have little to say to each other. Raoul and Barduc wear pistols all the time.

After many days of rough and lonely sailing, I am back on Gibraltar. An RAF Spitfire returns me to the U.K. MI5 people meet the plane and escort me to a conference room. The British Colonel Fort-Blaine and the American Colonel James join us. I am not greatly surprised as they reveal Madeleine was to have been arrested as an enemy agent immediately on her return to England. But, as far as they know, she has not come back. She would have been detained when she left England to join Colonel Elliott in the U.S. However, Elliott interceded and protected Madeleine.

There are no new intelligence reports at this time. No further information. MI5 agents are searching for her in France and in Germany.

Does Colonel Elliott know about this? MI5 isn't sure. Colonel James admits he learned about Madeleine's activities only after we boarded Raoul's trawler and were en route to France. It was then too late to stop us. And, "Yes, I have been in touch with Washington about this stinking mess."

So, the Maquisards and I were the only players who had not known the truth. And, we were the ones who had the most to lose. Now...what, who waits for me back in New York?

Chapter Seventeen

A deep breath, a straightening of the shoulders, a quick hand-smoothing of my jacket, and the elevator speedily delivers me to Colonel Elliott's office. Praise or condemnation, I am ready for whatever comes.

In response to my knock, a deep voice, not Colonel Elliott's, tells me, "Open!"

I enter and slowly remove my hat as I stare in uncontrolled surprise. "Beg pardon, sir. I am...I'm looking for..."

"I know. I know. You are Wortman. Right?"

"Yes, sir."

"Shut the door, please." He moves from his chair and offers his hand. "I am Joe Franken, Bill Elliott's replacement."

His smile seems genuine and friendly. He is well over 6' tall and has a heavy-set frame. Salt and pepper hair. His lapel insignia tells me he is a full colonel. "Glad to meet you, sir." I guess my puzzled expression is eloquent.

"Wondering where Bill Elliott is? Sit down and we'll talk about it."

I sag in the chair and Colonel Franken frowns. "Captain. You look like hell. When was the last time you had a good night's sleep...and some fun?"

"Slept for a few hours...on the flight back...on the plane's floor, sir. I apologize for my crummy appearance. Sorry, colonel. I just can't stop yawning. Didn't take time to stop at the hotel to freshen up. Wanted to get here as quickly as possible. Can you tell me, sir, where is Bill...er...Colonel Elliott?"

He produces two cigars. Hands one to me. "Light up first."

"Mind if I save this for after dinner, colonel? I'm not sure my lungs and stomach can deal with a cigar right now."

He nods in the affirmative. Studies my appearance. "Loosen your tie while I call for coffee. How do you like yours?"

"No matter. As long as it's hot."

In a few moments the door opens. I am too tired to turn around. A kakhi uniform, blouse and skirt, no stripes, comes to the colonel's desk and sets down two big steaming mugs.

"This is my aide, Merry Bounty. She came up from Washington with me. In fact, we both came up about 36 hours ago to take over this...this..." He searches for an appropriate word as he looks with revulsion at the bare walls, stained floor and discolored ceiling.

I suggest, "Shitbrindle...color...sir?"

The colonel and his aide smile as he enjoys the sound. "Shitbrindle. Shitbrindle. Exactly!"

The lady offers her hand in friendship and I have the opportunity to look at her without embarrassment.

She's no Madeleine, physically. Red hair. Green eyes. Bold body. "Bold body?" I must be more exhausted than I realize. She is built like the proverbial brick outhouse. On the husky, very healthy side. No mistaking her gender. She is a zahftig woman! Do all colonels select their own aides? Or is it the way things work for you when you become a colonel? It will take me a long time, if ever, to make colonel. In the meantime, I will have to seek aid and comfort from the colonel's aides.

The distracting Merry Bounty leaves the colonel's office and I try to pick up our conversation. "You were saying something concerning Colonel Elliott's whereabouts?"

"Not exactly, Wortman. I started to tell you we have to be in Washington, D.C. tomorrow morning for a conference with General Leblanc and his staff. You met him before you and Madeleine Brouillard left for the U.K. He was very impressed with you. Can you wait for the whole story until tomorrow morning when we meet with the General?"

I try unsuccessfully to stifle a deep yawn. "Can't keep my eyes open." Stiffly, painfully I rise from the chair. "With permission, sir, I'll head for the hotel."

"We leave from there at 0830 precisely. And one more thing." He's not smiling. "Do you have your gun?"

I pat my right trouser pocket. "Yes, sir."

"Good. Keep it loaded and handy." He talks very slowly and points directly at my pocket. "Do not—I repeat—DO NOT go anywhere without it. That's an order, captain!"

Chapter Eighteen

My brain is in a whirl. I stare out the plane's window but my mind is incapable of focus. Colonel Franken, sitting at my left, is buried deep in paperwork. I am aware that every once in a while he looks over at me. Thank goodness he isn't trying to make conversation.

This morning the General's staff gave me a lot to think about. I feel slow in absorbing the facts. Really, I should not feel this way. I'd had misgivings about Madeleine; serious doubts about Colonel Elliott, too. Perhaps my state of shock comes from the realization my instincts were right on target. My instincts had seemed a bit preposterous and I had no power to follow up on the strange messages they sent me.

Madeleine had been "captured"—been "taken prisoner"—or "rejoined her Nazi buddies"—however one wants to describe the events in Marseilles. G-2, working with MI5, had suspected Elliott for some time. As a matter of routine security, they had been secretly monitoring and investigating his movements and communications. Most ominous, he disappeared the night orders for his immediate arrest had been written; didn't show up at the hotel or at his office. How did he know he was under an arrest order? He must have contacts inside G-2, *iDIV* or the Signal Corps. Obviously, he had been alerted and went underground at once.

Geez! Who the hell can I trust?

My desire to work alone is justified. However, now I hear myself silently questioning, wondering about everyone with whom I have come into contact. But I cannot be effective in my assignments if I become paranoid about the General, the colonel, the major...everybody. The objectives for me are to help win this goddam war and live to tell about it.

Maybe I should chuck the whole thing and wait to be drafted as a buck private. What am I thinking? I'd make a lousy buck private. Besides which, I do have a fair amount of freedom in this job—this job of chasing after and catching shadows. The General and his staff told me I did a "damn good job." And so did Colonel Franken.

One of the General's staff cautions me. "Be aware you're probably a prime target for Bill Elliott's revenge. He knows your real and undercover names. Decide what armament you want to carry and you shall have it. Unless you request it, we won't assign security personnel to guard you. We'll keep you posted on anything we learn concerning Elliott's whereabouts. Our borders are being watched. We expect he will try to get out of the country; go to Germany."

Colonel Franken awards me some leave, a furlough. "Go up to The Farm, relax, just walk around the hills, do a little shooting, and feast on Pop's good food. In about a week, when you feel well rested, we'll talk about your next assignment." "Yes, Wortman," he reassures me. "You will continue to work solo as much as is possible."

Chapter Nineteen

Relaxing around The Farm's kitchen table late at night, Pop fills me in. "Colonel Franken has always been referred to as The Chief. To his peers and superiors he is Colonel Joe Franken, of course. The Chief rarely shares a coffee break or socializes with his subordinates."

"Is he a snob? Or just too busy?"

"Well, in most opinions, he is both a snob and an unusually busy guy. He rarely smiles or holds still for small talk. If he has or ever had a sense of humor, it's been laid to rest for the duration. I don't know his actual age, but I estimate the middle fifties. He never mentions family. What did he do before he joined the service? He never gives a hint. I know he can be tough, but he's a fair manager. Obviously he wants no one to develop a personal relationship with him."

Next afternoon, the fifth day of my so-called "leave," I receive a message from The Chief on our private radio link. He orders me to return to The Office in New York. He will send a car to take me to the Albany Airport tomorrow morning at 0700.

Pop is the only person on The Farm privy to an individual's comings and goings. When I tell him I have been called back to The Office and a car will come for me next morning, he shows no surprise. It is as though he already knew about my leaving. Oh, well. This is a strange business—that's for sure. I decide to spend what little time remains of today stretching my legs and doing a little target practice in the woods about 1,500 feet back of the main house. Haven't had much opportunity to practice the knife throwing techniques taught to me by my Marine Sergeants. It's still light enough to get in a couple of hours, or maybe three.

The Farm's armory boasts some excellent knives. I select three 16-ounce Bowie-style throwing knives made by Harry McEvoy and one of Harry's unusual holsters designed, so he told me, by a man who hunts wild boar in Florida armed only with these knives. The holster is fitted with straps that place it between one's shoulder blades. The handles of the three knives naturally protrude at the back of the wearer's head. Then, without losing sight of his target, the experienced thrower can grasp one of the knives, pull it up and out in a continuous, sweeping arc at the top of which he releases and launches the knife with great speed and force. A split second later, the sharp point of the knife forcefully penetrates the target. This is the knife thrower's counterpart of a gunfighter's fast draw.

Well, I won't find any wild boar here in the Catskill Mountains but tree trunks at 30 feet will do for now. So armed as a determined knife-throwing hunter, I set out for a relaxing walk in the woods.

As a youth spending my summers on a farm in these same Catskill Mountains, I used to walk light-footed through the forests, my BB-Gun at the ready for anything that might try to attack me. The childhood memory makes me feel warm, secure and comfortable. I walk in a half-crouch position, just as I did back then when the thought of a war never occurred.

But, this day, my senses tell me I am not alone in these woods. I feel someone is behind me, stalking me. I think I hear a rustle and crackle of leaves being crushed on the floor of the forest. I stop. And the forest is silent.

As soon as I move forward again, the talking leaves tell me I am not alone. Start…Stop. Start…Stop. I increase my pace. The pursuer keeps up with me. No doubt about it, I am being stalked. I dart behind a stout, Sugar Pine tree and look down the path. I cannot, at this moment, be absolutely certain in the dimming light of the forest whether it is friend or foe. The crackle of the stepped-on leaves continues and comes closer. I suddenly step out from behind my hiding place to face my stalker.

It's Elliott, my former Chief, now an outlaw and fugitive from the military police! He's startled by my unexpected move. But, with a "Now I gotcha!" expression, he slowly raises his arm and points a revolver at me. My reaction is defensive, automatic. In a single movement, I advance into a crouch, grasp the handle of one of the concealed Bowie-knives and throw it with all my might directly at his solar plexus. It hits the mark with a sickening, muffled thud!

Elliott's eyes are wide open, staring at me in astonishment. His gun hand drops suddenly to his side. I race to him and wrench the revolver from his grip. The man grunts, exhales and drops to his knees. He looks up at me, scowls, mutters something in German and pitches forward onto the handle of the knife. His body shudders violently and then becomes still. His eyes are open, but they see nothing. I cannot find a pulse. Blood pours from his mouth and nose…and I get sick.

Breathless, I race back to the main building, tell Pop to grab a blanket and follow me. Together, we put Elliott's body on the blanket and drag it back to one of the farm's buildings. Over the private radio-link I tell Colonel Franken all that has just happened. Calmly, no doubt with a smile, he exclaims, "Good! Tell no one, absolutely no one about this incident."

"Okay. But what about the body?"

Long pause. "Instead of a car, a panel truck will take you to the airport in the morning. Put the body in the back of the truck. I'll notify the military police who will probably fly Elliott's remains to Washington for verification, examination and disposal. Good work, Jacques, er Brevier, er Wortman. Dammit! You know who I mean. Well done! See you tomorrow, in my office."

There is one major concern: I am a civilian who technically committed a murder. Will the Army handle this situation as an internal affair? Or am I on my own—at the mercy of the civilian judicial system?

Chapter Twenty

The Chief motions me to sit down.

I do feel some anxiety and cannot avoid taking the lead. "Chief, what do I do now about last night's happenings?"

He looks up at me and frowns. "What do you think you have to do?"

"I really don't know. I am still technically under the juridiction of the..."

"Look Leon. You were doing your job as an emplyee of the Army. Also, wasn't your action entirely in self defense? There's only one more thing you'll have to do."

"I'm listening."

"Write a confidential report of the incident. Address it to me. I'll handle it with the military police and G-2. Can't imagine anything further will have to be done. In fact, the MPs and G-2 owe you for solving their nasty problem. This is entirely a military affair."

Reaching across the Chief's desk, I shake his hand and express my gratitude.

Avoiding small talk and ignoring yesterday's events, he reaches into the knee-drawer of his desk, pulls out a document and hands it to me.

Boldly stamped *CONFIDENTIAL*, it is titled "Acoustic Aircraft-Detection Equipment." A photo of the box containing the radio section of the device dominates the cover. The document includes comprehensive descriptions, specifications and trouble-shooting suggestions. Comprehensively described but not illustrated, the instrument that detects the sounds of approaching aircraft is an array of phased microphones that mounts on top of the tallest mast of a ship equipped with the system. The system is intended for ocean-going merchant ships. A built-in audio-amplifier and loudspeakers in the ship's bridge provide early warnings of approaching aircraft.

In theory, the ship's officers would hear an approaching aircraft's engines through the loudspeaker installed on the wall of the ship's bridge. Although the sound is easily identified, there is no provison to help the listener determine the aircraft's point on the compass, height, direction or distance from the ship. Nor is there any way to tell friend from foe. Not with this gear. Crude? To say the least. Effective? It is so new it has not yet been tested under combat conditions.

My instructions are to locate and bring back the *CONFIDENTIAL* document or an exact copy. "This is a security check—as well as a test of your resourcefulness. Start right now and return within 24 hours." No, The Chief isn't going to hide and have me seek the document he showed me. Yes, I am to find another just like it, if one exists. I am completely on my own.

The Chief offers a hint. I can see the equipment installed on a specific merchant ship making ready to sail in a convoy leaving New York Harbor. He gives me the ship's name and pier number. I will have to figure out for myself how to get by security, the Marine guard posted at the pier, board the ship and enter the bridge where the equipment is installed in a closet.

I move fast. No time for sophisticated planning. I change into my civilian suit and pocket my FCC commercial Radio-Telegraph license. A cab ride takes me to the Marine Radio Officers' Union in downtown Manhattan. I know there is a serious shortage of FCC-licensed radio-telegraph operators. The Merchant Marine is really hurting. Each ship requires a minimum of two radio operators. Three are even better for covering 24-hour radio watches. Sometimes the U.S. Navy supplies radio operators when commercially-licensed civilians can't be found—if the Navy has any to spare.

The union's business manager begs me to join the union and sign on a ship right away. He points out I also have to get Seaman's Papers from the Coast Guard office down the street. "Go and come back right away" and he'd tell me what ships are waiting for a chief radio officer. I could take my pick of ships by name. No, he does not know their destinations. By Federal law a U.S. ship cannot sail without at least one FCC-licensed radio officer on duty.

I pay the fees and become an instant-member of the union. I race to the Coast Guard office. There I display my FCC license and union card. I'd have to apply for a Seaman's Passport. No problem. With a birth certificate, I'd have mine in less than 24 hours. Coast Guard seaman's papers are issued on the spot. They even take my photograph and fingerprints right there.

This takes approximately one and one-half hours out of my quota of 24.

I hail a cab and arrive at the ship's pier 15 minutes later. Marine security checks my papers and allows me to board the ship. I flash my Coast Guard papers to the seaman on duty at the gangway and identify myself as a radio marine inspector. No problem. He directs me to the ship's bridge on the top deck.

Ten minutes later I locate the closet in which the equipment is housed, open the unlocked door and, sure enough, there it is, bolted to the wall. The nameplate on the front of the equipment's box confirms the manufacturer's name, RCA Radio Marine Corporation. More than I expected, in addition to the Navy classification number, it displays the unit's commercial model-number.

Moving quickly after leaving the ship, I find the address of the RCA Radio Marine Corporation's Service Depot in a telephone directory at a pay phone at the ship's pier and take another short cab ride. The Depot is only a few blocks from the waterfront, close to its customers, the ships of the Merchant Marine.

The Service Depot is a store front. As casually as I can, I saunter to the counter. There is a push-button with a small *Push For Service* sign. I push and hear a bell ring behind the partition that separates the counter from whatever they do in the back rooms.

A man in a gray jacket, typical garb for a bench technician, comes out. "What can I do for you?"

Calmly, I ask if he could let me have the "service manual" for the RCA Radio Marine Corporation's product, which I Identify by its commercial model-number.

With a deceptive look of annoyance he says, "Sorry buddy, but I can't 'let you have' you one of those." I thought my mission was at a dead-end until he continues with a smile, "They cost $1.75."

I fake amusement, hand him the money, and walk out with an exact duplicate of The Chief's document without the *CONFIDENTIAL* stamp on its cover page.

So much for security.

Less than three hours after the start of this assignment, I hand the document to The Chief. He appears totally astounded. Facetiously, I apologize for the fact it isn't stamped *CONFIDENTIAL.* He silently compares the two documents and confirms they are identical. The task has been completed the same day it is given to me. I feel triumphant, as one can imagine.

The Chief asks, "How'd you do it?"

"Sorry, Chief. That's confidential information."

Silently, he glares at me with an expression that loudly says, "I don't appreciate your sense of humor, smartass."

So, I tell him what my rationale, logic and actions have been since leaving The Office this morning. I never mention how lucky I had really been. Neither does The Chief.

My reward is a slight smile. "This is too easy for you."

Me and my big mouth.

Chapter Twenty-One

A hot shower, relaxation and a solid night's sleep are to be relished. However, they are not to happen tonight. A soft knock at my door.

"Who's there?"

"Me."

I open the door for Colonel Franken.

A master of the poker face. One never can tell The Chief's mood or message from his expression. Tonight's "face" is no exception. However, a personal visit to a field agent's hotel room is unusual. Unheard of.

Without a word he sits down, opens his well-worn briefcase and pulls out a bottle of fine Scotch whiskey. He holds up two fingers. I produce two glasses from the bathroom. He pours a small amount into each glass and raises his in a polite salute. I imitate him and wait for the other shoe.

It drops.

"You've heard of government agencies such as [(1)]C.I.C., C.O.I., O.W.I., O.N.I., and G-2." He doesn't wait for a response. "Of course you have. And, probably, you never quite understood or have been unable to differentiate their functions.

"In the rush to gear up for war, practically every department, bureau and agency in Washington has been in a hurry to set up its own intelligence gathering section. Each group has been trying to do its own thing. There has been absolutely no interaction or coordination. These are facts.

"We've not had a centralized intelligence-gathering agency. No formal, central international-espionage or counter-espionage group at all. No strategic analysts. The FBI is the only federal agency with a clear charter to investigate, expose and arrest foreign espionage agents here in the U.S and in Latin America. But the war is being fought *overseas*. Roosevelt recognizes the need to correct the situation right away!"

The Chief and I maintain tight eye contact. Neither of us blinks.

His voice drops almost to an inaudible whisper as he continues. "Have you ever heard of Colonel Bill Donovan, World War I vet...Congressional Medal of Honor...successful civilian attorney?"

"No. Before my time."

"Well, Wild Bill and I have been good friends for many years. Sometimes we worked together as law counselors for the same clients. Other times we were on opposite sides. But we've always had a strong admiration for each other's skills. He's stubborn. Very stubborn. Often opinionated. Guess I am a little like that, too. Fact is, he's usually the one who is right."

I don't know where The Chief is heading. This is the first time he has ever revealed his profession to me. With his poker face, intelligence, impressive powers of observation and cunning ability to make his point, The Chief must have been a darn good litigator.

He goes on to describe how Donovan had gone to the President with a plan to create and set up an international network of intelligence agents and strategic analysts drawn from the military, government and selected civilian sectors. The President gave the okay and named Donovan head of this new group to be known as the Office of Strategic Services, the O.S.S.

"Now, the main reason for this conversation. Donovan has moved our group out of the Signal Corps and..." A long pause adds emphasis. "...we are now the Foreign Information Section of the new O.S.S."

I blink. The Chief stops talking and allows me a moment to digest this information. He refills our glasses. We raise them in a salute to each other.

Suddenly I have a distressing vision of me as part of a tight group of operators despite my outspoken preference for solo action. I sip my drink. "What do we do now, Chief?"

He counters, "What would you like to do?"

"I want to continue to work with you, Chief. Stay with this operation, no matter what its initials are. But I want to remain a civilian employee and work alone in the field."

As he stands up to leave, The Chief betrays a slight smile. "That's what I've already put on your transfer paperwork. You are now with the O.S.S. Be at The Office at eight in the morning and we'll go into more details...including your new overseas assignment."

I can't let that last item go unnoticed. "My new overseas assignment?"

No more conversation. He shakes my hand and leaves. No doubt, before morning, he will make many hotel-room visits and have more discussions like the one we have just concluded.

[1]C.I.C., Counter Intelligence Corps; C.O.I., Coordinator Of Information; O.W.I., Office of War Information; O.N.I., Office Of Naval Intelligence; G2, Army Intelligence.

Chapter Twenty-Two

A very long night. Thoughts race. In anticipation of a day filled with new, exciting adventures, I do not get much sleep.

Who can wait until eight? I arrive at the Office at seven in the morning. Knocking before entering, but not waiting for "Come" I open the unlocked door to his office.

The Chief greets me with "You're too predictable. Work on that, please."

Seated in The Chief's office are five other men I have not seen before. Introductions are brief. I am told the two Lt. Commanders are from O.N.I. I estimate their ages at mid-forties The two Majors are from G-2; ages approximately the same as the naval officers. The fifth man is in civilian clothes. Somewhat older than the others, perhaps in his mid fifties, he is introduced as Monsieur Charles Dejuin from the American Embasssy in Dakar, French West Africa.

The first to speak is Monsieur Dejuin. He turns in my direction. "*Trés heureux, Monsieur Wortman, de vous faire la connaissance. Ça va*?" **[1]** He addresses me in French. Not American French. The real French de France, including the accent.

I suppress my surprise at his greeting and reply without hesitation, "*Bien merci, Monsieur DeJuin. Enchanté de faire la vôtre. Pour moi ça va trés bien. Comme toujours. J'èspére que tout le monde et vos amis marchent bien a vôtre côté*?"**[2]** Deliberately, this is an overly polite, lengthy and almost meaningless reply.

M. Dejuin responds with a broad smile. "*L'enchantement...c'est tout a moi*."**[3]**

For the next 10 or 12 minutes, he and I exchange pleasantries mingled with impersonal bits of information, all in French. Then he turns to the others in the room grinning from ear to ear and, in a stammering mixture of English and French, declares: "Congratulations *mes* A-A-A-American f-f-f-*amis*. At my opinion Monsieur *le Capitaine*, Wortman *peut-peut-peut*—ah, c-c-can do it! Non! *Je n'en doute pas! Pas de tout*! No doubt at all!"

I look at this gathering of five strangers and The Chief. I ask no one in particular, "Can do—what?"

The military men smile and say nothing. The Chief finally speaks up as he waves in the direction of the O.N.I. and G-2 officers, "These four gentlemen have been your observers from the day you joined *iDIV*. Meet Lieutenant Commanders Forest and Johnstone, and Majors Collings and Hurst. Monsieur Dejuin has been brought in from Dakar to give the final OK. He gives it. So now we can talk in some detail about specifics—your new assignment—where and why and for how long you're going over."

Monsieur Dejuin, obviously an experienced diplomat, glances at his watch and rises from his chair. He takes both my hands in his. "*Ça veut dire, mon ami de guerre, c'est l'heure! Bonne chance! À la prochaine. Au'voir. Que le bon dieu vous garde bien*!"[(4)]

With a smile and a wave of his hand at the others, he moves swiftly to the door. In a moment he is gone.

Endnotes (freely translated):

[(1)] "Very happy to meet you. How're things?"

[(2)] "Many thanks Monsieur Dejuin. Things are going very well for me, as always. A pleasure to meet you. I hope everybody and your friends are doing well."

[(3)] "The pleasure is all mine."

[(4)] "That means the time has come! Good luck. Until we meet again. May God watch over you."

Chapter Twenty-Three

An uncomfortable, almost eerie, feeling comes over me more than once in the next several weeks. My instructions change as often as every day. I assume The Chief is only reacting to what his Chief, Bill Donovan is telling him. For reasons I cannot comprehend, they seem to redirect him continually. I hope someone, somewhere knows the answer to "What the hell is going on?" One doesn't dare think otherwise. Privately, I consider the possibilities.

One, our work is so confidential to the outside world, it is necessary to keep even me in the dark until the very last moment. Could be so, although weird.

Two, they, whoever "they" might be, haven't quite bought into my capabilities and, therefore, are holding back on details and time tables. Possible, but I hope it isn't so.

Three, they haven't fully developed their strategy. Perhaps it will take more time than I expect.

Four, I am just being overly sensitive. This could be, too.

A few things are quite clear to me. Most certainly, I will be working in a French speaking country. Maybe even in France, which is partially occupied by the Nazi Army, primarily in the north. The southern provinces are not formally occupied because the French leaders based in Vichy are thoroughly friendly to the Nazis, entirely opposed to the Allies. Eighty year old Marshall Pétain is a figurehead put in place by the Nazis. A puppet of the anti-Ally French military and the Nazis, Pétain demonstrates he can be easily directed to transmit anti-Ally commands to the French armies in Africa. The French underground, the Maquis, has become more active but, because of limited resources, only barely effective in southern France.

Among the varied sets of possible operations I hear most persistently are: "You will be taken to Dakar, French West Africa. You will then proceed to Brazzaville in the Belgian Congo. From there you will head north to Algiers, a seaport on the Mediterranean. You will be taken across the Sea to southern France, probably to Marseilles where you will tie in again with the Maquis to provide an intelligence link with O.S.S. agents in North Africa who are in daily contact with our bases in Gibraltar and England."

"How do I get to Dakar?"

"You'll learn in due time" is always the response to my push for more specific data.

Don't they know? Probably they do not.

In this business one is supposed to have unlimited faith in those who are one's support and backups. My experience with Madeleine and Bill Elliott proved that assumption to be dangerous. It is unproductive, a waste of time and energy to press for more information. Certainly, I will "learn all—in due time."

Yet, despite the boundless height of my self-confidence, the suspense is difficult to bear.

The advantage of my youth, I am now 21 plus a few months, makes me believe I am invincible. On the other hand, my immaturity puts me at a disadvantage. Impatient. I want to know the whole story. Nonetheless, the elders do hold me at bay.

Finally, at the beginning of October a conference is called in The Chief's office. The same two O.N.I. and two G-2 officers are at the meeting. M. Dejuin is absent. Another Army officer I'd never met or heard of before is also in The Chief's office. He is introduced as G-2's Second-Lieutenant Bud Corval.

Bud looks even younger than I. He is actually my age. Six inches shorter than I; not quite 5'6" in height. He has a naturally ruddy face, sand-color hair, blue-eyes and a yards-wide smile he never tries to hide. We have good chemistry at once.

We exchange small talk and pleasantries. Bud comes from Virginia. In civilian life he had been a trainer of race horses. Nobody interrupts our chatter. This in itself is unusual. They observe us closely, listening purposefully to our dialog.

"Do you speak any foreign languages, Bud?"

Bud smiles disarmingly. "Only Virginian, suh!" He doesn't have to exaggerate his conspicuous southern drawl. His patois identifies his origin: very American.

Major Collings speaks. "Looks like you two can get along together. That's good because you're in this together."

"Hey Bud!" I ask. "Do you have any idea what 'this' is you and I are 'in together'?" My question is meant to be heard by everyone in the room.

"No. I was hopin' you'd tell me!"

The Major continues. "It's important for you to know each other by sight and sound. Lieutenant Corval is going on a mission to Dakar, for which he has been especially trained, as you have."

At that point, Bud and I exchange a brief glance. Neither of us speaks. Time for listening.

"You'll be a counter-intelligence team. Spy Catchers. Shadow Catchers, if you prefer."

G-2's Major Collings continues. "With Wortman's knack for survival tactics and the French language and Bud's natural appearance as a naive youth...plus his very special training...we think you can succeed as a team to rapidly identify French and other Nazi agents we assume are operating under some sort of cover."

"Please explain?" I query. "Why French rather than German?"

"According to what we have learned, the West, Northwest, and Mediterranean areas of French Africa have been flooded with Vichy-French agents loyal to the Nazis, or who prefer the Nazis and dislike the Allies. Yes, of course, there are many of Germany's agents in those areas, too. And we have other teams working on that problem."

The wheels start turning faster. I ask, "On which side are the local military and government officials of French West Africa on?"

"Well...that's one of the things we're not sure of. They claim to be neutral. But they despise, literally hate the British for what they did to the French fleet in 1940. So, the probability as well as the possibility is their neutrality could change to open hostility with the slightest provocation. The British are sensitive to the relationship and have gladly given the counter-intelligence job to us.

"What's the plan?" Bud and I ask the question almost at the same instant.

"It's not fully developed. We're uneasy about the French in North Africa. It's a not-so-funny circus. You'd be wise to trust no one who doesn't have official approval from one of our government agencies or the military."

"Who has the 'authority' to give 'approval'?" The answer. A shrug of the shoulders.

Major Hurst joins in at that point. "Your objective is to identify and disable as many of the anti-Ally pro-Nazi people, French or German, as you can—in a very short time period—and then get yourselves the hell out of there as quickly as possible!"

Bud speaks for both of us. "More, please."

Major Hurst tries. "We don't know much more. Just a little bit. Bud, you'll be assigned to the American Embassy at Dakar. You'll fly in, probably from Gibraltar. Wortman, you'll be delivered separately, by sea, the same day—if we can coordinate everything." He holds up crossed fingers to emphasize his uncertainty.

"What then?"

O.N.I.'s Commander Forest answers. "That's what we want you to tell us. We want you to spend the next couple of days huddling and chewing on the whole idea. Then, when you think you have a workable strategy, we'll get together and, if we can't shoot it down, we might give your plan the go-ahead." O.N.I. and G-2 must have spent considerable time, more than they would ever acknowledge, working on today's scenario.

The Chief has been silent through all the conversation. Now he displays his unique leadership skills. "We think, if you develop the details of the Plan yourselves, it will have a much better chance to succeed." He continues to be the master of brevity.

Somewhat overwhelmed and unaccustomed to this rare, open demonstration of confidence, Bud and I share a hearty handshake. It is an impulsive moment. Without the need for discussion, we declare it would be best if we were not seen in public together. We prefer to do our thinking, planning and talking together in the carefully controlled security of the shitbrindle office. The Chief comments on the correctness of our very first decision. The other four men nod in the affirmative.

"How much time do we have?" Bud directs the question at the G-2 Majors.

I focus on The Chief. "When do we go over? What's our deadline?".

The answers are vague, as ambiguous as ever. Bud is as accustomed as I to receiving clouded messages.

Obviously uncomfortable, the O.N.I. and G-2 officers look at each other and at The Chief as if to say "Shall we tell them?" They must have known our last questions would come up. With only the slightest hesitation, The Chief looks down at his desk calendar and announces "It's now October third. Be ready to leave no later than two weeks from today. Possibly sooner. Right now we don't have the exact date, time and point of departure." Looking directly at Bud and me, "Of course you'll have your Action Plan ready for our next meeting in this Office."

"When's that?"

The Chief rises from his chair. "Four days from today, October seventh. This meeting's over. Let's all go back to work!" There's his humor again.

The Chief, Bud, the four officers and I stand up, and shake hands all around.

As the four men turn to leave, Bud speaks up in a strong voice, "Sir!"—and salutes.

The uniformed officers return his salute. Nobody smiles.

The next three days fly by. Bud and I are intent on coming up with a foolproof Plan. Well, a creative Plan, at least. We feel like a pair of writers developing a script for a mystery radio program. The difference in this script is that we are also the actors. I tell Bud I had been the studio engineer for a radio program called *The Avenger*, a rival of *The Shadow*. Bud allows, "That's mighty good news. Then you-all must know how to make us both invisible!"

We are trying to keep a sense of humor.

Within the secure walls of the Office, we are able to write as well as talk out our thoughts. Bud and I play devil's advocate to each other's ideas. Strange, in retrospect, the thought we might fail never occurs to us.

As Bud and I see it, he will always be in his U.S. Army Officer's uniform and, if caught or discovered, Bud can expect to be expelled from the country or treated as a prisoner of war—depending on the hostility or hospitality of the French military and the government.

On the other hand, I will be in civilian clothing and, therefore, outside the protection of the U.S. Government. If I am "caught," I might just...disappear. Or, maybe and more likely, they'd hold me as trading piece. One of theirs for one of ours, so to speak. I had never learned to play Chess. Now I am learning a human version of the game. In fact, I might very well become one of the "pieces."

The unfolding of our Plan becomes fascinating. I set aside, at least temporarily, my strong desire to work alone. Bud, as my partner, does much to modify my position. We create a story-line filled with new challenges. Frankly, I never have been one to look for a fight. Violence is not in my nature. Nonetheless, I have never run from a fight. This adventure enables me to see a totally different side of my own personality. I have no sensation of fear. In fact, I feel elated about the future. And Bud shares my excitement.

Our imaginations run wild. He accuses me of being a frustrated actor, a ham. I say he has been reincarnated as a gun-slinger from the old west, but misplaced in Virginia! Both of us are absolute patriots. We love our country and our flag—and we passionately hate an enemy we've never seen in person—not yet! Neither of us could find any other reason for volunteering for this kind of service. No one forced us to join. Creating our own scenario is the fun part. Bud knows as well as I the hard part is coming.

On October seventh, the same group meets in The Chief's Office...The Chief, Lt. Commanders Forest and Johnstone, Majors Collings and Hurst, Bud and I. For this special occasion, Bud had his uniform cleaned and pressed. I bought a haircut and a new khaki shirt and tie. After all, we are now in "show biz." Bud and I sit next to each other. We have carefully rehearsed the presentation of our Plan. No script, papers or pads. The others stare at us, expressionless. They expect us to do the talking.

I speak first. "Our Plan makes several assumptions. Bud is in uniform, attached to the U.S. Embassy staff. Probably an assistant Military Attaché. I'm a civilian. An unarmed French citizen from somewhere in France, or perhaps from Belgium. I have no *papiers d'identité*. In the confusion of the Nazi occupation and moving about—rumors of an invasion from England were persistent—I lost my papers. I'm not sure exactly where, or when. You bet this caused serious problems in my search for work. It was time for me to leave Europe.

"The Captain of the trawler, a *chalutier* I paid my way onto, asked to see my papers. However, the generous fare I offered to pay diverted his attention from the need to see my papers. Yes, he's going to French West Africa at once from Marseilles. And, yes, for a few more hundreds of francs he would take me directly to Dakar. He estimated we'd be there in about seven to ten days, maybe two weeks.

"The trawler was in bad shape. The voyage took many days—days of miserable, heavily salted food and rancid undrinkable water. We drank a bitter red wine instead. I had to sleep on a narrow wooden bed. We arrived in the middle of the night and, according to the trawler's captain, to evade inspection by the Dakar port officials, I was literally, physically, ungently dumped onto the beach a few miles north. That's why I have nothing. No razor. No toothbrush. Still no papers. Just the clothes on my back and my hat. *Zut! Merde*! I'm lucky they let me keep *mes chaussures et mes chaussettes qui sentent très mauvaises*, my smelly shoes and socks!"

That's my cover and general strategy. I quickly add I will have to invent the tactics on a minute-by-minute day-to-day basis. I detect slight nods of approval. No disapprovals so far.

Bud picks up the description at this point. "As soon as you supply us with a map of Dakar, Wortman and I will select a public meeting place. I'll keep my eyes out for Wortman who'll be walking slowly, with hands in his pants pockets, unshaven, filthy, depressed and hungry, jacket collar turned up to keep warm. I approach this miserable looking guy and, in a loud voice, ask him if he'll be my guide around Dakar. 'I'm new around here. I want to see the local sights and, especially, the cafés where the local French ladies hang out.' He agrees. We haggle. Finally, we settle on a price. Without disguising my movements, I hand him some money, francs. He stubbornly insists on American dollars. So, reluctantly, I pay him in American dollars. Wortman has no American dollars on him but he does have some French francs. We expect you'll provide those before we start out."

Looking at the others for agreement, Major Hurst declares "Okay so far. What's your next move?"

Bud continues eagerly. "I'll get the name and location from the Embassy of a cheap hotel off the beaten track, just outside the Arab Quarter. A possible good place to start our investigations. I'll go there with Wortman. He'll haggle, animatedly, like a Frenchman, for a low-cost room. He'll get it. And the *concièrge* will sell him a razor and a toothbrush and what ever toilet supplies he'll need."

Bud passes the story line to me.

I answer the question before it is asked. "No! We haven't forgotten the cologne. To a Frenchman that's second only to bread, cheese and a glass of wine. Then we'll head for a café. How do we find one? The *concièrge* will be most accommodating, cooperative and helpful, especially after I hand him a couple of American dollars wrapped in a French franc. If the *concièrge* gives me a suspicious, puzzled look I will point to Bud, an American officer waiting outside for me, and wink and whisper to the concierge 'I am this guy's Official Guide.' Yes. I will be aware that we don't know the concierge's loyalties and alliances. But you bet before the night is over I will know a lot more about him, the hotel, the people in it and the neighborhood.

"What'll I do if he asks for my papers and passport? Again, I'll use the influence of the American dollars. I will generously *partager*, share with him. The black-market dollar-exchange rate will end all such questions. If he asks where did I get the dollars? Again, I'll point in the direction of the American officer who hired me to be his guide. I'll touch a finger to my lips and nod. Letting him in on my secret; and a bit of greed on his part, should work. He'll become my *copain*, my pal, I expect. I'll let it be known that my American Officer drinks too much, which implies he talks too much! My *Officier*

Américain will be most attractive...*attirant* to the right people. Or are they the wrong people in this case?"

"You have some doubts about your first day?" The Chief directs the question to me.

"*Bien entundu, patron*! And I will have doubts about every day."

"Good!" The Chief's caution is heard loud and clear. "Don't ever get cocksure, Wortman. You'll be very much on your own. And don't get overly friendly in public with your American Officer. Appear to keep your relationship purely business. We'll see that Bud has plenty of money, American dollars, in his pockets. And both of you will become most 'attractive' people."

I assure him that Bud and I do not intend to become public buddies. "I need an identifiable source of income...and, of course...a reliable point of contact with O.N.I. and G-2 in Dakar to whom I can report any discoveries or risks, get emergency help and an escape route—if I should need them. Bud will be the only one who can fill these needs in Dakar. You bet we'll take good care of each other." Bud smiles back at me and I conclude my monologue with "*C'est tout.* That's the whole thing."

The Chief responds, "You've got it! But. You know the quotation, 'The best laid plans of mice and men...' Suppose things do go astray, don't match your script?"

Bud and I look at each other. "We'll have to do some fast ad-libbing, won't we?"

Bud and I are instructed to stay in the office every day while we wait for orders to head out to our transportation. We'd have all our meals in the office; breakfast, lunch, dinner and coffee breaks. Go directly to our hotels only to sleep and shower. Don't come or leave together. A well worn set of badly fitting "Made-in-France" clothes will be assembled for me.

"What do we do for relaxation in the meantime?" I ask.

"Read romantic novels about spies!" The Chief's sense of humor is as unfunny as ever.

A question comes to mind. "Chief. Do I come back here to the office after I've done all I can in Dakar?"

"Probably not. As we told you. You may have to go to Brazzaville, French Equatorial Africa. It's neutral, so far."

"And do what?"

You'll be met there by another O.S.S. field-agent who will arrange for you to make the trip north to a Mediterranean port."

"And then?"

"I have the feeling I'm repeating myself. You'll probably be taken by submarine to a French port where you will join the Maquis, the French underground in southern France."

"What role do I play there?"

"Only the Maquis Chief will know your connection with the O.S.S.. To all others, you are a young, happy Frenchman, overtly faithful to the government at Vichy, but with questionable morals. By the time you arrive, we should have an O.S.S. radio operator in place with the Maquis at Marseilles. He'll be your communications link to us...if you can find a way to reach him."

Raising an imaginary glass, "Good luck, Wortman!"

Chapter Twenty-Four

"Come on in and shut the door, please."

"What's up, Chief?"

"One or two things. Maybe three. First, all concerned are pleased you took care of Elliott. It's being treated strictly as a military affair. However, do not relax your guard. We do not know how much he has told his Nazi contacts. We do not know all of his connections inside the service or in the field. And, your undercover name, Jiraud Brevier has to disappear. Think of a new one soon as possible."

The noise I make as I exhale startles the Chief. I feel doubly relieved. Not just for myself, but it is good to know Elliott is out of action and can do no further damage to our War program. After a long pause and a deep breath, I ask, "Other than you, Chief, who will know my undercover name?"

"Bud Corval has to know it. No one else."

"Good. The thought of changing my name had occurred. I would like to be known as *Léon Dejacques*. I write it on the Chief's scratch pad. "No particular reason. I just like the sound."

"Okay. Léon Dejacques. Give me your Jacques Brevier ID card. It will be destroyed. A new one issued to Léon Dejacques." He sits back in his chair and looks intensely at me as though setting the stage for a change in scene. "I have your travel orders. Are you ready for this?"

"What do you think, Chief?"

No reply to my question. "You'll take a commercial flight to the airport in Norfolk, Virginia. Bob, my administrator, will drive you. At the Norfolk Airport you will be met by an O.N.I. man in uniform, a Lt.jg Pedersen. He will have a Jeep and one or two Shore Patrol sailors with him. That night they'll escort you onto a U.S. destroyer. It will be at night to assure that very few people will see you come on board."

"Is the destroyer taking me to Dakar?"

Again, an evasive reply. "Let's assume it is. The skipper of the destroyer will have your specific orders in a sealed envelope. He'll turn them over to you as soon as the ship is in its duty position at sea."

I start to ask a question. The Chief holds up a hand to stop me.

"Wortman, I do not know any more than what I just told you about your route."

I believe him and slump back in my chair. "When do I leave for Norfolk?"

"A seat is reserved for you on a noon flight out of Floyd Bennet, tomorrow, October 22. Until that time, you will not telephone, you will not visit anyone. You'll stay here and have your meals in the office. We'll set up a cot here for you to sleep on tonight.

"Now, there are some important details you and I have to go over together. Merry Bounty will sit in on this part of the conversation to make sure I don't overlook anything. She'll take notes for the confidential files."

This must be serious. Merry had never, up to now, been party to any of the conversations between The Chief and me. He steps outside his office and returns with Merry. I'd never really noticed her friendly smile before. At this very minute, I wish I were 20 years older.

"Hi, Wortman. How are you, dear?" See what I mean about friendly?

I notice she is carrying her notepad, the *CONFIDENTIAL JOURNAL*, and a small suitcase which she hands to The Chief who looks closely at me as she quietly closes the door.

"Ready? Start taking notes, Merry. Wortman will have to remember all the details. No notes. Right, Wortman?"

"Right, Chief."

"This suitcase contains only the clothes specially made for you to wear when you get to your destination. There's also an oilskin, a waterproof packet of French francs to get you started."

"I'm listening, Chief." This reinforces our eye-to-eye contact.

"You'll take no idents with you when you leave from here to go to the airport."

"Suppose someone challenges me? If I have no draft registration card with me I won't get very far."

"You'll memorize a telephone number I'll give you. Use it if anyone arrests you while in the U.S. It's a direct line to O.S.S. headquarters in Washington. When the phone is answered, give your name, your location and a brief description of the problem. Hang up and wait right where you are. Within an hour, or less, someone will be there to help. If you are challenged while you're with Pedersen and the Shore Patrol, he will claim you are his prisoner."

"What shall I wear while en route to Norfolk?"

"Civvies. Just what you are wearing right now. Empty your pockets of all idents. Give them to Merry. She will lock them away for safekeeping. You can get a tooth brush, tooth paste, razor and shaving stuff from the ship's store. Anything else?"

Merry and I exchange quick glances and smiles. I daydream. *The condemned man's last request is...*

"Hello captain! Hello!" The Chief snaps me back to reality.

"Anything else you can tell me, Chief?"

"Yes. Someone, a psychologist, I don't really know who, will soon be here."

"Isn't it a little late for that kind of exam, Chief?"

"No, no. Not an 'exam.' He's going to brief you on how to avoid sleep problems you may have in the field. I think they call it 'auto-suggestion.'

Supposed to teach you how to train yourself to relax and fall asleep anywhere, anytime you want to. Don't ask me if it works. You tell me later if it does."

"Shall I try on the suit?"

"No matter. It is not supposed to fit well or look clean and pressed. You will exchange what you are wearing for a set of khakis after you're on board the Destroyer. You will turn the suit, your shoes, underwear and anything you have in your pockets over to Pedersen who has been instructed to deliver them to this office. That way, when you get back here, you will have an immediate change of clothing."

Well, this is the first time The Chief has implied he expects me to return from overseas! It is reassuring, to say the least. "What about armament? A handgun? Or a knife?"

"On board the ship, the skipper will offer you a short-barrel revolver, ammunition and a combat knife...if you wish. I suggest, to help kill time until tomorrow morning, you read the records of the men out of this Office who have been in serious trouble overseas...and did not survive. There may be some lessons to learn on what not to do. Okay?"

"Yes. I'm always willing to learn—the easy way."

The Chief reaches into one of his desk drawers as he declares "Let's drink to that!"

We sip our drinks. We look down at the floor. Neither of us speaks. We avoid eye contact. I feel he is holding back, hiding personal feelings. At any rate, The Chief's silent companionship is perfectly timed, couldn't be more appreciated.

The night is long. I lie on the cot. It's a good time to try the auto-suggestion instructions. They don't work. Too much adrenaline to counteract, I suppose. Oh, well. This isn't the first, nor will it be the last sleepless night for me. Many thoughts whiz through my mind: mother, sisters, brother, cousins, aunts, uncles, school buddies, girlfriends. The experiences of the past ten months. The circuitous route from linguist to engineer to counter-intelligence. Survival training. Did I make the right choices? Can I do the job? What will tomorrow be like?

I must have fallen asleep sometime during the night. I get up from my cot. Jason, our security man greets me. "Hope you had a good nap, sir. How about some hot coffee, orange juice and doughnuts?"

"Sounds great to me, Jase, old buddy." He looks about 45 years old. Everybody over 30 looks "old" to me. I marvel at his rugged skin color. Superb posture. Standing or sitting, he's always straight as a ramrod. Hope I look so good when I get to be an old man.

"Hey, Jase, where'd this nectar and ambrosia come from?"

"The Chief dropped them off just about 15 minutes ago. You were asleep so he left them for you."

No real father could have been more thoughtful.

"What time is it?" Don't know why I ask. I still have my wrist watch. I must remember to leave it with Merry.

"It's 7:45 A.M.. The Chief said he'd be back in half an hour, sir."

"I'll go wash up and brush the night taste out of my mouth. See you in five. Join me then for coffee and stuff?"

"Thank you, sir."

Ten minutes later, I'm breakfasting at Jason's desk. "Boy, this has to be the best breakfast in the world!"

"Okay, okay. Let's not get emotional about it!" It's The Chief standing in the open doorway to his office.

Jason jumps to his feet and salutes. I often wondered whether Jason is a military man in civvies. He never would admit to any identification. So, now I know.

"G'morning, Chief. Hey, thanks for the eye openers. Perfect timing. Hits the spot."

"Good. Bring your coffee into my office for a quick review of today's plan. You'll be on your own in about two hours."

I follow him and shut the door behind me.

"In exactly one hour, Bob will escort you to a car. Leave all your IDs with Merry before you go. Bob will stay with you until your flight is off the ground. Remember the password or Lieutenant Pedersen will not want to recognize you.

"The plane lands at Norfolk, Virginia. Pedersen meets you at the gate. You'll know him because he's with a couple of Shore Patrol guys. Introduce yourself with the password, 'Hey! I'd sure like to ship out.' Immediately the two SPs will surround you. And all of you will go immediately to their Jeep. The rest depends on Pedersen. His assignment is to escort you into the Norfolk Naval Base after dark and deliver you on board a destroyer. Remember that password. 'Hey! I'd sure like to ship out.' Forget it or say it incorrectly and you'll find yourself very much alone in Norfolk, all of a sudden."

"Then?"

"When you both are on board the destroyer, you turn all your clothes over to Pedersen which he delivers to Merry in this office. You will be given a set of khakis, underwear, socks, shoes, a wool cap and a short coat to wear while you are on the destroyer. Okay so far? Good. Now you tell me. What will you be carrying in your hand?"

"The small case with my made-in-France outfit. Incidentally, I tried it on last night. Who selected that horrible green color for the suit and the hat? I think he hates me!"

"It happens to be the best we could do. Quit bellyaching!"

"Just kidding, Chief. Just making a funny!"

"Very funny. Go take a shave."

I do so and it's time to leave. In my office, which I now give up, Merry accepts the few personal things I offer, puts them in a small lock box, and gives me a warm, lingering hug. I enjoy this. Merry slowly breaks away, smiles and busses me on the cheek.

The Chief takes my right hand into both of his. "The best to you, Wortman. I'll be waiting for your reports. They'll come to me through G-2 and O.N.I. I'll expect you back here in a couple of months. Remember, no diary, nothing written, only verbal reports until you give up your cover. Any questions?"

"Yes. One. How would you describe my assignment?"

"Well, I suppose we do need a label." Pause. "How about...your assignment is...to catch a shadow?"

Chapter Twenty-Five

Bob wears his customary frown as we walk briskly to the car. I have no idea how much The Chief tells him. Or how much he reports back to The Chief. I don't want to be quoted or misquoted. So, we have an uneventful, wordless, one-hour drive to the airport deep in the heart of Brooklyn.

Several hours later, at the Norfolk Airport, I give the password to Lieutenant Pedersen and the two Shore Patrolmen who offer to carry my case. "No thanks, fellows. I'm holding onto it myself." Then I realize I am not just holding it, I am gripping it as though my left hand were a vise. I am tense, I suppose.

We take off in the Jeep. Our destination is a late lunch. This is my introduction to the inelegant White Tower chain and its equally graceless hamburgers. We take our time. It won't be dark for a few hours.

Lt. Pedersen is 23 years old. Nordic. Blond hair and blue eyes. Probably a lawyer, a 90-day wonder. *I'm a veteran of ten months. Does that make me a 300-day wonder*? Eventually he's going overseas assigned to some safe O.N.I. field office. No doubt he's engaged to his high-school sweetheart. *I never had a "high school sweetheart." I went to Boys High in Brooklyn.*

To preclude conversation of a personal nature, I don't query him. In return, he doesn't probe me. The conversation is limited to "How's your hamburger?" "Great!" "Mine, too."

Night falls. We are stopped by the armed guards at the gate. Pedersen shows papers, which are carefully scrutinized. By flashlight, they slowly scan the Jeep's interior and temporarily blind me. A snappy salute from the sentries and the gate is opened for us to continue on through. The docks are filled with Navy ships of all kinds. I've had no training in ship recognition. But, I am truly excited by the awesome sight of such a large number of military ships.

Finally, after much zigging and zagging and getting nowhere, Pedersen stops two SPs and asks for directions to Dock #DD-17. We locate the dock and the destroyer very easily now. Everything is well lit. It might as well be daylight. There's no such thing as "sneaking" on board this destroyer.

The destroyer looks very small. However, my frame of reference is luxury liners, the *Ile de France*, the *Normandy* and the *Queen Mary* which I have often seen tied up at Hudson River piers. Sleek, rakish, elegant and huge. Now, those really are ships. I change my frame of reference to the *Staten Island Ferry*. This makes the destroyer look enormous.

We find the ship's Captain, Commander Millen, on the bridge. He's been expecting me. One of the seamen escorts me to a cabin, my "home" during the trip. The cabin is actually one of the ship's sickbays. Two bunk beds. I have my choice: upper or lower. Instead of a door, there's a canvas curtain. No windows, I mean portholes. It's as impersonal as my office had been for the past several months. A swivel chair is bolted to the steel deck. A small panel on the wall—er, bulkhead to my right folds down to become a mini-desktop. Two lifejackets and battle helmets hang from a wall hook.

I turn to the seaman. "Expecting anyone else?"

"No, sir. The captain will be here in a few minutes." With a smart salute to Lt. Pedersen, the seaman leaves and, five minutes later, the ship's skipper pushes aside the curtain and squeezes his six-feet-plus frame into my new, private quarters. The top of his head almost meets the bottom of the ceiling. Pedersen salutes him. I shake his massive hand.

The skipper has a strong, cultured New England accent. "I don't know our destination. I expect Ship's Orders this evening. Yours haven't arrived yet. When I open the Orders Envelope, I'll know our route and destination. We move away from the dock at 0530 tomorrow. If your orders arrive, I'll see you get them—after we're at sea and at our first rendezvous. One of my men will bring a fresh change for you. Right now I have to return to the bridge and also find time to get a few hours' sleep. Tomorrow's going to be a bit rough on all of us."

"Thank you, sir."

Fifteen minutes later a seaman brings two pairs of khaki shirts and trousers. A belt. Two pairs of black socks. Two sets of underwear. Two khaki handkerchiefs. A Navy-blue short coat and a knit seaman's cap. Toothbrush and toothpaste, razor, shaving mug, soap and a couple of towels. This is fine, for a two day trip. However, Dakar is more like two weeks away. Well, I'd better get used to doing without. Or, learn to do my own laundry.

Lt. Pedersen looks nervously at his wrist watch. The time is well past midnight and, I guess, he doesn't want to sail to Dakar with me. Quickly, I spring to life, remove all my clothes and put on the khakis. Lt. Pedersen stuffs my things into a small duffel bag he'd brought from the Jeep. I keep my sunglasses. He points out there is a small storage drawer under my bunk, shakes hands and wishes me well. I thank him and wish him well. He salutes me, more out of habit than of honoring me, I'm sure. After all, I'm not sporting any insignia of rank on my shirt. I return his salute as he disappears through the curtained doorway. I lie down on my bunk bed and think about the immediate future.

Chapter Twenty-Six

The child in me wants to roam about the destroyer, explore and see all the new and exciting things. It would be nice to spend time on the bridge, watching and listening to the Navy in action. I'm especially interested in the combat communications center which, I think, must be well below decks. On the other hand, the adult in me believes it is most important to minimize contacts with the officers and personnel of the ship. I shudder at the thought of one of the ship's officers or crew running into me and my green suit ashore in Dakar. If one of them should see me and greet me while I am trying to maintain the cover of a Frenchman...well, it wouldn't help the cause. Better stay to myself. Restrict the encounters as much as possible.

This enclosure to which I have been committed is smaller, more confining than a jail cell. How will I keep my sanity? I'll do a lot of reading. The destroyer probably has a store of books. They'll help the time pass. I'll change my sleep habits. Sleep during the day. Exercise; do calisthenics on deck at night. But, inside my windowless cabin, how can I distinguish between night and day? I'll explain my logic to the Captain and ask if it is possible to have my meals in my cabin. I don't have any appetite at all right now.

As I lie there and gaze at the ceiling, which is the bottom of the bunk above me, I can hear the hum of equipment. I don't know what equipment is generating the sound. But it is a reassuring hum, a hypnotizing drone.

I am awakened abruptly by the ship's movement. Apparently, we are under way. Sure. The clock on the wall reads 5:35 and we are scheduled to leave at 0530 hours. I have to control a great sense of excitement. Oh, how I'd like to go on deck and observe the maneuvers, and go to the bridge to listen to the convoy's radio communications.

One of the captain's aides opens the curtain and introduces himself, Lt.sg Thomas. "Captain's compliments, sir. Would you like to have breakfast now? In your cabin or at the officers' mess?" Nice, friendly sort.

I explain my privacy-viewpoint and he agrees to see that meals are brought to me. He'll bring me a stack of paperbacks, too. Have I ever been on a destroyer before? I admit the biggest boat I'd ever been on was a ferry.

Lt. Thomas advises me to hold onto my mess-tray very tightly at all times. "When we do a maneuver, we do it sudden and fast. In a tight turn, this ship can list hard over, display her keel and snap back to her upright position. Tie everything down and hold on tightly, sir."

The toilet, the head is only about 10 feet from my cabin. I brush my teeth. But I skip the shave. I don't want to look freshly shaved when I am put ashore. My goatee looks good. Did Narcissus have one, too? Silly thoughts do come when both the mind and the body are idling.

Breakfast is okay. *N'importe de quoi.* No importance. I hear the destroyer's engines speed up very distinctly. Whoops! Lt. Thomas's advice was absolutely correct. I should've held on as soon as I felt the change in the destroyer's speed and direction. The coffee made a mess. No room service. I go to the head to find a roll of paper to clean the mess.

I must take a peek at the outside world. I put on the short coat, seaman's cap and my sunglasses and walk down the passageway toward the open door at the end. I lean out to see what I can.

Wow! Ships! Ships! Ships of all kinds! A convoy of ships spread out as far as my eyes can see! I learn there are actually 107 ships in the convoy. The biggest armada in military history! The destroyer is racing around the convoy. Suddenly it slows to a crawl. Just as suddenly it leaps ahead and turns. Hold on! The turns are so swift and formidable, I have trouble keeping a secure grip on the doorway.

Oh, oh! I'm getting a headache. Stomach's queasy. Nauseated. Am I seasick? I go back to my cabin, sit and hold onto the edge of my bunk. Maybe auto-suggestion works to prevent seasickness. It seems to because in half an hour the symptoms are completely gone. I feel so good. I quietly sing a French folk song I learned, heaven only knows where. Judging from the humming sounds, the destroyer has slowed down. No turning or listing hard over now.

Lt. Commander Millen appears in the doorway. He has a large, thick envelope under his arm. "Here are your orders. Before you read them, I learned from the Ship's Orders we are part of Operation Torch. We're going to invade French Morocco at three points. Rear Admiral Hewitt is in command of the ships while we're at sea. General Patton is in command of the troops in our convoy. The admiral and the general are both on the battle cruiser Augusta."

"Pardon me while I look at my orders, sir." I open the thick, heavy envelope and dump its contents onto my bunk. There's another small, sealed, white envelope with my real name on it. I open it right away.

> For your eyes only. Read and destroy
>
> Your operations are to be centered in the city of Casablanca, Fr. Morocco. When conditions permit, including weather and combat, and in your judgment it is feasible to attempt a nighttime landing on the beach approximately one mile north of the port of Casablanca, you will change into the special clothing you carried on board and advise the commander of your ship you are ready to go ashore. He will move the ship as close to shore as he deems secure. The commander will launch a rubber scout boat and, as quickly as possible, take you directly to

> the beach where you will exit the boat. The boat and its personnel will immediately return to the ship and move rapidly out to sea. At this point you alone are responsible for your actions. A detailed map of Casablanca, the city and the port, is part of this package. Your G-2 associate is receiving a similar envelope at this moment. We suggest you plan to make your initial contact inside the city in plain sight on the Boulevard de la Gare. Bon voyage!

That last bit, "bon voyage," gives me a chuckle.

"Amusing?" It's the commander's voice.

"I'm being told to have a good trip. I think that is amusing. Also, surprise! I'm going to work in Casablanca, not Dakar! However, my plan isn't really affected. Only the location changes."

No comment on that last observation. He picks up the thread. "I've been instructed to give you whatever weapons, side arms and ammunition you ask for. As soon as you know what you want, they're yours. We expect to arrive and reform our group for battle about eight miles off the coast of French Morocco between Casablanca and Fedhala at approximately 0100 hours on November 7. So far, we seem to have outfoxed the Nazis. None of the escort has detected a U-Boat. According to our HF Direction-Finders, they've congregated in large packs around Dakar, a thousand miles south of our target position. We might make this work without having to fight off the wolves."

"Is there any new intelligence about the French military in Morocco? Friend or foe? Any idea what to expect? Cooperation? Resistance? My orders just advise me to be on guard."

Commander Millen shrugs. "*Quien sabé*? Or however you say 'who knows' in French."

"*Qui sait! Je ne suis pas au courant.*"

"What's that last bit?"

"Who knows! I'm not in the know."

The commander disappears through my curtained doorway. And, once again, I am alone.

Nothing of special interest happens for the next 14 days. I've read a stack of Tarzan of the Apes stories. I try to read, but do not really comprehend or enjoy "Bowditch's Manual of Navigation," the thick bible of every seaman who wants to learn the art of the sextant, so I am told by Lt. Thomas who proudly confesses to me he is the destroyer's navigator.

En route there are frequent calls to general quarters accompanied by the unmistakable sounds of running feet and slamming steel doors. We have many drills on the way. In the absence of verbal orders, I can never tell without looking whether or not each general quarters alarm is the real thing. However, no one has to tell me the smart thing to do is believe each drill is "real" and react accordingly. The first time I am utterly startled by the loud bells and deafening klaxon horns. I experience a moment of confusion, akin to panic I suppose; but just for a moment. I put the lifejacket on over my coat, the helmet over my knit cap and carefully step through the doorway at the end of the passage...my gateway to the outside world. The second, third, fourth, fifth...I lose count of the number of times...I don't even flinch. Gunnery practice is frequent. The rapid, automatic firing of the 50mm anti-aircraft guns on the steel deck directly over my head is something else. The cannons fore and aft of my small room actually aren't as bad. Each time they fire it feels as though a giant sledge hammer is smashing at the top, bottom and all sides of the destroyer. Still, I find they are easier to take than the sharp, deafening crack-crack-crack of the anti aircraft guns. No depth charges. Good indicators: no submarines.

It is now November 7, 1942. We must be at or near our rendezvous off the coast of French Morocco. About a quarter hour before midnight the General Alarm sounds and I hear the usual sounds, running feet and slamming doors. No one is right there. I step all the way out and look all around the horizon.

The night's dark. No moon. I can see a few stars which, no doubt, means the navigators know exactly where we are with relation to our target ports; Fedhala to the left, Casablanca to the right. No lights are showing anywhere. The destroyer's guns all point in the same direction, which I assume is shore.

The destroyer moves very slowly, quietly, in a large circle. The guns rotate counter to the ship's motion, as if to keep some invisible target in their sights. I grip anything solid my hands touch, in case of sudden acceleration. This continues for several hours. My eyes grow accustomed to the dark night. Still, I see no other movement in the ocean around us.

I think I can see the silhouettes of many ships. I hear muffled noises. The effect reminds me of the sounds made by birds and squirrels coming to life as the sun breaks over a forest of pine trees. But these are metallic noises. To my left. Now to my right. The sounds intensify. As the sky slowly brightens, an eerie luminescence comes over the scene. There they are! I see landing craft jam-packed with men, tanks and other military materiel as they move past us at full speed toward the beaches. I see the tops of sand dunes and low cliffs. Silent, still, somber silhouettes against the sky.

Suddenly, searchlights go on beyond the beaches. They rapidly scan the skies. The French must have heard the noises of the landing craft and think the sound is coming from the sky. They believe they are having an air raid. But I don't see any planes in the air. No matter. This is a hostile act and I am told the hills around both Fedhala and Casablanca are heavily fortified with powerful coastal-defense batteries.

The commander of the convoy gives the coded order to fire. The cruiser to the left of the destroyer looses a deafening broadside! The immediate response from the French coastal batteries in both Fedhala and Casablanca is a loud series of salvos. Tall plumes of water rise where the shells land. I can't tell whether any direct hits are scored.

The destroyer is doing a series of full-speed maneuvers, turning this way and that, circling the cruiser and zig-zagging like an excited puppy teasing its master. More strong cannon blasts, these are big ones, come from the direction of Casablanca. Not from behind Casablanca, but they appear to come from the port itself. Our guns return the fire with amazing accuracy. The cannons in the port are silenced.

More cannon fire from Fedhala. Some of the landing craft are hit as they reach the beach. Must be General Patton's forces. I can barely see them from my position on the destroyer's deck. The troops are advancing rapidly across the beach, climbing on the tanks and whatever vehicles they can grab onto.

The cruiser continues to pour fire into the Fedhala batteries. Amazing how stubbornly the French return the fire. However, their aim isn't very good. They inflict no damage I can see. But, I am hardly an expert in these matters. Shrapnel falls on the destroyer's deck but I feel neither need nor desire to go inside where I would be more safe. I feel a sense of elation! Invincibility! Isn't this ridiculous? What's going on? I want to do something! Anything! Well, my turn to play will come soon.

Full daylight now. Airplanes overhead. Ours. The big guns in the port of Casablanca that had been silenced start up again. Once more, our battle cruisers quickly silence them. Throughout the day, after the heavy firing stops, intermittent sounds of small arms, automatic rifles and machine guns continue. Amazing how sound carries across the water. There's a scientific explanation for the phenomenon, no doubt.

Right now, the action seems to have stopped and I am interested in a nap. Nobody's had any food for hours I am sure. However, other, more important concerns of the moment distract one's thoughts from hunger.

A seaman with a tray of hot food awakens me. An hour later Lt. Commander Millen comes in carrying two mugs of coffee. He sits in the swivel chair and I accept his invitation to share the coffee.

"Well, you are now a veteran of a land-sea engagement. What's your reaction?"

I tell him where I stood when it all took place; but I didn't really know what was actually happening.

He tries to fill me in. "Reports aren't complete, of course. Essentially, we've knocked out and captured all the coastal batteries around Fedhala and Casablanca."

"What were the big guns from what I think was the port of Casablanca? Not from the hills."

"The French Battleship, *Jean Bart*, was at anchor with her entire escort fleet in the port when the action started. She fired on our convoy, without accuracy. Our cruisers silenced her promptly. Somehow the French fixed her guns. When she started firing again, the cruisers really let her have it. She's probably sitting on the bottom of the harbor."

"What's happening inside the cities?"

"Fortunately for everyone, the French have no stomach for a last ditch fight with us. It could have become a bloody hand-to-hand street-by street situation. They surrendered as soon as the coastal batteries and their pride, the *Jean Bart*, were knocked out. Some of the *Jean Bart's* escort, including cruisers and submarines came out to engage us. They were totally outgunned. We'd have preferred to have their Navy join ours. They would have been welcomed. But it didn't work out that way. I'm certain you'll have a chance to see all the destruction there must be inside the Casablanca harbor. I have other orders to go elsewhere with the fleet."

"What's the situation now? I have to estimate the time for my own invasion."

"Patton's staff is going ashore to accept and sign the French military government's surrender agreement. I suggest you wait a day or two until we have confirmation the situation is under our total control. Say, you must be restless, even a bit bored. You've spent more than two weeks in this cabin." He makes a statement but is actually asking a question.

"To say the least, sir! I am very restless and bored. But I guess I can take a day or two more of this luxurious life in my stateroom!"

He accepts my humor and, with a strong pat on my shoulder, takes our two empty coffee mugs and disappears through the curtained doorway.

From this point I try to think in French. I talk to myself in French. Even when I talk to myself in English, it's with a strong French accent. *What's the name of that school of acting? The one in which the actors learn to live the parts they play? Maybe, after the war, I shall go on the stage...play French parts exclusively, of course.*

It's night. Time for my routine of fresh air and calisthenics. I need both.

0110, November 11. It's been absolutely quiet for the past two days. No sounds of gunfire. No General Alarms, although the destroyer is constantly moving. The skipper has been checking with me regularly. The next move is up to me. If he doesn't object, I'll start my personal adventure right now.

I take the suitcase out of the drawer under my bunk, quickly strip out of my khakis, underwear, socks and shoes, and put on my *Fabriqué en France* clothing. The oilskin packet with the French francs goes inside my green suit's jacket. I remove my wrist watch and, after a quick study of the map of Casablanca, stuff all my discards into the suit case and snap it shut. With care, I double and triple check to make certain I have no identification, no labels anywhere on my person.

Hope I look as grubby as I feel. It'll make my tale of how I got to Casablanca more credible.

"Going somewhere?" It's Lt. Commander Millen.

"Thought, with your help, I'd take a stroll on the beach. It's time, Captain. Don't you agree?"

"I do. I brought a short-barrel revolver, ammo and a knife for you." He hands them to me.

I spread the weapons on my bunk and stare at them for a moment. "Commander, before I left my home base to join you, I read the profiles of all the other guys in my section who have disappeared. I especially noted they all had one thing in common: they always carried a gun or a fighting knife, sometimes both."

"How do you interpret that?"

"If my opposition knows I carry a weapon, he's going to feel life-threatened by me. He might try to get me first. I know I'd feel the same way if I were to discover my opposition carries. So, I think I'll go in unarmed. My partner...*gad I hope he's ashore*...will carry for me. If I need a gun in a hurry I'll have to find him in a hurry. Make sense?"

"No. But you're the one who has to deal with it. It's going to be cold on the beach until the sun comes up. The wind's going to be real chilly during your ride to the beach in the rubber scout boat. Wish I had something to offer you. At least take the short coat and seaman's cap with you and drop them into the scout boat as soon as you touch shore. Then run like hell to the sand dunes and make yourself invisible."

"I'm ready."

"Okay. We are as close to shore as I dare bring this ship; about two miles. We'll ready the scout boat. Lt. Thomas will navigate and control the rudder. Two seamen will handle the oars. They'll have rifles, just in case. The night's fairly dark. I think we can get you to the beach without being discovered. We are approximately two miles north of the edge of Casablanca. The current and wind should bring the boat into the beach about one mile north of the city."

Thomas spreads Sesame's veil, pokes his head in and half whispers: "The scout boat's in the water. Starboard side. In exactly five minutes...quietly, please." He's wearing a black short-coat and seaman's cap.

I immediately put the black coat on over my green suit and wear my green hat. Things are moving at express speed. I exit the passageway, cross the deck, and climb down a Jacob's ladder into the small boat. Two seamen, dressed in black, are at the oars. Thomas is at the rudder. He points and signals to me. I move to the bow and crouch down as far as I can. We push off from the destroyer and the oars dip into the water. It sure is cold, especially when an ocean spray hits me in the face. I'm breathing hard. I can feel my heart pounding.

Thomas's navigation brings us right to our mark. I see the surf breaking on the beach. Shedding the short coat, I crouch on my haunches, ready to leap out the instant I feel the boat's bottom scrape the sand. I don't feel the cold water in my shoes. I don't wave. I don't look back.

I just run like hell for the sand dunes.

ENDNOTES

Many years after the end of World War II the facts and some of the truth were revealed. The invasion of French West- and North-Africa, "Operation Torch," was imminent. It was a huge military expedition; one of the largest in military history. Extreme secrecy was vital. Misinformation was deliberately circulated to prevent the Nazis from learning where the invasion would actually take place. The U.S. encouraged the Nazis to believe Dakar was the location. It was not Dakar. Fortunately, the Nazis believed the invasion was to be at Dakar.

Many of the military officers of the highest rank who were involved did not know the details and would not know them until "Operation Torch" was under way.

Technically, the Operation was a success; however, there were many logistic errors and breakdowns of communications. It was rumored that, while on board a Navy warship off the coast of French Morocco, General Patton, commanding officer of the invading U.S. Army Forces, had to endure many hours, if not days, of not knowing exactly what was taking place, where or when during the actual landing of his troops.

Chapter Twenty-Seven

Cold? The night air is teeth-chattering cold! Nervous? Scared? I have to admit it. Absolutely yes! The ocean spray must have soaked me through and through as I crouched in the scout boat. I didn't realize how wet I'd become until this very moment of quiet and reflection. Dry off in the middle of a cool—no, COLD—French Moroccan night? IMPOSSIBLE!

To strengthen, to make more credible the scenario Bud and I created, I haven't shaved or showered in a week. Oh, what I'd give for a wraparound blanket. A long, hot shower. Well, this is an opportunity for me to test the exercises in autohypnosis.

I must have dozed. Immediately, I scan the beach. Not a soul, human or animal, is in sight. Good. Luck is on my side. I raise my wrist to see what time it is. OOPS! My watch is on the destroyer. The night sky is less dark than before I had shut my eyes. The sun's coming up. It is time for me to leave the beach, walk in the open, the last mile directly into Casablanca. Come on, Léon. *Don't think in terms of "last." Call it "the first mile inside French Morocco." Ça vaut mieux, Léon! Much better.*

I can hear the traffic on the road above; sounds of a series of small convoys of trucks and jeeps heading north, away from Casablanca. Probably Patton's troops on the move, scouting for any persistent enemy combatants. As soon as the light is bright enough to make me fully visible to anyone I might meet on the road, I'll climb up from the beach to the top of the sand dune and casually start hiking.

But how do I explain to any one who sees me emerge? Just what was I doing below the road? If they stop me and ask me to identify myself, I could be in deep s—t! How ironic it would be for me to be arrested by Patton's men. Perhaps to even be shot right here on the road to Casablanca as a suspected enemy spy. It's possible some of the guys in the O.S.S. who disappeared were put out of business this way. If I were to shout "Don't shoot! I'm a spy!" They'd say "That's why we're shooting you—you Nazi bastard!" A miscommunication ends it all!

But, suppose, as I emerge, I immodestly adjust my pants, tighten my belt and button my fly. It could be interpreted I had gone down to use the beach as a toilet. No questions. No explanation necessary. In fact, the sky is bright enough right now. And I do have to relieve myself. So, no acting is necessary.

I wait for the sound of an approaching convoy. As casually as I can, I climb up, stand erect and slowly, deliberately adjust my clothing. The GIs in the personnel carriers laugh loudly and point at me. What a show I must be putting on for them. Even the officers smile and offer a friendly salute. I smile, wave my hat and shout, "*Bonne chance! Bonne chance!*" Good luck, buddies!

A dozen convoys, 50 or more vehicles, at least 500 officers and men must have passed me, all going in the opposite direction, north toward Fedhala. No one stops me. Nobody challenges me. I suppose the popular belief is that spies never look as crummy as I do. And I feel as crummy as I must look!

I see short buildings straight ahead. The edge of Casablanca City, "Casa" as the locals call it. The map I had memorized identifies this as the beginning of the main street, Boulevard de la Gare, which terminates at the railroad station. I haven't heard a train all night. Not surprising. The railroad serves for both transportation and communication. It is one of the first things to be captured and controlled in a military action. No doubt the trains will start rolling again as soon as U.S. Army intelligence gives security clearance to the personnel—if the French military and government are now on our side. And if we can trust them. They were shooting at us a couple of days ago.

Even ignoring my serious need for shower, shave, goatee trim and a change of clothes, my stomach noisily demands to be fed and watered. The sidewalks of the wide Boulevard de la Gare are protected by arcade-like superstructures. I see many window-front stores under the overhangs; mostly boarded up, but no shattered or broken window-glass. Almost no signs or identifications are visible.

A long time ago I learned that one of the characteristics of Frenchmen, whether Parisian or Moroccan, is their social activities usually center around bistros and cafés. They love to chat, exchange ideas, converse and shout at one another—switching their wine glasses or coffee cups and chunks of bread and cheese from hand to hand while using the free hand animatedly to punctuate their exclamations and declamations. War or peace, bombs or bird songs, the cafés and bistros stay open and in full operation. It's a question of national pride. I must find such a café and, despite the way I look, use some of my francs to refill my empty innards.

Walking slowly, close to the buildings and store fronts, I listen carefully for the noises of a café in action. Except for a few stalls operated by Arab natives, the streets are almost empty. But, the day is very young. The sun is still low in the sky. The Arabs do not try to sell me anything, which is a good sign they take me for a franc-less Frenchman. All my senses are totally alert.

Within 1,000 feet of my cautious entrance into Casa, I am rewarded by the sounds of loud conversations in French on the other side of a closed wooden door. It's locked. I knock hard. No response. Maybe the loud voices are drowning out the wrap of my knuckles on the door. I pound the door with the flat of my hand. A short, fat man with a drooping, black mustache, a dirty gray blouse and a badly stained waist-apron cracks open the door.

"*Ouvrez*! *Ouvrez*! Open up" I shout impatiently. "*Je veux manger*! *Je veux boire*! *Ceux sont vos affaires, n'est ce pas*? I want to eat. I want to drink. That is your business, isn't it?" At the same time, to prevent him from shutting the door, I place my right foot firmly between the bottom of the door and its frame.

He's obviously very annoyed and suspicious. "*Oui. Oui. Ceux sont mes affaires. Et quoi de vous? Quel sont les vôtre*? Yes. Yes. That's my business. And what's yours?"

Softening my tone (after all, I really am very hungry and thirsty), "*J'ai beaucoup de faim et de soif.* I am very hungry and thirsty." And in my most friendly voice, "*Est ce que vous permettiez que j'entre*? Won't you let me in?"

He hesitates and scowls as he looks me over from the top of my battered hat to my unpolished shoes. I certainly must look like a destitute street bum. Maybe he's concerned about my ability to pay.

I implore with flattery. "*Je vous en prie, chèr aubergiste.*"

The innkeeper's manner changes as soon as I display a few crumpled francs. He whispers hoarsely, "*Entrez! ENTREZ! Vite! VITE!*"

I quickly step inside. Just as quickly, he closes and locks the door behind me.

The room is small. Crowded. Very quiet now. All eyes are fixed on me.

Are these allies or enemies? Friends or foes? What have I stumbled into?

The innkeeper directs me to a table around which five men are seated. He introduces each one by first name. I give my full name: "Léon Dejacques."

One of the men queries, "*De Maroc? De France*?"

"*Ni l'un ni l'autre. Je suis né a Bruxelles.*" To discourage in-depth queries about my birthplace, I'd rehearsed "Brussels, Belgium" quite thoroughly as my birthplace. My assumption was accurate. Nobody comments "I've been to Brussels" or asks "What district in Brussels are you from?"

A chair is brought for me. Smiling broadly now, the *aubergiste* brings me a small glass of white liquid and motions for me to drink it right down. I do...and struggle to conceal my nausea. It's cognac or brandy; never could tell the difference. Unaccustomed as I am to hard liquor for breakfast, its rawness scorches my parched throat and uninhabited stomach.

I force a smile and lie, "*Très agréable.*" My host bows and returns my smile.

Rubbing my belly and looking a bit sad, I send a message for food.

The *aubergiste* takes one step back. "*Pardon, M'sieur Dejacques. Tenez. Je vais_chercher de bonne chose pour vôtre petit déjeuner.*" He is going to find something good for my breakfast. He passes through a narrow archway. The stringed-bead curtain sways and rattles noisily. I hear kitchen-type sounds.

I turn my attention to my new friends at the table. They do seem amicable. My tale of how I got out of Marseilles and was dumped on the beach last night seems to satisfy their curiosity.

Naturally, the small room is full of spirited talk of the action of the past few days; the invasion; the agreement to work with the allies (no one calls it a "surrender"); the noisy bombardments from sea and, with pride, the formidable French battlements. I get the impression this group is more affected by the loss of the battleship Jean Bart than any other aspect of the invasion. Very few make political comments. They seem to ignore the fact that, less than two years ago,

France had surrendered to the Nazis after just a few days of weak fighting. Acceptance seems to be a characteristic of the 1940s French personality. Napoleon must be spinning in his grave!

At long last the *aubergiste* brings me a plate of bread, nuts and fruits, predominantly raisins and, best of all, a demitasse of hot, dark liquid. My hunger is so strong I really want to devour them in one gulp. I restrain myself and eat all the goodies Moroccan style; bare fingers. The demitasse contains very hot, very bitter Moroccan or Arabian coffee. It doesn't resemble in the slightest the American-style coffee I drank aboard the destroyer which, itself, bore absolutely no similarity to good old Horn & Hardhardt's nickel coffee in New York. Nevertheless, the hot liquid is satisfying.

One of my new friends at the table offers me a cigarette. I accept. Another has a small box of wooden matches, strikes one and lights my cigarette. I feel relaxed, but alert.

As I scan the room and the men in it, one man in particular arrests my attention. The dark shirt, no tie, under his suit jacket emphasizes his blonde hair and fair complexion. Definitely not Moroccan. Nordic? Bavarian? German? He seems to be more a listener than a talker.

I'm fully aware he's been staring at me, studying me ever since I came into this tiny café. He doesn't indicate nor can I detect any feelings of hostility. Perhaps he's just curious, as are all the others. On the other hand, everyone else has resumed drinking, munching, smoking and vocalizing.

The group seems to have accepted me. Or, perhaps they've chosen to ignore me. French Morocco has always been a rendezvous for irresponsible Frenchmen, young ne'er-do-wells and society's outcasts. Morocco offers a nice climate. Easy-going citizens. Low cost-of-living. A laissez-faire environment. And a visually beautiful country filled with interesting places to visit. If they've put me in this category of young men...good! Laissez-faire suits me fine.

I focus my attention on the man who's been studying me. After introducing myself to the men at one of the other tables in the café, I saunter toward the "blonde man's" table. He sits back in his chair, smiles broadly, accepts my handshake and initiates a conversation.

"*Salut, Léon Dejacques. Je m'appelle Robert. Ça va*? Hi, Léon Dejacques. I'm Robert. How're things?" His accent is native French. But, then again, they tell me mine is, too.

"*Ça marche. Mais...pas bon.* Things are not good." This negative response is a bid to draw him out by converting a ritual greeting into one that invites dialog and details.

He moves aside and motions for me to bring my chair over. "*Pourquoi 'pas bon'*?"

I explain why things aren't going well. I've lost my papers. Had a rough trip at sea across the Mediterranean and down the coast to Casa, dumped on the shore. There's nothing in my pockets except a few francs. I turn my pockets inside out to emphasize my poverty. Of course, I don't turn out my jacket pocket in which the packet of francs is quietly resting.

"*Est-ce qu'il y a un barbier à Casa*?" I rub my face to emphasize my need for a barber who can give me a shave. "*Je me faut un rasoir.*" And, adding an extra bit of information, "I need a job right away so I can rent a room, get a good night's sleep, buy some fresh clothes and eat properly."

Robert rises, winks at me, shakes hands with the men at the table and waves at me to follow him as he heads for the door.

"*Pardon, Robert. Je dois faire mes au'voirs à l'aubergiste. Un m'sieur très gentil.* Must say so long to the kind innkeeper and pay for my breakfast."

"*Bien entendu, Léon. Je vous attends au dehors du café.* Of course. I'll wait for you outside."

L'aubergiste and I say our farewells. I promise to visit his tiny establishment again. I join Robert outside the café.

We head south, deeper into the central part of Casa. Robert is not much of a talker. He comes from the school who's slogan is "You learn only by listening. You can't learn a thing while you're talking." I get the impression he and I are from that same school. But, sooner or later, one of us must talk.

Walking side-by-side at a brisk pace, Robert leads me along the Boulevard de la Gare toward the center of Casa. My contribution to the conversation is limited to exclamations about the elegance of Casa. I'm quite sincere. He explains, Marshal Lyautey, the French military governor of Casablanca in 1912 made certain Casa would be one of the most beautiful of cities. Lyautey proclaimed, "Wherever the eye rests it shall be pleased." Mine are very pleased.

At that moment we come to Maréchal Lyautey square, at the center of which is a statue of the governor heroically mounted on a high-spirited horse. The facades of the buildings surrounding the square are handsomely inlaid with many small multi-colored tiles. They glisten in the sunlight. *La gare*, the railroad station lies just beyond.

However, as I move my eyes and turn my head to take in the lovely sights, I'm actually searching for Bud, my G-2 counterpart and primary contact. We had agreed to search for each other near the railroad station on the *Boulevard de la Gare* in Dakar, our original destination. The Plan should remain unchanged. The city's name is now Casablanca instead of Dakar. Every important French city seems to have a *Boulevard de la Gare*. I want to make the contact as soon as possible.

Robert stops suddenly, turns to me and says he has to go now, reaches into his pocket, pulls out a piece of note paper and a stub of a pencil. He scribbles quickly, hands me the paper and directs me to the Hôtel Monte Carlo. In a whisper he adds "*Dites lui que Robert vous envoies.* Tell him Robert sends you and you need work. He'll help you." Robert shakes my hand and hurries off in another direction.

The paper has a name, Jean-Paul Duval, and a room number, 23.

I stroll slowly around the area of the railroad station and, after a short while, I see Bud walking at a leisurely pace all spruced up in a freshly pressed lieutenant's uniform. I raise my jacket's collar, shove my hands into my pant's pockets and stare down at the ground as I walk toward him.

Bud stops me. "Parlay vous American?" His deep southern drawl sounds beautiful.

I am indignant! I raise my voice to assure I will be overheard. In heavily French-accented English, I respond, "*Oui*. I speak American! I'm in a hurry. So, *allez*! Go away *Américain*!"

"Hol' it, Frenchie! You look like you need work." Bud adds in a whisper, "An' a shower. Phew!"

"You have work for me?"

Bud answers in a loud voice. "Sure do. I've got some free time an' I want to see the sights of Casablanca. Y'know what I mean? Cafays. Drinkin' places. Maybe some friendly French girls...if'n you catch my meanin'."

Bud's playing it to the hilt. He openly displays U.S. dollars. "I'll pay well for yo' time, if y'all show me the right sights."

"*Bien sûr, Américain. Premièrement*...first I have to go somewhere. You may accompany me, if you wish."

Bud shrugs, puts his money back in his pocket and follows closely behind me as I hurry toward the Hôtel Monte Carlo.

Bud catches up to me and looking up at nothing he whispers very slowly, "Shit! You stink!"

I grumble quietly, "Funny, the French didn't mention it."

We stop and reverse our direction to make sure we aren't being followed. I hustle him into an Arab stall. As we both examine the cheap goodies, I slip him the note so he knows where I'm going. He reads it quickly and slips it back to me.

I gesture, "*Allons*! Let's go *Américain*."

Our conversation continues as we walk quickly toward the hotel, about one-half mile beyond the railroad station. Bud keeps his left hand in his pocket. I notice he's carrying a holstered pistol, a Colt-45, on his right side.

I'm waving my arms like any Frenchman does to punctuate his chatter.

The vertical sign of the Monte Carlo comes into sight. It's a flat-roof three-story building in a corner location, which is good; offers more escape routes in case I have to, as The Chief put it, "Get the hell out of there in a hurry!"

I suggest Bud wait outside for me. The hotel has a glass-paned, wide, front door. The concierge glares at my disheveled clothes and unshaved face. I tell him

I want to see Jean-Paul Duval. He points toward the stairs. He is not smiling. I sense his eyes are following me.

I climb the stairs slowly to give me time to search for a path to a sudden exit. There's none I can see. The second floor has a large foyer, a central hall around which are the doors to the separate rooms. Some of the doors are numbered. I take a deep breath, exhale slowly, and knock on the door to 23, the room of Monsieur Duval.

Chapter Twenty-Eight

Pressing my ear to the door, I listen for sounds of activity. Knock again. Sounds of chairs shuffling and a door closing. Within a few seconds a man's voice on the other side of the door asks "*Qui va? Qui frappe*?"

"*M'sieur Duval? Robert m'envoie. Je cherche du travail.* Robert sent me. I am looking for work."

"*Moment, s'il vous plait.*"

The door opens a notch and a man's face appears. "*Qu'est ce que vous disez*?"

"Robert gave me a note for Jean-Paul Duval."

A moment's hesitation and the door is opened wide. The man looks up and down the hallway. Apparently assured I'm alone, he motions me to come in. He softly closes the door behind me and asks "*Quelle note? Montrez le moi.*"

Exercising deliberate caution, "*Peut être M'sieur Duval, c'est vous? Je l`espére bien.*"

"*Oui, je suis Jean-Paul Duval.*"

I hand him the note. He studies it, although it appears to have nothing more than Jean-Paul Duval and number 23 written on it. I must have missed some code, a scratch mark or some other device to authenticate the note. He's satisfied.

"*Asseyez.*" M. Duval sweeps his arm across the room to indicate "sit anywhere."

Quickly, I memorize the scene. There are 11 chairs, all but one with hard seats and straight backs. One resembles a small, cushioned sofa, big enough for a wide person. The room is large. I estimate it to be 12 feet by 15 feet. There are two heavily curtained windows on the 15-feet long wall which, as I orient myself, overlook the hotel's corner entrance and offer a wide view of three streets, left, right and straight ahead. A door, now closed, is at the mid-point of the 12-feet wall to the left of the windows. The ceiling is high, approximately 10 or more feet. A single, uncovered light bulb hangs by a thin chain from the ceiling. No sink or wash basin. Looks like this is a meeting room and badly in need of painting. But I'm not here as an interior decorator.

M. Duval settles into the sofa. "*Comment vous appellez vous*? What's your name?"

"*Je m'appelle Léon. Léon Dejacques.*"

"Tell me where you met Robert. And what can I do for you?"

Jean-Paul Duval, whoever or whatever he is, would make my Chief proud of me. This is as efficient as the time he sent me on a 24-hour mission in New York City to obtain a genuine copy of a confidential document.

Duval is a husky six footer. In his forties. Receding gray-blond hair. Suntanned complexion. He listens, without expression, as I repeat the tale of my miserable voyage from Marseilles to Casablanca, although I had paid for a trip to Dakar. His expression changes to a slight smile when I describe the café, my chance encounter with Robert, our walk and brief chat along the Boulevard, scribbling the note and directing me to the Hôtel Monte Carlo.

Without giving him time to evaluate my monologue, I repeat the urgency of my need for work so I can get enough money to clean myself up, buy clothes, get a shave, rent some lodgings and eat regularly. Finally, I stop prattling and give him an opportunity to respond.

He stares silently at me. I search for signals of hostility, friendship, doubt or belief. He's a hard one to read. Then, still staring at me, his voice is deep-toned as he starts a series of probing questions.

"What are your politics?"

"Me? Politics? I haven't any."

"What's your reaction to the invasion of Casa?"

"I heard the loud explosions as we came down the coast of Morocco at night, but I didn't know the noise was a military 'invasion'."

"Do you care that the Americans have taken control?"

"*C'est dommage.* Too bad. *Pour moi—Américain, Français ou Allemagne—c'est tout la même. Ma loyauté se sert personne qui me paye.*" Thus, I declared myself to be totally neutral, not caring whether the Americans, French or the Germans are in charge of Casablanca. Apparently, my expressions of dedicated neutrality, disinterest in politics and loyalty only to whoever pays for my keep satisfy M. Duval's probe.

He nods affirmatively. "There is work for you. Right here in this hotel."

"*Oh là là! Je vous remercie! Milles fois, M'sieur Duval*!" I am really stimulated. Whether Jean-Paul Duval is benign or evil, merely a petty crook, an arch criminal or a master spy, at least I have an anchor in the Casa community. I speak rapidly, excitedly. "When do I start? Where can I get lodgings? What work do you want me to do?"

He rises, smiles and extends his hand. "*Premièrement, Léon. Non pas Monsieur Duval. Je suis simplement Jean-Paul. C'est tout.*"

To display intense gratitude for his permission to be informal, I enclose his hand within my two hands and shake vigorously.

"*Vous pourrez rester ici a l'Hôtel Monte Carlo. Ça va*? You could stay here at the hotel. Okay?"

"*D'accord! D'accord! Mais, pour moi, ce n'est pas à bon marché*! Stay at the Hotel? You bet it's O.K. But, it's not cheap." I look into his eyes, literally pleading for sympathy.

"No. No. Calm down. When you work for me, you do not pay a thing. Here is some money." He tells me to buy new clothes, toilet accessories and whatever I need.

I pocket the money. "*Vous êtes très gentil. Un vrai ami*!" I declare my gratitude with grand gestures. Don't pay anything while working for him? He's paying me. Strange. I can hardly wait for the job description. I am eager to learn how I am expected to repay his generosity. "*Qu'est ce que je peux faire. Comment payer de retour, Jean/Paul*? What can I do to repay you?"

"We'll see. I need an energetic young man who can move freely and swiftly through Casa, possibly travel to other cities inside French Morocco. I think you might do. Do you know any of the Americans, the military people now in Casa?"

"I know only one, an American Army Lieutenant. *Zut*! *Merde*! He's waiting for me outside the hotel right now!" I had completely lost track of time. I still don't have a watch. No doubt Bud's waiting for me and wondering if I am in a jam. He might become concerned, impatient, and burst in to rescue me. That'd blow it for sure! I jump from my chair. "*Quelle heure est il, Jean-Paul*?"

However, at the mention of an American Lieutenant waiting for me, Jean-Paul's eyes open wide. For a moment, I detect alarm in his face. Just for a moment. Then he restores his calm. His curiosity boils over. "*Expliquez. Je vous en prie*. Explain."

So, I describe my chance meeting with this U.S. Army Lieutenant who wants me to guide him around Casa. That is amusing to me because I just got here myself. But, I explain with a smirk, since he's going to pay me in U.S. dollars, I have instantly become an expert guide to all the sights, sounds and good times of Casa.

Jean-Paul is amused. He urges me not to keep the lieutenant waiting, but return here to Room 23 before dark. He points out many of the Arabs of the old city are dangerous thieves and cutthroats, especially hazardous to non-Arabs; even more so to French people.

I stand up to leave, but at that moment, I hear sounds of a person, a woman, coughing lightly, clearing her throat. They come from the other side of the closed door along the shorter wall of the room. I try to ignore them, pretend they haven't happened. However, Jean-Paul looks in the direction of the door, then back at me.

"*N'importe de quoi, Léon.* It is one of my friends who lives in these rooms."

One of his friends? Female, of course. Who lives in these rooms? Are all of them women? Are they, too, Jean-Paul's employees? Employed to do what? How many of them are there? How many rooms do they occupy? Is this hotel a headquarters? Headquarters for what? En garde, Léon! Watch out for hazardous Arabs...and watch out for your new French friends in Casa, too. They can operate 24 hours 'round the clock, night or day. *Fais attention*! *Prends garde*! *Méfie-toi*! *Trust no one*!

The door opens abruptly and the unexpected happens. A woman comes into the room. She's not just pretty. She's beautiful! Rubbing the sleep from her eyes, she covers her mouth and stifles a yawn in mid-flight when she sees me and realizes she's interrupting our conversation.

Jean-Paul smiles and stands as he introduces his *amie*, "Georgette." She explains she's been making *un petit somme*, a nap, and didn't know Jean-Paul has a visitor. Georgette is tall, almost my height. Probably in her early thirties. A stunning brunette in any country, her dark hair is neatly brushed, long, bright and lush. She's wearing a peignoir, opaque but tight enough to reveal a curvaceous body.

Georgette slowly, gracefully, langorously sinks into the sofa Jean-Paul had been occupying. "*Cigarette*?" She's looking at me and I am wilting fast.

I pat my pockets, "*Non, Georgette. Pardon. Je n'en ai pas.*" I haven't any. I feel nervous. Not because of any sense of danger. It must be my age and...it has been a long time since Madeleine and I...

She turns to Jean-Paul. He draws a cigarette case from his shirt pocket and lights a cigarette for her. Jean-Paul tells her I am now working for him and will be staying at the hotel. This brings a seductive smile to Georgette's lovely face. Georgette sure knows how to tantalize.

I clear my dry throat and remind Jean-Paul the lieutenant is waiting for me. He briefly tells Georgette about my meeting the lieutenant this morning and how he has hired me to guide him around Casa. He and Georgette share a laugh when I add the bit about the wonders of being hired to guide anyone in view of my own very recent arrival in Casa.

"*Il faut que je prends congé, chère Georgette. Mon lieutenant m'attend.*" Patting my filthy clothing, I add, "I must go. My lieutenant is waiting for me. And my dirty clothes embarrass me." I bow and bend over to kiss her extended hand. Georgette acknowledges my discomfort and good manners with a smile and a backward tilt of her head. She slowly exhales a long stream of cigarette smoke in my direction. Nothing like this seductress had ever been discussed in my months of training in New York. I've never been a fast one with the ladies, especially beautiful ladies. I must get out of here "*Salut. Au'voir*!"

"*À bientôt, Léon*. Bring your lieutenant up here sometime. We'd love to meet him." Jean Paul nods. Georgette smiles and wiggles her fingers at me as I make my retreat through the door of Room 23. "*Tout à l'heure*. Soon."

Chapter Twenty-Nine

This can't be real. They skipped this stuff in my training. What really is this all about? Random thoughts race through my mind as I turn left toward the stairs leading down to the first floor, the exit and, I hope, Bud.

I recover control as I pass the concierge. He leans over his desk and follows me closely with his eyes. His right arm appears to be hanging down as though he might be hiding something in his right hand. A gun? A knife? An exotic weapon at the ready? He glances anxiously at the stairs. To see if anyone is chasing me? He moves his arm as though he were releasing whatever he's holding onto.

I smile at him, wave and say, "*Salut, monsieur le concierge*!" in as friendly and calm a voice as I can fake. "*Je rentre plus tard.* So long! Back later." Bet on it.

He returns my wave. No smile.

Bud's waiting. Very relieved to see me, he looks at his watch and shouts out loud, deliberately I hope, "Dammit, Frenchie! Don't ever keep me waitin' like that! I ain't got fo'ever, y'know!" And in a very quiet voice, "Five minutes more and I would have brought in the MPs an' raided the place. What'n hell happened?"

I appreciate his concern for me. Waiting can be tougher than doing. I shout at him, "*Tais tois, Américain.* If you cannot wait for me, do your business with some other 'Frenchie.' I'm sure the Arabs would like to show you around. *Avec plaisir.* With pleasure."

As we start walking at a fast pace uphill on the street to the right of the Hôtel Monte Carlo, Bud whirls on me. "Let's get some food before I fall apart from starvation."

Now it's my turn to do some whirling. "Before YOU fall apart? You know what *merde* means? That's what I feel like right now! I haven't eaten a substantial meal in more than 24 hours. I've been soaked, frozen and gone without enough food or water to keep me alive since I left the destroyer. Don't talk to me about falling apart."

"Sorry, Frenchie, Dejacques, or whatever you call yourself. Tough times for both of us. So, now, let's put on the feed bag."

That's right. Very à-propos. Bud's a horse trainer in civilian life, which must have been years ago. "*Suivez moi, mon Américain. Nous cherchons the dinner—tout ensemble.*" I put my hand on his shoulder and squeeze hard to assure him I'm still on his side. We're together.

I keep looking around for landmarks so I can find my way back to the hotel "before dark." Street-name signs are not often visible. The ones I do see are aged plaques mounted high up on the side of a building's corner wall. Many are in Arabic. No help to us. A few are in French. I see some bilinguals. Streets are not laid out in a square pattern, North, South, East and West, as they are back home. Here they curve, bend and appear to go any which way, without any plan or reason.

I tell Bud, my fellow virgin in Morocco, we'll use the same method I did when I entered Casablanca this morning. If we don't see an eatery, we'll listen for sounds of life à la bistro. Above all, Bud, I've been told I must be careful not to wander into the Medina, the old city, the Arab quarter. "More people go in than come out." So, they say.

Bud looks serious. "I know. The Medina's off limits for military personnel. It's so bad. Whenever it's necessary for personnel and officers to go into the Medina on official business, they must go in groups of at least six. Those are the orders. Seems the Ayrabs never surrendered. Guess we didn't think to ask 'em to. Although it's their homeland since way back, the French have governed 'em for years and treated the Ayrabs like they didn't belong here. In a way I can't blame 'em for not taking a shine to us. They expect us to be just as miserable toward them as the French. Maybe we will be. I don't really know." Pause. "An' I won't guess."

All the while Bud is delivering this monologue, I swing animatedly from left to right, gesticulating as though I were pointing out things of special interest. They actually are of "special interest" to me. I am seeing them for the first time.

As we walk along, several U.S. Army vehicles loaded with American troops pass us by. They're moving fast. No foot soldiers. A jeep or two and personnel carriers. Bud returns the salutes and initiates some.

"*Regardez! Un barbier! Pardon, s'il vous plait.* I do not like to interrupt, but here's *un barbier. Dans ce kiosque. Vous attendez. Il me faut*...Wait. I must clean up my face."

"Yeah. I'll wait right here. But, hurry up. I could eat anythin'...long as it isn't movin'."

Fortunately, the barber shop is empty and I can get immediate attention. The "shop" is actually a very small kiosk, about five feet wide, six feet deep, with walls on three sides and open at the front. As with other Arab-operated kiosks, when the shop closes, the keeper merely draws an opaque drape across the front. Apparently this method of closure is honored. Or, perhaps, anyone with criminal intent quickly finds he has offended and angered the entire Arab population and...well...that criminal's life is very likely to come to a sudden end when he returns to the Medina. An effective method of crime control among the Arabs in Casablanca.

The barber's "chair" is a pile of soiled cushions. The "sink" is a bowl of water; probably the customers share the same water all day. I see a straight razor, a tired cake of soap, a shaving brush, a chipped mug and a small bottle of unidentifiable green liquid. A tattered rag is slung across his left shoulder. Must be the "towel." I shudder.

"*Bon jour, monsieur.*" The barber greets me with an exaggerated smile. He could use a shave himself.

"*Oui. Très bon jour. Comme vous voyez, rasez mais ne touchez pas le menton. C'est mon vrai goutée.*" I tell him to leave my chin-beard alone. Who knows to what diseases I am about to be exposed.

"*Oui, monsieur. Je comprends.*" His French accent is strange, but interesting. Must be a combination of dialects, Arabic and street-learned French.

I settle onto the cushions. Not too uncomfortable. The barber dips the mug in the water, wets the shaving brush, rubs the brush across the cake of soap and vigorously massages the inside of the mug. Not much of a lather is created, but he does manage to transfer what little there is onto my cheeks. I take the rag-towel from his shoulder and use it as a bib. Force of habit, I suppose. It doesn't really matter whether any soap or beard shavings get onto my filthy, stained shirt or rumpled green jacket. What's one more stain? They probably wouldn't be noticed. Right after Bud and I find food, I intend to search for a kiosk where I can buy clean, new clothes. Hopefully, there's a bathtub or some equivalent luxury at the hotel.

I admire the barber's skill with the razor. Swift. Painless. He wipes my face with the towel. Then I discover what the green liquid is as the barber splashes it all over my face, forehead and beard and steps back to admire his artistry. The liquid has an odd, heavy fragrance. Not too unpleasant. Moroccan cologne? The barber tells me all his French customers enjoy it. One of the French words for customer is "client." He uses the French word, and I feel I am participating in a satire on *usages sociaux des Français*. Social uses of French. It would have been ungracious of me to laugh out loud. Bud's silently watching the action from the entrance to the kiosk. My bodyguard.

Bud can't resist the opportunity. "You still stink, but its a different kind of stink."

I look up at the barber. "*Tous les Américains, sont ils idiotes? Je crois que oui! Tout à fait à lier*!" Of course, I mean Bud is, like all Americans, raving mad.

The barber plays it wisely. He shrugs and doesn't comment. "*Moment, monsieur.*" He presses my shoulders to keep me seated, picks up a pair of shears...they certainly couldn't be called "barber's scissors"...and makes a few strategic snips at the hairline around my ears and neck.

"*Ça va, m'sieur*? Okay?"

"*Oui, ça marche.*" I hand him French money, *argent français*, which he rejects.

He signals toward Bud who has reappeared. "*Argent Américain*?"

"*Bien entendu. Attendez.*" I turn to Bud and relay the message.

Bud pretends annoyance. "Goddammit! What d'you think I am? Fort Knox?"

I tilt my head pretending not to understand. "*Quoi? Quoi*?

"Oh nuts to you, Frenchie!" Bud dips into his pocket and hands the Arab a dollar bill.

Now the barber is all smiles and bows. I ask him where can I find a new suit, socks, shirt, shoes, razor and all the *accessoires de toilette* a man needs? He motions and steps outside the kiosk. Pointing, he directs me to his friend's shop, not a kiosk; two streets, turn right and Achmed's tailor-shop is on the right side of the street, which has an unpronounceable Arabian name. He adds, "Tell Achmed, Bahrouhn sent you, please."

Like being back home in New York. You can always make a deal!

"*Au'voir, Bahrouhn*!" I leave the kiosk smelling like something inhuman. Bud puts three feet of space between us as we walk toward Achmed's place.

Just as Bahrouhn said, there is Achmed's shop. Relatively luxurious, it has a sign above a real doorway. Trouble is the sign is in Arabic. Ah! Beneath the Arabic are the welcome French words: "*Marchand. Fait. sûr mesure.*" The equivalent of custom-made clothing.

Achmed welcomes us profusely. Bows repeatedly and smiles. I introduce the U.S. Army Lieutenant who doesn't speak French. *N'importe*! Any friend of Bahrouhn is a friend of his. Achmed is a short, pudgy man. He could use a good dentist. Dark hair peeks out beneath the edge of his bright red, rimless, tassled tarabich. His clothes, the typical loose-fitting, wide seraweel trousers and leather sandals, are clean. I don't have to tell him what I need. It's quite plain to see.

He moves to a table on which are some stacks of cloth. No, I don't have time for a custom-made suit. He shrugs and moves toward another table, looks me over, estimates my size and, from this stack, he withdraws a dark kind of gray suit. Pin-stripes again! The jacket's tight, the trousers are baggy. But, Achmed makes it clear this is his very best suit, practically an import from France, whatever that means. Now he produces a *chemise*, a shirt. I want two. No problem, if you aren't fussy about colors or patterns. Underwear? Naturally. Never mind the color and fit. How about a coat for the chilly nights? No problem. "If you don't mind wearing a horse-blanket" is Bud's contribution to this moment of sartorial elegance. Socks? Sure. Two pairs, please. Off white is all he has.

"No problem" is Achmed's response to any and all requests. Shoes? Again, no problem. He can brush the one's I'm wearing and they'll look as good as new. Okay. A new hat? All he has are tall, brimless tarabiches. "Here's a nice orange-red one in exactly your size, monsieur." No, thanks. I'll do without a hat. I need a razor, shaving brush and soap, toothbrush and hairbrush. With a toothy smile, Achmed tells us to wait right where we are. He bows hurriedly and dashes out of the shop and returns in a matter of minutes with a cloth-wrapped package of toiletries for me, including the inevitable cologne I had neglected to mention.

Judging from his enthusiasm and excitement, this is probably the biggest sale Achmed has made this year. His enthusiasm boils over. "*Vive les Français*!"

"*Et quoi des Américains*?" I nod toward Bud.

"*Vive les Américains*! *Vive les Américains*!" Achmed's overdoing it now.

How much does all this cost? Achmed is typical. He names an outrageous price, which he doesn't really expect to get. I name a price that's half the amount. To Arab merchants, it's an important part of the game. Pay the asking price and he'll accept of course, but without a smile. No fun unless you drive hard for a "bargain."

"Well...you were sent by Bahrouhn...okay!" Achmed's all smiles. He even accepts the payment in French francs.

I don't see a dressing room. Without asking permission, I strip right there and put on the new things. Achmed ties a large cloth around the rest of my new purchases and, with much fuss and smiles and bows, he accompanies us to the door. He gratefully accepts my battered green hat, which he probably will sell to another client as a hat imported from France! "*Très bon marché.* Very low price. Cheap."

Bud and I continue further up the street in search of a café or a bistro. We find a likely one just inside an alley. A jeep with three officers, one of whom is in a French uniform, and a driver whizzes past us as we take seats and sigh deeply. Bud sighs from hunger. I sigh from both hunger and exhaustion.

"Damn! I forgot to ask Achmed about a wristwatch!"

"Here, take mine. I'm sure I can buy, beg or steal another one at the base."

We eat our fill. No food shortage here in this bistro. Bud points out it's probably because we didn't have to blockade Casablanca and the invasion itself didn't take very long. However, he adds the information that no one is allowed to leave or enter Casablanca without military-approved papers. But this condition excludes food and medical transports.

I'm amazed there's little or no evidence of the naval bombardments.

Bud explains, "They tell me the hills east and south of the city where the French batteries are located have been heavily hit. And the ships in the port itself were demolished—including the battleship *Jean Bart* and its escort. I'm gonna to take a look for myself tomorrow. Should be quite a sight! Also, one of the surrendering French officers claims there is a prison camp about 50 miles northeast of Casablanca. A squad's on its way to scout it."

My curiosity's aroused. "What kind of prisoners?"

"Mostly political. French officers an' others who spoke out against the Nazi alliance with the government in France...an'...a lotta Jews."

"Let's eat and get the hell out of here, Bud."

Chapter Twenty-Thirty

Bud and I go our separate ways. He ostentatiously hands me some money and waves good-bye at me. I'm alone—again. That's okay. I don't feel lonely.

Jean-Paul Duval, Georgette and whoever the others who work for Duval may be, could be involved in dark-scheme intelligence-work for Vichy France or even directly for the Nazis. Could be they are in a non-political profession...such as drug smuggling. At this time I don't really know. However, I have the feeling I am about to get more definitive clues as I enter the hotel, pass the concierge who seems to be the only one who works the desk, and climb the stairs to Room 23. I knock on the door. Wait. Knock again, and the door is opened by a face I have not seen before.

"*Qui va?*"

"*C'est moi, Léon Dejacques.*"

Jean-Paul and Georgette are here. I am introduced to the door opener, Michel. He's a beefy guy. Mid thirties. Light hair. Piercing, blue-gray eyes. Neatly dressed. An ominous bulge under his jacket's left breast pocket. A "hit" man? Or just a bad tailor? He smiles slightly, makes direct eye contact and squints at me as we shake hands.

I take one of the straight-back chairs facing Jean-Paul in his cushioned sofa. Georgette is on his left. Michel is at his right, close to the door.

"Well, *Léon, mon ami*. You've shaved and bought some clothes. Looks good. You feel like a new man, eh?"

"*Merci bien, Jean-Paul.* I sure feel like a better man, now. How do you like my cologne?"

"Strong. Not bad. But I think we can provide much better cologne for you."

Small talk. Direct questions. "Where have you been?" "Meet anyone, other than your lieutenant?" "See any U.S. troops?" "Any French troops?" "Ship movements?"

Unhesitatingly, I give direct answers. "I wasn't near the port. Couldn't see the ocean." The truth makes it easy for me. Yawning involuntarily, I add "What I need now is a good night's sleep. How do I get a room for myself? In this hotel, I hope. I don't think I can stay awake long enough to walk to another."

"We've set you up in Room 29, across the hall—just to help us keep in close touch while you work for me. Okay?"

"Thank you very much, Jean-Paul. *Vous êtes encore très gentil.*" I can't stifle my yawns. My eyelids are as heavy as they've ever been. I excuse myself. "*Je prends congé.*" I really do have to lie down. I rise. Shake hands all around and leave Room 23.

The hall is in semi-darkness. There are no windows to let in any outside light; only one small electric bulb in a crude fixture on the wall of the hall opposite the stairs. One stairway goes down to the lobby. The other goes up. To the next floor? The roof, perhaps? I'll have to investigate the "up" stairs...after I've caught up on some sleep; one of the conditions for my survival.

I open the door, search in the darkness for a light switch. Ah, there! Again, a single bulb hanging from the ceiling provides adequate, not luxurious, light. Room 29 is ample for me; about 10 by 10. There's a bed; full size, with two pillows, clean sheets and a blanket. Oh boy! One chair, a low, marble-topped narrow chest with a pitcher and a bowl on it and a small wardrobe-closet are the total furnishings. A dingy brown towel is suspended from a hook on the wall alongside the chest. A short drape alongside the bed covers the window. It's too dark outside for me to see anything. The window's stuck but, with a grunting effort, it opens enough to provide some ventilation. Forget this as a possible escape route; too big a drop to the street below.

My wrist watch reports the time as 2022 hours. I toss my clothes onto the chair...

The sound of the door being opened awakens me. I must have fallen asleep.

"*Bon jour, Léon*! *Réveilles-toi, mon cher*! *Je t'apporte le petit déjeuner*!" It's Georgette with my breakfast.

I sit up in bed and check the time; 0731. Georgette puts a tray of food on my lap. Looks like scrambled eggs, bread, no butter, a small glass of clear liquid and a pot of, I hope, hot coffee. Georgette sits on the edge of the bed and indicates I should drink the clear liquid first.

Argh! It's the raw brandy, cognac or paint thinner again! Hazards of war! If the Nazis don't get me, the breakfast liquor will!

The scrambled eggs are real, though not the freshest. The bread is good; real fresh-baked French bread. It would be even better if there were butter. Georgette tells me she hasn't seen butter in several weeks. "Maybe your U.S. Lieutenant can bring us some butter." She squeals with delight. "*Oui*! *Oui*! Invite him to our rooms...with the butter!"

Good. An excuse to bring Bud directly into the scene.

"Jean-Paul wants to talk with us this morning. In 15 minutes, in 23."

"I'll eat and dress quickly. Where's the toilet?"

"It's the door between Rooms 27 and this one. Turn left when you leave this room. It's just the next door. Come quickly. You can shave later."

"Good. See you in 15."

Georgette slowly, tantalizingly rises from the bed, wiggles her fingers at me and, with a seductive smile, leaves the room.

I get out of bed and look out the window. Can't see much. The street's quite narrow. Casa's a city of exaggeratedly wide boulevards contradicted by its narrow streets.

Putting on my underwear, trousers, socks and shoes I make my first visit to the important room, the one with the door next to mine. Apparently the toilet is the French-Moroccan version of a "hall bathroom." It's small, very small, no larger than needs be to contain a sink and a small mirror on the wall above it. The French-style commode or bidet next to the sink amuses me for some reason. Against the wall at my right is an oversize basin for taking baths—if you don't mind doing it while standing. This is actually a *salle de bain*, a bathroom; a bit more than just a toilet. A hose rests in the basin-bathtub. Probably one attaches it to the sink's faucet and, in this way, fills the tub. A flimsy drain-stopper retains the water in the tub. A metal rack, I suppose for hanging one's towel, is mounted on the side of the sink.

Mon dieu! There's actually running water, slowly running water, at the sink's faucets. Only one works. Naturally it's the cold water. I presume hot water is rationed for use during certain hours; probably in the middle of the night when everyone's asleep. Must find out about this. I still haven't had a hot, not even a warm shower since I left the destroyer. How long can a body get by on cologne alone?

"*Il faut que je me dépêche*!" Gotta hurry! Can't keep the boss waiting on my first day of work! I skip the shave. Brush my teeth and hair, wash my face and hurry back to my room where I can splash a bit of cologne and finish dressing.

"*Ah, bon matin, Léon.*" Good morning. Jean-Paul expresses interest as he closes and locks the door behind me.

"*Oui*, thanks to Georgette's kindness, I've had breakfast."

"You'll soon discover she has many skills most useful to our tasks."

Our tasks. What in hell does that mean? I recognize and greet Michel. Two faces are new to me. How many more are there who work for Jean-Paul?

Jean-Paul introduces Philippe and André—two more of his "team"—as he sweeps his hand in the direction of Michel and Georgette. "*Asseyez.*" We all sit facing Jean-Paul who, as seems to be usual, sinks into his sofa. Philippe and André express interest in knowing more about me. Philippe, the older of the two takes the lead in the questioning. "Where are you from? Have you been in Morocco very long? How'd you meet Jean-Paul? How old are you?" And so on. Natural questions.

I counter with a few similar questions. Philippe and André are actually from Algeria. They were visiting Jean-Paul when the invasion began and haven't been able to leave. However, they think transportation is becoming available and expect to get back in a day or two. Philippe appears to be in his mid forties. André could be 10 years younger. Again, both have blond hair and blue eyes. Amazing how many of Jean-Paul's "workers" have the classic, handsome Nordic look. Or is it Aryan? Not sure I can tell the difference. How did they travel all the way to Casablanca? It's prudent not to ask.

The two are well-dressed; however, their clothing has become a bit rumpled. They weren't prepared for an extended stay in Casablanca; didn't bring enough changes with them. I tell them about Achmed's shop. They're say they are glad to know this. They'll visit his shop before they leave Casa. However, I think they know more about Casa than I.

A knock on the door followed by "*C'est moi. Claude.*" The door is opened by Michel. Claude, the concierge, comes in carrying a large tray and a folding table to support it. The pitcher's steaming. Coffee, I hope. There's a plate of croissants and enough mugs for all of us. I remark again, "There's no butter, sugar, cream. *Rien*!"

I'm being stared at as though I'm from a distant planet. I'm reminded of *la disette*, the food shortage. Then I mention my lieutenant to them and say with a wink and a smug smile, "Maybe he can obtain some of those rare *délicatesses* for us."

"*Oh la la*! *Ça serait merveilleuse*!" A group reaction, sentiment and expressions of delight at the thought. Someone adds "Cigarettes, too, please."

I modestly lower my head. "*Pas de quoi, mes amis*. I'll ask him when next I see him."

Jean-Paul is the first to speak. "When do you expect to see him? Do you have a rendezvous?"

"Yes. We are to meet at the port at approximately 11 A.M.. He told me he has to examine the damage and make a report. He has invited me to accompany him and act as interpreter. He doesn't speak, read or understand a word of French. Official translators are scarce."

"What's his duty? What division of the U.S. Army does he belong to? Artillery? Quartermaster? Cavalry? Infantry? Security? Is he an intelligence officer?" Jean-Paul leans far forward. His questions come at me like a rifle on full automatic.

The group watches me closely for reactions. "*Je ne sais pas*. He hasn't told me. I haven't asked. After all, we've only known each other since yesterday morning. Is it important to know these things?" I marvel at my pretext of naiveté and not seriously caring about the lieutenant's assignment. The possible significance of this line of questions doesn't escape my notice.

"*Oui, Léon. C'est très important. Il est nécessaire, absolument, qu'on fait ça; que vous...que vous savez ces choses...en long sûr*." Jean-Paul repeats and says the last part with deliberate slowness "*...en long sûr...*" in the long run!

I sigh, "*Okay, mes amis. Je veux faire ce qu'il faut*." Very interesting, but why is it so important, in fact necessary for me to know all these things...in depth and detail? I promise to do my best, to do whatever is necessary.

"No. Not your 'best', *cher Léon*. you must do everything possible to learn as much as you can about your lieutenant's tasks. In fact, I...we are very interested in any military activities in this area. Do you understand?"

"I guess so." Although the need to learn about "any military activities" reveals a lot to me, I must sound only mildly curious. Perhaps holding back, restraining my enthusiasm will eliminate any residual doubts about my low level of interest in politics and current affairs and cause them to reveal more and more to me about who and what they really are. I have to gain their confidence. Smiling gratefully at Jean-Paul, I add, “I want to repay your many kindnesses to me.”

Jean-Paul smiles and sits back on his sofa. This is a signal for the others to relax. I imitate.

Chapter Thirty-One

Bud is waiting for me at the end of the street leading to the seaport. The port itself is "C" shaped, a crescent-moon. Just left of where we stand, it begins a broad, clockwise sweep to a breakwater that extends into the Atlantic. I estimate the far end is a good mile from shore. This forms a bay, a weather-safe harbor.

On my left, immediately at the port's entrance, is a long series of colorful buildings with shops and apartments. A well-worn street separates the buildings from the "bay" by about 50 feet. I've seen this kind of view in panoramic paintings by modern French artists. Very charming. However, the most dramatic sight is that of the destruction of ships caused by the bombardments from our naval armada.

Also to my left is an ocean-going ship; black hull, red waterline, and a white deck. The name is clearly visible, "Porthos." No flag flies. The ship's been capsized and lies on her starboard side, leaning against the quay. The keel appears to be resting on the mud-bottom of the bay. Porthos was probably driven ashore by the continuous impacts of shells hitting the water. There are no signs of damage to the ship itself; some scratched paint but no major dents. Weird.

Close to shore, the bay is crowded with sunken vessels resting on the bottom; everything from submarines to destroyers. Only the superstructures and conning towers show above the water. The prize, the battleship *Jean Bart*, is at the outer curve of the breakwater, quite a distance from where I stand. She's resting on the bottom, too. Her topmost deck is above water. Most of her superstructure's gone, blown away. I can see people riding bicycles around her deck; probably a French search, rescue and salvage team.

A short distance north of the breakwater a large flotilla of U.S. Navy ships moves back and forth across the area. The Nazi U-Boats must be aware of the invasion of North Africa and, no doubt, will try to attack. A moving target's harder to hit. So, the Navy keeps moving. Just inside an imaginary line between the end of the breakwater and the shoreline, a large group of Navy supply-and Merchant Marine ships lie at anchor. The Navy units provide a protective screen. Cargo and some troops are being off-loaded onto landing craft and numerous barges, which shuttle back and forth from ships to shore. Bet the U.S. Army's fabulous Corps of Engineers already has new piers and docks under construction for greater efficiency in transferring cargo and personnel.

To the right of the street from which we entered the port area, a barbed wire fence at least eight feet high has been erected. At the wide entry gate are several armed MPs. Bud tells me this is the military compound. It's where he bunks. It's also HQ for the MPs, SPs, standby security forces and a field hospital. Bud's taking notes as we walk along the quay. He looks up only long enough to take quick snapshots with his eyes, then back to his notepad to record his observations. There's a lot to observe and write about.

I marvel, with obvious pride, at the incredible accuracy of our Navy's gunfire. As I look down the row of buildings adjacent to the water, not a single building seems to have been hit. There are some deep and wide gouges in their pastel colored walls, but no direct hits, no visible structural damage. "Maybe the pockmarks are from some other action in Casablanca's long battle history."

"Not so." Bud points to the buildings. "These are fresh wounds. Notice their color's different from the painted walls." He buries his face in his notebook.

We continue our slow walk along the street, gazing up at the buildings on our left and studying the numerous small berths on our right that must have been docking places for fishing boats and privately owned small craft. The water is murky, dark brown and opaque; quite impossible to see any object more than an inch or two below the surface. No small vessels are visible; they've probably been blasted, capsized or sunk and now rest on the bottom. Even with Bud's field glasses, we can't begin to develop a tally or descriptions of any of the multitude of vessels whose super structures stick up above the surface of the bay. The statistics will have to be developed by people in small boats moving in and out of the wreckage. There's no room for a destroyer or an escort vessel to maneuver safely.

Bud surveys the scene. "Dam' good shootin'!"

I whistle a few bars of the Marseillaise. Then, I drop my voice to a whisper as I pretend to point out the sights. "Must talk to you, Bud. I think we've found what we came for. I'm not 100 percent sure, but it looks like my new friends are our enemies."

"How come?"

I tell Bud about Jean-Paul Duval's intense interest in military information and his instruction to report to him my observations of U.S. and French troops as well as ship movements. I also describe Georgette.

Bud looks at me and whistles softly. His leer is as "loud" as a smirk can be. "War sho' nuff is hell. Ain' it?"

"It might get to be 'hell' before long! They asked me to invite you to meet them."

"This French lady, is she southern or northern France?" Bud's incorrigible.

"Okay, Bud. She says she's from Paris. That's the north. Too bad. Enough! If we plan it right, this could be a heck of a break for our side." Although I don't have many details, not yet, I tell Bud about Michel, Philippe, André, and Claude the concierge who seems to be part of the group. I reveal "Georgette wants to meet you because she thinks you can bring her some butter. They've plenty of bread and croissants but no butter for them. They haven't had any for a while. Also, they have no cream for their coffee. If you really want to make a hit, and I know you do, you patriotic rebel, get them some American cigarettes!"

"Hey! I might be able to find some nylon stockin's for Georgette!"

"My mind reels at the thought of how she'd personally express her gratitude to you." I put emphasis on "personally."

Okay, pal. Y'all call the shots. When should we do this?"

"I've an idea to help us determine if they really are our targets. I'll tell them you're a cargo security officer. You're the guy who keeps track of supplies and, because you are the guy, you know what's arriving, how, when, where and all that good military stuff, like ship and troop movements in and out of North Africa."

"Funny you should say that. It's my next assignment to General Patton's command after we clean up here. Patton's pushin' on into Algiers right now. He's itchin' real bad to hit Rommel's tanks."

"Coincidence. It just means we're only lying a little. Tell you what. They'll want to hear all about my meeting with you today. Bet Duval calls me to his special Room 23 as soon as I get back. Bet, too, Michel, Philippe, André and Georgette are in that meeting. I have no idea how many more are in this group. Personally, despite my first impressions, I think we need more evidence. Also, we should try to locate their contacts and methods of getting critical information out of Casablanca. Let's play their game for a little while. See what happens."

As we continue our casual walk close to the edge of the quay, I develop a simple plan. Bud listens closely as I ad lib the scenario.

"You can put on one helluva drunk act. I've seen you do it. I'm not always sure it's an act. In fact, at any one time, I'm not always sure whether you're really drunk or sober. But, I've never seen you lose your self-control. When I get back to the hotel, I'll tell them about your assignment to cargo security and all it signifies. I'll suggest I invite you to join us tomorrow night in Room 23 for coffee and cake. Of course, you'll have to bring the coffee and cake. Throw in some sugar and canned milk. Bring a couple of cartons of cigarettes. They're for Jean-Paul to distribute. Pack a couple pounds of butter. Hand them to Georgette. Then, if you have any nylons and chocolates, give them to Georgette—and stand back!"

"Not too far back!" Bud wisecracks.

"Be careful of the colorless stuff. Cognac, or brandy? I don't know. Tastes like paint remover. Maybe they'll bring out some wine. Don't hesitate if it's white wine, but drink slowly if it's red. I have been warned about the red stuff. Might be poisoned or doped; a Moroccan Mickey Finn. Anyway, in the disguise of celebrating a new friendship with the U.S. Army, they'll probably try to get you drunk enough to spill your talkative guts. Got it, *Américain*?"

"Gotcha, Frenchie."

It's now mid-afternoon. We search for food and find a small bistro close to the railroad station. The other customers in the bistro glare at Bud in a most unfriendly way. Their eyes dart repeatedly from Bud to me and back to Bud. I get a message from all this unspoken hostility. "*Français! What are you doing with this Américain? Are you a collaborateur?*"

"Careful, Bud. We're not exactly welcome."

"Screw them, too!" Bud pats the 45 automatic on his hip.

The waiter pretends not to notice us. I raise my voice and, in French, demand "*Service. Immédiatement*!" He wipes one of the tables, stalling. Eventually he comes to ours and with a sneer says, "*À vôtre service. Qu'est ce que vous desirez, messieurs?*"

"*Naturellement, monsieur le garçon, nous avons beaucoup de faim. Qu'est ce qu'il y a*? We are very hungry. What do you have to offer?"

His shrug is meant to say they're out of everything. I don't buy it. When we came in we saw a couple of men eating sliced ham, cheese, bread and white wine. I speak loudly and firmly. "*On veut de jambon. Beacoup de jambon, du pain, de fromage et de vin blanc. Tous nous deux*. Ham. Lots of ham, bread, cheese and white wine for both of us." I return his sneering attitude. "*S'il vous plait...garçon*!"

Without a word, the waiter heads to what I hope is the kitchen. I notice Bud moves his hand defensively toward his hip. I whisper, "Don't hit me! Wait 'til I duck before you shoot!" Bud responds to my reassuring smile and puts both his hands on the table.

The waiter's in no hurry to feed us. In his own due time, he brings two platters of ham and a yellowish cheese, a basket of bread and two large glasses of amber liquid. Bud raises one glass and toasts everyone's health. He is totally ignored.

Loud enough for all to hear, I toast Bud. "*À la vôtre! Américain.*" Then, for Bud's ears only, "Eat. Listen. Don't talk."

Finally, it's time for me to return to the hotel and make my report to Jean-Paul Duval. Bud has a jeep parked at the railroad station. He says its been signed out to him for as long as he needs it. While we drive in the direction of the hotel, I ask Bud if anyone else, Army or Navy, knows I'm here or what I'm trying to do?

He tells me the base commander and the commanders of the MPs and the SPs know somebody's here from the O.S.S. doing "what I'm trying to do." But they don't know who or where I am. They're ready to act the moment he, Bud, tells them to. They recognize the importance of neutralizing Nazi agents in French Morocco, putting them out of action.

"One more thing, Bud. I still have no papers, no ID. Frankly, I don't want to run up against any U.S. soldiers, MPs or SPs. Can you figure out a way to get me some kind of papers."

Bud chuckles. "Remember the westerns? The soldiers always had friendly Indians on the payroll as scouts. Helped 'em find other, hostile Indians."

"Yeah? Whatcha thinking?"

"I'll get you papers tomorrow identifyin' you as an official interpreter for the U.S. Army with permission to move freely everywhere, except within U.S. military compounds."

"Neat! Who'll write and sign them?"

"I'll write the papers an' my C.O. will sign them!"

At that moment we reach the hotel's entrance. Bud shouts "So long Frenchie!"

Someone may be observing us from a window. I give him a French salute; chin thrust out; arrogantly flicking my fingers in his direction upward from my throat. Mustn't appear to be enjoying his camaraderie.

I wave as I pass Claude at his desk. He's still not smiling at me. I climb the stairs and, once again, knock on the door of Room 23.

Chapter Thirty-Two

Jean-Paul, Georgette, Michel and Claude are the only ones here. Although I am eager to know more members of this group, I have a good feeling about meeting several in so short a time. Claude hasn't attended any of the meetings I've been to in Room 23. In the true sense of the word, the concierge, Claude seems to be the caretaker, the doorkeeper. Based on his secretive movements when I pass his desk just beyond the entrance to the hotel, I include him as the security guard who makes sure only the correct people are allowed to enter and leave the hotel.

Although I am pleased with the group's apparent acceptance of me as one of them, I know I shouldn't hurry myself or make incorrect assumptions. So far the only reasons I have for suspicion are the missing description of the work I am expected to do and the overtly friendly but questionable behavior of those I've met and especially their profound interest in U.S. and French military activities.

Then, again, probably all French people in French Morocco and north and east into Algeria want to know exactly what the allies have in mind. Will there be roundups and mass arrests? Are the water and food supplies to be severely rationed or even cut off? Will the telephones be cut off or will they continue to work as I'm told they always did before the invasion...although with a questionable degree of reliability? How long will this recent friendship continue among the U.S. and French military and the civilian population? Should the French people in Casablanca plan to evacuate or escape the region? Or continue going about daily activities, business, family and chores as before, as though there is no war? Stay? Run? Anyone with accurate answers to these questions would know how to plan. But one can only guess about the future. And that includes me.

I can understand some of the emotions and uncertainties when war comes so close. Here they are exacerbated by the peculiar circumstances surrounding the French military government's belligerent response to the invasion, which was followed quickly by total acceptance of the invaders. It's a strange sort of surrender. Who's really running the show? How does one tell the difference between pro-Vichy French and pro-Ally? Friends and enemies look alike. My Chief isn't here to advise me. I'm not sure he could advise me anyway. This is not a theoretical situation. It's real and I'm on my own now.

"*Heureux de vous voir, Léon.*" Jean-Paul snaps me out of my silent soliloquy. I'm very much aware he still uses the formal "*vous*" in addressing me. I believe my strongest clues to acceptance into the group will be revealed when the formal "*vous*" becomes the informal pronouns "*te* or *tu.*"

"*Moi aussi! Enchanté*!" Greetings all around. Georgette is nicely dressed; as attractive as can be. I remove my suit jacket, primarily to reveal I have no weapons. Michel doesn't imitate me. He wears the same suit with the bulging breast pocket; same squint-eyed, silent, unsmiling, grim and untrusting expression.

Jean-Paul tells us we're going to have an early dinner in the hotel's dining room then we'll have a nice meeting of the group in Room 23 and you, Léon, can tell us all about your day's affairs.

I nod and smile appreciatively. "Where's the dining room?"

"*Oh, c'est au dessous de cet étage. Ça sera à vôtre gout.*" It is directly below this floor. You'll like it. Claude is preparing something special."

He did say "meeting of the group." This should be most interesting and instructive. To say the least, it's probably another test of my credibility. Jean-Paul doesn't ask me any questions. He must want everyone in the group to hear about my day.

"*C'est bon. Ça me va.*" Suits me fine. I heave a deep sigh, clasp my hands around the back of my head, slouch in my chair and stare up at the ceiling; the picture of a carefree guy. It's really difficult for a man with a lot on his mind to act as though he hasn't any troubles. But I try.

Not much conversation. Jean-Paul offers cigarettes all around. We light up and blow smoke rings, figuratively and literally. I'd give a lot more than a penny for their thoughts. How much would they give for mine? I close my eyes and drift off. *Un petit sommeil. Une sieste.* I've conditioned myself to napping anywhere at any time. Given ten minutes of nap-time, I can awaken instantly at the slightest sound; fully refreshed.

The sound of a knock at the door triggers my clock. It's Claude. He has a tray with five small glasses containing equal amounts of a red liquid. He cheerfully announces "Dinner's ready."

Jean-Paul salutes us with "Santé!" We reply as though we had rehearsed it: "*À la vôtre*! *Salut*!" Claude, unsmiling, without comment, waves his glass around, chug-a-lugs the beverage and leaves the room.

I watch the others and wait for Jean-Paul to drink his first. This is sipping stuff. Pretty good. Kind of sweet. Georgette volunteers it's a locally manufactured apéritif good for the stomach, the mind and the appetite. Nothing's wrong with my appetite, but this is a very nice beverage to start stomach juices flowing. I must make it part of my regular dinner ritual—when the war is over and I come marching home again.

"*Allons, mes amis. Mangons*!" Jean-Paul signals it is time to eat. And, like the faithful group members we are, we follow our leader out the door, left, down the stairs to the ground floor, hard right and through the wide doorway.

Each time I'd come in or left the hotel, this area had been totally dark. I couldn't see beyond the doorway. Now, there are chandeliers, bright lights, several round tables, one with a white table cloth and dinner utensils, and lots of chairs. Automatically, we head for the table which is covered with a white cloth.

Everyone knows his and her place. Michel's at Jean-Paul's right. Georgette, as usual, is at his left. This must be a practiced ritual. Jean-Paul points to a chair for me, directly opposite his, and waves at us to sit. There are enough chairs at our table for eight. A clue to the size of Jean-Paul's group? I expect I'll know soon enough. While we're settling in, I do a quick study of the room. In it's day, this must have been a posh hotel.

Georgette notices me turning my head right, left and behind. "*Bon, n'est ce pas*?"

"*Oui*. Quite pleasant. Where does the door on the far wall lead to?"

Georgette laughs. "To the kitchen, dummy!"

"Of course. *Que je suis bête*!" I apologize for my apparent stupidity. Could this be another way out? Through the kitchen? It must lead to another exit to the street; an entrance for deliveries and trash removal. I'll have to explore when I can do so unobserved.

Jean-Paul looks at his watch. Frowns. He glances in the direction of the doorway to the dining room. Looks at his watch again, then at Michel who gives an "I don't know" shrug. But Jean-Paul appears concerned. Obviously he expects some one, perhaps several more to fill the empty chairs at our table. Claude appears suddenly in the doorway, nods affirmatively at Jean-Paul and disappears. Within a moment's time, two men I've never seen before enter the dining room and come directly to our table.

Everyone makes happy noises; hugs, embraces, handshakes and other signs of a welcome reunion. I meet Henri and Jules. Both men are modestly dressed in suits without suspicious bulges. They carry light overcoats. The night air gets chilly here; how well I know it!

Henri is at least six feet tall. I estimate his age at the middle thirties. His swarthy complexion and dark eyes look Latin, Italian or Arabic, rather than French. His voice is hoarse but, since nobody comments, it must be his natural voice. Jules is shorter, about five feet eight, and a little younger. He has a swarthy complexion and dark eyes, similar to Henri's. His voice is clearer and higher pitched than Henri's. They could be brothers.

Jean-Paul signals them to sit down at the table. This accounts for six of the eight chairs. Two more to come? Two more in the group? Where are Philippe and André? Jean-Paul is becoming worried. It's getting dark and unsafe on the streets. Henri says they weren't stopped by any patrols. However, there are many hostile Arabs in the streets. Jean-Paul deliberately breaks into Henri's chatter. "*Restez tranquil, Léon.* We don't want to alarm Léon? He recently arrived from Marseilles. He knows Robert." Then looking directly at me, "Léon, I'm sure Henri and Jules would very much like to hear about your brave escape from France and uncomfortable arrival in Casa. *Encore une fois, s'il vous plait.* Please, tell us about it again."

Moving my eyes back and forth from Henri to Jules, I describe the misadventure; losing my papers, locating the fishing trawler's Captain, paying him to take me to Dakar and, after many days in rough seas, being unceremoniously and ungently dumped on the beach about one mile north of Casa. The Captain and his crew were not nice; no, not nice at all. As I describe my fortunate meeting with Robert and my introduction to Jean-Paul, I'm aware of the concentrated attention being given me by Jean-Paul and, particularly, by Michel. This, for me, is a memory test. The description, the words may change, but not the details.

"*Malheureux ça*!" Henri offers sympathy.

"*Oui, malheureux ça*!" Jules echoes the sentiment.

"*C'est la vie. Ou, peut être, la guerre*." I nod affirmatively at Jean-Paul. He acknowledges me. "However, M. Duval has been kind enough to offer me work and lodgings."

Everyone looks at Jean-Paul and, almost in unison, quietly says, "*Bravo. Bravo Jean-Paul Duval*!" He's the boss all right.

Claude brings two bottles of wine, one red and one white, glasses and bread. The glasses are actually large tumblers, not delicate, stemmed, wine glasses. These people are seasoned wine drinkers. I must be careful not to try to keep pace with them; mustn't miss a word or a clue.

Henri speaks up. "We have to talk with you and the others, Jean-Paul. *Il nous faut des instructions nouveaux.*" He's quite agitated as he ask for new instructions.

Jean-Paul smiles with obviously forced patience. "Henri. Jules. Where are your manners? We don't want to bore Léon with the dull details of your activities." Jean-Paul turns to me. "Henri and Jules are located in Rabat. This is the first time we've been able to get together since the invasion started. When was that, about a week ago? I'm sure we have much to talk over—but it can wait." He turns to Henri and Jules with a stern expression. "*N'est ce pas*?"

Sounds more like a command than a question.

Henri catches on quickly. Heaves a deep sigh. "*Bien sur*. Of course it can wait. *Plus de vin rouge*?" He holds up his empty glass.

Claude reappears periodically to clear the plates and add new ones laden with all sorts of very tasty items. But Claude never sits at the table with us. And when he's not in the kitchen, I don't hear very many kitchen-type noises. Claude seems to be the entire kitchen crew.

The remainder of dinner time passes quickly with a swapping of tales about where each of us had been when the invasion began. Innocuous weather reports are exchanged. Casa and Rabat share the same climate. Geographically, they're not far apart. Seems, at this moment, there's not much to talk about. Conversation is difficult.

How are the natives, meaning the Arabs, taking to the changes? Oh, they don't like the Americans any more than they do the French. Even though he's been a puppet ruler for many years, they do worship the Sultan. His main palace is in Rabat. How many palaces does he have? Only Allah knows! Everyone laughs at that. Frankly, I don't get it, but I join in the laughter. Wish I could think of a good Sultan joke. The only Sultan in New York is Babe Ruth, the Sultan of Swat, the baseball home run king. But how would a young man from Belgium know about Babe Ruth? I can't think of anything funny, so I just laugh on cue.

Dinner proceeds calmly. Not much conversation. A few French or Moroccan jokes and laughs are shared. I don't actually see the humor; a weakness in my disguise. The coffee's strong and dark, satisfyingly hot.

We finish, bring out our cigarettes, light up and, after a few audible belchings from my table partners, we draw back our chairs on cue from Jean-Paul and follow him out of the dining room, left up the stairs, and turn right into Room 23. Not a word is spoken as we seat ourselves facing Jean-Paul. Like faithful watchdogs, Michel and Georgette are at his side. Henri, Jules and I sit facing the trio and the door. Nobody smiles. It is official meeting time.

Chapter Thirty-Three

Clearly, these members of the group have been working together for some time. I'm the newcomer and they're feeling some discomfort with my presence. However, Jean-Paul did not explicitly exclude me. So, here I am.

Michel, in response to a knock, opens the door for Claude and his tray. I count the glasses quickly: six. If Claude doesn't take one, I'm included in the count and, possibly, expected to stay for the conversation that follows. Claude bends over and offers the tray to Jean-Paul; no ladies first here. However, Jean-Paul chivalrously motions in Georgette's direction. Claude makes a quick, emotionless apology to Georgette, "*Pardon*," and offers her the tray. She doesn't conceal her contempt for Claude, grunts a "hunh!" sound and takes the first glass. Then the hierarchy is made obvious by Claude who turns back to Jean-Paul, then to Michel and the others. I'm last. None for Claude himself.

Facing Jean-Paul, Claude bows abruptly, stiffly from the neck, clicks his heels loudly together and leaves the room. I pretend not to have noticed what could be a give-away of European military training and respect for a superior officer. A Frenchman's *au revoir* often includes a slight, smoothly controlled bow from the waist. It certainly excludes heel clicking. I realize his peculiar way of speaking French is with a German accent. If Claude were a Frenchman and personally friendly with Georgette, he might even bring his lips close to her extended hand, smile and say something flowery. But Georgette doesn't extend her hand nor does she even look in his direction.

While this mini-drama between Georgette and Claude is playing, Jean-Paul's eyes flash in my direction and our eyes meet briefly. No doubt he's wondering how much I had noticed just then. I can't ignore the event nor dare I ask what's going on here? I cover myself with an overt shrug and a simple soft-voiced statement directed at Jean-Paul, "*Rien*." Nothing at all. So they're not lovers. Who cares? Frankly, I couldn't care less.

Jean-Paul, without any change in facial expression, holds onto the meeting of our eyes for a moment longer. He releases our visual contact and turns to no one in particular. "*Bien. Parlons.*" Okay. Let's talk. "Henri. You first. Talk freely. Léon's working for me now. What's on your mind?"

Henri and Jules look at me before beginning. "We're puzzled and need your instructions. The U.S. and the French soldiers have become buddies. My French government contacts are nowhere to be seen. The Americans and French are patrolling the streets in groups, U.S. and French together. There's been no disarmament of the French troops; none I can see. The French officers, especially, are always in the company of American officers, both wear their sidearms and share cigarettes, exchange small gifts and in every way seem to enjoy each other's companionship. Very unusual, I think."

Jean-Paul looks at Jules. "Is this what you observe, too?"

"Yes, sir! Exactly. I don't know what to make of it. It's not the way it was before the Americans landed. I can't locate many of the French officers who were in command. Most of my important contacts have disappeared."

Jean-Paul is quite patient. And, although I do my best to appear inattentive, I'm concentrating on every word and mannerism. So to speak, I'm "reading" between the lines. It's becoming obvious the nature of the "*travaux*," the work this group does for Jean-Paul is some form of gathering of military intelligence. And, surely, they do not collect information for the benefit of the allies.

Jean-Paul instructs Henri and Jules to remain in Casa for a few more days. "I'll have to figure out how we can best continue to serve our country."

This is my opportunity to become more deeply and openly involved. "*Jean-Paul, mes amis*. Perhaps I can help."

Jean-Paul smiles. His facial expression encourages me to say what's on my mind.

"I'm not too well known around Casa, or any other part of French Morocco for that matter. I can try to get Lieutenant Corval to tell me what's happening to the military government and the officers who used to be in charge. Can't hurt, eh?"

Silence. The others are looking at one another, waiting for some one to restart the conversation. Naturally, it's Jean-Paul who's first to speak. "Can you do this without arousing Corval's suspicion? We're still not sure of his official post in the Army."

"In my opinion, Corval's an 'American playboy', as they call it. He is in the U.S. Army but I don't think he takes the war very seriously. He doesn't seem to think about anything except spending money and having a good time. As Georgette suggested the other day, I can invite him to come here for wine, coffee and cakes after dinner one evening soon. He's very sociable. It's my guess he'll jump at the chance to visit and talk with some real French people. I'll suggest he bring the coffee and cakes. Eh?" I laugh at my own impromptu joke. Jean-Paul laughs. Everybody laughs.

"Great! Great idea, and so simple, too!" Jean-Paul appreciates me. "Also, I know how we can make good use of your time."

"You mean the work I will do for you...for the group?" I'm sounding excited.

"Exactly, Léon. I need someone, a courier who can travel freely between Casa and Rabat; possibly to Fes." Jean-Paul frowns. "But, you have no papers. You don't dare leave Casa and even here you can be picked up because you can't prove you belong here. I'm afraid you don't fit. Right now, I'm not sure I can obtain false papers for you."

"*Alors! Pas de problème*! *Nous avons un coup de veine*!" I sit up straight and exclaim we have a stroke of luck! Lt. Corval has offered to get authentic papers identifying me as an official interpreter for the U.S. Army with freedom to move around Casa.

"And onto military bases, too?" Henri's eyes are wide with excitement.

"*Je n'en suis certain.* I'm not sure about that part. Not likely. However, he does want to visit, go sightseeing outside Casa before he's ordered to move on to another assignment. He and I have developed a good, though formal, relationship. If he wants me to go with him, maybe he can get papers allowing me to travel within a radius of 50 or even 100 kilometers of Casa. It can't hurt to ask him. How's that, eh?" I don't mention Bud's on standby to move to Algeria.

Everybody's smiling and chatting excitedly. I bring new opportunities to the group...Everybody but Michel smiles and chats. He just continues to squint at me.

Jean-Paul asks "When are you meeting the lieutenant again?"

"He told me to come to the compound at the port at about 10-hundred hours tomorrow morning and ask the *Police Militaire* to let him know I am waiting for him at the gate. He'll come out as soon as he can. So, unless you have something, some other assignment for me..."

"No, no, no. Do as he told you. Go to the port. Can you bring up the subject of the identification papers tomorrow morning? We are enthusiastic about this idea. A fine opportunity for our...for us!"

"Sure. I'll do it casually, as though it's for his benefit, not mine."

"Wonderful!" Georgette screeches. "He won't regret it. I'll see to it!"

"When shall I invite him to come visit us here in the hotel?"

"*Demain soir.* Tomorrow night suits me fine!"

With a downward movement of his left hand, Jean-Paul gently shushes Georgette's excitement. and says, "Let's leave it to Léon. We don't want to appear too eager, do we?"

"Good. I'll make the proposal and leave it up to Corval to set the day."

"Evening, please. We may not be able to gather the group at one time if it's during the day."

"That's best. Corval tells me he sometimes has administrative work to do during the day. But he can always procure a jeep and get away from the compound at night. Who'll be here to meet Corval?"

Jean-Paul gets up from his sofa, stretches his arms, heaves a huge yawn. "We'll see."

Everyone rises. *La séance se termine*. The meeting's over. And, assuming the night is over and everyone is retiring, I go to my room, switch on the light, undress, switch off the light and get into bed. I lie here wide awake, wonder what's going to happen next. My eyelids are heavy now. Relax. Give in. There's an old Russian saying, or maybe it's a Ukrainian proverb: "*Ootroh vyetcher radmudno-nyayee.*" My mother never spelled it for me, but it translates into "The morning is brighter than the night." As I try to doze off, I tell myself "Wait for the brilliant morning."

I almost succeed in falling into a sound sleep when I'm aware my door is being opened. The hallway is dark so I can't see anything, not even a silhouette. Should I lie still? Remain quiet? Or jump up and challenge the intruder. I'm ready to fight, if I have to. The door closes and Georgette's voice whispers softly, almost musically in the darkness, "*Léon! Est-ce que tu t'endormes*?" I whisper "*Non, Georgette. Pas du tout*." I've just lost all interest in sleep.

Chapter Thirty-Four

Fifteen minutes after I ask the MPs at the gate to tell Lieutenant Corval I am here, Bud greets me with a loud "Bonn joor, Frenchie!" I return the greeting, "Oakee Doakee, Yankee Doodle Soldier Boy!" The MPs cough, grin from ear to ear and look away.

Bud is in a great mood and I'm feeling pretty good, too. Yes, very good after last night's sessions at the hotel. Bud doesn't realize what he is in for.

We turn the corner and head in the direction of *La Gare*. A few GI patrols pass us and salute; Bud, not me, of course. Traffic's pretty heavy this morning. Jeeps pass by heading to and from the direction of the compound at high speed. We don't meet any unaccompanied French foot soldiers; they're always with American soldiers. Nobody stops me and asks for my ID. I'm okay as long as I'm with Bud. But patrols are heavy today.

Bud makes certain we are out of sight of the sentries. "Big doings. You've noticed, I'm sure."

"What's up?"

"Patton's moving out, transferring his base to Oran."

"How come?"

"I guess he realizes Rommel's Afrika Korp is not coming to French Morocco. So, he's moving in Rommel's direction, North and East."

"Fantastic guy, Patton!"

"Yeah. His men love him for his courage an' leadership. But they hate him for his heavy discipline. Have you noticed all men in uniform are wearin' ties, shirts or blouses an' jackets fully buttoned in this scivvy climate?"

"Now that you mention it, yes."

"It's not classified military information, but you can always tell when the General is around. Discipline. Discipline. This means you can tell when he's moved away. too. Ties and jackets come off. Shirt collars are wide open."

"Hey, *Américain*! Would you like to change places with me? All you have to worry about is your own ass!"

"Jus' fine the way things are, Frenchie!"

The street's clear for a moment so I quickly ask Bud, "Got my papers yet? I told the group you were getting some official papers for me and this makes them very happy because they make me more useful to their purposes."

"How so?"

I tell Bud about Philippe, André, Henri and Jules who are supposed to be based in other French Morocco cities, Rabat and Fes. "And I believe they want me to be a courier between them and Casablanca—if I can persuade you to get me papers permitting me to travel outside Casablanca. Can you do it?"

"I've got the ID for you in my pocket, but it restricts you to Casablanca. Let's go back to the compound for your new ID. No trouble. My C.O. has been instructed to give me all the cooperation I need. He's an okay guy. Comes from Georgia; not as good as Virginia, but still neighborly."

We go back and about half an hour later, Bud reappears at the gate flush with excitement. "Got your ID right here." He pats his breast pocket. "The big hustle and bustle is we've located the camp where political and religious prisoners are being held. I don't know exactly where it is, or where they are. There's more than one. Troops are goin' to check out the info. If it's accurate, they'll verify the prisoners' status an' release them right away."

"Wow! What kind of 'political' prisoners?"

"Some of the French Moroccan Officers refused to go along with the Vichy government's policies. So, I guess they had been arrested for disobeying orders, or something like that."

"What about the ones who wouldn't cooperate with the U.S. invasion?"

"I understand we're going to make an exchange." Bud smiles. "We're gonna release our friends an' replace them with Vichy Frenchies."

"This is an intelligence job, Bud. Are you being told to go on this one?"

"Yeah! I leave today at 1300 hours. But I should be back tomorrow afternoon."

I steer Bud down an empty looking street. "Let's talk fast. When can you come to the hotel to meet Duval and the others. Can you make it for sure tomorrow night?"

"I'll make a point of it. I'll be there. I think I can get my own jeep so I don't have to depend on a convoy's movements."

"Great! I'll tell Duval you'll come to the hotel after dinner for coffee and stuff. He'll pull the gang together for this special event. You bring the coffee and stuff...like butter, canned milk, sugar, cartons of cigarettes and matches, and something nice for Georgette. She's so damn horny...who knows what a goodie or two might do for her social glands."

"What time should I show up?"

"Any time after 1900 hours should be okay. I bet they feed you lots of wine. Stay away from the red wine and the short glasses of clear liquid. It's horrible stuff. The drunker you get, the more pressing their questions and the closer they'll listen to you. What a deal this is going to be!" I can't help but laugh to myself as I visualize the setup in Room 23! Wow!

Chapter Thirty-Five

Back in my room at the Hotel Monte Carlo, I have time to do some mental grazing, bring my thought processes up-to-date.

There is something to be said for working in partnership with another field agent, meaning Bud specifically. When I started on this adventure I made it clear I wanted to operate alone. My Chief said "Okay, if that's the way you want it."

I had only one reason for this manifesto. Frankly, I didn't know anyone I could or would believe in, no one reliable or resourceful enough to trust in a critical situation. But, Bud is made of different stuff. Wonder how he got into this activity? Probably the same way I did...at someone else's option. Well, enjoy it while you can, Léon. It could be a very short career.

Thinking about the bizarre series of events that changed my career from professional-engineer/amateur-linguist to cloak-and-dagger agent...without a dagger.No doubt I and the other guys and the few gals in the New York office are considered essential but expendable. Organized intelligence activities are being invented on a day-to-day basis. Our Chiefs, it has become obvious, are learning their jobs by practicing theirs every day; O-T-J, On-The-Job training. Their approach is to throw young bodies at the enemy and reap whatever harvest of knowledge and wisdom they can from the meager information filtering back from the field.

Well, I get the impression there's a missing link somewhere between me and the strategists back home. As far as I can tell, Bud is the only one who has any knowledge of what's been going on at the Hotel Monte Carlo. I don't think he has told his C.O. in Casablanca everything. Bud said his C.O. knows an O.S.S. guy is here but doesn't know who or where he is. Bud! Take very special care of yourself. You're the only link I have with home. You're my security, my insurance policy.

Do I miss my family and friends? No, not really. How come? My family wasn't much fun. Guess we never had the time or never took the time, or didn't have the wisdom to support each other's emotional needs. It was tough for a fatherless family during the depression. Guess, depression or no, it is always "tough for a fatherless family." Perhaps because we left each other alone to survive his and her emotions, I developed the personality of a man alone. My sisters and brother probably arrived at similar personalities. This is life's pattern—in my family at any rate.

I never felt close to any of my so-called childhood friends. I was lousy at team sports; couldn't throw a ball or run fast, which kept me out of neighborhood baseball, knuckle ball and basketball games. I was too skinny to be any good at football and touch-tackle. So, I learned to grow up alone, work and play by myself.

Hobbies became my "family and friends." I could draw pictures, sketch with pen and pencil, charcoal or pen and ink. Told I was good at it, too. I thoroughly enjoyed museums and classical music. The Brooklyn Museum of Art offered free art lectures and concerts every Sunday. President Roosevelt's W.P.A., the Works Progress Administration, provided work for unemployed artists and musicians and I took full advantage of their free performances. Oh, what delicious pleasure. What welcome relief they brought to my loneliness. Then, for no obvious reason, in my early teens I became interested in two-way radio comunications. I taught myself to understand Morse code. I didn't have the money to buy an actual telegraph key and a tone generator. I would simulate the operation of a telegraph key by tapping my fingers on any convenient, hard surface and silently pronounce the sounds, "Dah-Dit-Dah-Dit. Dah-Dah-Dit-Dah. I would read billboards, posters, and car cards on the subway and noiselessly translate them into Morse code. I worked hard to build my speed and fluency. And it worked for me.

The first time I heard the real sounds of Morse code was the two successive Saturdays I showed up for official tests at the Federal Communication Commision's offices in downtown Manhattan. The first Saturday I took the test for the Amateur "Ham" Radio Operator and Station license. The second was for the much faster Commercial Radio Telegraph Operator's license. Happily, to my great surprise, I passed both Morse code tests. This made me eligible to take the theory tests for the Commercial Radio Telegraph and Radio Telephone licenses.

My family wasn't aware of my radio ambitions. I'd discovered the best place for me to read and digest the theory books, which I borrowed from the public library, was in the quiet of a cemetery about 2 miles from my house in Brooklyn. In retrospect, it does seem a strange place to study. The theory portions of the tests for the licenses consisted of a succession of six written exams, called "Elements." I passed each element the first time I took the exam and, in due time, I received my precious licenses, known as "tickets." I knew someday they'd be my tickets, my passports to a career and independence. I did, completely on my own, gain a career in commercial radio communications. I didn't think I'd ever want to or be capable of working at anything else in life...

"*Léon, mon cher. Tu es là?*" Georgette calls out as she opens the door to my room.

"*Oui, oui. C'est moi. Je faisais une petite sommeil.*" Better to claim I was napping than tell her the truth about this private moment. I'm not ready to end my present career.

Looking at her wrist watch, Georgette softly whispers into my ears, "*Six heures et demi de l'après midi*. I have a wonderful idea for dinner. For just you and me." She's all smiles.

"*Dites moi, je te prie*." I really can't imagine what she's creating for the two of us.

She doesn't wait for my imagination to get up to speed. "A few kilometers south of here, there is or was a magnificent, charming restaurant built on the edge of a cliff overlooking the Atlantic Ocean. Not only is the view wide and wonderful, the food used to be incredibly delicious. And the table service, *très elegante*! It's name is *La Falaise*." She continues to bubble. "*La lune est bien clair ce soir*. The moon is bright tonight. Makes it especially wonderful for us!"

"I like it. I like it. How do we get there?"

"The taxis are operating again. We can go there in style!"

Taxis? Could they have a fleet of Checker Cabs way out here in French Morocco? "Great, Georgette! Give me a few minutes to shave and change my shirt and we'll go! Does Jean-Paul know? We should get his okay, don't you think?"

Georgette smiles with self-satisfaction and tells me he already knows. In fact, it's his idea for us to go there and notice who the customers are, listen to the conversations going on around us and report to him everything we see and hear tomorrow morning. Georgette gives a silly, self-satisfied laugh as she hands me a wad of francs. "*Il le paye*. He's paying for it, too."

No time for real relaxation. Agents, Nazi and American, work 'round the clock. Even having a fine dinner is part of one's duty! Thus, we are both fervently serving our countries' needs. I don't know about other wars...but this surely is a strange one! *Quel jeu*! What a game!

At this point in my association with Jean-Paul and his group, there's been no hard evidence they are engaged in espionage. Admit it. Everything has been inferential. Maybe I've been wasting my time and Bud's. Maybe my inferences will become realities. Perhaps they are just "lying low," taking time to allow things to cool down, giving the French and American forces in Casa a wide berth while Jean-Paul develops a new strategy and tactics. Jean-Paul's signals and non-committal statements indicate I can expect to soon become directly involved in their "work." Jean-Paul's direct orders to Georgette to observe and listen tonight and then report it all to him is certainly a strong implication of the kind of work Jean-Paul is involved in. Still, hard evidence is needed before I can put an end to this group's activities, assuming the activity is espionage. And, if it is, how will I "put an end" to this group? Right now I haven't the foggiest notion. One thing is certain: When the "end" does come, I can expect it to come quickly. This thought brings a sudden shiver down my back.

"Léon! *Mon chéri*!" Georgette's calling me. "*Es tu prêt*?"

"*Oui, chère Georgette. Je me dépêcherai. Tout d' suite*!" I assure her I am hurrying. I must have lost track of time. I pull on and adjust my trousers, put on my one clean shirt and jacket, socks and shoes. With a quick swipe of my shoes on the backs of my trouser legs, I hastily brush my hair and grab my overcoat. Trying to sound as nonchalant as possible I whistle "*Sur le Pont d'Auvigon*" as I exit my room. Now it's my turn to call out. "*Georgette, es tu prêt*?"

I hear her voice coming from downstairs. "*Zut*!" She sounds annoyed with me. No wonder. I had reversed the traditional dating behavior. I kept the woman waiting. And Georgette is very much a woman.

It's not yet dark outside, but soon it will be. There are no streetlights. But there's a bright moon in the sky. I don't know how she found it, but our taxi's waiting at the front of the hotel. The "taxi" is a funny looking vehicle drawn by a horse; definitely not a thoroughbred animal. The driver's wearing a tarabich. He's an Arab and he's perched high up at the front of the vehicle. I can't see much more of him than that. The taxi looks like an oversize wooden box. It's painted an orange color, about four feet in width and length, and five feet high. Not terribly aesthetic. The passenger entrance is a narrow door at the back of the "box" reaching from the floor right up to the roof. A single footstep extends out from the doorway, half way between the vehicle's floor and the street. Georgette takes my arm, which I present to help her up and into the interior of the "passenger compartment." I climb gingerly up and join her. My head hits the roof. Georgette thinks it's funny. She's laughing at me. I guess it is funny. I feign great pain and collapse onto the seat.

Our seat's a hard, uncovered wooden board. It runs along the inside of the vehicle's interior. There's another seat, the same kind, along the opposite side. Georgette must have told the driver where we are going because, at the rap of her hand against the forward wall of the taxi, the horse starts off at a brisk walk. The night air is already developing its chill. Georgette snuggles against me for warmth as the taxi heads toward the ocean and south down the road to our grand restaurant.

The drive's like something out of a Hollywood set, moonlight, a beautiful woman, a romantic environment. All that's missing is a 100-piece soaring-string orchestra and a choir. Except for a few expressions of pleasure and comfort, Georgette and I are quiet as we go clip-clopping along the road. I'm enjoying the tranquillity, the freedom from stress. Perhaps she feels as I do.

What's this? Looking toward the open back door, I see three Arabs dash out from the side of the road, racing on foot as fast as they can to overtake the taxi. Georgette gasps. This is one time I wish I had a weapon. I position myself for a fight and shout to the driver "*Vite*! *Encore de vitesse*! *Vite*! *Merde*! *Plus de vitesse*!" He ignores my orders for more speed! The taxi's pace does not change. The Arabs are gaining, rapidly closing the distance. Georgette has her hands to her face and her eyes are wide open with fear. I tell Georgette not to be afraid.

One of the Arabs is poised to jump through the back door. I stand as upright as I can, block the doorway and shout at him loudly in French, "*Qu'est ce que vous voulez*! *Allez vous en*! *Je suis un Officier Américain*! *Allez*! *Allez vite*! *VITE*!"

Startled by my outburst, the Arab jumps away from the doorway and, along with his companions, takes off at full speed away from the taxi! The angry sound of my voice may have stopped them. Or, was it my shouted command, "I am an American Officer! Get out of here! Quick! QUICK!"?

I sit down, turn to Georgette and calmly ask "*Ça va*?" Is everything okay?

Georgette draws back, takes a deep breath and looks at me with an extremely troubled expression. "*Oui. Ça va.* But, tell me why you shouted you were an American Officer? Are you really an American Officer?"

I hoped she hadn't noticed that slip-up. I try to cover up. "*Vraiement, je ne sais pas*. I don't really know, Georgette, *chérie*. I wasn't sure what they would do if I had said I was a French anything. So, I hoped they would back off if they believed I might really be an American Officer." With a smug smile I add, "*C'etais bon*? It worked, didn't it?"

Georgette smiles and snuggles closer. "*Oui, mon cher*. It worked."

Perhaps she's as great an actress as she is a beautiful woman.

Chapter Thirty-Six

Certainly, Georgette is irresistible. Specter of Mata Hari, the great German seductress of World War I; that's how Georgette might fit into a modern, organized espionage activity. Except for the one flash of fear I saw in her eyes at the moment the Arab tried to get into our taxi, she's always calm, cool, in full control of her expressions and gestures. The speed of her recovery from what probably was a life-threatening situation is truly astonishing to me. I'd like to have such people on my side but, if Georgette is in fact an enemy agent, we can never be on the same side.

At any rate, this brief episode tells me to be even more *en garde*, cautious! "*Gardez vous bien, Léon*!" While in training, I had heard the advice many times in both English and French. The corny phrase "experience is the best teacher" has just proven to be true...and I learn quickly. Tonight, clearly, one of us is the cat. The other is the mouse. More accurately, we're taking turns being cat and mouse.

The way Georgette reports this incident to Jean-Paul will tell me a lot about her real identity. Is she a 1942 version of Mata Hari or just a woman trapped in French Morocco by this strange new war? I sense tonight's ostensibly social event plays an important part in my relationship with Jean-Paul's group. Thoughts and possibilities race through my mind.

Am I, rather than any patron at *La Falaise*, the one who's being observed tonight? Have I and the tale of my arrival in Casablanca not been completely accepted by the group? Are they still dubious, suspicious? Is this evening part of a test? Do they have other tests in mind for me? Are they searching for evidence my verbal credentials are real or phony? Is my relationship with Bud too close for comfort? Is it casting doubts? Should I advise Bud we'd best be spending less time together? There's only one answer to these questions: Yes!

In this case I must carefully consider how much time I have in this disguise? I recall Monsieur Dejuin's estimate when I met him in my Chief's office in New York: "two weeks." I'd better move more deeply into this task and be ready to bail out in a big hurry at any moment. It's going to be hard to keep up the pretext I'm a devil-may-care young guy. However, I must now assume I'm on target: Jean Paul's group is my objective. I'm working my way into the group. Physically, anyway.

We arrive at our destination. My wrist watch shows we left the Hôtel Monte Carlo half an hour ago. It seemed much longer than that. Estimating the taxi's speed at an average of 6 miles per hour, *La Falaise* is approximately three miles, less than five kilometers south of Casablanca. It's now on our right, between the road and the cliff overlooking the Atlantic. A beautiful site. I've never seen anything quite like it. Hardly a sound other than the surf can be heard. *La Falaise's* low, single story structure is exquisitely silhouetted against the light of the moon reflected from the Atlantic Ocean. Access is by a narrow dirt road exiting from the poorly paved road we'd been traveling. The dirt road disappears to the right and left of the building. Parking in the rear? Probably. The building's architecture is closer to modern French than old Moroccan. None of the characteristic colorful mosaic tiles.

Here's a strange contrast. The doorman is dressed in what must be a costume designer's overheated notion of how a royal eunuch would be clothed. Reminds me of some of the New York City hotel doormen's getups, more elaborate than a highly decorated Cossack General. This doorkeeper is tall, much taller than any Arab I've seen in Casa. He wears a fiercely arched set of dark mustaches, a large turban on his head and a wide waistband around his long kumsan. Moroccan seraweel trousers and leather sandals complete the costume. If he is a Moroccan Arab, how does he explain all this to his wife? I'm amused at the thought. He plays the role of an Arabian Nights doorman with an extravagant series of low bows while muttering some unintelligible sounds, which I assume are greetings in Arabic. At the same time a young Moroccan boy with a nice smile, probably the doorman's son, grasps the horse's bridle and exchanges words with the Arab taxi driver.

I step out of the taxi and, in an exaggerated and most elegant display of gentlemanly manners, turn to assist Georgette. She rewards me with a soft "*Je te remercie mon Léon.*" Georgette tells the driver to wait for us. We'll return to the hotel in about an hour. We'll pay for his time. A simple "*d'accord*," okay from the driver and we enter the wide doorway to *La Falaise*. Is the driver one of the group? Egad. I am becoming paranoid!

"*Ah! Très bon soir, monsieur et madame. Bienvenu chez La Falaise*!" The maître de's greeting, deep bowing and tooth-exhibiting smile are gushy enough to make one grimace.

Georgette more than settles the score by imitating his gushy smile and making a direct and decisive statement. "*Mademoiselle, maître. Entendez*? *Mademoiselle*! *Pas madame*!"

He sure rubbed her the wrong way. This is the second time tonight she's revealed new emotions. The first was the moment of fear in the taxi, now this abrupt, sharp flash of temper. This is the first time I've seen her openly display hostility. Georgette's more complex than I realize. There's more to this woman than physical charm and beauty. It's possible the fearsome moment on the road to *La Falaise* left a nerve or two raw and exposed.

Of course, I'm not very well acquainted with the dining-out customs of Casa; however, with regard to tipping, or gratuities, they are probably the same in Casa as in New York. The maître d's flourishing acceptance of the several franc notes I place in the palm of his open hand assures me they are identical. At the same time I give him a brief instruction. "*À la mur.*" Two, against the wall. He personally escorts us to an appropriate table and takes our coats. Excellent. From this spot Georgette and I have a panoramic view of the establishment, including the entrance, all the tables and their occupants.

As soon as we are seated, Georgette resumes her very feminine ways. She places her hand on mine, squeezes gently, looks directly into my eyes and smiles. "*Tu me donne beaucoup de plaisir, cher Léon.*" I give her much pleasure.

"*Enchanté, chère Georgette. Je ne désire que...*" I hesitate for fear I'm overdoing things. Then I hold her close and tightly. "*Tu me donne aussi plus grand plaisir.*" Georgette purses her lips and presents me with a silent kiss. I swear I'm blushing.

She's very quiet now. Her expression is seriows and sad. Her eyes fill with tears as she tells me it is not easy to find some moments of happiness during these strange hours of the war. It's difficult to believe in anyone or anything. She has many memories of good times. It is hard to keep them fresh and strong. "And, Léon, I've had special, happy times back in Paris."

I'm eager to hear details of her background. Other than the fact she once told me she lived in Paris until the German occupation of the city, I know nothing about her, really. I remind myself repeatedly I must not get too close. Be aware at all times of my objective. I must be careful not exchange too much information with Georgette—listen closely—talk no more than is necessary.

It's impossible to tell how honest she's being with me. However, to demonstrate empathy and encourage her to continue, I place her left hand in both of mine. With her free hand she delicately wipes a tear or two from her eyes. What a performance she's giving!

What a performance I'm giving! I don't say a word. I just continue to look into her eyes with what I think is tenderness and compassion. As I wondered earlier in the evening, are we here to observe the goings on at *La Falaise*...or am I the one under observation? At any rate, as much as I would like to visually sweep the restaurant's clients and personnel, I force myself to give Georgette my undivided attention.

"Few people know my real story. You are such a kind person, I want to tell it to you."

I softly stroke her hand and nod encouragement.

Georgette tells me she was born in Germany, near Berlin, before the first World War. Her mother was French and her father was German. He was a career diplomat in Germany's Foreign Service Bureau. The family moved to Paris in 1934. Georgette entered the Sorbonne as a history student in 1935 and graduated in 1939, not long before France declared war against Germany. But there was very little work for an inexperienced history student, certainly not in Paris at that time. However, there was a lot of good-paying work for fashion and photography models. She was lucky and soon made top money as a model.

Face or figure, fashion or photography, Georgette must have ranked among the top models. So far, her story is believable. She's talkative now, warming up to her "life story."

Her father was called back to Germany and her mother went with him to Berlin. Georgette preferred Paris. With her father's influence, after the Germans took over Paris, she soon worked again as a model.

This story's got to have a twist. Even an amateur story teller usually puts a surprise curve into the series of events. I'm still holding her hand in mine and looking at her with my saddest eyes.

"*À vôtre service*." The waiter is figuratively throwing ice water on us. "*À boire*?"

I order two apéritifs. Without taking her eyes off me, Georgette nods her approval. I try to get her back on the track. However, the mood's been broken by the waiter's intrusion. She withdraws her hand from mine and excuses herself to powder her nose, of course. Well, this leaves me alone at the table with time to look over the place and the people.

The room is essentially a hexagon, only about 25 feet across its widest point. The lighting's low, as one would expect in a romantic place such as *La Falaise*. But no music. I hear the chatter of the customers' conversations, the waiters' commentaries and the inevitable clatter of dishes and tableware. The kitchen must be to my left. Waiters and helpers quickly disappear and reappear through the swinging door. I count 14 tables, some large enough to seat eight or ten and a few small tables for intimate pairs, which is the appearance Georgette and I give. Georgette is the only woman in the place.

Alors! I'm a bit startled. At one of the tables are a U.S. Army colonel and two majors; his *aides-de-camp*, no doubt. Between the colonel and his majors are two French officers. The five men are obviously having a good time. They are smoking and drinking heavily. All the others in the dining room are in civilian clothes. Hold on. Here comes the U.S. Navy. A captain and two lieutenant commanders come in and go directly to the colonel's table, shake hands all around, exchange greetings and move on to a table that had obviously been held in reserve for them. I'd heard the first thing the armed services do when they occupy a town or a city is open an officers' club. The second thing is get the name and location of the best restaurant in town and "occupy it." However, I didn't believe those tales...until now. I successfully resist the urge to shout, "Hey, you guys! Look at me. I'm an American, too! Tell me, please, where is the Officers' Club?"

As Georgette crosses the floor to our table, all eyes are on her, especially the Americans'. Every man likes to be seen with a beautiful woman. I'm no exception. Ridiculous perhaps, but I'm proud to be her escort. Good for my ego.

Georgette accepts my offer of a cigarette. As I move closer to light her cigarette, she looks at the flame and whispers to me, "*Écoutons, mon cher. Écoutons bien*. Listen well." She reminds me we came to *La Falaise* to listen.

I smile and avoid her eyes to enable me to focus intensely on the sounds of the conversations at the nearby tables. My ears become directional antennas. I am especially interested in the conversations at the Americans' two tables. Are they discussing military affairs? If they are, they could be jeopardizing the Allies' positions. Treasonable acts. If they are, how can I stop them? I can't, of course. Judging from their facial expressions, they're not talking about the war. Probably swapping the latest French and American Army and Navy humor. I hope so! I can't hear the punch lines, but they laugh loudly together. No point in trying to tune into their tables. That's the job of the internal affairs sections of Army and Navy intelligence.

What I really want is to tune in on the French dialogs. My credibility would benefit greatly if I were able to report some interesting conversations to Jean-Paul or, at the very least, corroborate anything Georgette might summarize.

The aperitifs are sweet and very tasty, give a bit of warmth to the depths of my stomach. The waiter comes over. There's no menu. The waiter defends *La Falaise*. "It's impossible to predict from day to day what food supplies the *propriétaire* will be able to buy at the market."

"Of course. *Nous comprenons bien*. What does the *propriétaire* offer tonight? *Non, non. Ça ne fait rien*. Just bring us two of your best dinners, please. We have confidence in *La Falaise.*"

Georgette applauds quietly. "*Très bien fait*. Very well done, Léon." She rolls her eyes to the right and to the left. We must resume our listening.

I'm intensely hungry for news of what's been going on since the invasion of French Morocco. Nothing of consequence reaches my ears. The others in the room seem to be local ministers and city officials concerned with *les affaires de Casa*. Clearly, they are very happy to openly support France's pre-Nazi days. They're glad the Germans have left Casa. Glad the Americans caught the German Commission in Casa with it's pants down.

According to the conversation I've tuned into, a commission of high-ranking German officers staying at a hotel in Casa underestimated the secrecy, speed and effectiveness of the invasion and didn't bother to get the hell out of the city. They are now being held as prisoners of war by the Americans. The French are congratulating themselves. Georgette and I exchange looks. I can't tell whether or not she feels congratulations are in order. The whole thing's quite ridiculous. The Americans are the ones to be congratulated, not the French! Beside that, the war isn't over. Far from it. Well, it's over for those imprisoned Germans and for the Vichy French in Casa who probably will spend the remainder of this war safe, secure and well fed under the protection of the Americans.

"*Très intéressant, eh Georgette*?"

"*Très égoiste. Ils ne parlent que d'eux-même. N'est ce pas, Léon*?" They talk only about themselves.

We resume our listening. The waiter returns with a huge tray. I draw back a bit to give him all the room he needs. I'm starved and don't want to delay him for a single instant. First, he places a bottle of champagne on the table and tells us, as he indicates the table, the *Officiers de l'Armée Américain* ordered the champagne for us and send their best wishes. "*Très gallant*" Georgette says as she turns toward our American benefactors, flutters her eyelids and gives them her most enchanting smile. I stand up and bow to them. The champagne is warm. No ice.

"*Est ce que je suis trop gallant*? Am I, too, gallant? I pout deliberately.

"*Tu es toujours gallant. Mais je croix que tu sois jaloux.*" Georgette taunts me.

"*Oh là là. Non. Pas du tout!*" I protest. I am not jealous. Well...not very.

Georgette smiles. "*Cher Léon. Je t'aime.*" And she blows me a kiss again.

I glance at the officers' tables to make sure they saw that. I think to myself "Eat your hearts out, *Américains. Pour moi, c'est mon butin de la guerre.*" My spoils of war.

The waiter has been standing at our table observing this social exchange. He places our platters of food, elegantly concealed under silver lids, in front of us. With a smile bigger than Columbus must have worn when he heard the cry "Land Ho!", the waiter carefully removes the platters' lids, stands erect and holds them in a stance reminiscent of a cymbalist in a major symphony orchestra waiting for his cue. With an emotional tremor, he says, "*Voici*! *Quelle grandeur*! *Quel arôme*!"

What histrionics! To keep from laughing out loud, I tear my eyes off him and focus on my platter of food. The cause of all this passion is a large, grilled steak sharing the platter with an equally large lobster tail and some unidentifiable vegetables. Is this the food shortage they complain about? A young boy brings a basket of bread; no butter. Ah! *La disette*. There's the shortage! I feel compelled to make a dramatic speech of gratitude for such abundance.

Georgette stops me with a slight smile and a brief but unmistakable admonishing expression. "*Ici, à La Falaise, toujours on mange bien.*" One always eats well at La Falaise.

We are eating well, I suppose. So, I settle down and slice my steak. I'm fully aware Georgette is watching me closely. I cut the meat deliberately with the knife in my right hand and do not shift the fork from my left to my right hand. Georgette starts her meal, too.

The waiter pours the champagne. Georgette and I toast each other's health. I hold my glass aloft in the direction of our American hosts. They return the gesture and call out in unison, "*Santé*!" Georgette and I nod our thanks.

The rest of the hour at *La Falaise* is most pleasant, but unproductive as far as reportable events and overheard conversations are concerned. I call for the bill, which I pay plus a generous gratuity.

Georgette doesn't smile as she tells me I am too generous. "*Vite gagné*! *Vite perdu*! *Eh, Léon*?"

"*Oui*. Easy come! Easy go! *C'est l'histoire du monde donc je suis venu.* That is how I was brought up. *Allons, Georgette.*" Time to go.

We collect our coats. The *maître d' of La Falaise* bows repeatedly as he invites us to return soon. We finally escape his overdone gratitude, step outside and in a jiffy the Arab boy comes from the far side of *La Falaise* leading the taxi directly to the front door. I give him a franc. Judging from Georgette's *tsk-tsk-tsk* sounds, it must be another of my generous moments.

I smile and shrug. "*Ne rien*. It's nothing."

The ride back to the hotel is uneventful. The abundant food, the warm champagne and the peaceful mood have made us both drowsy. I move to the forward wall of the taxi's passenger compartment and position myself so I have a clear view out the back door. Georgette snuggles against me and, judging from her even and deep breathing, she falls asleep almost immediately. I struggle to stay awake and alert. It isn't easy. Not one bit.

After what seems like hours of riding, we are back at the hotel. The front door is locked. Georgette raps on the glass window. In a moment, Claude appears at the door near his desk. He's rubbing his eyes as though he'd been asleep. He looks as mean as ever and has a large club in his right hand as he approaches the hotel's front door. He recognizes us, smiles and unlocks the door for us and quickly locks the door behind us.

Georgette remarks that one can't be too careful with the Arabs running about all night. *Eh Claude*?"

"*Gute nacht. Schlafen sie...*" He hesitates for a moment and then quickly reverts to German-accented French. "*Bon soir. Dormez bien. Jusqu'au matin.* Jean-Paul wants to see you at 8 o'clock in the morning."

I pretend, but Claude's brief lapse into German does not escape my notice.

Georgette and I together return Claude's goodnight. "*Dormez bien.*"

I go upstairs to my room. Georgette goes to hers. I wearily undress, turn off the light and collapse onto my bed. Just as I drift off, my door opens and Georgette whispers, "*Léon*! *Est-ce que tu t'endormes*?"

"No, Georgette. I am not asleep." Here we go again.

Chapter Thirty-Seven

Eight-ten. Uh oh! I'm late. Georgette's gone. Must hurry. Skip the shave for now. I pull my shirt onto my arms, drag my trousers over my legs, manage to put on my socks and shoes, open the door, take a long deep breath, cross the hall and knock on the door to room 23. Michel, again, glumly opens the door for me. Jean-Paul's there, neatly dressed and hair slicked back, as usual. Georgette's there, too.

Georgette smiles wickedly. "*Il'y a longtemps, Léon, depuis que*...It's been a long time, Léon, since..."

She's making some sort of joke I suppose. All I can say is "*Oui*. Too long, dear lady." I apologize for my appearance; I overslept. Apology accepted.

Jean-Paul smiles. His mouth smiles but his eyes do not reflect it. He's in a serious mood. "*On a beaucoup de choses*...we have much to talk about as soon as Claude brings our breakfast."

Breakfast! I can use lots of coffee. Claude arrives with his welcome tray of food and beverages for Jean-Paul, Georgette, Michel and myself. There's no conversation as we gulp our alcohol shots, pour our coffee and scoop up portions of scrambled eggs and bread. The coffee's bitter. But it's hot. The eggs are lukewarm. Where do they get them? The bread's great, as usual, despite the lack of butter. There's no conversation while we finish our meal. We light our horrible Moroccan cigarettes, settle back and wait for Jean-Paul to speak.

"*Bien mes amis*. Well, my friends, I believe we are now ready to resume our tasks. It's fortunate Léon showed up when he did."

I add, "*Heureusement*...very lucky for me to have met Robert and then all of you on my very first day in Casa."

"*Assurément*...'Lucky' all around. I expect some very interesting things to come from your acquaintance, your apparent friendship with Lieutenant Corval. What time shall we expect him this evening?"

"*Il m'a dit que*...he had some important work to do. I don't know what or where, but he said he'd be here at the hotel about 7:30 tonight." I glance at Georgette and say slowly, "With butter...and cigarettes...and other goodies!" She nods vigorously and smiles broadly.

Jean-Paul continues. "*C'est bon*. It is possible Philippe, André...maybe Henri and Jules, too, will be here for this occasion. It's a very special event for us to meet an American Officer. We shall have an outstanding evening, all of us. *Bien fait*! Well done, Léon!"

I thank Jean-Paul for his generous compliments and ask, "Did Georgette tell you about our pleasant but unproductive soirée at *La Falaise*?"

"Yes. However, I'd like to hear your impression."

"*La Falaise* is a fine establishment. *Élégant*. We had a tasty apéritif and a delicious dinner. Three American Army officers and two French officers at one table. Three American Navy officers, were there, also. I tried to listen to their conversation, but there was too much talking going on at the same time in the room. Anyway, judging from their expressions and gestures, they were not discussing anything important."

"*Même que Georgette*. Exactly the same as Georgette's report. Let's set that aside for now."

No doubt, I was the one under observation last night. Evidently, I passed this test.

Looking directly at me, Jean-Paul continues. "Did you get the papers from Lieutenant Corval as he promised? If so, may I see them." He extends his open hand, palm up.

"They're in my coat pocket, in my room. *Vous voulez que je les apporte*? Shall I get them?"

"Yes, please."

"*Je reviens*. Right back!"

I move briskly and return in a few seconds. I hand the "papers" to Jean-Paul. Actually, the "papers" are a single sheet, a few sentences in both English and French on a U.S. Army form giving my name, Léon Dejacques; my age, 21 and a brief description; address in Casa, the *Hôtel Monte Carlo*—and a statement of appointment as a civilian translator/interpreter to the U.S. Armed Forces based in Casablanca. It also limits my travel to within a radius of 120 kilometers from my present address in Casablanca. It's signed by Lieutenant B. Corval and Colonel S. Hauser.

Jean-Paul asks "Who is this Colonel Hauser?"

"*Je n'ai pas aucune idée*. I've no idea. Possibly he's Corval's commanding officer?" That's the truth. I don't know whether Col. Hauser is real or a figment of Bud's imagination. But it was a good notion. Bud's creativity, no doubt.

Jean-Paul hands the paper to Michel, then to Georgette. They read it for what seems an especially long time. Georgette hands it to Jean-Paul and he returns it to me with a broad smile. "*Très bon*. He saved us the trouble of preparing special documents for you, which also saves time and means you can get to work with us at once."

"*Oui*. At once!"

"*Oui*." Georgette echoes my expressed sentiment. Michel grunts.

"We'll have special work for you tomorrow, Léon. So, give yourself a vacation for the rest of the day. Eh?"

"*Merci*, Jean-Paul. *Bien Merci*. I think I'll just hang around the hotel and rest up a bit." My motive is not a need to recuperate from the past day's activities. They weren't very fatiguing. I do want to explore the rest of the hotel. It's a big place for so few people to inhabit. I'm still searching for quick exits in addition to the hotel's front door. Staying in the hotel for the day without surveillance could give me the opportunity to explore the place.

"*Si vous le désirez, je donnerai des instructions à Claude.* If you want to have lunch here, I'll tell Claude you'll take your lunch today in the dining room. You arrange the precise time with him. We'll all have dinner together in the dining room. Again, what time is your Lieutenant coming?"

"*Il m'a dit*...He said 1930 hours."

Jean-Paul rises, signaling the end of our meeting. "*Ainsi*...we'll have dinner at 6."

It's now almost 1000. I go to my room. I need a shave. If there's warm water, which would be a pleasant surprise, I need a shower, too. Cologne goes just so far in general hygiene. First, I need a nap. Didn't get enough sleep last night.

Sounds of angry voices awaken me. I get out of my bed, listen at my door. The voices are not coming from the hall. Carefully, quietly, slowly I open my door just a crack. The voices are coming from Jean-Paul's room and they are not speaking French. They're speaking German.

I recognize Jean-Paul's voice and Georgette's. I think another voice is Claude's. There's a fourth. Michel's? I've rarely heard him speak; only grunt. They're talking or arguing in German. Most significant of all, I hear my name; sometimes in anger. This would not be a good time to interrupt. But, if this is an argument and if they're arguing about me, which of the four are my defenders? Which are my prosecutors? It's important for me to know. It isn't easy. It could be critical. So, I continue to listen, stretching my limited knowledge of German to the edge, depending on my childhood experience with Yiddish, the non-grammatical version of old German, the common language of the Jewish people.

I can't hear enough of the dialogue. It's muffled by the closed door. However, the tones of the voices indicate my defenders are Jean-Paul and Georgette. Claude and Michel are doing their best to condemn me. Well, the only way get through this is to maintain my apparent dedication to the group and demonstrate my eagerness to do whatever work they ask me to perform...within reason, of course.

As I had told The Chief back in New York when I was in training as a "shadow catcher," I want to work alone. I don't want to get into trouble because of another agent's mistakes. I'm willing to take the blame or suffer the consequences for my own errors. At this moment, I feel very much alone—and tense.

The voices are calmer now. Must have arrived at a consensus. I shut my door just as the door to Room 23 opens. I hear two pairs of feet descending the stairs. This is my cue to visit Jean-Paul and Georgette to gain some sense of the direction or a change in the direction of affairs. Again, as casually as I can, I cross the hall and knock on Jean-Paul's door.

"*Qui*?" It's Jean-Paul.

"*C'est moi, Léon.*"

"*Ah bon. Entrez.*"

Jean-Paul and Georgette are in the room, sipping some sort of clear, amber-colored liquid. Wine, I suppose. They offer me a glassful with "*santé*," as usual. It is wine. I sip, sit back and smile at my companions. "*Mes très chers amis*. It is so good to be here with you. Today I feel relaxed and ready for an assignment."

Jean-Paul's attitude toward me seems as positive as he has ever allowed it to be. So, with his expressed approval—it's apparent no one does anything of which Jean-Paul does not expressly approve—Georgette excuses herself to freshen up. Now, Jean-Paul and I are alone in the room. He and I wordlessly sip our wine for a few moments. We both start to speak at the same time. However, he is *le patron*, the boss of this outfit, so I interrupt myself with a short apology.

He continues. "Léon. In this short time we've known each other, I've grown to like you. Your spirit and enthusiasm are most refreshing to me and Georgette."

My natural curiosity prompts me to ask, "*Et quoi de Cluade and Michel*? What about Claude and Michel? Sometimes I get the feeling they resent me, do not trust me. It bothers me deeply." I hope for a revealing answer. My hope is quickly satisfied by Jean-Paul's response.

"To be honest with you, Claude is a frightened man. He distrusts everyone. I imagine he's always been like that."

"And Michel? Is he, too, frightened or is he just filled with hatred for all mankind?"

Jean-Paul hesitates for a moment, probably thinking over my question and his answer. "*Très pénétrant, Léon.* You are very perceptive, Léon. I think there are very few people he trusts. This translates into a kind of hatred, a reaction to his own private fears. Perhaps that's why he behaves as though he isn't afraid of anyone or anything. I know he conceals his true feelings."

"But he has no reason to fear or hate me. Or, am I doing something I shouldn't?" Oh, how I lie!

"I'll be very honest with you about Michel. He doesn't like you. You are new. You are unknown. This alarms him. However, it is entirely up to you to convince him you are okay." Jean-Paul looks intently at me. "Your quick friendship with Georgette upsets him. He's in love, or thinks he's in love with Georgette. But, she can't stand Michel."

I exclaim, "*Zut*! *Alors*! *Merde*! Georgette and I are not in love! I'm much younger than she and I don't have anything, any security to offer a woman. I have no real job or dependable income. Georgette and I have become good friends. I'm flattered by her attention. That is all."

"Are you sure that is all?"

Jean-Paul catches my attention with this question. What does he mean by "Am I sure that is all?" So, I plead innocence. "*Bien entendu*, Jean-Paul. *Oui*. Certainly. It is the truth."

Georgette comes back into the room on a cloud of perfume. Jean-Paul smiles at me, “Lucky you.”

Yeah, some luck.

Chapter Thirty-Eight

Lunch time. I go downstairs and greet Claude. He's expecting me for lunch and escorts me to a table in the dining room. This display of friendship is unexpected but I accept it...with suspicion. "*Très bon jour, mon ami. Ça va*?" I can match his friendly display.

Claude reacts. "*Oui. Ça va bien.* I've prepared something nice for your lunch. *Un peu de vin*?"

I decline the offer of wine. He might bring some red stuff and I could suddenly feel little or no pain. The rest of lunch time is uneventful. The weather is our most serious dialogue. Amusing. The weather is almost always predictably fine in Casa. After a hot cup of bitter coffee, I express my interest, with flattery, in seeing his kitchen, "from which emerge the most delicious dishes I have ever been privileged to taste and enjoy."

Claude reacts with a smile. Compliments are probably something he rarely hears. I'm invited to see it now. My real interest is only in locating "emergency exits" through the kitchen. As Claude escorts me everywhere in his well-equipped kitchen, I note there is only one exit/entrance door. It is a metal door with a thick iron or steel bar, a locking device that slides horizontally from right to left. Not exactly a hasty exit, but it is another way out. This leaves the third floor, which I must find a reason to visit. While Claude's in this overtly friendly mood, I press my luck. I invite him to join me in an American cigarette. He is grateful and sits at the table with me.

"*Claude, mon ami.* I've never seen the top floor of this fine hotel. May I have a quick look, perhaps go out on the roof and admire the view of Casa?"

He thinks this one over and then says "*Bien sûr*. Okay, but do not enter any of the rooms on the third floor. They belong to other guests."

Other guests? One must be Michel. Georgette's room is on the same floor as mine. Others could include Henri, Jules, Philippe, and André. What about the mysterious Robert? No one refers to him nor have I seen him since the morning I landed on the beach and located the café. Yet, he must have some strong relationship with Jean-Paul. He recruited me. Is that his assignment? Does he report to Jean-Paul? Or vice versa? Okay for now. However, the immediate task is to get onto the roof and see where it leads me.

I shake hands with Claude. His hand is larger and stronger than mine. I'd lose an arm-wrestling contest with him, no doubt. However, for the moment, we are friends and that's a notable advance. We casually move together out of the dining room, pause at his desk and shake hands again. "*Salut, Claude. À bientôt.* I'll enjoy the warm sun and the view of Casa from the roof. Is there a door to the roof on the third floor?"

Claude grins smugly. "Yes. Turn left when you get to the third floor. It's at the top of a short stairway. It's usually unlocked from the inside. But don't let the door close behind you. It'll lock itself and I'll have to come up and open it for you...if I can hear your calls for help from down here."

"Thanks, Claude. I'll be careful not to lock myself out. I won't be long. But just in case, if I'm not back in two or three days, please look for me on the roof!" My sense of humor isn't wasted. Claude bursts into loud laughter.

I climb to the third floor. It's a duplicate of the second floor. Even the doors to the rooms are spaced in the same sequence. Only the numbers are different; 39 instead of 29. Logical. I turn left and climb the 10 steps at the top of which is the self-locking door. A triangular wood block hangs on the inside of the door. Practical. I use it to prop the door open and step through onto the roof. The light is almost blinding. I have been indoors too long lately. My hand shields my eyes until I can adjust to the bright sun and exquisitely blue sky.

To my surprise, the roof is wooden and looks as though it could use some repair. The tireless sun is hard on the exposed wood. The roof is flat with a low wall around its outside perimeter. Casually, hands in pockets, I slowly, deliberately stroll around the roof, moving toward its edge. Never know who might be watching. I try to appear to be up here with no specific purpose.

The view is great. I stop to enjoy it. The port and the breakwater with the Jean Bart battleship are clearly visible. To the north I can also see the approximate area where I landed on the beach. The foothills of a mountain range extend northeast and southwest. The battlements our Navy ships put out of action are on the mountain slopes several kilometers east and south of the hotel. The roof of the hotel is higher than the others on either side. I could break my leg, or worse, in a jump to an adjoining roof. This is definitely not the way out. There's no basement. Unless I've overlooked something, the only quick way out is the front door of the hotel. So much for getting "the hell out of there in a hurry!" And I would still have to pass Claude, the watchdog, on the way to the door.

As I scan the roof, I notice something else. A thin wire with another cable connected at its center is stretched between two five-foot bamboo poles; a basic doublet-type radio antenna. The wire runs approximately northwest to southeast. Its orientation would give it some directivity toward Germany and could include the area in which—last time I heard—Rommel's Afrika Korps is operating. The feed line connecting the center of the antenna to the receiver or transmitter is a twisted pair of insulated wires. The type is known in the United States as "EO-1 cable." It is moderately flexible, electrically efficient and very cheap.

I saunter over to the edge of the roof on which the cable rests. I lean over and see the cable enters a room through the top of a window just below the roof. My guess it is a window to room 35. If my conclusion is correct, if this is an antenna for two-way radio communications, the antenna's length would put operations optimally in or near the 40-meter radio band; good for daytime communications.

Bet the radio set is operated by one of the occupants of the third floor whose rooms Claude cautioned me not to enter.

There is no way for me to monitor radio communications made from inside the hotel. Although I am quite competent and experienced with Morse Code, their transmissions would probably be in German Morse, not International Morse. My mother had urged me to learn German. I now regret my stubborn refusal. I just did not like the unmelodic sound of spoken German. On the other hand, if all my assumptions are correct, they must use headphones. I couldn't hear the signals anyway. How about the click-click of the telegraph key? Usually they are not loud enough to be heard in another room.

After half an hour of contemplation, I leave the roof, shut the door behind me and return to the second floor from which I announce to Claude, "I think I'll go to my room and take a nap." He acknowledges my announcement. And I do take a nap.

Chapter Thirty-Nine

There are a few surprises at dinner. Everybody is here to meet Lieutenant Corval of the U.S. Army. Michel and Georgette are, as usual, on either side of Jean-Paul. Too, in the room are Henri, Philippe, André, and Jules who never seem to have anything to say...and a gorgeous, mature lady who is introduced to me as Christine. I have never heard her name mentioned before. She is about five to ten years older than Georgette. In her prime, she must have been a knockout. In fact, she is still exceptionally elegant. Georgette says she and Christine worked as models for the same fashion house and photographers in Paris; "before the war, of course."

No one pities poor Claude. He appears to revel in the multiple tasks of maître de, chef and garçon. He dashes in and out of the kitchen, brings trays of plates and glasses to our table, returns to the kitchen, emerges within minutes to repeat the procedure again and again. However, the biggest surprise of all arrives 15 minutes after Claude serves our apéritifs.

The mood in the hotel's dining room is as festive as ever I've seen it. Can all this be because Bud is expected? Or is everyone here for a strategic meeting? There's a loud rapping at the front door. It is too early for Bud.

Everyone at the table pauses, looks around at one another and smiles as Jean-Paul rises from his chair and, with the biggest smile of all, excuses himself. Must be someone of great importance for Jean-Paul to personally go to the door. Curiosity overwhelms me. I can hear a great commotion of friendly greetings being made by Jean-Paul and another man for whom he opened the hotel door. I seem to recognize the newcomer's voice. I know it from somewhere. No wonder! Jean-Paul returns with the visitor. It's Robert! Well, the count of the members of the group is now 10.

"*Ah, mes amis*! So good to see you again!" Robert is charming. His manners are almost *élégant* as he shakes hands enthusiastically with the men, all of whom are standing, and softly kisses the hands and cheeks of the two ladies who remained seated. He saves me for last.

He grasps my right hand in his. "*Léon*! *Comment va tu*? I've heard you'd been accepted as a member of our group and are ready to take on some very interesting assignments. *À ma plus grand joie*! Delighted!"

The theatrical entrance is over. He slows his pace and I have an opportunity to express myself. "*Oui, Robert*. I can never forget your kindness in introducing me to these good people. I was very much in need of friends...in addition to the other more material things." Everyone laughs at the dramatic tone of my voice and applauds my performance. "How can I thank you. I am sure one day I will demonstrate what all of you mean to me." More laughter and applause as I sit down and cover my eyes, to wipe away the false tears. Everyone sits.

Claude comes from the kitchen, sees Robert, gasps, puts his tray down and salutes. Definitely not a Frenchman's or a French soldier's salute. He clicks his heels and starts to speak in German, "*Mein lieber freund! Meine...*" Jean-Paul and Robert both hasten to interrupt and remind Claude: "*Ici on parle seulement en français*! We only speak french here!"

Of course, I pretend not to notice this episode. But, it registers; convinces me more than ever that I am on the right target and had better give some specific thought to how I'm going to arrest them and get out of here. The thought is ridiculous. If I were to concentrate on just one of the group, I might trick him or her to get far enough away to enable me to take some sort of aggressive action. I do not want Georgette. Not Claude. I want key people.

As the hubbub of conversation fills the dining room, I try to rank the attendees. First in importance is Robert, perhaps Jean-Paul. I do not know enough about Robert but I suspect he ranks with Jean-Paul in knowledge of the group's activities. He is probably a recruiter for the group. And I happened to be in the right place at the right time. Am I lucky, or what? Next in rank is the enigmatic Michel.

Claude brings a chair for Robert. He places it between Michel and Jean-Paul. Robert and Jean-Paul are in deep, whispered conversation all through the rest of dinner. I cannot hear a word of what they're saying. Are they speaking French or German? I'm totally unable to make out any of their conversation. Their faces tell me its a serious one. The rest of the group is talking very loudly in French as though they were providing a sound screen for Jean-Paul and Robert. Michel is doing very heavy smoking, very little talking. He frequently looks at me and frowns. The big bulge in his suit jacket is still there. It seems to get bigger and more conspicuous every time I see him.

Jean-Paul announces to no one specifically, "It's a little past seven. I suggest we go to my room and relax until the good Lieutenant Corval arrives." Robert agrees. Jean-Paul must have told him we were going to have a special visitor.

Bud, don't disappoint me! Be here at 1930! *And come bearing asssorted gifts and goodies*!

Robert and Jean-Paul lead the way up the stairs and into Room 23. The room's been redone. There are large, lounging chairs and end-tables for all of us. A few potted plants and soft lights in the corners of the room make the atmosphere altogether warm and pleasant. Must be Claude's work. What will Bud think? I don't live like this all the time, you know.

Jean-Paul gives everyone instructions, like a stage manager. "Look relaxed. Feel relaxed. Look friendly. Be friendly. This is a new and rare opportunity." Jean-Paul points to me. "*Grâce à Léon*."

Applause from everyone. Georgette comes over and kisses my cheek. "*Bravo, cher Léon*!" I wish she wouldn't do that. Not now. Michel glares with obvious hatred.

Claude's been alerted to keep the front door open for the Lieutenant. At a few minutes after 1930, Claude knocks on our door and announces "*L'invité est arrivée.* Your visitor is here." Bud is prompt, thank heaven.

Michel opens the door and Bud steps in. His hair is neatly slicked back. The cut and trim of his uniform and the high polish on his shoes would make General Patton happy to acknowledge him as "one of my best men." On top of all that, Bud wears a great big smile and an innocent, wide-eyed expression. As a Virginia gentleman, he goes to the ladies and greets them warmly. He blushes when Georgette and Christine kiss him on both cheeks.

Enough! I interrupt and introduce him to our host, Jean-Paul, then to Robert, Michel, Henri, André, Philippe, and Jules. Bud makes a brief apology, which I translate into French. "*Le Lieutenant ne parle pas francais. Pas du tout.* However, if you need me to, I will translate for you and for him."

"*Oui, merci, Léon.* Translate for us. Don't miss a word, please."

"*Bien entendu, Jean-Paul.* I will do my best." Fortunately, it is Bud's nature to speak slowly; a southern gentleman's habit.

I direct my French-accented English to Bud. "Mr. Jean-Paul Duval, our host, wishes to express his gratitude to you for paying us the honor of your visit tonight." I pause for Jean-Paul's next social, ritualistic remarks and then translate. Discreetly, I add a few comments of my own. One can't be sure. These people could disguise their linguistic skills. I do ask Bud, with a French accent and a smile on my face, "Where are the goddamn goodies you were supposed to bring?"

"Y'all gotta forgive mah forgetfulness. I've had a very busy couple'a days. Conferences with O.N.I. and G-2 an' all that stuff. Whew! Sure tuckers me!" That's Bud. His sense of humor never slows down. I translate and, clearly, the group's appetite has been whetted. Like children waiting impatiently for the cutting of the party's cake, they glance back and forth at one another. They anticipate a very productive evening. As for me, I'm a bit worried about how far Bud might go in an effort to be convincing.

Bud's southern drawl gets heavier. "Ah've got some things in mah Jeep parked out in front of the hotel. I hope you don' mind mah parkin' in front o' yo' hotel? I'll be right back with them. Hey, Frenchie, how 'bout givin' me a hand?"

"Sure, *Américain.* Let's go!" I translate and add for the benefit of the others, "He's a bit crazy, like all Americans, I think. Be right back."

Jean-Paul says, "*Entendu, Léon,* go with him, but Claude should go, too...to carry any heavy packages. Okay?"

So, in silence, Bud and I go downstairs where Claude joins us. Bud's outdone himself. He must have raided the quartermaster's stores. The three of us struggle back to Room 23 under the weight of numerous cartons and boxes of all sorts of shapes.

"Tell yo' playmate Claude to get the hot water ready. We're goin' to have some real American coffee 'n stuff. Tell him to bring a bunch o' cups and glasses. I got some real whiskey here. Bourbon 'n Scotch, too." I could have shouted for joy as I translate. Claude races out of the room with an armload of bags of coffee and everyone shouts various forms of joyous greetings. *Vive la guerre*! *Joyeux Noel*! *Bonne vacances*! I think I even hear some absent-minded greetings in German.

Georgette and Christine gather close to Bud as he opens boxes. Wow! Even the real Santa Claus never is so generous. Out comes the whiskey. Several bottles. Next a dozen cans of evaporated milk. Two-pound packages of butter. Bags of sugar. Boxes of chocolate candy bars. Cartons and cartons of cigarettes. Even my favorite brand is among them. And matches...and on and on—gifts in a quantity one might reserve for a royal visit to the Sultan!

Bud puts on a corrupt expression as he brings out several boxes of ladies' personal items. Perfumes, lipsticks, face powders. And...nylons! Where'd he ever get those! Georgette and Christine squeal with excitement. As they divide the booty, the two jabber and giggle loudly like spoiled school girls until Jean-Paul good naturedly shushes them.

Everybody, at the same time, asks me to tell Bud how much they enjoy meeting him. What else can one say? "*Monsieur le Lieutenant* Corval, you have brought much joy to my good friends. I wish to add my own personal thanks to those they ask me to express to you."

"Heck. This's the least I c'n do fo' mah allies in this terrible war." He can lie like hell, too. "I want y'all to come visit me in Virginia after we win the war." Oh, oh! That was a bit too much. They expect to own Virginia after they win the war. Nonetheless, I translate Bud's invitation. A potentially embarrassing moment, but Claude's arrival rescues us. He enters the room wheeling a large serving-cart with pitchers of coffee and plates of cheeses and breads. He drags in a large table on which he sets cups and saucers, spoons and small knives.

With the large chairs, the serving cart and table, the boxes brought in from the Jeep, and all the people, the room is packed, crowded. And that is an understatement.

"Hey, Frenchie. We could use glasses for this here Bourbon and Scotch. It's all fresh from my personal still."

I translate but I can't find a French word for "still." Claude dashes out of the room and returns in no time with a tray of glasses, obviously including one for himself. Why not? So we settle down to real coffee, genuine sugar and canned milk which, when you don't have the real thing, isn't so bad. We all enjoy the genuine whiskey along with our coffee and cheese. Georgette and Christine haven't relaxed their hold on the nylons and the other female things.

I toss encouragement to Bud. "*Hey, Américain.* You are a...*qu'est ce que c'est le mot en Anglais*? *Ah, oui*. You are a big hit with the ladies."

To which, Jean-Paul immediately adds, "*Aussi aux hommes*!"

Well. Surprise. I didn't even have to translate my broken English into French. How much English does Jean-Paul actually understand? I hope Bud caught that tip-off. I think he did. Bud goes into high gear. He appears to drink the whiskey quite fast. Actually he's sipping, and with each sip he appears to get drunker and drunker. His naturally red complexion enhances the effect. His next bit will be to become talkative. Sure enough. Bud begins to "reveal" military information. The group hangs on to every word. Side conversations suddenly stop each time Bud says something, anything.

"They're workin' mah southern ass off. They think there are spies everywhere. Shit! I haven't seen one!"

I encourage Bud to keep it up. "I haven't been to the port in several days, Lieutenant. Is there any activity down there these days?"

"Activity? Not much. But plans? A whole lot. They're even talkin' about floatin' the battleship Jean Bart an' puttin' her back into action as part of the U.S. Navy. That's a laugh!"

Nobody in the room is laughing. They are trying to calibrate Bud's truthfulness.

I press Bud for more information and hope he will slow down his tall tales. "How are they handling supply convoys?"

"Hey! Where's the Bourbon? Oh, thank you mah frien'. The Army Corp of Engineers built temporary docks about half a mile north of Casablanca for troop ships 'n freighters. They're comin' in as fast as they can. One ship docks, unloads, pulls out and another comes right in. Hah! The Ayrabs are makin' more money than they've ever had before...unloadin' the cargo, y'know. The troops and heavy tanks are mostly hittin' the beach from some new kind of landin' craft." Bud swallows coffee and munches some cheese. "Hey, friends! I'm sure glad y'all invited me here. I surely needed a night out, away from the base and the salutin' and all that shit!"

"How much free time do you have?"

"Overnight. Gotta be back at the base for a breakfast meetin' with the security staff."

Jean-Paul, in as friendly a voice as he can present, invites Bud. "*Tiens. J'ai une idée._Vous pouvez rester ici, à l'hôtel, jusqu'au matin.*" Looking at Christine, "*Christine. Le bon Lieutenant peut rester ici en vôtre chambre. Oui*?"

I translate the invitation for Bud to spend the night here at the hotel...in Christine's room. Bud's eyes light up.

Christine smilingly responds, "*Bien entendu.*" She looks seductively at Bud as I translate. "Wouldn't you like to spend the night with me?" Her tone of voice and the expression on her face require minimum translation into English. Christine is speaking with a universal voice; woman to man.

Bud leers at Christine. She has her answer and moves over to sit on the arm of his chair. She presses against Bud. His response is predictable. "Honey, I'd sho' welcome yo' companionship."

Georgette displays no envy. Michel is stone-faced. Claude just listens and betrays no emotion. Robert sips his drink and smiles. Jean-Paul nods to Christine; he approves. The rest just leer and flash meaningful looks at one another. Everyone enjoys the scene. Me, too.

I bring the discussion back on track. "Hey, *mon ami Américain.* How long before you have to move out of Casa?

"Ah'm not sure for certain. Probably in a couple o' days."

"*Ou va tu*? Where are you going?"

"Probably to Tunisia." Bud's lying, appropriately.

I press on, giving Bud more cues. "Are General Patton and his troops going there, too? Are you assigned to him?"

"Yeah, dammit. I'm havin' such a good time here I hate to leave."

He continues to drink and appears to get drunker; so drunk I am not entirely sure how much of his act is fake. "Very interesting. What's your assignment to be?"

"Oh, ah'm gonna head up an intelligence activity. Well...I'll be part of a group, anyway."

Not credible. Bud's overdoing it. Michel sniggers again. The others give no signs of reaction. The Army would not likely hand such a task to a green, gabby second lieutenant.

However, I say without sincerity, "You should be good at that, *mon ami.*" Tonight is a good, non-threatening practice session for Bud.

The group overacts, too, when they respond to my translation with "*Oui. Oui. Très bon. Très bon*!"

Bud, still hamming it up, looks me squarely in the eye and arrogantly says "You, Frenchie, are a playboy. Good for nothin' useful. Ah'm sho' glad you're not in a U.S. Army uniform. How'd you escape the French draft anyway?"

With a jest, I try to pick up on Bud's lead. "We Frenchmen are all playboys. I think when they start a French Playboy Division, I will become a high-ranking officer. In the meantime, I'm quite happy working with my friends right here." My translation into French brings laughs. Even Michel laughs; not heartily, more like a cackle.

No response from Bud, so I continue. "Ah, *mon ami.* Any idea when Patton will move to Tunisia?" I pretend not to know he's already in Oran and his troops are fighting alongside the British in Tunisia.

"Beats me. I should know more after tomorrow mornin's staff conf'rence."

Now it's up to me. "Lieutenant Corval, I've learned about some more interesting places for you to visit in Casa. What time shall we meet tomorrow?"

"Well, the conf'rence is at 0815. Come to the gates at 1000 hours and let the MPs know you're waitin' for me. I'll join you soon's I can."

"I'll be there *mon ami*." You bet I will.

Bud rubs his eyes and gives a jaw-breaking yawn. Jean-Paul nods to Christine. It's bed time for Bud. Christine takes his arm. It is time to go upstairs.

"Jus' one more." Bud pours a small shot of Bourbon, adds some water, and downs the mixture in one gulp. We're all standing now. Bud burps as he bows to everyone in the room.

"*À bientôt. Salut. Salut*!"

Bud takes the French word "*salut*" literally and salutes the group. We all chuckle as Bud, supported by Christine, leaves the room.

He's in for one helluva sleepless night.

Chapter Fourty

Ten hundred hours and I'm waiting at the gate for Bud to appear. The sentries at the gate are nice guys. "Parlay voo American?" is the extent of their French vocabulary. I shrug and say in my practiced broken English, "Yes, a little...when I have to." For some reason they get a kick out of this and offer me a cigarette. I look at the package and recognize the picture of an animal. "*Ah. C'est un chameau*! How you say this word...*SahMELL*...*CahMELL*?" This is funny to them. In fact it gets funnier to them each time I mispronounce the word with exaggerated emphasis on the last syllable 'MELL'.

Bud's here now and he looks very serious and stressed. He takes me by the arm and hustles me onto the street alongside the capsized liner, *Porthos*. "I've got some bad news. I'm movin' out in two days to join Patton's intelligence staff in Oran. So, pal, in two days you're on your own."

"Any possibility of getting a delay?"

"I tried this mornin'. They're considerin' givin' me an extra day in Casablanca. My C.O. knows we're workin' on what we think is a sure-thing group of Nazi agents."

"What's the reaction?"

Bud looks at me intensely. "Wrap it up!"

"Wrap it up?"

"Yup. Those are the exact words."

I move Bud away from the *Porthos*. "Let's walk and talk. If that's your C.O.'s orders, we'll have to do just what he says. Won't we?"

"We've no choice. Okay?"

"Okay, Bud. Any suggestions?"

"It's your show. You tell me what you want me to do and I'll do it. Better make it a fast show."

"Let's toss around some ideas, Bud, and see which one might work out. Trouble is, as we both learned at the start of this little adventure, *rien se passe comme prévu*."

"What's that mean?"

"Paraphrasing Robert Burns: The best laid plans usually get screwed up. Bud, I think all I can do is what I've been doing. Play it by ear—but at a faster tempo."

Bud nods his agreement. "What can I do to help?"

"Stick close to the hotel with a Jeep. I may need transportation out of here in a helluva hurry. Any problems with that?"

"None. What about a gun, a knife, a pair of scissors or a sharp pencil? Anythin' that can be used as a weapon. If you're goin' to take greater risks, you've got to be prepared to defen' yourself until I can get to you, assumin' I know where you are and that you are in a jam."

"I know. But if they should find out or detect that I've armed myself—in a mysterious, all-of-a-sudden way—I would be in a jam up to here."

Bud pats the holster on his hip. "Yeah. Right. Tell you what I can do. In addition to my G.I. 45, I'll have a short-barrel 38 in my pocket. But it only holds 5 shots." Bud stops and looks at me quizzically. "I've never seen you shoot. You do know how to, I hope. Did you get any firearms instructions while you were in trainin'?"

I describe the Marine Sergeants at The Farm who, I think, were damn good at their trade: guns, knives, hand-to-hand combat and fixing up makeshift weapons on the spot. Bud and I agree I might have an opportunity to use some or all of those skills. I welcome his offer to carry for me.

Bud's only half kidding when he asks "What brand of gun would you like? Colt? Smith & Wesson? Maybe a Luger?" His humor's in high gear now. "But you can't have Colt six shooters with pearl handles. Patton's got those reserved as his personal trade-mark."

"So I've heard, Bud. Probably any shooting, if I have to do any, will be at very close quarters. Get me one with the shortest barrel and the slimmest shape—better as a hideout. And, please, make sure it's loaded and works."

"You bet. I'll select it, load and test fire it myself."

"Couldn't ask for more. Even my own mother couldn't do as much!"

"From now on I'm gonna stick close to you. I'll park my Jeep on the street...what's its name...the one that runs in a northerly direction from the hotel?"

"*Rue du Moissonier*?"

"Yeah. That's the one. I'll park in the alley, the one on the east side of the street, about half a block, 300 feet from the hotel. I'll be in the jeep waitin' for you. If it's okay with you, I want to tell my C.O. who you are an' what's happenin'. Okay?"

"I guess it's time to alert the MPs. Sure, tell your C.O. And tell the C.O. of Navy intelligence. Might just as well have the SPs standby, too."

We continue our walk; me, the official tour guide and translator, and Bud the crazy American tourist. I'll have to look him up back in the U.S.A. when this whole thing is over. I'd like to continue this friendship.

"Incidentally, Bud. How'd it go for you last night?"

Bud slaps his forehead and grabs his right thigh. "You son of a bitch! I thought I was good. But that Christine could take on the whole U.S. Army an' have energy left over! Wow! She's somethin' to write home about! Well, not to my mother, please."

Conversation makes Bud and me hungry. We find a bistro and order some food. We eat without any further conversation, a rare moment of silence.

I walk Bud back to the compound at the port and we exchange powerful handshakes. As he goes through the gate, he returns the sentries' salutes. I watch him walk very slowly, hands in his pockets, he appears to be staring down at the ground.

Me? I'm going back to the hotel.

Chapter Forty-One

Time now is 1430 hours. I wander downstairs, hoping to get into a friendly conversation with Claude. We've never once had a real chat in the more than two weeks since I first met the group. As usual Claude is at his desk. He looks up at me as I approach.

"*Bon après midi, Claude. Comment ça va*?" He nods and shrugs his shoulders but doesn't look away. I take this as an invitation to continue.

Finally, after a very long pause, he speaks. "*Alles gut...er, ah...ça va bien, monsieur*."

"*Das gute, Claude*!" It would have been foolish of me to totally ignore his lapse into German. It's possible he and I haven't conversed because he doesn't speak French fluently and I don't know enough German to sustain a dialogue. At any rate, Claude is greatly amused at my attempt to speak the language. He laughs! We try to out-laugh one another. He easily wins this contest.

"*Ja*! *Das ist gute*! *Du habst gutmutigkeit, Léon*!"

I think he's telling me I have a good disposition. He continues to smile at me in an unusually friendly kind of way. Anyway, I've just about exhausted my German vocabulary. I've got to be careful not to lapse into Yiddish! I switch back to French.

"*Tiens, Claude*. I have to get some clothes from the store. Shirts and socks and underwear. Things like that."

He gives me a look that says "What's that got to do with me?"

"I'd enjoy your company. It won't take more than half an hour. The clothing store isn't more than five minutes from here. Can you take the time off? Come with me?"

He apologizes. "I must not leave my post at the desk. I can't go out of the hotel without Jean-Paul's or Robert's permission." He frowns for a moment, holds up a finger to signal "just a moment," and rushes up the stairs to the second floor. I hear a door open and close; probably the door to Room 23. After a few suspenseful minutes the door opens and closes again and Claude comes back down the steps with, of all people...Michel.

"Léon, Michel will go with you. He wants to learn as much about Casa as you know. He's only been here for six weeks and hasn't spent much time outside the hotel. Isn't that right, Michel?" My request for Claude's companionship has backfired.

This time, Michel smiles at me when he grunts. Perhaps he, too, doesn't speak much French. I can't refuse his companionship. "Excellent, Michel. We can get to know each other better, too."

Although he seems to understand when anyone speaks in French, Michel's personal French vocabulary seems to be limited to a grunt. At least now he's smiling. As his chronological junior, I hold the door open for him as we leave the hotel. I seem to do all the talking, as a tour guide would. We turn right, head up the street, pass Bahroun-the-Barber's place and turn right again onto the narrow street where Achmed's clothing shop is located. Everything's fine.

Suddenly, I'm stopped by a man I'd never seen before. He's about 40, badly in need of a shave and clean clothes. I expect he's an Arab beggar. However, this man is not an Arab. He's a dark-skinned Caucasian. Michel and I stop and wait for the man to speak. He does. In Yiddish!

The man points at me. "*Du bist ein Yid*?" In view of the fact that Michel is standing next to me, the man couldn't have said anything more shocking than to ask me if I am a Jew. He repeats it several times as a statement. "*Du bist ein Yid*! *Du bist ein Yid*!" The man grasps my hand and grips my arm.

Michel hears and understands the four words addressed to me in Yiddish, which is similar to German. I quickly glance at Michel who has moved back two feet from us. He's looking at me with a deep frown and very visible anger. I don't think it is an expression of surprise, more of sinister satisfaction. His frown abruptly changes to a "now I gotcha" grin.

"*Quoi*? *Qu'est ce que vous disez*? *Je ne comprends pas du tout*!" I protest and rudely remove the man's hand from my arm. "I don't know you! Go away! Leave me alone! *Je ne vous connais pas*! *Allez vous en*! *Quittez moi*!" I move away and wave at Michel. "*Allons*! Let's go!" I continue toward Achmed's. I can feel my pulse pounding. Michel has stopped the man and is talking with him. I yell, "*Allez*! *Allez*! *Allez*! Go away!"

As I walk off, he shouts back at me in Yiddish. "The Americans just now released me from a prison camp with a lot of other Jews. I only want to be friendly and introduce you to my family. My daughter. There aren't many young Jews in Casa now!"

This can't be real. I'd very much like to see a Moroccan Jewish family. But, goddamn, this is the worst possible time. "*Michel*! *Ici Achmed*! *Viens*! *Viens*! Come here!"

Michel waves and catches up to me. I take a quick look back. The Moroccan Jew is standing there looking very forlorn, abandoned by one of his kind. I feel distressed, filled with conflicting emotions—and, for the first time, I feeel sickening fear.

If I had been alone, the least I'd have done is press some francs or dollars into his hand. Who can tell, under other circumstances I might have even taken him into Achmed's shop with me and fitted him with new, clean clothing. I might have even prevailed upon Bud to deliver some of his goodies to the man's house or room in the *Mellah*, the Jewish Quarter. But this encounter is a frightening and totally threatening experience witnessed by Michel, the one who wears the suit with the bulging left breast.

It is very hard for me to concentrate on clothing. I don't really hear Achmed's greeting. Michel is standing about three feet behind me. My pounding pulse and his heavy breathing are echoing loudly inside my head.

I think it is time for me to get that revolver from Bud. If Michel really wants to liquidate me, this incident surely has eliminated Michel's doubts concerning who I am and what I claim to be. This event, plus his obvious hatred for me, are all the motivation he needs to act on his own even without Jean-Paul's or Robert's permission.

I select several items from Achmed's tables, pay him and start to leave. Achmed doesn't realize the significance of his question. "How is your good friend, the American Lieutenant?"

Oh, what awful timing! I nervously tell Achmed, "Haven't seen him lately. Have you?" But I recognize the situation is hopeless. Michel walks behind me all the way back to the hotel. All I can think about now is how to get the hideout gun from Bud. He is only a half block away from the hotel—I hope. That "half block" seems like a mile.

Michel holds the door for me and we enter the hotel. Claude greets us with "Glad you came back. Everyone is here now. Jean-Paul wants to see all of us in ten minutes. Big things are happening, I think!"

If I don't act now, I may never have another opportunity to get them all at the same time. I tell Claude and Michel I will take my new things to my room and join them in ten minutes. Michel is very quiet; not even a grunt. Claude just says "*Ja*" and goes into his room behind the desk. Michel heads up the stairs.

I quietly put my bundle of clothing on the floor alongside Claude's desk and run like an Olympic sprinter down the block toward the alley. *Oh, Bud. Please be there*! He is. "Bud! This is it! Give me the gun, quick! And keep the engine running!"

Bud responds instantly. He presses the gun into my outstretched hand. "I'll move the jeep to the right of the hotel door...with the engine running."

I pocket the gun, run back to the hotel, pick up my clothes, climb the stairs, go to my room, wash my face and hands, wet my hair, leave my room, take a deep breath and knock one more time on the door to Room 23.

Chapter Forty-Two

Yes, they are all here. Jean-Paul, Robert, Michel, Georgette, Christine, Henri, Jules, André and Philippe. Only Claude is not here. Probably hasn't been given permission to leave his post. If I have to get out in a hurry, and the only way out is the front door of the hotel, this means I will have to pass him. The most significant thing is the group's visible change in attitude toward me. Georgette isn't blowing me kisses or wiggling her fingers at me. Jean-Paul and Robert are frowning. Henri, Jules, André and Philippe look as empty-headed as ever. Christine? I didn't get to know her at all. But Michel has changed severely, for the worse. He looks like the proverbial cat that swallowed the canary. My pretend-to-be-happy "*Salut*!" is returned without enthusiasm.

This looks bad...for me. I put my hand in the right pocket of my trousers and gain some comfort from the feel of the gun's steel.

After what seems like an interminable period of silence, Jean-Paul speaks. "*Cher Léon*. We've been having some very serious discussions about how you can best fit into our organization." His tone is sarcastic.

I try not to betray my nervousness. "Very good! Jean-Paul, as you know, I am eager to get some important assignments from you and Robert." I'm not smiling as I study the two men for reactions.

Jean-Paul continues. "We now have an assignment for you. Everyone thinks it is perfect."

Robert smiles at me as he picks up the thread. "Yes. It's so important we've asked Michel to give you the details...privately."

Jean-Paul and Michel nod in agreement. Everyone else in the room is absolutely quiet, motionless. Michel rises and, with a smug smile, points a finger at me then at the door. I stand up and follow him into the hall. My adrenaline is pumping. My right hand is in my pocket, gripping the gun, feeling the trigger with my finger. Michel opens the door to my room and goes in. I follow, remove the gun from my pocket. With my finger firmly on the trigger, I cover the gun with my left hand.

As soon as we are inside the room, Michel whirls on me. In his right hand is a Luger pointed directly at my forehead! He's about an arm's length from me, close enough for me to see death in his eyes. My death!

He hoarsely demands, "*Jetzt aber schnell*! *Wer bist du*? *Scheisskerl*! Quick! Who are you? Shithead!"

I am pure reaction. I rapidly duck to the left and fire from the waist. Michel's gun goes off at the same instant. I'm deafened and feel an excruciating burning on the right side of my head. Michel doubles up, falls backward and hits the floor hard.

I dash into the hallway. The others will have thought both gunshots were a single blast and are waiting for Michel's report of the successful completion of his assignment. "*Auftrag vollstændig, meine Herren*! The task is done, gentlemen!"

I'm not sure how many flying steps I take as I rush down to the first floor. Claude comes out of his room and sees me racing for the front door. He reaches under his desk. I point my gun at him and, without stopping or slowing down, shout in German, "*Halt*! *HALT*!"

I am on the street now and, bless him, Bud's standing alongside his Jeep, engine running. He jumps in behind the wheel and we take off at maximum speed! Still gripping the revolver in my right hand, I tightly grip the windshield's metal rim with my left hand and press the side of my head with my right hand. The pain is piercing, burning.

I shout, "I'm hit! Get the MPs and SPs rolling right now! Get those ten Nazi bastards!"

As we speed toward the military compound, Bud has a walkie-talkie in his right hand. He's giving some kind of code word and the number 10 to whoever's on the other end of the radio. He also shouts, "My passenger is wounded. Standby with the medics! We'll be there in three minutes!"

Chapter Forty-Three

No more than two minutes after Bud's radio instructions, six jeeps and a troop-transport truck loaded with Army and Navy officers and rifle-armed MPs and SPs race by in the opposite direction.

Anxiously, I look at my right hand. No blood! How come? If I've been hit in the head, there should be lots of blood. On the other hand, if I've been hit in the head, I shouldn't be conscious and riding in a sitting position in a Jeep! I am very dizzy and seriously nauseated.

"Hol' on we're goin' into the compound now!"

An officer at the gate jumps aside and waves us through. I'm sure Bud would have run right over him. He's not slowing down for anybody or anything. The Jeep screeches to an abrupt stop at one of the Quonsets. Several men, officers and enlisteds, are outside waiting for us. Two of the enlisted men grab me. They're trying to carry me out of the jeep. I shout "I'm okay. It's my head that's been hit!"

They let go of me. But I can't keep my balance and start retching as I lean on one of the soldiers. They hurry me into the building. Apparently, it's the hospital. I'm hustled onto a gurney. Several people shout and race about, moving all sorts of tables loaded with equipment up to my side. Someone's checking my blood pressure; another's counting my pulse.

An officer with medical insignia on his collar, pulls my hand away from my head and looks into my ear canals with one of those pointed-end flashlights. I remember the device well from my childhood, when doctors made house calls and my mother would call the doctor to come look at my earache. The one I have now is the "grand-daddy" of all earaches! It extends from the back of my neck to the top of my head. The doctor brings out a tuning fork, strikes it on the edge of a table, places it against my temple and asks me if I hear the tone. "No, I can't."

The doctor announces "You must have taken quite a loud noise in this ear. A gunshot? Take these pills, two now and one every three hours. They'll help you with the dizziness and nausea, a natural loss of equilibrium when the inner ear's been severely shocked. Take these aspirin as you need them for pain. You may have trouble with your hearing for a day or two. But, it will gradually improve."

Bud looks relieved. "My C.O. wants to see us as soon as you can make it."

"I can make it now...if you let me lean on you so I don't fall over. Where's your C.O.?"

"He's waiting for us in a room down the hall. Okay? Can you handle it?"

An officer, a major, stands up as we enter the room. Bud salutes and introduces another man. "Meet Colonel Hauser."

I can only say, "Hi. Mind if I sit down?" So, there really is a Hauser who signed the papers Bud got for me. "Happy to meet you, Colonel. In fact, at this moment I'm happy to be able to meet anybody!"

Hauser sits. Bud sits. Both are staring at me.

"Something wrong?" I ask.

Colonel Hauser speaks first. "No, no. I'm delighted the way this has turned out. Commander Humphries of Navy intelligence will be right over. He's eager, as I am, to debrief you while the whole thing's fresh." A knock on the door startles me. I jump instinctively and fall back into my chair with dizziness and nausea. But this knock only announces it's "Hot coffee time."

Commander Humphries comes in right behind the coffee mugs. Introductions are made. And the debriefing starts. I recite the entire chain of events, starting from the time I met Bud and we planned this venture. An Army officer comes in and reports to Hauser that, besides a dead man who was shot at close range in the stomach area and clutching a Luger in his right hand, they arrested nine other people in civilian clothes. So, this must have happened within minutes of my escape from the hotel. I am filled with admiration for the MPs and SPs, really. I give the names and descriptions of the ten members of the group. These match the people arrested at the hotel, including the dead man. They found a short-wave radio transmitter and receiver on the third floor and an antenna on the roof.

Commander Humphries says, "Mister Wortman, I think we had better get you out of Casablanca as fast as we can get you on a ship going anywhere! We can't be sure we've got the whole lot. And if not, you can bet one of them will be gunning for you."

Colonel Hauser agrees and says to the commander, "We'd better change his appearance as much as we can while you locate a ship."

So, my goatee, my favorite adornment must come off. My hair is cut short. Commander Humphries says he can round up a uniform and IDs for me. He picks up the phone, gives orders, looks at me and asks, "Hope you don't mind becoming a Lieutenant Senior Grade, USN?"

I try to appear nonchalant about the whole affair. "Okay with me. Sometimes, during the past two, or is it three weeks, I've not always been sure who I really am anyway."

The uniform arrives. A set of suntans, handsome tropical worsted, beige, with twin epaulets, two gold stripes and a matching cap. I point at my well worn socks and shoes.

"What size?"

"Ten and a half, C."

Another phone call. In less than fifteen minutes I'm completely reclothed, including khaki T-shirt and skivvies, black socks and black shoes. The uniform fits; well...the fit is pretty good.

The phone rings. It's for Commander Humphries. "A ship, a freighter is leaving in a convoy within the hour for the Mediterranean, probably Oran. We've told the officer of the armed guard to expect a Lt. Leon Wortman to come aboard in ten minutes."

To myself I say, *Rest in peace, Léon Dejacques.*

Commander Humphries announces, "I'm going to suggest to your chief he recommend you for the Distinguished Service Medal."

Bud is teary-eyed. I am all choked up. We give each other bear hugs and shake hands good-bye.

Bud slowly drawls, "Those were some mighty nasty shadows y'all caught!"

Will I ever have the pleasure of seeing Bud again? *Qui sait?* Who knows?

Chapter Forty-Four

The freighter sails north and east from Casablanca in a convoy under the protection of a large number of continuously zig-zagging U.S. Navy warships. I don't think anybody on board the ship sleeps during the run to the port of Oran. Certainly I don't. We pass through the relatively narrow, only 12 miles wide, Strait of Gibraltar. The night is moonless, dark. It is open sea between the northern tip of Spanish Morocco and the Rock of Gibraltar, a highly productive area for Nazi scouting planes and U-Boats on the prowl. We come through without incident.

By morning, the freighter drops anchor a mile or so outside Oran's harbor. As at Casa, possibly more so, the port is filled with debris from the invasion. Enemy submarines, destroyers, freighters, large and small craft lay on the bottom of the harbor with only the tops of their conning towers, bridges and masts visible. I understand the invasion of Algeria, especially at Oran, was strenuously resisted by the French. Although no major French warships were involved, the French fought with surprising energy to defend the port.

Today, the sun and sky are bright and clear. The earache is tolerable. No more nausea. The Mediterranean is slightly choppy. A lovely day, nice enough to make one forget the tension of Casablanca and think about the future. I'm sure Colonel Hauser and Commander Humphries, one or the other or both, will advise my Chief back in New York City about the conclusion of my French Morocco adventure and my present whereabouts.

I do feel some eagerness to get back to New York. Wonder how my family is. All I can do now is wonder. I'm on the bridge-deck of the ship, and what do I see as I lean over the ship's starboard side, gazing without purpose at the shore? A liberty boat, the open type generally used to transport men and light materials between ships or to and from the shore, is approaching. Three sailors in fatigues are on the boat. One is the coxs'n, who controls the steering and the engine, and two ordinary seamen who act as aides. One of the three calls out, "Is Lieutenant Leon Wortman on board, sir! We've come to take him ashore."

The only supplies I own, other than the uniform I'm wearing, are my overnight acquisitions from the purser's slop chest: a tooth brush, tube of tooth paste, sunglasses, a pipe, matches and a small pouch of tobacco. So, in a matter of minutes, I'm all packed, shake hands with the ship's Captain and the officer of the Navy Armed Guard, scramble down the Jacob's Ladder and drop onto the liberty boat's deck. Away we go, toward the shore of Oran!

This is one of the loveliest day's I've seen in a long time. Even the white caps of the lazily breaking waves seem peaceful and quiet. I fill and light my pipe. I climb onto the boat's narrow gunnel, seize the waist-high pipe-railing with my left hand, grasp the visor of my tropical worsted uniform cap and puff contentedly on my pipe. Now I really feel like John Wayne, powerful, masculine, even immodestly handsome as I direct my tiny, gallant "armada" toward shore. A bit like the famous painting of George Washington crossing the Delaware.

The coxs'n stammers. "Er, sir. I, I shouldn't s-stand up th-there if I were you!"

Before I can look at him and reply, the liberty boat catches a wave on its beam, slams down and tosses me ass over teakettle into the Mediterranean! I come up with the officer's cap on my head, the pipe clenched in my teeth and my sunglasses still perched firmly on my nose.

The coxswain turns the craft in a circle and draws alongside me. The two other sailors hold grappling hooks, extending them for me to grab hold. Finally, dripping wet, soaked through and through, I take the coxs'n's advice and plop down on the boat's deck. The three sailors are grinning, mouths closed, gasping for air, making suffocating sounds as they stare wide-eyed at me. The absurdity of the picture gets to me.

I call out, "All right! Officers don't have to listen to coxs'ns!" And I break into loud, raucous laughter as I fall backward, arms outstretched and look skyward. This makes it impossible for my three rescuers to hold it in any longer. They literally explode into great and uncontrolled howls of laughter.

By the time we reach the dock, we calm down a bit. The three sailors salute as I step out of the boat. My "drowned rat" appearance tells everyone at the dock a very complete story.

Two MPs and a jeep are waiting for me. "Lieutenant Wortman, sir?"

"Yes?"

"We are to escort you to Colonel Diederich's office."

"Whose office?"

"Colonel Diederich, sir, is the C.O."

Adopting a devil-may-care style to match my appearance, I wave at my audience of smiling sailors as I climb into the jeep. We drive off.

The Colonel is waiting impatiently at his desk. One look at me and he slams his pencil down on his desk and shouts, "What'n hell happened to you?"

"Would you believe I'm rehearsing a comedy routine?"

"Okay, wiseguy. I doubt very much Patton will find it funny. The general's command staff has already started its meeting. Get your damp rear over to Building-D as fast as you can. They're expecting you to participate." He looks down, slowly shakes his head and then waves me toward the door. "I don't know, in fact I don't care what you tell them. But, one thing for sure, if Patton's there, you'd better have a damn good story to tell or you'll be busted to the lowest rank in the forces. They'll invent a low rank just for you!"

I'm a spy, a species considered by many career military people to have already attained the lowest possible rank. What's more, I'm wearing a borrowed Navy officer's uniform. However, when he says "I'll have new military IDs made up for you. You'd better pick them up on your way out," I realize he knows who I am. Casablanca must have notified him that I am on my way to Oran for new orders. Does he know I report to the O.S.S. in New York City? I don't ask any questions. Not now.

The Chief back in New York City must be wondering why he hasn't heard from me. I hope he hasn't sent someone to notify my family, as he once sent me to the Hotel Lafayette in New York to break the news to the wife of a field agent who disappeared in North Africa. When I return to pick up my IDs I'll ask the C.O. to set up a contact with The Chief...ASAP.

I'm very much lost in my own thoughts. The C.O.'s voice sounds as though it's coming from inside a hollow log in an underground pit. "I'll phone ahead so the guard will let you through without papers."

Where do I go from here?

The hollow log tells me, "Out the door, turn right, and walk straight ahead about 500 feet. You won't miss it."

Chapter Forty-Five

Building-D is a gigantic Quonset hut. Although not as tall, in this place it's as easy to find as the Empire State Building in New York City. The concentration of Jeeps, Army and Navy sedans, armed troops, MPs and SPs shout the presence of top brass. I'm not used to being saluted so my right arm begins to cramp as I briskly walk to Building-D. The guards and the officers at the door step aside to let me pass, unchallenged.

I am escorted inside the building to the staff's meeting room. The door is opened for me. There, clearly visible through the haze and pungent aroma of thick cigar smoke, is a long, very long conference table. Its top is barely visible under layers of maps, briefcases and forearms. The walls are covered with uniform jackets representing the major services and hats laden with brass and military insignia. I've never seen so much scrambled eggs. When all this started for me back in New York City, I was the guy who declared "I don't want to wear a uniform!" I think I'm in shock!

Forgetting my bedraggled appearance, I stand still and straight, uniform hat in my left hand, elbow bent. I'm pressing my hat tightly between my upper arm and the left side of my chest. This is intended to give the impression of an officer of the U.S. Navy at attention.

It's very quiet. All talk has stopped. The officers who have their backs to me and the door realize something is going on behind them. They swivel in their seats to see what's happening. I continue to stare directly ahead. Actually, I am waiting for someone to say something to me. I haven't the foggiest notion what this is all about, but it must be big. Finally, the officer in command, an Army man with one general's star on each collar tab, loudly declares "What'n hell happened to you, mister? No, don't tell us. You're the guy who took a swim in the Mediterranean!"

I am terribly, acutely embarrassed. This kind of recognition I don't need. "Yes, sir!" is my straight-face reply.

Everybody convulses with laughter, unrestrained. Loud laughs lead to coughing fits. I am convulsed with mortification. Oh, to have the power to make myself invisible! This unexpected informality relaxes me a bit as one of the Navy officers, captain's rank, steps up to me, smiles broadly, shakes my hand vigorously, leads me to a chair against the wall and hands me a cigar.

"Best joke since the war started!"

"Funniest thing I ever heard!"

"We needed a good laugh!"

Those are typical of the comments I hear and acknowledge with weak smiles and nods of my head. As I look around the room I realize I am, by many years, the youngest person in this assembly. Seems, invariably, I am the youngest.

Word travels fast. These men are remote from my level, but they are close enough to the action to have heard about my Frank Merriwell adventures in Casablanca. They've been completely briefed, including the details of my impressive ride in the liberty boat to the shore of Oran. Well, that last part really is funny.

The laughing and coughing die down and the general continues. "We've heard about your duty in Casablanca. Congratulations. Well done." The officers at the table interrupt the general with a brief round of applause. This is unbelievably gratifying. "General Patton specifically asked for you to attend part of this meeting. Fortunately, he's not in Oran at this minute. I'm not sure he'd find your appearance amusing. He parked his sense of humor when he took command of Operation Torch."

"Thank you, sir."

"General Patton's moving fast and, as usual, he wisely insists on planning far ahead. Strategies must include every possible contingency. It's no secret we're going into Italy as soon as we...and the British...eliminate Rommel's Korps, which shouldn't take too much longer."

"Yes, sir. Do I have a part in all this?"

"You do. Not a very big part, but it's a full-time part."

I'm eager to learn more. "Thank you, sir."

"Right, son. You'll get some of the details later. Right now you only need to know we'll want you to go into Italy in advance of the invasion, link up with the underground and feed back intelligence information directly to this command."

"I'm not fluent in Italian, sir."

"You look Italian to me. We hear you do a pretty good imitation in just about any language. And you can think on your feet, even when under pressure. We wanted to see how you'd react under the pressure of coming to this meeting looking as you do. Some of the officers at the conference table mumble approvals. I quickly look in the direction of the Navy captain. He catches my glance and with a slight movement of his head, signals he, too, approves.

What can I say but "Thank you, gentlemen!" At this point I'm excused, stand up, walk briskly to the door, do an about turn, put on my cap and give a smart salute as though I am a graduate of the naval academy.

I make straight for Colonel Diederich's office. He asks me how it went and especially enjoys hearing about the reaction of the staff. I confess to mixed feelings about Patton not being there. I'm one of his admirers. However, if the general had been there, he certainly would not be one of my admirers. He might have shipped me off to Italy this very afternoon just to get me out of his sight.

I request a telephone call or some reliable ability to contact my office in New York City. The best the C.O. can do is give me time to transmit a Morse code message to some receiving station near New York. That's okay with me. How soon can I do it? He'll contact the communications officer and we'll know in a couple of minutes. The colonel picks up one of the many phones on his desk and asks the communications officer to break away for about 15 minutes.

While we're waiting, I learn both Army and Navy intelligence people want to debrief me today. Okay. I'll hang around the base for the rest of the day. Can they put me up? I left all my money and papers with my civilian clothes at the Casablanca compound when I hastily departed. Sure. No problem. They'll provide me with a supply of American dollars along with my IDs before the day is over. Of course, I'll have to sign for the money. Regulations, you know. They'll quarter me in the Hotel Algeria for as long as I need it. But, I should plan on spending most of my time for the next few days on the base with O.N.I. and G-2. I intend to do that, at least until I hear from my Chief. Can the colonel arrange for another clean and pressed uniform, underwear, socks and stuff? Even a civilian suit will do.

"No, no! You'll do much better in a uniform in Oran...at least while Patton is around."

A knock on the door and the communications officer, a major, is introduced. Yes, if I can handle a telegraph key he can give me 15 minutes on a frequency that will get me into the communications center in New York City. Propagation's good in the direction of the northeast at this time of day.

"Son of a gun!" I fairly shout.

"What's the matter?"

"I know the very room where the message will be received. I've been in it before." *I remember the cryptic message I copied in unencoded English the first time I saw the room in the New York City Communications Center. And the message: "Get me the hell out of here! Get me the hell out of here!"* Great! Colonel Franken will probably send some young recruit from the Office to that mysterious, undecorated, isolated room to copy my encoded Morse-code message. Maybe they'll even telephone the text to him. It is written to be innocuous, inoffensive, of no value to the enemy; important only to me and The Chief. I expect in a short time, an answer from Colonel Franken, will be sent to me via the same route.

I didn't realize, as I do now, the full significance of that bizarre room and Colonel Bill Elliott, who was then my Chief, introducing me to it; of course, now I know it is one of the remarkable methods to his extravagant madness. However, the situation is very different this time. I don't want him to "Get me the hell out of here!" I like rubbing shoulders with the brass.

Chapter Forty-Six

Time drags. However, it is not wasted. I'm drafting the message for The Chief. Nothing's been said about encrypting my transmission so I assume I'll have to send it in cryptic English. I write and rewrite at least a dozen times before I have it down pat; brief and notably innocent. I don't feel I can identify my exact location. Perhaps the communications officer can insert the code name for the base. The Chief has to have the code name, at least, or he won't be able to send a reply, which is the entire point of this exercise. The message tells all he has to know at this moment.

> JF. ROOM 37. 224 WEST 57 STREET, NEW YORK CITY. TASK COMPLETED. WAITING INSTRUCTIONS. REPLY SOONEST. LW. SK

The "sk" at the end, keyed as one continuous series of letters, *dit-dit-dit-dah-dit-dah*, is the international symbol for end of transmission. Sending at the customary speed of 15 words per minute, all I need is less than a minute and a half on the air.

A telephone call from the communications officer to Colonel Diederich's desk summons me. "Come to the communications building now." It is a large hut behind the C.O.'s. About 300 feet beyond it is a cluster of radio antennas pointing in assorted directions; a genuine "antenna farm." A camouflage-painted mobile-communications van designated SCR-299 is parked alongside the communications building. I recall hearing reports it has a 500-watt multi-band transmitter and assorted receivers. The Signal Corps had been developing and refining it early this year. An Army sergeant is waiting for me. He directs me to enter the van and gives me brief instructions.

I sit down at the small, metal desk-top at the center of a rack of equipment. When I am ready to start, I am to put on the headset and wait to hear a voice: "go-ahead." Use the manual telegraph key to make my transmission. Wait for a voice to acknowledge the message left here okay and was received okay at the other end, then leave the van. However, first thing, my message must be written out beforehand and given to the communications officer for encryption and scheduling. I hand the sergeant the sheet on which I had scribbled the message.

"Won't take more than a couple of minutes, sir. Be right back."

In less than 10 minutes the sergeant is back with my message neatly typed. Code groups have replaced The Chief's name and address and the amusing English-language word "gobblegobble" substituted for my location. Must say the base's code name is very American. The sergeant tells me the code name is changed several times a day. It will be checked at the other end, the receiving end, verified and delivered within minutes.

I put on the headset and, while waiting for the "go ahead," my mind recreates the scene in the secluded room in New York City. If The Chief hasn't developed a different scheme, his operator will copy the message in longhand, grab a cab to the Office and hand the message to The Chief. He might have it as quickly as fifteen minutes after I send it.

Let's see. It's now about 1120 hours here—7:20 A.M. in New York City. If I start sending at 1130, allowing time for decoding and verification, The Chief can have it in on his desk by, say, between 8:00 and 9:00 A.M. He'll probably take half an hour to prepare his response and send one of the guys to the Communications Center to transmit it back to gobblegobble. Allow another 15 minutes for the cab ride. This brings the time in Oran to 1230 or 1330. Another 10 minutes for encoding the message. Give communications at gobblegobble 10 minutes to decode Joe's reply; five minutes to get it to me. So, in about an hour and a half or two hours from now, I might learn what happens next. Oh, the fabulous wonders of modern communications in December 1942!

"Standby, please!" It's a voice in my headset." Pause. "Go ahead!"

A minute later, after I key the *sk* ending, the voice says "That's all. Thank you."

I quit the van and return to the C.O.'s building where I'm taken to a small, windowless room furnished only with a small desk, a telephone, a chalk board on the wall and half a dozen chairs. It's hot in here. Nothing to do but wait. Sit down. Tap my fingers on the desk. Stand up. Do a small fox-trot around the room. Now a rumba. Then a tango. Gad, I'm bored. The coarse ring of the telephone explodes violently in the room. My reveries return to realities. No one else is in the room so, naturally, I pick up the phone.

"Hello?"

"Hello, Wortman." It's Colonel Diederich.

"Any word yet from New York City?"

"No. Maybe later. But you do have some visitors."

"Me? Who?"

"I'll send them to you." Click.

In a few seconds, there's a smart rap of knuckles on the door. Before I can ask "Who's there?" the door is opened and four men come in, two in Army and two in Navy uniforms. Introductions all around. They're from G-2 and O.N.I. Can we chat for an hour or two? Sure. They sit down and open their briefcases. Take out pads and pencils. Close their briefcases. Set them alongside their chairs. Look at me with friendly smiles. As I return their silent offers of friendship, their faces dissolve into those of Jean-Paul, Michel, Robert and Claude. I rub my eyes to wipe away images I'd just as soon forget. I'm with my own people now. A thought flashes. The Casablanca experience has been more disturbing than I have been willing to admit to myself. I need some recreation. I'll spend my free time sightseeing. I can be Bud this time. Let somebody else be my guide.

The senior G-2 officer breaks the quiet. "Well, sir. Captain Wortman. Leon Wortman, isn't it?"

"Yes. Correct."

The senior O.N.I. officer adds, "We understand you've just returned to Oran from Casablanca. That right?"

"Not exactly. I just *arrived* in Oran for the first time, *from* Casablanca." I'm feeling tired. No silly questions, please. Silly? Heck, no. They're probably lawyers in civilian life. We are all 90-day wonders. They're checking out my sense of reality. Okay. I can buy the approach.

We, the five of us, spend the next three or so hours in a dialog, mostly their questions and my answers. We're having a series of exchanges interrupted frequently by deliveries of coffee and doughnuts. They have maps of French Morocco; even a map of Casablanca I've never seen before. It's a lot more detailed than the one I read on the destroyer. Nuts! Why didn't The Chief get one like this for me? I indicate all the points on the map I'd been to and why I'd been there. Who I'd met. What we talked about. On and on, in the style of four prosecutors and one tired defendant. This debriefing seems to have no perceptible end.

At last we're finished. The scene goes into reverse motion. Open briefcases. Insert pads and pencils. Close briefcases. Stand up. Shake hands. Put on hats. Open the door. Turn to leave the room.

"Oh, by the way, Wortman, let's do this again tomorrow. Same time and place. Okay?"

Instinctively, I want to say "no." But, I have no other appointments, no excuses, and they have a job to do. "Sure. See you in this room. Tomorrow. Same time. By the way. Can you help me find Army Lieutenant Bud Corval? I'd very much like to thank him for his help in doing the Casablanca thing. I left in one helluva hurry, you know."

The senior G-2 officer replies. "He's G-2, isn't he? Sorry. Even if we knew his whereabouts, we're not permitted to reveal them." They leave. I leave and go to the C.O.'s office. The colonel hands me my new IDs, a pocketful of money and a form to sign. My eyes ask the question.

"Sorry, Wortman. Nothing yet from New York City."

Colonel Diederich directs me to the quartermaster building. They are out of Army officer uniforms. If I don't mind, he's arranged for me to be outfitted with a new Navy uniform, couple of shirts, a black tie, cap, shoes, socks, underwear and toilet articles.

"Come back to my office for transportation to the hotel. Want to have dinner on the base or at the hotel?"

Frankly, at the moment, I don't feel social or conversational. "I'm more used to hotel food. So, if you don't mind...raincheck?" What's more, I'm sorely in need of a good night's sleep. No Michel. No Georgette. Just solid, uninterrupted, restful sleep.

Damn you, Chief, for keeping me waiting.

Chapter Forty-Seven

What a luxury! Twelve hours of unbroken sleep! I awaken slowly, yawning, stretching and thinking about the marvels of a steaming hot shower. Last one was on the ship from Casablanca; a delicious experience. A quick check of my room and I realize the next hot shower will have to be somewhere on the base. No hot water in the hotel. My discomfort, hearing and sense of balance are recovering nicely from the blast of Michel's Luger.

The Chief must have sent me an answer by now. I am eager to get back to the C.O.'s office and read it. First, I'll wash and shave as best I can. Second, I shall grab a quick breakfast in the hotel's dining room. I have no desire to spend time wandering around in search of a café, not right now. As soon as I get official business out of the way I can wander to my heart's content. It would be outstanding to locate Bud and do the tourist bit together. I'll ask Colonel Diederich to help me locate Bud. After a breakfast of something resembling the appearance of but not the taste of fresh scrambled eggs washed down with strong, thick, bitter and dark Algerian coffee, I head for the base.

Marvelous weather, every bit as nice as—no, even better than—Casablanca's. I walk at a fast pace in the direction of the base. Can't miss it. All military traffic, and there's lots of it, focuses on one direction. I follow the herd, saluting as I go. Everybody's in full uniform, wearing ties. Patton's men, obviously. Wonder if his crews wear ties and jackets while inside their tanks and armored vehicles in pursuit of the enemy! Don't think I'd like to be one of them. But, I do seem to be getting closer and closer to becoming part of that kind of picture. Patton says he wants me, but The Chief may have some other priorities in mind.

My IDs check out okay at the gate. The MPs salute and step aside. I walk into the base and head for the C.O.'s building. He greets me with an offer of a cup of coffee, which I need to dilute the taste of the Arabian stuff.

"No word from New York City, Wortman."

"Maybe my Chief's out of town. He does practically commute between New York City and Washington. He's a lieutenant colonel, you know." I'm bragging. In the military hierarchy, there is status in making it known you report directly to brass.

Colonel Diederich looks me over, rubs his chin and frowns. "Maybe we've put you in the wrong service. You should be in Army khakis, not Navy blues. Shall we make the change? Won't take but a minute."

I dramatize my reply with a negative shake of my head while tightly wrapping my arms around each other. "Not necessary, sir. In fact I think, for the moment, I look much better in Navy blue color than I do in khaki."

The Chief and I once had a half-serious discussion about our preferences between the two services. He's for the Army. I favor the Navy, if I had to make a choice. But I don't have to. Matter of fact, the O.S.S. is predominantly Army. Perhaps it is because Bill Donovan is a decorated veteran of the World War I Army and, when he was given the okay to start the intelligence activity, he concentrated his recruiting among former buddies. The Chief obviously chose the Army. As far as I know, I'm the only one from the New York Office who is dressed Navy. I have the uncomfortable feeling The Chief doesn't really like my attitude, as far as Army/Navy go. But he tolerates it.

Heck, this isn't the only conflict the O.S.S. has to deal with. Before I left on my assignment, it was well known around the Office in New York City "Wild Bill" Donovan continuously has friction with both the Army and Navy commands in Washington. Everybody wants to have the intelligence responsibility. They don't buy Donovan's approach—a central intelligence group. Donovan won't buy any other resolution.

Donovan, they say, isn't exactly buddy-buddy with J. Edgar Hoover either. Hoover argues the F.B.I. should have jurisdiction and responsibility for all intelligence and counter-intelligence work overseas as well as in the United States. They compromised. In addition to its usual domestic U.S. activities, the F.B.I. is responsible for Latin America surveillance, detection. surveillance and apprehension of enemy agents. The rest of the world belongs to the O.S.S.

All this is hearsay as far as I'm concerned. I haven't been invited to participate in interagency politics, nor do I want to. For my part, all the Army and Navy execs I've met overseas have been completely friendly and cooperative. Ignoring that murderous vermin, Lt. Colonel W. C. Elliott, not one single exception. Couldn't ask for better relations, which is more than I can say for any O.S.S. execs who might be in the area. I've never heard a word from them. Well, as far as the O.S.S. goes, maybe I'm more alone than I realized I'd ever be.

"Colonel Diederich, mind if I hang around while I wait for the answer from New York?"

"Not one bit. As long as you don't make my office your hangout. This is going to be one helluva day for me. Just look at those convoys out there! American. British. Dutch. You name any one of our allies. They've probably got a ship or two trying to drop anchor here. The Mediterranean has enough ships in it right now to raise the level of the sea!"

"I'll stay out of your way, sir. I'll wander around here and there until I hear from New York." I move toward the door. "I have to be back here about 1430 this afternoon for more debriefing with G-2 and O.N.I."

"Stop at communications. I'll telephone and let them know you're available. You'll pick up your mail, if any, at the communications officer's desk. Okay?"

"You bet...er, yes sir!" I leave and head for communications.

The major makes me feel welcome, even though the traffic of men and women in and out of his office is a bit staggering. He's okay. "The channels to New York should open up in about an hour. Your message might come in then. Hang around, if you want to. Find a chair for yourself—right outside my office."

Of course! Shame on me. I hadn't thought of it. The band might have gone dead right after my transmission. Nobody can win an argument with the heavy-side layer and its effect on radio-wave propagation!

Sure enough, about an hour and a half further into the day I see a sergeant carrying several sealed brown envelopes go into the communications office and close the door. He's delivering the "mail." The sergeant comes out of the office in a few minutes, empty handed. Fifteen minutes later, the colonel's aide opens his door and signals me to come in.

"You've been waiting for this, I believe."

I literally snatch the envelope, tear open its flap and remove the single sheet of paper.

LW. FIND TRANSPORTATION TO HOME OFFICE IMMEDIATELY FOR NEW ASSIGNMENT. CHIEF. SK

Short and direct. Nothing ambiguous. He's still stingy with praise. Typical. Not surprising. However, he doesn't know his instructions have just put me between the proverbial rock and a hard place. Patton wants me in Oran and Italy. The Chief wants me back in New York. If I don't return, The Chief might have me bumped off for disobedience. If I do return, Patton can have me shot for desertion! Both can get me for impersonating a military officer in a combat area! Ouch!

Chapter Forty-Eight

I present the drama of my dilemma to Colonel Diederich. The colonel smiles. "There's another option. You can tell your Chief about Patton's demands on you and you'll gladly respond to your Chief's orders...provided he puts them in writing. Then act accordingly...and officially."

"There's still one more," I suggest. "I can ask you to convey my regrets to the command staff but I actually have received written orders—the radio message I received in writing this morning from Colonel Franken. And meaning no offense Colonel Diederich, sir, you are obliged to arrange immediate transportation for me in the next convoy departing Oran for the United States." This combines my choice of options with an indirect request for a berth, without delay, on a ship, any kind of ship headed in the direction of the United States.

Colonel Diederich gets the message. He swivels his chair, opens the door to the steel security-safe behind him, takes out a folder, shuffles some papers, returns the folder to the safe, shut its door and swivels to face me.

The colonel looks me straight in the eyes and smiles. "A convoy assembles at sunup tomorrow morning. Some of the ships are going directly to New York City."

My eyes open wide. This is good news.

"You realize their destinations may be changed at any time. The final decisions about specific ships are made in...well, somewhere in the United States. Best I can do is put you on a ship *possibly* going to New York City. Okay?"

"Great with me! Oops. I'm scheduled for more debriefing this afternoon."

"We can still put you on board a ship later today."

"I'm for that, colonel!"

"I suggest you go to the quartermaster and exchange your Navy blues for a couple of plain khaki shirt and pants...without insignia."

"I'm busted from Navy Lieutenant to civilian?"

"That's war, Wortman." He has a sense of humor about the whole thing, too.

"Will I board a freighter or a warship? It doesn't really matter to me."

"Let's wait to see. I can't identify the ship for you until you leave Oran. Security. I'll have a Navy Officer escort you to the ship with special orders for its skipper. I'll set up the paperwork. Go to the quartermaster and come back here after the debriefing. Did you leave anything of value at the hotel?"

"No, sir."

"Good. Let me have the Navy IDs I issued you. We'll check you out of the hotel. You can have lunch in the room where you'll be debriefed. I'll have food sent in about 1300. That way we won't have to get involved in complicated paper work...new IDs and extra documents. I like to keep things simple—when I can."

He gazes off into space. "It isn't always this easy. Better go now, Wortman. See you later today." He picks up a telephone and looks away.

I'm excited about this turn of things. I leave the colonel's office and head for the quartermaster's building. They've been alerted and know what to do. I swap my uniform for unmarked khakis and stroll around the area for some needed exercise. Nobody salutes me now.

Lunch is unexciting. A salty ham or spam sandwich on tasteless white bread and a big mug of unsweetened coffee. There should be a special medal for this unsung hero: coffee. No American can function without a regular ration of hot coffee. Never mind the flavor. Just make it American and hot!

The four 90-day wonders from intelligence are prompt. The interrogation continues. Most questions are the same as yesterday's...rephrased. So are my answers.

As soon as they leave, I go to Colonel Diederich's office. The colonel's aide, a major who doesn't offer a handshake or his name, intercepts me. He carefully looks me over, points to an empty chair and tells me to sit and he goes into the colonel's office. I feel very unimportant. Quite different from the lofty status I enjoyed yesterday.

The colonel's voice startles me. "Good luck, Wortman."

I stand and accept his handshake. "Thank you, sir. It's a special pleasure to know you. Maybe we'll meet again. In Italy?"

"Not likely. Even though you made the correct decision, I wish you had decided to stay here. That's a personal opinion. Nothing official."

We both laugh and shake hands again. The major doesn't really understand what's going on. Perhaps the colonel will fill him in.

The major looks directly at me. "I'll introduce you now to the Navy Officer who'll escort you to the ship right away."

The colonel's face wears a superficial smile. "And, Wortman, please don't wet your pants in the Mediterranean on the way out!"

I salute and turn to follow the major out of the building. I smile, but I feel a bit sad.

Without conversation, we wait a few minutes at the entrance to the C.O.'s building. A jeep with Shore Patrol markings and a SP driver pulls up. The major and I shake hands. He points to the jeep. I climb in alongside the driver and wave at the major as we quickly drive off. At the gate to the base we are joined by a Navy Lieutenant and another SP, both wearing sidearms. We drive to the dock where a liberty boat and crew are waiting. Colonel Diederich is one hell of a good organizer.

A lot of freighters are anchored out there. I can barely make them out but I do see several warships slowly circling the area beyond the merchant ships. They're providing a protective screen, no doubt. This time I definitely sit down in the liberty boat.

The ride to the freighter is uneventful. The lieutenant carries a briefcase. He takes a sheaf of papers out of the case and, with a worried expression, repeatedly shuffles and reads them. He says he's trying to locate the ship. Ah! He's found it! He gives navigating directions to the coxs'n and settles back.

It's not a merchant ship we've been looking for. It's a Navy Supply Ship, a mother ship for the escort vessels. Even better than a merchant ship. In case of attack, it will be hugged and protected by the escort.

The coxs'n brings the liberty boat around to the starboard side of the ship. A Jacobs Ladder hangs over the ship's side. As we come in close to the ship, I become impressively aware of, almost mesmerized by the Mediterranean's movements. Although the sea isn't choppy, there are continuous wave swells at least six feet high. The liberty boat behaves like a cork bobbing up and down in an unsteady tub of water. As we get close to the Supply Ship's Jacobs Ladder, the coxswain tells me to stand up, estimate the movement of the liberty boat and, when the boat reaches its peak height, grab the Ladder tightly with my hands. When the liberty boat starts to drop away, scramble quickly up the Ladder.

I position myself. Arms outstretched. The movements are very rhythmic, like doing a slow motion tango with the liberty boat and the Supply Ship. The coxs'n shouts "*GO!*" I lean forward, grab the Ladder and scramble up to the top. A couple of sailors grab my arms and drag me over the side onto the deck. I am thoroughly soaked by the sea spray and chilled by the wind. The Navy Officer escort comes on board right behind me. A ship's officer calls for an aide and the lieutenant and I are escorted to the executive officer's cabin. A manila envelope is taken out of the briefcase and handed to the exec, a lieutenant commander. He reads its contents and looks up at me with a severe expression.

"Your name, mister?" He seems annoyed.

"Wortman, sir. Leon Wortman.

"I am Philips. You're a passenger on this ship, mister. You know that?"

"Yes, sir."

He stands up. He's over six feet tall. A full head of salt 'n pepper hair and a robust, sunburned complexion coupled with a toothy smile give him the look of a healthy, outdoor man in his late thirties or early forties. He appears to have a solidly muscled body and an upright posture. The commander is in superb physical condition. He offers a handshake. I accept. This friendly gesture almost crushes my hand. My Navy escort asks Commander Phillips to sign his log book to verify he's delivered me as ordered. He salutes the commander, shakes hands with me, and leaves the exec's cabin. *Au'voir Oran. Au'voir North Africa.*

The exec turns to me. "When we're alone, call me Don. Otherwise, I'm Commander Phillips. Let's see, where can I put you?"

"Close to the showers and the dining room will do just fine."

Don glances at me and ignores my attempted humor. "I know how we can handle this. The communications officer is short handed. Had to transfer some of his men to shore duty in Oran. He probably has a spare bunk, too. I'll ask him to come to my cabin as soon as he's off watch." He makes the phone call to communications and tells me the "junior" will be with us in ten minutes.

"This ship's scheduled to join the convoy sometime between 0400 and 0500 hours. We have been given a number, our position in the convoy. The navigating officers have the rendezvous points in their sailing papers. It's up to them to get us into our station as the convoy heads out of the Mediterranean into the Atlantic. Chow's from 1700 to 1900. You can sit at my table in the officers' saloon. There are coffee and substantial snacks available 'round the clock in the officers' saloon."

He's my kind of guy! An amiable disposition. Good thing, too. We'll be on this floating island for at least the next two to three weeks. It can be hell, I'm sure, to be on a ship with people you don't like or who try to give you a hard time. I don't expect, once the ship gets under weigh, Don will have any time for companionship or any activities not directly related to running the ship and its crew. I've heard that, on a military ship at sea, the executive officer is one of the busiest people.

The exec has one foot out the door of my quarters when he stops and turns his head toward me. "One more thing, Wortman. We're carrying a several young French women as passengers for work in the U.S. They're quartered in the sick bay down this deck's passageway." He points in the direction to the right. "There'll be no nonsense for me to have to deal with—I hope."

I shrug and tell him "Not from me Don. No sir."

A short time later, resting on my bunk and feeling very bored, a female form appears at the door to my room. She looks confused and with a most charming French accent and an umistakeable smile, apologizes. "Pardon, monsieur. I am confused by all these passageways and doors. *Je me sens perdu.* I feel lost. Can you help me locate my room?"

Time for me to revert to the French language. *"Non, non ma'amselle. Je crois que vous soyez à vôtre propre chambre.* No, no young lady. I believe you might be in the right room. Please do come in and sit down."

Her friendly smile and the lowering of her eyes tell me this trip home will be a most comfortable one. Certainly, not at all boring.

No doubt, in his drab New York office the Chief is carefully, meticulously planning my next overseas assignment. No need to hurry—not now.

Chapter Forty-Nine

Docking a large, incoming ship is a slow, laborious process. It demands the total concentration of officers and crews, both aboard the ship and those who work the tether-lines on the dock. Finally, the tugboat's lines are let go. With a reassuring toot-toot of its horn, the tug backs away, turns to port and steams off. Our gangplank is lowered and we are officially in the United States.

Don and the skipper appear in full uniform. They must file reports immediately. Several jeeps and pairs of SPs are waiting. Don confirms one of them is for me. "When you leave the gangplank the SPs will call your name." He extends his hand in farewell. My feelings are mixed as we have a prolonged handshake. He salutes me. I'm very moved by this gracious gesture. After all, I am not in uniform, not even disguised as a uniformed officer. I almost hate to go, but I can't stay.

My SP escort asks, "Where to, sir?"

"To a public telephone, first, please."

The SPs look at one another and simultaneously say, "Mike's!"

Mike's is a bar and grill, a small building just outside the compound. There's a pay phone just to the left of the structure. I borrow a nickel from the SPs and tell the telephone operator, "I want to place a collect call to New York City, Evergreen 9360." That's Merry's desk. "My name? Leon." I hope they remember who Leon is.

"Hello? Merry? Yes. It's really me...What?...I'm at the Navy base in Norfolk, Virginia...What?...Sorry, Merry. The connection's bad. Is Joe there? Great! Gotta talk to him. Yes. I might see you late this afternoon...if you can arrange transportation for me from here to there. Thanks, Merry."

Joe gets on the line. "Where the hell are you now?"

"Hi, Joe. I got your message and came as quickly as I could. I'm almost out of money, Joe and I'm in plain khakis. No...No papers. Can you fly me out of here to New York? You can? I'm to go to the military transportation office at Norfolk? Sure, Joe. Where am I right now? Outside the gate to the Navy base. I'm being escorted by two SPs and a jeep. No, no! I'm not in a jam. They're helping me get home. Okay. I'll wait at the airport at Military Transportation. Bob will meet the plane in New York? Will you fix me up with a hotel room? No, no, Joe. I had a good night's sleep. Dinner with you? At The Office? Sounds good to me. Bob will bring me directly to The Office? What's that? Okay. Bye, Joe."

The SPs stomp their cigarettes and I tell them specifically where I have to go. Of course, they know the location of the Military Transportation Office much better than I do. They've delivered and picked up prisoners there many, many times. I smile. They smile.

The drive to the airport's pretty wild. Through force of habit and in compliance with their orders, the SPs walk with me into the office, one on either side of me. It gives me a wonderful feeling of safety. They present two slips of paper to the sergeant at the desk. A receipt for delivery of the "goods," me. He signs them and hands one back to the SPs. Task completed, the SPs touch their index fingers to the side of their hat brims, a non-com salute for the sergeant. As they turn to leave the office, they give me a full salute. They're not sure who I am, obviously.

"What can I do for you, Mister er ah..." The sergeant looks down at the receipt and back up at me. "...Mister Wortman?"

No. He hasn't had a call mentioning my first or last name. Sure. I can sit here and wait for the call. The transportation office is open 24 hours. No. No message or calls from anyone named Joe. No. None from a Colonel Franken or a Merry either. A smile would permanently fracture his jaw. In civilian life, he must have been a clerk, one who dealt only with things, not with people. So, I'll just wait here in silence, ignoring this personality dynamo. He has a dull job. Well, it's a good match.

There is some activity. SPs and MPs drop in for a smoke and a cup of coffee in the back room. Nobody offers me a cup. I can wait for more gracious company. A woman of about 40, in a civilian dress, comes in, looks around the room and walks over to me. She looks down at me with a frown. "Your name, please."

"First or last?" I'm a little irritable. "Sorry, ma'am...Leon Wortman."

"May I see your ID, please?"

"Will a birthmark do?" Before she can answer, I add "I have no papers; none of any kind."

"Then you must be the man I'm looking for. If you had tried to fake an ID, I would have turned around and walked out. Here's a message for you from Joe." She hands me a brown envelope and leaves immediately without waiting for me to read whatever is inside. She's the first American woman I've seen in months. Probably she is O.S.S. I step into the empty washroom and open the envelope. There's a 20 dollar bill and a short message.

> Wortman. Air Corps DC3 leaves Norfolk at approx 2:30 p.m.. This is your travel pass. Show it to the sergeant. Bob meets you at Floyd Bennet. Lt. Col. J. Franken.

The sergeant cracks a miniature but detectable smile when he reads the note. "You got a couple more hours to wait, mister."

"I'll stretch my legs a bit around the airport."

"That won't take much stretching. This is a small airport."

"Is there any place inside the airport I can get a sandwich and a coke?" I'm fairly safe as long as I stay within the boundaries of the airport, which is mostly used by military people. There's not much civilian transportation available in this Navy town and, not being able to prove I'm legal, I still must avoid the local police.

"A sandwich counter's to the left about 200 feet."

I'm back in 30 minutes. Wish I had a tooth brush and strong tooth paste to get rid of the terrible taste that sandwich left in my mouth. The sergeant offers me some hard candy mints. They, and a glass full of cold water, do the job.

A sudden flurry of activity breaks the monotony. Four SPs with two sailors and two MPs with one Army man come into the room. The two sailors are handcuffed to each other. The Army man is handcuffed to one of the MPs. The sergeant confirms these are my traveling companions. I don't ask, I really don't want to know why they're in handcuffs. I study my wrists, wondering whether or not I'm more free than these military prisoners.

Chapter Fifty

The plane is on time. The SPs, MPs and their prisoners board first. I'm next. I still remember my first flight on an Air Corps plane last year when I flew to Albany, New York and Steve drove me to the Farm for survival training. I'll never forget the stormy weather sitting on the airplane's hard deck...and the terrible misery of air-sickness.

This time there are real seats. I don't have to sit on the bare deck with nothing to hold on to keep from being bounced around. This winter's weather is clear all the way north to the airport in Brooklyn. Bob's waiting with a car. We never did have much to say to one another. Our relationship hasn't changed. We exchange social rituals.

"Hi, Leon."

"Hi, Bob."

"Good flight?"

"Yeah. Good flight."

"The Chief's waiting for you."

"I know."

"Also, a friend of yours, Bill Brady, is with our outfit now."

"The hell you say! That's wonderful!"

We're both silent the rest of the ride into New York City. Bob drops me off at at a building just west of Fifth Avenue. Without hesitating, I go directly to The Office. Jason, the security man at the door recognizes me but asks for my ID anyway. Fortunately, Merry spots me at the door and clears me. A warm hug and a few kind words from her are the first nice things that have happened to me all day.

"You look great, Leon! Go right in. Joe's waiting for you."

Merry looks very, very nice. "How about a date sometime this week?"

"Sure. Sometime."

I knock on Joe's door and hear the familiar word from the unceremonious voice, "Come."

Joe gets up from behind his desk, comes around to the front and intercepts me with a vigorous handshake, steps back and studies me from head to toe.

"You smell like the sea."

"Well, I'm not surprised. I've been at sea for weeks. I need a hot fresh-water shower."

You can relax now. "Tomorrow you can buy a complete new wardrobe, on the expense account. Tell me all about what happened to you from the time you joined the destroyer and Operation Torch in Norfolk. No, no! Begin with how you got to Casablanca from the destroyer."

I'm curious about just how out-of-touch we've actually been. "Have you had any reports about me from Casablanca or Oran?"

"O.N.I. and G-2 let me know they had debriefed you but they wouldn't give me any details. Joe makes a disgusted expression. "Everything's classified these days. Other than that, from the time you left here for Norfolk, we've had no idea whether you were dead or alive."

"Did Colonel Diederich contact you from Oran?"

The Chief breaks into a smile. But doesn't answer my question. He can be exasperating.

My mouth's dry. "Joe, can we have a cup of coffee while we talk?"

He looks up at the door and shouts, "Merry! Coffee! For two, please!"

I'm not sure of the time. I've been through several time zones and, as a result, I've lost complete track. I comment on this to the Chief. He says he's not surprised. He can lose track of time without passing through time zones. He's been spending most of his time racing between Washington and New York.

"Chief, I've been on the move since land was sighted from the Supply Ship, maybe two days ago. I hear my buddy, Bill Brady, has joined us. Is he here or gone overseas?"

"No, Bill's still here. He's been asking about you ever since I received your message from Oran. He's become my right arm. Doing a good job for me. For us."

"I'd sure like to see him again."

"Tomorrow."

Of course I'm eager to hear about my next assignment. But one thing's certain. The Chief won't tell me what it is until I complete my report to him and he hears all the details about French Morocco and Algeria. He asks Merry to join us to make notes of my monologue.

I put on my best weary expression. "Frankly, Joe. I'm a bit tired of telling the story. I've told it once in Casablanca and several times in Oran." The Chief isn't moved at all.

"Too bad, Leon, but you aren't officially debriefed until you tell it to me."

"You're right, Joe. I'll give you the complete, unabridged version."

"Don't leave out anything. I want it all straight from you."

He dictates to Merry, "Official Debriefing. Leon A. Wortman, Field Agent, F.I.S., O.S.S., date, time and all the usual cover info."

I just heard some new initials. "What's F.I.S., Chief?"

"Foreign Information Section."

I look at Merry and apologize for some of the scenes I'll have to describe.

She smiles. "Don't give it another thought, Leon. I've heard it all before."

Joe leans forward for emphasis, looks me in the eye and slowly repeats himself. "Don't leave anything out. Not a single thing."

"Before we begin—it's a long story—can we order some food. I'm starved, especially for a corned beef sandwich from the Stage Deli, a bottle of Dr. Brown's Cel-Ray Tonic and a big, big glass of ice cold milk."

The Chief tells Merry to order food for three. "Corned beef, Dr. Brown's and lots of milk." She does so, telephoning from the Chief's desk.

I can taste it now. "Two sandwiches for me, Merry. With cole slaw on them."

For the next three hours I talk nonstop, between bites of corned beef sandwiches washed down with Dr. Brown's Cel-Ray Tonic and greedy gulps of milk. Wonder where Merry found the milk? The Stage Deli claims to be kosher, never serves milk with meat.

Joe wants details. I give him details. Hours of them. Merry's yawning, fighting cramped fingers and looking at her watch. I'm rubbing my eyes. The Chief gets our messages.

Mercifully, he announces, "Okay, Leon...for now. See you here in the morning, 0700."

Merry adds, "You're registered at the Henry Hudson Hotel on 57th Street."

"G'nite, Joe. G'nite Merry." I'm bushed.

Chapter Fifty-One

Promptly at 0700, Joe, Merry and I settle around the desk and my monologue continues. We take a stretch an hour later and I search for Bill Brady. This wonderful Irishman, one of my favorite people from civilian life, is champing at the bit to shake hands again. He's still in civilian clothes.

No words are necessary. We hug and growl sounds of satisfaction.

Bill tells me he introduced his mother to mine and they've become great friends, which I am delighted to hear.

"How is my mother, Bill?"

"Fantastic! In good health. Misses you. Doesn't know where you've been. My mother doesn't know either. I told my mother I may have to go overseas any day. She's learned not to ask questions, as your mother has learned. But, they've both guessed pretty close to the truth. We're goddamn spies."

"I don't know about you, Bill. But I'm a Shadow Catcher. I'm going to visit my mother soon as I can get a few hours to myself. Say! How about you and me taking our moms to dinner? I've never had the pleasure of meeting your mother."

"I like! I like! You'll get a kick out of my mother. Happy woman, like all Irish mothers!"

"Your Irish-Catholic mother and my Russian-Jewish mother together? This I have got to see!"

The Chief steps out of his office. "Okay, you guys. Continue your love affair later. Let's go, Leon. Merry. Ready?"

We resume where I'd left off and go straight on into lunch time. No phone calls are allowed to interrupt us unless, of course, they are from Washington, meaning Donovan. Sandwiches are brought in and the Chief suggests we talk while we chew our food. So much for "don't talk with food in your mouth!"

We quit the debriefing at the point where I call Joe from the transportation office at the Norfolk Airport. The three of us stand up, push our chairs back, stretch, yawn and sound off with deep sighs of relief. Finito! Accompli! Done!

Merry starts to leave the room when I remember, "My things, Merry? The stuff I left in The Office when I got my orders to leave?"

"Yes. You want them now, dear?"

"Not right now. They just came to mind. I'll get them later. Oh, Merry, I'd better have my IDs." I turn to the Chief, "Now, about the new wardrobe...on the expense account."

He scribbles something on a slip of paper and hands it to me. "The super-patriotic New York Police have been cracking down on young men not in uniform. Go to this place on Eighth Avenue, an Army and Navy Store. I'll phone the manager and tell him you're approved for a uniform. They'll have everything you need and bill us for whatever you buy. Get a uniform with—what rank did you say you wore when you left Casablanca and while you were in Oran?"

"Navy. Lieutenant. Senior Grade."

At the end of the afternoon, I return to The Office fully decked out in Navy blues, white shirt, black necktie, dark shoes, socks and, slung over my left arm, a Navy topcoat with shoulder boards. Jason stands up and salutes. Merry oohs and aahs! Most of the people in The Office are new and don't really know what to make of all this fuss. Joe steps out of his office to see what's causing the noise. He looks me over and nods his approval. I salute him. This is Caesar's Rome.

"How come you didn't get some ribbons for your jacket? Buy something. You look bare assed." He disappears into his office.

Bill suggests we have a reunion dinner together, tonight. "Invite Bob, too. He's loosened up a bit and wants to be accepted. You should get to know him better. He's really okay. Okay? You name the place."

Without hesitation, I suggest the Hotel Taft's dining room. It's as good as any, better than most. Vincent Lopez and his orchestra, if they're still playing the hotel as they've been doing for about 20 years, make nice music. But my real reason for the recommendation is his vocalist, Mary Elizabeth Sewell, a cute, petite reddish blond, a bundle of energy and fun I met while working at the studios of radio station WHN. She's not exactly "the girl next door." She hails from San Antonio, Texas, not Brooklyn. But it would be nice to see and hear her sing and laugh again. Just in case she's not there, I don't mention Mary Elizabeth to Bill and Bob. No point in all three of us risking disappointment.

We make a reservation for dinner at 9 o'clock and decide to head to the Hotel Taft's cocktail lounge where we can kick back and relax with a drink or two. I confirm Mary Elizabeth is on tonight with Vincent Lopez's Orchestra. Yes, the maitre d' will notify us at nine, when our table's ready. We check our coats and move into the lounge. How wonderful it is to be back in the United States having dinner with Bill. I'm even enjoying Bob's company. He's lost a good deal of the heavy reserve I associated with his overly serious personality. Good.

At about 9:10 p.m. we're advised our table is ready. The maitre d' escorts us to a ringside table so we can have a good view of the stage. Just when we've settled down to a pleasurable evening, a photographer comes over to our table and takes a photoflash picture of the three of us. We react instantly as though we were wired to the same power switch. "No pictures! Please!"

Bill clamps a firm grasp on the photographer's arm and touches the index finger of his right hand to his lips. He shushes me and Bob then signals us to sit down as he walks toward the kitchen door, never relaxing nor releasing his grip on the photographer. Bill will stay with the photographer in the hotel's darkroom while all the film in the camera is developed and printed. I signal the waiter and tell him to delay our dinner until our friend comes back to the table. "No problem, sir."

Bill comes back in less than half an hour holding two white envelopes in his hand. He hands one envelope to me and pockets the other. I open mine. It contains the photo of the three of us at the table. Each of us is in clear focus, which is not good for agents who have to work under cover. I'm pegged as an under-cover field agent. Bill and Bob may never work under cover, but one can never tell. Better not to have recent photos lying around.

"Do you have the neg, Bill?"

Bill pats his pocket. "Natch!"

"Any other prints of this one?"

"None. Let's eat. What's happened to the food?"

The waiter notices "our friend" is back. He catches my eye and reacts to my affirmative nod by disappearing into the kitchen. The orchestra's members come out, shuffle around a bit, take their seats and tune up for a few seconds. Vincent Lopez raises his hand and they start playing a lively opening song. On the second number, Mary Elizabeth comes out from backstage and sings one of her wonderful, peppy songs. She spots me and, eyes open wide, waves wildly in the direction of our table. Bill and Bob do double-takes when I stand up and wave back. Bill's as speechless as I've ever seen him. Bob's jaw is almost touching his chest.

At the end of her set of songs, Mary Elizabeth hops off the bandstand and rushes to our table, leaps up, hangs on with her arms around my neck and kisses me noisily on the lips, eyes, nose and cheeks. I'm not used to such public displays. It's a bit embarrassing. But I like it.

I place a chair for her between me and Bill and make introductions. My two companions are visibly stunned by Mary Elizabeth's excitement. She talks nonstop and breathlessly asks questions. "Where've you been? What've you been doing? Are you really a Navy officer? I'm so proud of you!" I try not to change my expression as she asks question after question. Bill's smile is slowing down to a frown. Bob's aghast, afraid of how I might answer her probing questions.

Knowing Mary Elizabeth as I do, I'm not concerned about her reasons for asking. She's always been like this. It's her way of making conversation. Nonetheless, I tell her I spend all my time on a supply ship, hiding inside a convoy of freighters. "Nothing exciting, Mary Elizabeth!" She accepts this and agrees to come back after her next set. She'll have coffee and dessert with us, then we have to leave.

"Leon! You rascal you!" Bill exclaims.

"Yeah!" Bob echoes with a grin.

A few days later, I am consumed with feelings of guilt. My family doesn't yet know I'm back in the city. In fact, they don't know I've been away. I should try to imitate a good son's behavior and visit my mother. The Chief agrees.

I don't completely know why, but I'm going to just drop in on Mom without calling ahead. Perhaps I've become so absorbed into this game of shadow-catching that I try to restrict all advance knowledge of my movements.

Merry brings me the things I'd left behind for my return from Africa. I change into my civilian suit. Bob lends me his overcoat. I don't want to have to explain the uniform. A quick subway ride on the Independent's "A" train to Brooklyn and a short walk from the subway station down Ralph Avenue brings me to 482 Decatur Street, my mother's brownstone house. I hope no neighbors are on the street. I don't want to have to answer any curious questions. My sister Rose answers the doorbell and stifles a scream of joy. She puts her fingers to her lips to let me know we should surprise Mom. Mom's in the kitchen cooking, as usual. The kitchen's aromas are fantastic! She makes the greatest cheese blintzes. I'm ready.

We have wine, some of Mom's happiness-inducing homemade, Concord grape wine produced by my Uncle Joe in our basement, an annual ritual for as long as I can remember. I ask about my cousins and hastily add, "Promise you won't ask me what I do or where or when. I don't want to have to lie—and I can't tell you about it." Although they're probably dying to know, Rose and Mom almost keep their promise.

A mother's curiosity and concern prompts Mom. "Tell me, at least, do you have to go overseas? To Europe?"

I answer with a half-truth. "No, I don't have to go to Europe." *Chief, don't make a total liar out of me*. Something about the way Mom and Rose look at me makes me realize they don't believe a word of what I just said. Mom gives me the latest news of the neighbors. But she regularly digresses into a game of questions I just cannot answer. I begin to feel uncomfortable and, although I enjoy seeing Rose and Mom, I conclude it may be time to end the visit. Too bad my brother and other sister aren't home, too. Who knows when—if ever—we will be able to get together again.

It's best to head for my hotel room in Manhattan and get back into the protective coloration of my uniform.

Chapter Fifty-Two

The next morning I'm back in the Chief's office. I sure do realize there's much I don't know about this field-agent business. So, I'm thankful when the Chief tells me "We've made some significant advances in the training we give our field agents, like yourself. We lack knowledge in important areas, as we've learned from experience, sometimes from unfortunate experience. With the reluctant help of the F.B.I. and the willing assistance of some of New York City's Detective Squads, we've been able to add to and round out a few of the skills. It would be to your advantage to take some of this new training. You've been lucky up to now, Leon. Your skills were just right for Marseilles and Casablanca. However, they may not be adequate for your next duty, which is completely solo—entirely on your own."

I sit up straight and react with wide open eyes. "You have a new job for me? Tell me about it, Chief!"

He turns away and shakes his head. "No. No. We *may* have a new job for you. The strategy's still being developed in Washington. So, frankly, there's no point in discussing it. In fact, it's still classified above your level."

My annoyance shows very clearly. "Everything I do is classified! Please Chief, don't give me that kind of talk!"

The Chief, Lt. Colonel Joe Franken, the former litigator, doesn't like to be challenged. I can feel powerful lightning bolts from his eyes and making direct hits on mine. "What kind of talk are you referring to?" He pauses and takes a deep breath. He's probably counting to ten, very slowly.

Softening his manner, the Chief looks directly at me. "Do we continue or no?" He pauses once more, leans forward to emphasize his seriousness and talks very slowly. "It's up to you, Leon."

I take a moment to consider the significance and seriousness of his reaction. Sitting back and upright in my chair, "Sorry. I must have temporarily lost the hearing in my good ear." A quick change of subject is appropriate. "Tell me about the new skill-training, Chief." I know it's useless to try to pump information out of him concerning my next assignment. He'll let me know in due time. This job beats any other option I can think of. It gives me a high degree of independence. The Chief needs me to accomplish his tasks and I need the freedom he allows me. We both win. We're fighting the same war. He and I are not the enemy.

The Chief sits back and visibly relaxes his tension, and mine. He calls for Bill Brady to join us. "You're going to like this, Leon. I'm being quite serious. I want you to think of what I'm going to tell you as a series of games, non-threatening games between you and a fictitious enemy."

My eagerness shows in my face. I lean forward to make sure I don't miss a single bit about these "games."

The Chief smiles. "Good. You've never had training or even practical experience in two very important actions. You've never had to tail anyone, follow him without being detected. Right? Also, suppose you think you may be followed, tailed. You're going to learn how to detect a tail and, just as important, you're going to learn how to shake the tail; get away from him."

I'm somewhat amused by the images this brings to mind. "Sounds like a plot right out of Hollywood!"

"Well, sometimes life imitates the movies. Sorry about that. I must've read it somewhere." He looks a bit embarrassed by his own words, but recovers quickly. "There's a third part to this game. You'll learn how to be the tail, how to follow someone with minimum risk of being detected."

"Who're the instructors?

The Chief smiles with self satisfaction. "I've worked out a deal with the New York City's Chief of Police. He's assigned four detectives to us for a couple of weeks. Two of them will be here in the morning to explain the procedure, how the police do it."

"What about the other two detectives?"

"I understand you won't meet them. They'll be your tails, as the police put it. You will have to determine whether or not you're being tailed by a person or persons unknown. Be here at 0900 tomorrow for our first meeting with the instructors."

"Gotcha, Chief!"

I start to get out of my chair. The Chief signals me to sit down. He's not finished.

"Hold it, Leon. There's more."

"Through Washington's contacts, I made a deal with the supervisor of the New York F.B.I. Office. You lucked out in Casablanca in the shoot-out with Michel. F.B.I. agents take continuous instruction and practice in handguns, combat and defensive shooting. They're outstanding guys in close action. Fast and accurate. I watched a demonstration of their techniques. They're something to behold. Amazing!"

I'm hanging onto every word the Chief says.

"The F.B.I agents and the New York Police, well, many of the detectives practice frequently at the Armory at 34th Street and Park Avenue. There's an excellent indoor range for handguns. "You're going to get some first class instruction from them."

"From who? The F.B.I.? The detectives?"

"Both."

"I don't have a gun, Joe. Remember? I left it on the floor of Bud's Jeep when we made our getaway."

"I know. I know. Merry!" He calls to her and asks her to come in.

Bill Brady excuses himself. "See ya!"

The Chief reaches into his desk drawer, opens a small lock-box and produces a key with an oversized tag tied to it. He hands the key to Merry. "Show Leon our handgun collection." Then, turning to me, "Pick out one of the guns, any one you prefer, and a holster. You can get the ammunition tomorrow. Bring the gun and holster in here. Don't let anyone see you with them, please. They might draw the wrong conclusions."

Merry leads me down the hall to another room. The door's locked but she has the key secured to what looks like a fancy shoelace around her neck. As we walk down the hall together, she's probably not aware she's pressing the key between her breasts. This exaggerates and enhances the full roundness of her figure. She notices me staring at the key and her bosom. She moves the key away from her body and smiles, a very knowing smile. Merry looks down as we continue walking and, in a hushed voice, "Leon. You're embarrassing me."

"Don't be embarrassed, Merry. Be proud!"

"Thank you, dear."

She unlocks the door and we enter the windowless room. She locks the door behind us. Inside is a large metal desk and several chairs. Against the wall is a large heavy-steel closet with a sturdy padlock on it. Merry opens one of the closet's doors and points inside.

There are a dozen or so wooden boxes. We put all of them on the desk. Each box contains a single, brand new revolver painted a non-reflecting black. Some of the revolvers have 6" barrels, big, heavy, hard to hide. Others appear to have short 4", 3", or 2" barrels. Here's one I've never seen before. A no-name hideout gun for sure. Literally, it has no barrel. Machined or sawed off. It probably has no accuracy at all. You might hit the side of a barn with it, as long as you're standing no more than an arm's length from the barn. It probably has one helluva recoil, too! A knuckle buster! Not what I want. Next time I may not be standing close to my target.

No effort has been made to conceal the trade marks of the guns' manufacturers. They're either Colt's or Smith & Wesson's. I favor the S&W with a 2" barrel. It holds only five cartridges, which makes it slim in girth; fits nicely in one's pants pocket without creating a suspicious bulge. An excellent hideout weapon with extraordinary accuracy for such a short barrel. It's been my favorite since we worked out with our Marine Sergeants during survival training on the Farm. And it looks like the same gun Bud smuggled to me in Casablanca. Can I be sentimental about a gun? "I'll take the 2-inch S&W, Merry and, for a holster, I like this soft, black leather job with the metal clip. I can clip it onto my belt and suspend it inside my waistband. Good concealment and fast access."

Merry urges me to end this fashion show. "Lovely. Let's get the Chief's okay. You'll have to sign for the gun and the ammunition, of course."

"Of course. Here. I'll clip on the holster and tuck the gun into it's resting place. Voilà! With my jacket buttoned you'd never spot the gun without patting me down. With my jacket unbuttoned, I'm ready to defend myself or attack the nearest bad guy!"

Merry's a bit tired and mumbles through a deep yawn. "It's been a long day, Leon." She padlocks the cabinet. Unlocks the door. We exit the room. She locks the door from the outside with that fortunate key. It hangs from her neck band and bounces happily against her breasts as we walk back to the Chief's office. Merry tries very hard to ignore my lewd glances. But I am very human.

The Chief snaps me back to instant-reality. "Let's go, Leon! Show me your gourmet selection. What'll you carry?" He approves my choice of the S&W hideout gun and hands me some sheets to read concerning the laws of New York City and its dim view of hand guns and the grave consequences of misuse, or unnecessary display, or threatening actions. I'm impressed. He also hands me a receipt to sign for the gun. It's government property, you know."

"Suppose I lose it in while operating in the field?"

"Better have a good explanation handy!" He doesn't seem to be kidding.

All papers read and signed, he hands me a box of 50 cartridges for the gun and offers several words of caution. "If you carry the gun, carry it loaded. If you draw it, intend to use it. If you use it, shoot to kill. If you miss your target, better have a very good excuse...if you come back alive."

"Chief. Suppose, just suppose, someone detects I'm carrying and calls the cops. If carrying concealed without a permit is against the law, I've got trouble. How do I handle it?"

"It's legal to carry if you're a member of the armed services in uniform, you know."

The Chief reaches into his bottomless desk and comes up with a card. He hands it to me. It's an ID card bearing my name and his countersignature. "Sign this card, Leon."

This the first time I've even heard of such a card. It explicitly identifies me as a Field Agent, Office of Strategic Services, an agency of the United States Government.

I notice the card has an early expiration date.

Chapter Fifty-Three

Several weeks later, the police and F.B.I. training/instruction have been completed. I've learned many new things I hope I will never have to use. I check into The Office early every morning, before and after lunch, and again at the end of the day before I go back to the hotel to stand by the telephone—just in case. The Chief is aware of my restlessness. Every time he passes me in The Office he shrugs his shoulders as a "No change" message. I'm bored. Plain b-o-r-e-d! I feel useless. I feel insecure. Have I been forgotten? Is anything wrong?

One morning at the end of March 1943, I'm in The Office's reception room drinking coffee, chatting with Bill Brady and Jason, our security man, waiting for the Chief to return from one of his many trips to Washington. The Chief bursts into the reception room, rushes past Jason and me without any sign of recognition, and noisily opens and slams shut the door to his office. Jason and I look at one another in astonishment. This is unusual behavior for the Chief. He often comes across as insensitive, but never rude. No more than five seconds after he bangs his office door shut, he opens it, apologizes to us and urgently signals me and Bill to join him.

"Come!"

"What's happening, Chief?" I'm filled with anticipation...about to hear either the worst or the best news.

"Leon. You're on! You're going out!"

I'm confused. "Going out? I'm fired?" I inhale deeply and hold my breath.

The Chief smiles. "No, Leon. You're far from being fired. You're assignment's been cleared for an immediate 'go'!"

I loudly exhale. "Go where?"

"This one's a stroke of good luck for both you and the O.S.S."

"Tell me, Chief. Please!"

He gets up from his desk, opens the door, looks around to assure there are no eavesdroppers, and quietly closes the door. "Here's all I know and why I hurried back from Washington. Bill Donovan has been in London meeting with British intelligence."

"How do I fit in?"

"You have the near-perfect cover for this duty."

"Meaning?"

"You're a good wireless operator. You have linguistic skills. You've demonstrated an unusual aptitude as a shadow catcher. You already have Coast Guard papers identifying you as a Merchant Marine Radio Officer. You have F.C.C. licenses for sea-duty. Do you get a picture from what I'm saying?"

I tilt my head and frown inquisitively. "Not quite."

"They tell me the radio officer is the first one to leave a ship as soon as it makes its port. And, he's the last one to come back on board just before the ship sails. Right?"

"Yes. Some friends of mine who've sailed in peacetime as radio operators tell me the radioman has no duties while the ship's at the dock. His duties stop along with the engine. They begin again as soon as the engine starts."

"Perfect! Perfect! It fits the plan! We want you to sign on a Merchant Marine ship as the radio officer. We picked the ship, one headed for the U.K. It's the *S.S. Collis P. Huntington.* As soon as the ship docks, you can leave and go to a hotel and, from that base, you can do your sniffing for shadows." He leans back in his chair and smiles.

I stop to evaluate what the Chief has just told me. "So simple, it's almost silly. How do I establish a contact in the U.K.? I have no power to arrest anyone."

"As soon as we know the ship's port, it's destination, we'll inform O.N.I. in Washington and they'll advise MI5 of the name of the port. So, carry your O.S.S. ID card with you this time for positive ID. Just in case you get in as deeply as you did in Casablanca, I recommend you take your revolver. I'll give you a full box of 50 cartridges to take with you. But, be extra careful. The British don't like the idea of the O.S.S. bringing guns into their territory."

"I'll be careful. This means I have to get a different uniform, too. Doesn't it?"

"Yup. You have to be in the uniform of an officer of the U.S. Merchant Marine. It looks exactly like a U.S. Navy uniform with a different insignia on the cap."

"Well, this is a different job. What language shall I speak?"

The Chief understands my joke and smiles. "Try American English."

I join in the humor. "Okay. You have a choice of Brooklyn, Bronx and Manhattan accents. Which do you prefer?"

"Try your natural accent. I can't tell what it is. Your accent is all mixed up. It changes all the time. Go to the same store where you bought the Navy uniform. I'll phone ahead. You can charge whatever you need, of course, and they'll make any alterations while you wait. See you here for lunch. Okay?"

"Okay...I guess."

"Incidentally, to complete the cover, your paycheck will be issued by the company that manages the ship. One of us in this Office will pick up your paycheck and deposit it in your bank account. Same amount you're now being paid."

About 1315 I return to The Office, still in Navy uniform but with a large, flat, paper package over my left arm—my new Merchant Marine uniform, white shirts and a Navy-blue great coat. The Chief, Bill Brady and I have sandwiches together at the Chief's desk while we discuss details and the timetable of my assignment.

It's not complicated. My assignment starts as soon as we finish our lunch which, the Chief says "Ends at exactly 1400." I'm to go from here to the hotel, change into my civilian suit, pack everything and check out. Carry the new uniform and new overcoat in plain paper wrappers, check out and return to The Office then leave my Navy uniform and overcoat here for safekeeping.

The Chief hands me a slip of paper with the name of the shipping company, American-Range Liberty Lines in downtown New York City. "Ask for the Port Captain. You're expected at 1500. He'll assign you to a ship scheduled to depart tomorrow morning. The ship's radio officer has become ill and they need a replacement. There's a Navy radioman already on board. He's young, but he's been to sea before. Federal law requires an F.C.C. licensed radio operator must be on board before the ship can depart. In this case, you will be the F.C.C. radio operator."

"What about the Radio Officer's Union? Don't they have to assign the operator to the ship?"

"I doubt they'll challenge the Port Captain's actions." The Chief looks at his watch. "It's 1400, Leon. You're now officially on assignment." He and Bill shake my hand vigorously.

Before we leave The Office, Bill Brady proposes a slight change of plan. I should change into the new Merchant Marine uniform and overcoat before leaving the hotel. I can put my other suit and accessories in the suitcase. Makes things more manageable. Simplifies the luggage. He'll square it with the Chief. At my request, Merry supplies a small, metal lock-box in which I can conceal my revolver, holster and a box of ammunition.

Bill suggests, "Let me go with you to the hotel to help you check out. I'll take your Navy uniform and overcoat to The Office and turn them over to Merry. I'll even accept, on your behalf, her hugs and good luck wishes." What a pal.

As we leave the hotel, I hail a taxi headed downtown. Bill walks away in the direction of The Office. Suddenly, I feel completely alone again.

At 1500 I meet the Port Captain of the American-Range Liberty Lines. "You're in luck, Sparks. Your ship's Captain's here right now. You can go to the ship with him. First, let me see your Coast Guard papers and F.C.C. license. Good. Everything looks okay. Come meet Captain Alfred W. Hudnall, skipper of the *S.S. Collis P. Huntington*."

Captain Hudnall is in his mid-70s, and a bit short of six feet in height. His complexion and craggy face are positive evidence he's a veteran seaman. His hair is white, eyes are blue and smiling, strong voice, authoritative. He's from Virginia and has the accent and gentlemanly manners to prove it. I like this man at once. We get acquainted in the cab on the way to the ship. He'd been a ship's Captain for more than 30 years; came out of retirement when he learned there was a shortage of ships' masters. This is his first ship since the war started. The gold braid on his cap shows no signs of green tarnish. It's as new as mine.

Captain Hudnall looks at my overcoat and the two gold stripes on its shoulders. "How long you been going to sea as a radio operator, son?"

"Never been before, Captain." He doesn't comment. Just looks out the taxi's window. The cab stops at the entrance to a Hudson River pier. A uniformed, armed U.S. Marine sentry asks for our papers. We produce them and climb the gangway to my my new home, the *S.S. Collis P. Huntington*, a freighter, a Liberty Ship, a floating freight train.

A new realization comes to me. No longer am I "Leon," "Léon" or "Mister Wortman." From now on, as long as I'm assigned to the Merchant Marine, I'll be known as "Sparks." Or "Spaahks." Or "Spawks." It depends entirely on what part of the United States you hail from. The name or title is traditional, dating back to the early days of marine radio when ships used equipment whose transmissions were generated by *electric sparks* jumping across an air gap between twin electrodes.

Aboard a merchant ship, it's normal, customary to address a person by his title or his function, not by his name. The only exception is the Captain. He's always addressed, respectfully, by title and, often, the last name is added—as in "Captain Hudnall."

"Sparks!" That's me, now. My title, job and name all in one.

Chapter Fifty-Four

Captain Hudnall leads me up the gangway. A ramp more than a stairway, the gangway is usually suspended from the starboard side of the ship. *Let me see. As I look toward the ship's bow, starboard is right, port is left. I've a new vocabulary to learn. Mustn't sound like a landlubber. Must try to behave like an old salt.* The lower end of the gangway rests on wheels touching the pier's deck so the gangway can move without self-destructing as the ship rises and falls with the sea's swells and the tide. The upper end of the gangway makes a turn of almost 90 degrees onto the ship's main deck.

With a tight grip on the banister, a wire rope that passes through pipes rising vertically from the gangway, I follow closely behind the Captain. Good thing I'm with the Captain. Otherwise my unsteady walk up the gangway might generate some laughter among the veteran officers and crew who are standing by on the deck waiting to greet Captain Hudnall.

The Captain is hailed with glad-to-see-you-sir enthusiasm. Everybody greets him with maritime salutes, quick movements of the right hand, two fingers together briefly touching the visor of the cap or, if no cap is worn, a touch to the forehead serves the purpose nicely. Not a military type salute, but just as much—no, more so—a sign of recognition and respect.

The lightning emblems on my overcoat's shoulder boards identify me as a radio officer. As an officer of the ship, I'm accorded the same courteous salute, but with significantly less enthusiasm. I intend to make a serious effort to be accepted by the officers and crew of this ocean bound, battleship-gray behemoth of a freight-train. Everything around me, every person and every object is new to my senses, my eyes, ears, nose and touch. By nature, I am very much a land-living and land-loving animal. Right here and now, stepping onto the steel deck of the ship, I resolve to learn to adjust quickly and thoroughly to this amphibious lifestyle.

Captain Hudnall calls out loudly enough for everyone to hear his order to me, "Follow me to the bridge, Sparks." We enter at the back (*I'll have to learn the nautical terminology*) of the midship housing, move along the narrow passageway past wooden doors and steel walls, turn right, and climb two more flights of stairs. Captain Hudnall's my tour guide. "We are now on the bridge deck." The Captain points to a door at the left-rear end of the deck, "Your cabin, Sparks. Drop your things and meet me forward on the bridge, please."

"Yes, Captain. Join you there in a second." I wonder if I should have said "Aye, Aye, sir!" Like in the movies.

Without taking time to study my accommodations, I literally drop my things on the bunk, remove my heavy coat, leave my cabin, close the door behind me and, just as I'm about to enter a doorway to what has to be the bridge, the

Captain arrives with a bulging briefcase. I step aside to allow him to enter first. He politely says "Thank you, Sparks." He's okay!

Some of the ship's officers and a Navy officer are assembled on the bridge, a wide, steel-enclosed room running almost the full width of the ship. There are three square, glass covered windows for observing the forward part, the bow of the ship. Wings, accessible through doors, extend on both the starboard and port sides of the bridge. By standing on either of these wings you can see the stern of the ship as well its bow. Of course, depending upon which wing you are standing on, you can also see the port or starboard horizon. A compass, the ship's large wheel for controlling the rudder's position, and the ship's telegraph for signaling the desired speeds to the engine room are at approximately the midpoint of the bridge's interior. A small handle, connected by a chain to the ship's whistle, hangs from the ceiling.

Captain Hudnall wastes no time in small talk. He introduces me. "Gentlemen, this is Sparks," but he doesn't introduce any of the officers to me. *I'm sure I'll have plenty of time to meet them individually.*

Pointing to the Navy officer, the Captain continues, "Mr. Wells, our Armed Guard commander and I've been to the convoy conference. This is what we've been told. We're scheduled to leave this dock at approximately 1000, depending on the availability of tugboats and New York harbor pilots. As soon as the tugs release their lines and the pilot leaves our ship, we move out of lower New York Bay and into convoy position." Captain Hudnall has everyone's undivided attention as he continues.

"I have the sailing instructions here." He pats and holds the briefcase firmly in his grip, and calls out to "Mister Bach," pronounced "Mistuh Batch" by the Captain. He's the 1st Mate, a short, white-haired, barrel-chested man who appears to be older than the Captain. "Please come to my cabin for your envelope. Our convoy position is shown on your papers in the envelope. Rendezvous points are also indicated."

The Captain opens his briefcase and calls out, "Mr. Thompson! He points to another man, just a few years younger than himself. "Here are your papers. Initial speed of the convoy is to be 11 knots until otherwise notified by the commodore of the convoy.

"Sparks!" *I seem to be the youngest one on the bridge*. "Here's your envelope with the BAMS schedule. Get together with Mistuh Batch and set up a daily schedule for receiving time signals. Bon voyage to us. Eh?"

We respond with "Yes, sir." Or "Bon voyage, Captain." The general attitude is serious, almost like a religious ceremony. I fully expect someone to suggest, "Before we separate gentlemen, let us pray." No one makes the suggestion. All minds are directed at thoughts of the many things to be accomplished between now and 1000 hours.

As for me, I have lots of questions and no one to answer them for me. "What's BAMS?" "What time signals for the First Mate?" I have the F.C.C. license that authorizes me to be the radio officer. I passed the tests, which I took in a landlocked building in downtown New York City four and a half or five years ago. The F.C.C. exams were all about radio-theory, never asked nor answered such practical questions.

First thing to do is find the radio room. Logic tells me it probably is next to my living quarters. Logic fails me. The cabin next to mine has a pair of bunk beds, an upper and a lower berth. No radio equipment. As I open the door, the noise it makes wakens a body sleeping in the lower bunk. The upper is empty. The "body" jumps up and salutes. He's a Navy man, even younger than I am. My guess is he's 18. "Radioman 3rd Class, Jeffers, sir." Even though his eyes are filled with symptoms of sleep, his manner and presence are the kind one doesn't mind being cooped up with for the next several months. Maybe he's been taught the things I don't know about maritime radio. Heck. I'll accept knowledge wherever I find it.

I offer my hand. "I'm Sparks. Nice to meet you, Jeffers. Can you take time to come with me to the radio room?" This is my way of asking him to show me where it is.

Behind the next door down the passageway, closer to the bridge, is the radio room. Surprisingly small in size, it's packed with equipment. Jeffers tells me this is his second trip as a radio operator aboard the *Collis P. Huntington*, which means he probably knows its radio equipment and the maritime radio procedures.

Couldn't be nicer. I've found my teacher.

A knock on the open door to the radio room and the short, elderly gentleman with the barrel chest, Mr. Bach steps into the radio room. Mr. Bach, the 1st Mate, is second in command aboard ship and may be referred to as "Chief," or "First," or "First Mate" or by his last name, as in "Mr. Bach." His clear, blue eyes twinkle to match his wide open, very friendly smile. The gold braid of his cap is crusted with green; a veteran of many years at sea. He doffs his cap to reveal a full head of very white hair. If he had a white beard, he'd look exactly like Santa Claus.

Chapter Fifty-Five

Mr. Bach asks me to come with him to the chart room. It's on the starboard side of the bridge deck, a small room between the Captain's cabin and the bridge. Mr. Bach points to three brass-frame round clocks mounted one above the other on the wall. *Must get used to calling a wall a "bulkhead."* The clocks are wind-ups. The brass-framed glass cover of each clock is hinged to provide quick access for manually making adjustments or corrections to the relative positions of the hour and minute hands. Mr. Bach is the ship's chief navigator, assisted by the 2nd Mate whom I haven't met yet.

A large, tilted shelf, more like a large waist-high table top with wide drawers is just below the clocks. Large marine maps, charts are spread out on the table top. A marine-radio direction finder is suspended from the ceiling. The wheel for manually rotating the direction-sensing antenna protrudes from the bottom of the direction finder and is parallel to the chart room's deck. Although I've never actually operated a direction finder, the F.C.C. exams thoroughly covered the theory of operation. I feel comfortable about using the equipment.

Mr. Bach points to the clocks. "These must be adjusted every day at the same time. I log their errors. You can get the National Bureau of Standards continuous time-transmissions on your radio receiver. Turn up your loudspeaker and I'll hear the time beeps and adjust the clocks. Shouldn't take more than 10 minutes at most."

"Absolutely, Mr. Bach. Every day at noon, 1200. Count on it. Why three clocks?" *I know this reveals my naiveté but, anyway, they'll discover quickly enough I'm a virgin seaman.*

"Because the clock mechanisms are not synchronized and are affected by humidity, the probability for an accurate time fix at any given moment is made better by averaging the time indications of the three clocks." Mr. Bach thanks me. We shake hands and I go back to the radio room, wondering where, on what frequency and when the National Bureau of Standards (NBS) transmissions are broadcast. Heck! The envelope Captain Hudnall handed me! Telling Jeffers, "Be right back," I dash to my cabin, retrieve the envelope and return to the radio room.

I close the door, lay the envelope on the metal table that is part of the radio equipment's housing and open it. Lots of things for me to read, all stamped *CONFIDENTIAL.* This is not intended to exclude Jeffers, I'm sure. We study the documents, many of which Jeffers says are the same as the ones the Sparks before me had showed him.

The material is virtually a complete set of "How-To" guides for the maritime radio operator. During the next hour of reading I become an expert of sorts, knowledgeable about where, when and what my duties are...but still without practical experience.

Ah! BAMS stands for *Broadcasts to Allied Merchant Ships.* These are Morse code transmissions originating somewhere in the United States on specific radio frequencies at scheduled times of the day and night. These transmissions are in encrypted groups of five characters sent at the rate of 15 words per minute. They are sent just once, so the radio operator better not miss any of the groups. This is fine with me. My copying speed is 25 words per minute with 100% accuracy.

Okay, now I have the code, which I've transcribed into readable but meaningless English. How do I decrypt the groups of characters? This, too, is explained. The code books are in the padlocked steel, gray chest on the floor to the left of the main radio-equipment housing. The key to the chest's lock is in my envelope. It has a large, metal ring so it can be hung on a hook installed on the bulkhead above the steel chest. The chest has a series of holes about 1-inch in diameter all around its sides. The instructions continue:

"In the event the order to abandon ship is given by the appropriate authority, the radio operator is responsible for destroying the code books. This is done by tossing the chest into the sea with the code books inside and the top closed and securely padlocked." The holes in the chest? Of course. So the water gets inside and makes the chest and its contents sink quickly.

"The radio operator shall continuously monitor 500 KHz, the international calling and distress frequency. A log shall be kept of the time and the name of the person monitoring the 500 KHz frequency. Any signals heard shall be entered in their entirety into the log. If nothing is heard, the radio operator shall enter NIL HRD, or NOTHING HEARD, at 15 minute intervals during the radio watch.

"Radio silence shall be maintained at all times, whether at sea or in port, except for emergencies. If a merchant ship traveling without escort is hit or attacked by a submarine, the radio operator shall, under explicit instructions from the ship's master, transmit a series of SSS signals, the ship's position and call sign. If a merchant ship traveling without escort is in distress or damaged by other than enemy action, the radio operator shall, under explicit instructions from the ship's master, transmit the international distress signal, SOS, the ship's position and radio call sign. If a merchant ship traveling without escort is hit or attacked by an enemy aircraft, the radio operator shall, under explicit instructions from the ship's master, transmit a series of AAA signals, the ship's position and radio call sign."

Jeffers points to a typewriter bolted to a small table secured to the bulkhead to the right of the radio-equipment housing. A swivel chair, its pedestal secured to the floor, er...deck, is provided for the radioman-typist. I'm not at all a good typist, but I think I can keep up with 15 words per minute, maybe more. The radio logbook, pads of paper and lots of pencils are in a kneehole slide-out draw in the longer table top attached to the front of the radio-equipment's housing.

Jeffers sees me rubbing my stomach, which is making "I'm hungry" noises. He suggests we break for chow. Good idea!

I add, "Let's get together here in about an hour. We can set up a watch schedule then."

He heads for the crew's mess. I go to the officers' salon, pronounced "saloon." I'm wearing my uniform jacket, and the insignia identifies me. The messman in the saloon is my age. He smiles and greets me, "Hi, Sparks!" and directs me to a chair at the second table from the right.

The first table is for Captain Hudnall, the Chief Engineer, First Mate, and the Navy officer in charge of the Armed Guard, all of whom I'd met this afternoon. My partners at the second table are the Purser, the 2nd Mate and the 2nd Engineer. I introduce myself to my table buddies. Chairs at a third table are occupied by the 3rd Mate, the 3rd Engineer and the Chief Steward. Getting up from my chair, I introduce myself to the 3rd. No doubt this seating arrangement reflects traditional, maritime pecking order. An unoccupied fourth table with four pedestal-mounted swivel chairs is located against the bulkhead directly behind me, alongside the refrigerator. This table is reserved for cadet officers, if part of the ship's roster. The refrigerator is always stocked with snacks, until the ship runs out of them, that is. Coffee is constantly brewing on a table to the right of the refrigerator.

The ship's officers' ages range from young, to middle age and seniors. Seated diagonally across from the Captain, the Navy Armed Guard Officer, Mr. Wells, is in his early thirties. He wears ensign bars on the tabs of his shirt-collar; a "90-day wonder." Mr. Wells doesn't seem to have anything to say to anyone. He doesn't chat with the Captain. He gives me the impression he's a loner; angry and depressed.

George Leitner, the Purser, is very short, quite thin. His hair is salt and pepper. He wears bifocals and, when he talks to anyone, tilts his head far back and peers through the lower segment of his spectacles. I'd say he's in his 50s. A delightful guy, he's always talking and joking. Before he volunteered for the Merchant Marine, he'd been sales manager for a ladies garment manufacturer in New York City. My impression is he must be good at his profession. Mr. Leitner tells me to call him by his first name, "George."

The 2nd Mate and 2nd Engineer, both in their mid 50s don't mention their last names so, to me, they are "Hi, 2nd!" Same thing for the 3rd Mate and 3rd Engineer. "Hi, 3rd!"

The tables are covered with white tablecloths and set with full complements of flatware, water glasses and cloth napkins. Pitchers of cream, sugar dispensers and bread baskets are placed on each table. Service is rapid. Compliments to the messman. Our dinner plates are brought to us already piled high with piping hot food. To my surprise, it's delicious! Compliments to the chef or cook, whichever he is called.

Probably we're all slightly nervous and tense, waiting for the time when we start the engines and the ship is pulled away from the dock. There's very little conversation while we eat. Each of us is off somewhere else, lost in private thoughts. I'm no exception. I don't know exactly where this ship is going or what lies ahead. I've no idea whether I'll get seasick. Maybe, if I just don't think about it...

Here we are. A bunch of men, not yet a team, confined to this gray all-steel freighter for a period of time officially and only defined as "the voyage." No doubt, we're different from one another. Different in our backgrounds, training, skills, ambitions, motivations and goals. Except for the Navy Armed Guard, everyone on board the *Collis P. Huntington* has volunteered to join the Merchant Marine.

Under attack from the enemy, some of us may remain outwardly cool, calm. Others may panic, display intense fear or even overt cowardice. How an individual reacts to the most serious threat to his life is not reliably predictable.

Soon, I feel we'll learn things about ourselves we'd never been able to imagine. Which of us will break down under pressure? Which of us can be depended upon to behave like a man? After all, only real men voluntarily go down to the sea in ships.

Chapter Fifty-Six

How different this lifestyle is when compared with my time on board the destroyer last October. At that time, the need for total secrecy kept me confined to a tiny, inside cabin and deprived me of the opportunity to see the extraordinary flotilla of ships of Operation Torch take their assigned positions in the North-Africa bound convoy.

While on the destroyer it was absolutely necessary for me to stay completely out of sight of the crew. My contacts with the outside world had been restricted to sensations of the sweeping and rolling movements of the destroyer as it shepherded the huge convoy of ships into assigned positions.

The formation of a convoy of huge, hulking merchant ships maneuvering for their assigned positions on an unmarked ocean highway—devoid of visible traffic signs or green-yellow-red light stanchions—must be a spectacle to witness. Large ships are not capable of fast turns. They require lots of room and time to achieve a simple maneuver. I have difficulty imagining dozens of freighters moving hither and thither without piling up, one on top of the other. Where's the traffic cop? Perhaps, this time, I'll be able to observe the intricate maneuvers of the convoy's ships and the naval escorts and gain some understanding of how this extraordinary feat is accomplished.

On board a merchant ship, the radio "watch" begins when the port-pilot leaves the ship and the Captain resumes complete control and responsibility. Navy Radioman Jeffers and I agree to stand the initial radio watch together. After the convoy has formed, we will begin to rotate our radio watch. When there are three radio operators on a ship, the watch is rotated four-hours on and eight-hours off for each operator. The two of us will have to do six on, six off.

The complement of officers on an ocean-going ship usually includes 1st, 2nd and 3rd mates for both the "deck gang" and the engine room's so-called "black gang." This makes watch periods of four-hours on and eight-hours off quite practicable. Three radio officers would work a similar schedule if, three were available for all merchant ships. Because of the shortage of licensed radio officers for the rapidly expanding Merchant Marine fleet, the Navy has tried to assign two assistant radiomen. But at this time the Navy has to strain to supply one assistant.

Kings Point, New York, among other Merchant Marine Academies, trains and graduates cadet officers at an incredible rate. After a short time at sea as cadets or as 3rd mates, they are qualified by proof of performance to take examinations for advancement to 3rd or 2nd mates. If they choose the sea as their career paths, they may eventually be examined and licensed to sail as ships' Masters, Captains. Some Kings Point cadets have earned Captain's papers in as little as two years.

I learn a new word to add to my rapidly expanding language of sea and ships. Among other administrative duties, the Purser is responsible for operating the ship's store. But it is not called a "store." It's the "slop chest" operated on this ship by the Purser, George. He correctly guesses I need clothing better suited to a sea voyage than my Navy blue uniform and one and only white shirt. He kindly offers to open the slop chest for me right now so I can properly outfit myself. Purchases are deducted from the paycheck I'll receive at the conclusion of the voyage. The slop chest is a cabin on the deck below the radio room. So, a few minutes after George extends the invitation, he's measuring me for shirt and trouser sizes.

"You have a choice of colors, Sparks. Khaki, or khaki."

I share his humor. "The correct decision will take more time, George. In the meantime make it khaki, please." I select several pairs of pants, half a dozen shirts, socks, undershirts, shorts, all khaki of course; a pair of navy-blue wool gloves, heavy navy-blue woolen sweater, navy-blue wool cap with a face mask and a heavy-duty navy-blue hip-length coat.

"George, what do I do for a laundry?"

He hands me a large bar of soap and a course brush. "You won't need a tub. You can use the one you'll find in the bottom of your cabin's closet."

"Just like being home. Isn't it, George?"

"What kind of home do you come from, Sparks."

"Goodnight, George."

"Goodnight, Sparks."

Blackout regulations take effect at sundown. Dim, deep red lights adequately illuminate the passageways. If a doorway to the outside deck is opened at night, a black drape is manually pulled across the exit to prevent the escape of light from the ship's interior. No lit cigarettes, pipes, flashlights or lanterns may be carried on deck at night. The same applies to the interior of the ship's bridge where the metal covers of the portholes are always kept open; no lights of any kind other than the dim light inside the compass visible only to the man at the ship's wheel.

This is my first night at sea. I'm on watch and thankfully I have not become seasick. I'm amazed at how quiet the ship is. The only audible sound is made by ship's engines—*thump-atta-thump-atta-thump-atta-thump*. It's a boring monotone—but I hope it doesn't stop until we reach our destination.

The Atlantic Ocean is absolutely calm which, logic dictates, is a near-perfect setting for U-Boat activity. The only thing that keeps the setting from being perfect for the U-Boats is the comforting presence of the naval-warship escort. Our ship carries some armament. She has a 3-inch-50 cannon mounted on a rotating platform on the her bow. A larger 5-inch-38 is at her stern. Ear-splitting 50mm antiaircraft guns are mounted on each of the four corners of the flying bridge, the steel deck directly over my head. If the guns are fired while I'm copying radio signals, the rat-tat-tat pounding of the guns will most certainly put me out of action. I won't be able to hear a thing coming over the radio. Right now, all guns are silent.

Using earphones for privacy, I copy the first encrypted BAMS transmission without difficulty. At the conclusion of the BAMS, I unlock the steel chest and remove the code book, a hard bound, green, cloth-covered volume about one-inch thick with oversized pages. For me, decrypting the message is neither fun nor boring. It's just slow. I think of it as tediously reading a story who's ending must remain completely unknown to me.

This particular BAMS is addressed to "All Ship's Masters." No specific ship or convoy is named. The message describes sightings of debris, sightings of mines, sightings of unidentified objects of such-and-such-shape and this-and-that-color. The locations of the sightings are given in latitude and longitude. I quickly type the translated message onto a clean sheet of paper and deliver it to Captain Hudnall's cabin. He's still awake and seated at his desk located just inside the entrance. He invites me to come in and have a seat while he reads the message.

I'm not familiar with the languages of latitudes and longitudes. I'm a bit disappointed and almost embarrassed when Captain Hudnall tells me "These sightings are in the South Atlantic Ocean. We are in the North Atlantic, thousands of miles away." Not my fault.

Sensing my embarrassment, Captain Hudnall adds, "You did exactly what you're supposed to do, Sparks. Every BAMS message should be brought to me immediately, as you did. Good work. And good night."

"Good night, Captain." He knows how to reassure a greenhorn. I feel better.

The rest of the night is uneventful. Jeffers takes the next watch. In the morning, before relieving Jeffers, I go to the officers' salon for breakfast. George is here. So, are the Chief Mate and the Chief Engineer. Captain Hudnall's already been here and gone to the bridge.

I'm served fresh-squeezed orange juice, fresh-baked muffins, fresh-cooked eggs, authentic butter, and hot coffee with real cream. Not at all bad. I ask Mr. Bach, "How long has this been going on?"

Mr. Bach replies, "More important, how long does this continue?"

How long do oranges keep? How long do butter and eggs and cream remain fresh?

George, the Purser, is either answering Mr. Bach's question or he's reading my mind. He smiles as he flicks the ash off his cigarette. "You'll find out, Sparks!"

Mr. Bach glances up at the ship's clock on the wall behind me and gets up to leave. "Come jaw with me in the chart room anytime, Sparks."

"I've 15 minutes before I go on watch. If you're going there now, mind if I come with you?"

I trail him up to the bridge deck and into the chart room. He opens one of the wide drawers built into the chart table, selects a map of the North Atlantic Ocean and spreads it carefully on the table top.

"Here, Sparks let me show you our position and proposed route to the United Kingdom."

I'm fascinated and grateful I'm being made privy to this information. Heck. Even if I were a Nazi agent, there's no way I could transmit these facts to anyone. There are probably 30, 40 or more radio receivers constantly monitoring all radio frequencies. There are probably a dozen or more people manning the RDFs, the Radio Direction Finders on board the ships. Any illegal transmissions can be heard and pinpointed before the transmissions are finished. So, Mr. Bach continues without concern for secrecy.

While drawing a pencil line, he tells me we're headed on a northeast bearing which will take us close to Halifax, Nova Scotia. According to his papers, a small convoy of ships will join ours with an escort of Canadian corvettes. Our position in the convoy won't change.

"Pardon the interruption, Mr. Bach, but is there any reason why our position in the convoy is at the end of the outermost starboard column of ships. I noticed we're in this position when I stepped out of my cabin and onto the deck. Our stern and our starboard side seem to be protected by two lone destroyer escorts keeping pace with the convoy's speed. Is there any special significance?"

Mr. Bach doesn't look up from the map. "Sure is, Sparks. This trip we're an ammunition carrier...tons of dynamite in hold number one. The other holds are filled with big-size cannon shells and other kinds of war-stuff. On deck, as you can see, were carrying partially assembled aircraft, fighter planes wrapped against the weather and the ocean's salt. If we go up, there's no way of predicting if any other ships'd go with us. So, they separate us from the middle of the convoy, put us on the outside column and corner. That's the only significance, Sparks."

Mr. Bach looks up at me and adds, "It's called 'coffin corner'."

Chapter Fifty-Seven

The section of the convoy out of Halifax joins us today in full daylight. The whole thing, the blending of the two convoys takes place without a single flaw. Maybe a professional seaman can find technical faults. But it looks just fine to me.

We all welcome the addition of the Canadian Corvettes to our small fleet of U.S. Navy warships. However our Chief Mate tells me the corvettes have replaced most of the U.S. warships. The result, Mr. Bach and I conclude, is a net reduction in escort power. The U.S. Navy has other demands to meet elsewhere, or perhaps they were ordered to return to New York to pick up another convoy. Mr. Bach and I magnanimously accept this state of affairs.

"It's a tradition of the sea," smiles Mr. Bach. He rises to his full height of 5-feet 5-inches. "And if you don't like it, you can get off and walk back!"

Several days pass uneventfully. Jeffers and I continue to copy the BAMS, decode and deliver them to the Captain. The convoy's route takes the flotilla close to the southern tip of Greenland. The sun is high. The sky is cloudless. The sea is smooth as a mirror's surface. No wind is blowing. I'm on the deck above the bridge, comfortable in my new sweater and heavy coat and admiring the contrasts.

The coast of Greenland is white with snow. Picture-card beautiful, but ice cold. The warmth of the sun reaches all of us on deck. Jackets, sweaters and caps are soon doffed. Captain Hudnall comes onto the deck. He's the only one wearing a hat; his Captain's hat, of course. He greets each of us by name and makes social comments about today's great weather.

"What d'you think, Sparks?"

"About what, Captain?"

"About the weather."

"I'm not sure."

"Not sure? What d'you mean, not sure?"

"If I were a U-Boat commander and I spotted this convoy, I'd consider this sight a superb opportunity. I'd put my U-Boat off the starboard beam of the convoy between me and the Greenland coast. I'd slowly maneuver for a good shot and, from a distance of a mile or so, let loose my torpedoes and..."

"And what, Sparks?"

"And I'd get the hell away from here before the escort can counter my attack. That's what, sir. On the other hand, if the ocean is rough and the weather stormy, I'd have to keep my submarine down below the rough water. I would not be able to come near the surface. So I can't use my periscope."

Captain Hudnall's expression doesn't change one bit as he leans over the deck's railing, looks in the direction of the Greenland coast, toward the bow of the ship, then toward the stern. I wait, anticipating his comments on my observations.

At last he speaks up. "Son, when we hit real North Atlantic weather, I'm going to ask you which you'd prefer, the bad weather or the U-Boats. Not as easy a choice as you might think, Sparks." He goes down the ladder to the ship's bridge, leaving me to try to understand what he means. I've never been in a North Atlantic storm, so I can't fully appreciate his last statement. A short while later I, too, descend to the chart room and visit with Mr. Bach.

Mr. Bach points to the map on the chart table. He indicates the convoy's position in the Atlantic. "We're about one third the way to the U.K. The convoy's speed's been reduced to 10 knots. Some of the older ships are having trouble keeping up. I'm glad it's been slowed down. Eleven knots is our top speed. We would have trouble maintaining 11 knots all the way across."

Within reason, the speed of the convoy is the speed of the slowest ship. The limits of "reason" are governed by the effect the speed reduction has on the general safety of the convoy. If a ship's engines lose enough power and the reduced speed jeopardizes the entire convoy, the lame ship has to fall behind. If an escort vessel can be spared, an unlikely possibility, it will circle about the lone ship, offering whatever protection it can against a U-Boat attack. If the straggling ship is unable to rejoin the convoy, its escort has to leave the freighter and return to its position as part of the main convoy's escort. A corvette's speed is about 16 knots so it can't remain very long with the straggler. If the corvette lingers, it takes a long time to overtake the convoy and resume its duty.

Mr. Bach tells me, "Sometimes a lame freighter gets through without being detected by the enemy. Sometimes it doesn't. You never can predict."

Right now, I'm glad the weather is good. No U-Boats, and our ship's engines are doing just fine. It's a comfortable feeling.

Suddenly, the quiet is broken by the ship's nerve-jarring General Alarm bells! This is followed immediately by four blasts of our ship's loud, deep-throated horn. The ships danger sound! I race to the radio room and turn on the power to the transmitter, ready to send any message the Captain may order. I wish we had a receiver tuned to the convoy escort's frequency so I might hear the battle-action communications and know more accurately what's going on. But we don't have one.

The radio room is on the port side of the ship. I open the porthole cover for a sight of the convoy. Jeffers is listening closely for distress signals on the 500 KHz radio receiver. He's a good radio operator. I'm glad he's on board. I glance at the chest and the location of the life-boat emergency transmitter to make certain they're in their correct positions. They are.

I tell Jeffers I'm going to check with the Captain on the bridge. "Right back!"

All three mates are on the bridge. Mr. Bach is on the ship's phone checking with the chief engineer asking about the condition of the engine room. The chief reports we are running at maximum speed. No spare "turns" of the screw, the ship's propeller.

Captain Hudnall's on the port wing of the bridge. I join him and tell him I'm standing by for instructions. The Captain is totally calm and unruffled, as though this is an everyday experience. He tells me our bow lookout thought he'd spotted a torpedo's wake and immediately telephoned the bridge. The second Mate instantly set off the General Alarm and blew the ship's horn. Using the blinker-signal light, I send the information to the commodore's ship. And then I return to the radio room. Escort vessels display a black flag and are moving at high speed on our starboard side. Perhaps our bow lookout actually did see the wake of a torpedo. The escort is dropping depth charges. No tell-tale signs of a hit on a submarine are seen.

The convoy continues its speed and direction. Captain Hudnall points out the convoy appears to be able to maintain the 10 knots forward speed. So can we. Everything's under control. No cause for alarm. Assured by the Captain we are out of danger the all-clear is sounded, a single short blast of the ship's horn. I suggest to Jeffers he take a break. I'll stand his watch for the next half hour. Actually, I want to be alone to review my reactions and actions.

There's a helluva difference between this ocean-going kind of thing and my experiences in Casablanca. This ocean's a lot bigger in size than Casablanca. The convoy has an armed escort, small but better than nothing, I suppose. However, despite all this protection, I feel more hemmed in, restricted and constricted by the ship than I ever did by the Hotel Monte Carlo. I could leave the hotel and still be on *terra firma*. Living on board a ship is something else. Step outside and you're on *aqua-not-so-firma*. As for my own reactions, the violent clanging of the General Alarm and the loud blasts on the ship's horn startled me. New sounds to my ears. But I felt no sense of panic. None. "*Hey, Chief! Yes, I mean you, Colonel Joe. This is the life*!"

Chapter Fifty-Eight

During the first several days of this voyage, airplanes had been flying in circles at a some distance from the convoy. Ensign Wells says they were part of the escort, sub spotters. Probably they flew out of Nova Scotia or Newfoundland or Greenland. Weather permitting, this kind of cover is provided for approximately one-third of the way across the Atlantic. Aircraft based in the U.K. cover us for the last third of the distance, again, weather permitting. I repeat this to Mr. Bach. He responds, "Weather rarely is 'permitting', Sparks!"

After the convoy moves out of the range of aircraft cover, Captain Hudnall calls for a lifeboat drill. In the event of an order to *ABANDON SHIP*! my station is in lifeboat #1 with the ship's Captain—and the emergency radio transmitter.

During breakfast, when the officers are assembled, Captain Hudnall looks at his wrist watch and announces in his strong authoritative voice, "We'll have a lifeboat drill sometime this morning. All hands. A staccato, on-off sounding of the General-Quarters bells is the signal for the simulated abandon ship. Do not, I repeat, do not launch the lifeboats or the rafts!" Captain Hudnall looks directly at me. "Sparks. Do not go to your lifeboat. You will join me on the bridge."

I'm puzzled by this instruction. Certainly, I won't throw the chest of code-books over the side in the drill. But I think it's important for me to practice lugging the emergency transmitter from the radio room and finding my way to the lifeboat. However, one is not inclined to argue with the ship's master.

The drill begins with the ear-shattering General Quarters bells. They make an appalling, extremely dreadful noise. You can't ignore the signals. Actually, in a way, the whole thing's very exciting. Adrenaline flows by the gallon.

I have the morning radio watch. Word's been passed throughout the ship, "We're going to have a lifeboat drill this morning. But, do not launch the lifeboats! Repeat. This is a drill! Do not launch the lifeboats or the rafts!" I'm pretty sure nobody, including those who are off-watch, is napping when the General Alarm bells ring and the cry goes out, *ABANDON SHIP*!

Jeffers rushes into the radio room as I wrestle with the portable emergency transmitter shaped as a "Gibson Girl." I shout "Go to your lifeboat, Jeffers!" Instead, he starts to lift the steel chest. I shout again, "Go to your lifeboat, Jeffers! Now!" He drops the chest and dashes out the door of the radio room, to his lifeboat station, I hope.

The Navy Armed Guard, merchant seamen and deck officers race for their stations. Seamen from the engine room are the last to reach the lifeboats. Some of the men of the Armed Guard and the merchant seamen assemble at the foot of their assigned, large, ramp-mounted floats. During the drill, the four engineer-officers remain in the engine room and man the controls. I expect my first requirement is to start the main transmitter and stand by for the order to abandon ship at which time I am supposed to get rid of the code books, grab the emergency transmitter and race to lifeboat #1. Seems logical. But reality and logic sometimes follow different paths. And such is the case during my first lifeboat drill.

Within a few seconds of the abandon ship call, I'm on the bridge with the emergency transmitter, the Captain and the seaman at the ship's wheel. Somebody has to keep the ship on course. The Captain races from one wing of the bridge to the other, shouting orders and watching the process of the simulated abandonment.

"When do I head for the lifeboat, Captain?"

Captain Hudnall pauses long enough to say, "Don't worry about the lifeboat, Sparks. You and I won't use it!"

So, I put the transmitter on the deck and join the Captain in his race from bridge-wing to bridge-wing. He is studying the action on the deck. I am imitating his race. After 15 or 20 minutes into the drill, Captain Hudnall briefly sounds the general quarters bells. The drill is over. Is it successful? Guess we have to wait for the real thing to determine whether or not the drill is effective.

I'm puzzled by Captain Hudnall's statement on the bridge, "You and I won't use it!" He doesn't explain. As I think about it and search for an understanding, a fantasy of images crosses my mind. It's an eyewitness report:

> *As word to abandon ship spreads throughout, Captain Hudnall and Sparks, the lone survivors, stand isolated on the bridge. As the ship settles into the ocean's depths, Captain Hudnall and Sparks can be seen side by side, bold, brave and erect, saluting the American Flag.*
>
> *Back in New York City, Joe reads the official message. It tells him of my noble last stand in the line of duty. Unlike his usual unemotional self, he wipes tears from his eyes and calls quietly to Bill.*
>
> *"Bill. I want you to pay an official visit to Leon's mother."*
>
> *"Chief! Not Leon! Say it isn't so!"*
>
> *"Sorry Bill. It is so!" He chokes on the words.*

Chapter Fifty-Nine

Clear weather. The convoy makes good time. Two days ago, one ship in our convoy dropped out; engine trouble, the Captain assumes. Jeffers and I pay special attention to the distress frequency on the radio. One feels a special kinship with any ship in trouble. It's a transference of personal fears. It could happen to us. A merchant ship traveling alone in the North Atlantic is automatically in extremely serious, grim trouble.

Night and day we hear many distress signals. SOS's report natural disasters. SSS's report submarine attacks. Each is able to include its call sign and position in latitude and longitude. Jeffers and I immediately deliver all distress signals to Captain Hudnall. Out of curiosity, I usually accompany the Captain to the chart room where he pinpoints the distressed ship's location. I must have explicit instructions from the Captain concerning our obligation to respond to any distress signal within a day's run of our own position. We are especially listening for distress signals within a range of 500 miles or so. We're all rooting and cheering for the ship, the unfortunate straggler, who had to leave the protection of our convoy. It's no laughing matter to us. Nobody talks about it. There's no need to talk about it. One SOS is only a day's run from our present position. No ship leaves the convoy.

As an individual ship in a convoy, there's nothing we can do about any of the calls. Obviously, each of us would get a sense of increased security, a feeble sense perhaps, if the straggler makes it to a safe port. And the only way we have of knowing if it does make it, peculiarly enough, is by the absence of a distress signal. One tries not to think about the possibility the lone ship, if it is hit, is unable to get off a distress message. The straggler's fate could be our fate. We continue to listen closely for a nearby distress signal. *Nil Hrd.*

Two thirds the way there. Full daylight. Mr. Bach calls me to the flying bridge. The commodore of the convoy is signaling. I grab a pad and pencil and race to the open top deck, port side, where one of our own two Navy-style signaling lights is located and from which high point I can easily see the commodore's ship and signaling light. There's also a duplicate signaling light on the starboard side of our flying bridge.

A lever on the right side of the light's housing operates the mechanism covering the face of the light, a shutter, a device resembling a venetian blind. By firmly flicking the handle downward, the blinder-slats open wide enough to allow the beam of light to be seen by anyone within a narrow arc of the direction in which the light is pointed. A set of large sights, a metal ring with cross hairs on the light's housing, makes it easy for me to aim the beam of light at the commodore's ship. One flicks and releases the handle in a logical series of long and short actions to emulate Morse code; a long light is a dash: *dah.* A short flash is a dot: *dit.*

I switch on the electric power to the light and sight on the commodore's ship. The operator of the commodore's light is sending the attention signal repeatedly: *dit-dah dit-dah dit-dah.* I hand the pad and pencil to Mr. Bach who's standing next to me. I'm not sure of Navy signaling-light communications procedure, however I respond with the *dah-dit-dah,* the letter *K*, the International Morse for "go ahead, start sending." This kind of communications is slow, but avoids the obvious hazards of breaking radio silence.

Surprised I can actually read and translate the blinking light' message, I call out the letters and numbers as they are sent from the commodore's ship. Mr. Bach writes them down. The communication ends with the International Morse SK signal, *dit-dit-dit-dah-dit-dah,* meaning "that's all." I respond with "*dit-dah-dit dit-dit-dit-dah-dit-dah.* Roger. Message received. SK." The commodore's signaling light shifts its focus to another ship and Mr. Bach and I turn to Captain Hudnall who's joined us.

"Well done, Sparks. Glad you can handle the blinker."

"Thank you, Captain." *I don't mention I didn't know I could. Never had to before.*

The message instructs the ships of the convoy to maintain positions and execute a 30-degree turn to port at exactly 1500 hours.

"What's it mean?" I ask the Captain.

"Could be an evasive action. The escort may have received reports of a wolf-pack dead ahead of the convoy. Okay, Mr. Bach. You're our navigator."

Mr. Wells, the Armed Guard officer, alerted by one of the Armed Guard lookouts, comes to the bridge. "What's happening, Captain?"

"Can any of your men read Morse Code sent by blinker light, Mr. Wells?"

"No, sir."

"How about your radioman. Can he do it?"

"No, sir."

Captain Hudnall turns to me, smiles and, for the special benefit of Ensign Wells, loudly declares, "Glad you're on board, Sparks!"

"Me too, sir." *Actually, I'm not "glad." I think I can be forgiven this little white lie.*

At 1500 hours we begin the slow process of changing course to our new heading. Jeffers takes the radio watch. Just in case the commodore has a new idea or a change of plan, the Captain and I stand on the flying bridge next to the port side signaling light. As the ships try to maintain their relative positions, I imagine a herd of pachyderms performing a synchronized, slow-motion ballet.

The air is extremely cold. It's quiet. The ocean's obligingly calm. Maneuvering a convoy of freighters is slow and serious work. Collisions must be avoided. And these monstrous pachyderms of the sea cannot possibly turn or change direction on a dime.

Two hours later, the signaling lights are in action again. The convoy is instructed to execute a starboard turn into a new compass heading. This is accomplished slowly, as before, without incident. By the time the convoy completes the maneuver, the hazy sun starts to disappear. It sinks into the ocean.

Or, was it torpedoed?

Chapter Sixty

Approximately three days to make port. We have no idea which port. Could be North Ireland, England or Scotland—any place in the United Kingdom. If communication systems are working, the local O.N.I. office will know our destination and will watch for me to step off the ship's gangway. I'm looking forward to working on dry land and trying to catch new shadows. It may not be entertainment, but it beats the monotony of shipboard life.

Another string of signals from the commodore of the convoy. We may hold gunnery practice, firing at will. Within minutes cannons boom from many of the ships in the convoy. Because of the relative closeness and spread of the ships, cannons must be aimed and fired at high elevations.

A few minutes after the practice has begun, the commodore orders an immediate cease fire followed by the information that a seaman on one of the ships has been fatally hit by shrapnel. I deliver each message to the Captain. Mr. Wells, the Navy Armed-Guard officer had been busy at the stern cannon issuing lengthy orders to his crew and had not yet fired a single shell. He was not aware of the cease fire order. I guess he thinks his crew is now ready to fire and came to the bridge. I've been observing from the port-side wing of the bridge. Mr. Wells comes out of the bridge onto the port wing followed closely by Captain Hudnall. They're involved in heated exchange.

"Captain, I will decide when we fire the guns! I am in charge of this ship's armament!"

"Mr. Wells! I am master of this ship and I will tell you when you may practice!"

"No, you don't control the gun-crew!

Maintaining his fabulous self-control, Captain Hudnall ends the argument. "Mr. Wells.

If you fire the guns at any time without my permission, I will put you in irons!"

Mr. Wells rushes past me, races down the ladder and sulks as he slowly climbs to the stern gun's platform. Captain Hudnall, I and all on deck who heard the angry disagreement with Mr. Wells, watch closely to see what he is up to.

Will he fire the cannon? He still is not aware of the commodore's last instruction. Fortunately, Mr. Wells recognizes the fact Captain Hudnall always keeps his promises. He dismisses the gun crew.

On the bridge with the 2nd Mate, Mr. Thompson. It is late afternoon. The sky is overcast, a dreary gray color. I gaze forward at the horizon, looking for nothing in particular. I become aware of a change in the shape of the horizon's line dead ahead. "What's that on the horizon, Mr. Thompson?"

Mr. Thompson picks up his heavy maritime field glasses and focuses on the horizon. "We're heading into a fog bank. I'd better notify the Captain." He blows into one of the speaking tubes on the wall. It's actually a hollow pipe about one inch in diameter. Blowing hard into it causes a whistle at the other end of the pipe to sound.

"Bridge, Captain. We're coming into a heavy fog bank, sir."

Captain Hudnall responds, "Be right there."

The Captain and the 2nd pick up field glasses and the three of us head for the open top deck where we can get an unobstructed view of the horizon. The fog bank almost engulfs the entire horizon and is closing on us rapidly. The Captain estimates we'll be inside the fog in 10 minutes. We return to the bridge's housing. Captain Hudnall tells the 2nd to ask the 1st and 3rd Mates to join us on the bridge right away. He blows into the engine room's speaking tube. "Chief. Can you come to the bridge, please."

A few minutes later all the deck officers, the Chief Engineer and his 1st are assembled on the bridge. Captain Hudnall points forward. "Gentlemen. There's a heavy fog and we're going to run straight into it. I've no idea how deep it is so there's no way of knowing how long it will take the convoy to pass through. Stand your regular watches please. Stay alert." He addresses the Chief Engineer. "Stand close by the throttle." Enough said.

The commodore's signaling light is pointed at us: *dit-dah dit-dah dit-dah*. Attention! The Captain, the Chief Mate and I race up to the top deck and our port-side blinker. I send the go ahead signal: *dah-dah-dit dit-dah*. GA.

The commodore instructs ships' masters to reduce speed to six knots, a safety measure while running through the fog. Also, under such weather conditions, it is necessary for each ship's fog horn to count off its convoy station number at intervals of ten minutes or less. The frequent blowing of the ship's number on the fog horn helps each navigator estimate his ship's position relative to those riding forward, aft and abeam. The ear is the direction finder. At the moment, there are no ships aft of us or on our starboard beam. All we have to do is keep from drifting aft or to the starboard outside the perimeters of the convoy. Or so I think.

Quickly, we are consumed by the ice-cold, dense fog. It's so thick I actually cannot see the ship's bow from inside the bridge. I run to the radio room to alert Jeffers and take over the watch myself. I suggest he advise Ensign Wells what's happening.

This is first time I've been in a fog this thick. It's as though someone had thrown a heavy blanket over the entire ship. We are cut off visually from the rest of the convoy. We're blindfolded. The spooky effect the thick fog has on sound is an amazing phenomenon. Everything sounds muffled. I whisper automatically. So does everyone else. I think it's because we're trying to listen intently while talking, listen for changes in the environment's sounds. Above all the muffled noises, the engine's *thump-atta-thump* sounds louder than ever. It's thumping at a slower rate now that we've reduced speed to six knots. The thumpings are part of the environment of sound. One tunes them out—until moments such as these. The steady, deep sound of the engine is reassuring—as long as it's steady and not interrupted.

The 3rd Mate has the watch. Everything slows down. Time drags. Listening closely, trying to shut out all other sounds, I hear the fog horns of the ships as they hoarsely sound their numbers. Now our horn raises its voice. *Six* blasts and *Five* blasts. Our convoy position: *Sixth column, Fifth row*. A fog horn directly forward of us blasts, *Six*! *Four*! Then a fog horn on our port beam counts off. *Five*! *Five*! The horns blast regularly. Everyone listens attentively for changes in the fog horns of the ships directly ahead and off our port beam. Monotonous, depressing sounds. Their deep throats fill one with anxiety. It's unavoidable. "You never get used to it," they say. Only the most experienced seaman can accurately judge distances at sea by the loudness and direction of sounds. Good thing we have at least two such men on board ship. Captain Hudnall and Mr. Bach, of course. I can't be of any help on the bridge. I go to the radio room.

I recall, as a boy, reading novels of the sea and the romantic, swashbuckling days of ships under real sails. The men were tough, sometimes even cruel to one another as they fought for survival against the overwhelming forces of the sea:

> *The Captain, gray and grizzled from decades of sailing the seven seas, peers into the dense fog, listening closely to the sound of the fog horn from the invisible lighthouse. He turns his head left and right, trying to sense the direction and distance of the fog horn and the rocky shore. The lookout, high up on the main-mast, frantically shouts, "Thar she is, cap'n!" With horrible crashing noises and agonizing groans of the doomed ship's timbers, the...*

I'm quickly brought back to reality by four short blasts from our ship's horn! *Danger*! I reach over and switch on the main transmitter. Jeffers comes running to the radio room. His eyes and voice are filled with alarm. "What's happening?"

At that very moment, the ship shudders and pitches slightly as though she'd been grounded. Remembering our forward hold is loaded with ammunition, I grasp the side of the transmitter's housing and try to hold on. But there's no explosion. Telling Jeffers to stand by, I race to the bridge. Captain Hudnall is already there. Mr. Bach and the 2nd Mate arrive just behind me. It's terribly quiet. Thump-atta-thump. Captain Hudnall is rapidly firing questions at the 3rd, a junior officer, graduate of one of the maritime academies with six months experience at sea. Recently promoted from cadet, this is his first trip as a licensed deck-officer.

He's flustered. Almost in a state of panic. Mr. Bach grabs the 3rd by the shoulders and shakes him very hard while shouting to him, "Speak up! Speak up, Mister!"

In a frightened voice, the 3rd Mate tells the Captain and Mr. Bach he thinks he dozed off and lost track of the fog horns. He wasn't aware that the distance between our ship and the one ahead was closing rapidly until the lookout man on the bow telephoned frantically. He could see the stern of a ship ahead of us! That's when the 3rd sounded the danger signal. Our bow touched and pressed hard against the stern of the ship ahead. A collision! Thanks to the convoy's slow-ahead speed, we didn't crash with great force.

The 3rd Mate buries his face in his hands and begins to sob. The Chief Engineer arrives at the bridge at this point. Captain Hudnall fills him in. The Chief Engineer says his 3rd had the watch and when he felt the collision, immediately slowed the engines and waited for instructions from the bridge—which didn't come. The Chief reports he was on the way down the ladder into the engine room and when he felt the heavy jolt of the collision. He continued down, got his 3rd's report, then came directly to the bridge for instructions.

Captain Hudnall takes a deep breath. I can see he's trying to control his anger. "Let's get things back in order. Mr. Bach, you and I will remain on the bridge." Pointing his finger directly into the 3rd's face, "You are relieved of your duties aboard this ship. You will go to your cabin and stay there until I give you permission to leave!" The 3rd Mate, head held low, shoulders stooped, leaves the bridge. Captain Hudnall scans our faces. "Thank you gentlemen for doing the right thing. Please go back to your duties. I'll attend to the 3rd Mate at breakfast, tomorrow. I'd appreciate it if you are all there. Just be thankful we didn't hit hard enough to set off our cargo!"

As though we are one relieved voice, we quietly respond, "Yes, sir. Yes, sir." And, except for the Captain, Mr. Bach and the man at the ship's wheel, we leave the bridge. The two engineers run to the ship's bow to assess the damage. None is visible.

The Captain's ceremony next morning in the officer's salon is short, sharp, unambiguous. All officers, including the 3rd Mate are here. Not a word is being spoken. The 3rd looks miserable, eats nothing. Captain Hudnall takes his time, finishes his breakfast and looks at each of us, one at a time. His eyes come to rest on the 3rd.

Captain Hudnall stands up, very erect. "I want you all to witness what I'm saying to the 3rd." He pauses, then continues with a detailed account of the previous night's happenings. "Is there any disagreement with the facts as I've stated them? Third, do you have any disagreement?"

Third, with head still bowed, stands up. He replies slowly in a hoarse whisper. "No, sir."

The Captain continues. "We don't have a brig or I'd put you there in irons. You are relieved of all duties aboard this ship until we reach port. When we do reach port, you will take your personal belongings and leave this ship in my custody. I will locate the port Captain and tell him exactly what happened, just as I said it here. You!" Pointing and looking at the 3rd, "You will never again sail on a ship with me! Whether or not you ever sail on any other ship...I leave that determination up to the War Shipping Administration's courts. In the meantime, I will make certain you get transportation back to New York. Understand me?"

The thoroughly dejected and remorseful 3rd Mate chokes back sobs and tears, hoarsely whispers and repeats over and over, "I do, sir. I do. I'm sorry. Very...very...very sorry."

I feel sad for the 3rd. All of us do. On the other hand, he did jeopardize our lives, the ship and, perhaps, the convoy. We do not discuss the situation among ourselves.

This afternoon the fog lifts. It passes by or we sail through it; whichever, the effect is the same. It's as though the thick blanket that covered us is slowly rolled back. Our blindfold is removed. Through field glasses we can see a large dent in the stern of the ship ahead of us.

Captain Hudnall instructs me to contact the damaged ship by blinker light. "Ask for a damage report." The other ship's Captain assures us the collision does not affect his ship's seaworthiness or steering ability. I send Captain Hudnall's compliments and wishes for a safe journey. All very formal, unhurried, and gentlemanly.

The convoy reaches the U.K. without further incident or contact either with foul weather or the enemy. Our ship drops anchor in the Clyde River off Gourock, Scotland, and we are told by signaling light to wait for an available dock where our cargo will be unloaded. My duties aboard ship will soon be over—until our departure.

I ask the Captain's permission to hail a passing boat and go ashore. Navy Radioman Jeffers remains on board. I can't tell Captain Hudnall why I am eager to go ashore. With some apparent reluctance, he gives permission.

"I'll keep in close touch with the Navy office, Captain. As soon as I get word at what dock the ship has discharged its cargo and, when the ship's scheduled to move out to an anchorage, I'll rejoin her, sir."

"I've never had to leave anyone behind because he didn't show up, Sparks. Don't be the first!"

"I won't, Captain."

Captain Hudnall dismisses me with a wave of his arm. I tell Mr. Bach I am going ashore for a while. I pack a bag, put on my Merchant Marine uniform, load and pocket my revolver and head for the Jacobs Ladder on the ship's starboard side, facing the shore of Gourock.

Within half an hour, I'm able to hail a passing Navy liberty boat. "Can you take me ashore?"

A Navy ensign on the liberty boat calls out to me. "What's your name, sir?"

I'm a bit surprised when, on hearing my name, he orders the liberty boat's coxs'n to bring the boat alongside the Jacobs Ladder. Within 15 minutes I step ashore. Terra firma feels good.

Chapter Sixty-One

I easily locate the Navy communications office southwest of Gourock and the Office of Naval Intelligence. There is a brief message for me from New York.

```
To: LAW
From: JF
Read this and destroy.

   Your  original  destination  postponed.
Return to Office for new instructions.
```

Chapter Sixty-Two

The Navy provides me with a liberty boat to take me back to my ship. She has been unloaded, filled with ballast materials and is making ready to sail back to the United States.

Back on board the ship, I go directly to Captain Hudnall to let him know I've kept my word. He's in his cabin, all smiles.

"I'm back, Captain. As I said I'd be."

"Never doubted it for a moment, Sparks. However, yesterday, when they called the convoy conference in Gourock—which you were supposed to attend—I did advise the Navy office I was short a radio operator."

"Sorry, Captain. Too bad. I never left Gourock."

He stops smiling. "I think the Shore Patrol and local police may be looking for you right now. I suggest you get on the signaling light, contact the Navy shore-lookout and report you're on board and they can stop the search." He waves me off. I do not reveal they already know.

I find Mr. Bach in the chart room. "Where in hell have you been, Sparks? We form convoy in the morning! Would have hated to leave you behind."

"I was doing some sightseeing and lost track of time." I cut off any further questions by asking him to give me the bearing for the Navy shore-lookout so I can signal that I'm on board.

He tells me there is some trouble aboard, "Again its with Mr. Wells. Every single day, regardless of weather, he assembles his gun crew on hatch cover #2 and lectures them endlessly while they are told to stand at attention. In my opinion, he's a sick man. Never says a word to any of the Merchant Marine officers or crew. Never greets anyone when he comes to meals in the officers' salon. Sparks, I want you to keep an eye on him. Please let me know if he appears to do anything improper to his men or equipment."

"I will, sir."

One night, on our return voyage, I am alone on watch in the radio room. A soft knock on the door. Three of the gun crew come into the room and quickly but silently close the door behind them. They are not smiling and present me with an impossible request.

"Sparks, sir. You probably know the ensign has made himself very disliked by the crew.

It's a fact...we hate his guts! We need your help, sir. Wells never comes out of his cabin at night. We think you are the only one on this ship who can get him to come out on deck. We'll take care of the rest."

I do not have to hear the "rest." I certainly will not be an accessory to the murder of Ensign Wells or his disappearance at sea. "Fellows. This conversation never took place. It will not be repeated to anyone, anywhere. We'll be back in the U.S. pretty soon. Please hold on until we are home. Then, as a group, file formal charges against him to the Navy authorities."

Chapter Sixty-Three

I don't know who's more surprised—Bill Brady or Merry, the Chief's secretary. I don't understand the unusual way the two of them keep looking at me with their mouths wide open.

Merry runs to me, throws her arms around my neck and presses her face so close to mine I'm afraid one of us will be permanently scarred. She bursts into tears. Bill comes over and hugs both of us. The three of us form a single mass of bodies rocking back and forth.

I steer our threesome into the privacy of Bill's office. "Okay, now. Why the tears? So much emotion? What's this all about?"

Bill composes himself. "We heard your ship had been sunk. We couldn't get any details. A storm? Submarines? Luftwaffe? I've been trying to figure a way to tell your mother. She'd learn for the first time, from me, how you were involved in the war. I hated the thought of going to see her with such bad news. I didn't know what...how to tell her..." He breaks off, choked with emotion and relief.

Merry sits down, wipes her eyes and nods her head. "It's been terrible for us!"

I sit down and try to comfort her. Bill, smiling now, pulls up a chair. The two of them are looking at me as if they don't believe their eyes.

"Hey! It's me. It really is me. Merry. Bill. I didn't think anyone cared so much whether I make it or not. It's nice to know somebody besides my mother cares."

Bill tells me the Chief is out of town for the next two days. "Let's the three of us—you, Merry and me—go out on the town tonight and tie one on, a light one. A kind of celebration."

"I like it. Bill! Merry! You're a couple of pals. What I need right now is some mid-morning coffee and doughnuts. No! Make it ice cold milk and doughnuts! I haven't had a glass of milk since two days after I shipped out. And a doughnut from Horn & Hardhardt's. I've been dreaming about it."

Bill suggests the three of us go down the street and for milk and doughnuts right now.

Merry is more practical. Before we separate, she calls the hotel and reserves a room for me. "He'll be there in about an hour. I don't care what your check-in time is. Mr. Wortman will be there in an hour!"

We stay at the Horn & Hardhardt Automat for almost two hours. While we chat about nothing in particular, I enjoy looking around the Automat. I get a kick out of watching the people go up to the lady behind the big, square central change booth and get their piles of nickels. It's amusing to see them put one or more nickels in the slots alongside the small, windowed cubicles in which the mouth-watering food items are displayed. Then the windows pop open and the lucky customers withdraw their selected items and march off to enjoy their goodies at one of the many tables. Five cent coffee comes from a spout. Put your cup under the spout, deposit your nickel, and turn the lever It always amazes me how the spout knows exactly when to stop the flow.

Merry looks anxiously at her wrist watch. She must return to The Office, "In case Joe calls."

Bill insists, "To hell with Joe! I'm going to help Leon check in. We'll pick up his things from The Office and I'll go to the hotel with him."

Bill, his arms laden with my "things," encourages me to precede him out of The Office. Merry gently plants a lingering kiss on my cheek.

In the hotel room, talking as quietly as possible, I tell Bill all about my *Scotland Non-Adventure*.

Bill shrugs off my nothing-happened report. "O.N.I. and G-2 will want to debrief you, I'm sure."

I remember how annoyed our leader was when I allowed O.N.I. and G-2 to debrief me before he'd heard the details directly from me. "Er, Bill. Can you hold off until I've made my report to Joe? You know how he is about protocol. He'll want to hear my report before O.N.I. and G-2."

"Of course, I can. Joe should be back in two days. I'll let him call the soldiers and sailor boys. "What would you like to do next? I mean now."

"Take a shower and a nap."

"Then?"

"Grab a sandwich—corned beef on rye with cole slaw on it and half-sour pickles—at the Stage Delicatessen, of course."

"And then?"

"Catch up on the latest French movie at the Apollo Theater on 42nd Street."

"And then?"

"Meet you and Merry at some nice restaurant for dinner. Preferably one that never heard of warm beer!"

Bill shakes my hand and heads out the door. "How's about 1900 at the Hofbrau, downtown?"

I think he's making a joke. "A German restaurant?"

"How about a French place?"

I think he's still making jokes. He can tell from my expression I'd prefer something else. "How's about a steak at Gallagher's?"

"You're on, Bill. Gallagher's Steak House. You did say 'Gallagher's Steak House'?"

Next morning, the Chief's back. He'd heard I was in The Office and cut his trip short to get back to New York City for my report. I know him better. He'll accept any excuse to leave Washington. Although he's thrown his body wholeheartedly into his job, he hates the politics of Washington and loves New

York and the freedom he has to run The Office. He calls for coffee for us, settles down at his desk and locks his briefcase in one of the drawers.

"Glad you made it, Leon." He calls Merry to come in with her pad. "Merry, take notes please as we listen to Leon's report of his Scotland holiday."

Thus, on the Chief's sarcastic note, I recount my experiences. I omit nothing. Deliberately, with excruciating detail, I describe every rise and fall of the ship, every movement of the convoy, including the collision with another ship in a fog; the torpedo-wake sighting; my conversations with the 1st Mate and the Purser. The long hours of a two-man watch are gloriously detailed. I wouldn't think of leaving out descriptions of the hours of copying and decoding the BAMS messages and their reports of floating mines sighted in the South Atlantic Ocean while our ship was in the North Atlantic. Finally, our arrival in Scotland, anchoring in the Clyde River and the liberty boat to Gourock's shore—and back.

Merry struggles to suppress laughter. She's more than a bit amused. She looks up from her pad frequently and winks at me. She's enjoying my game of "Some holiday I had!"

After several hours of listening to my monologue, during which Merry had to go to her desk for more pads and pencils for my never-ending tale, I finish with a description of "How amazing it is to discover the first sight of the United States we deep-water sailors have, as we near the end of an Atlantic crossing. It's the Parachute Jump, the entertainment ride in Coney Island. I haven't mentioned that important fact before. Have I, Chief?"

Am I serious or pulling his leg? The Chief isn't quite sure. But, my timing is trying the Chief's humor. The little he has left, anyway, is being sorely tested.

"Merry." He asks, "Have you notified O.N.I. and G-2 to come debrief our own Scotsman?

"No. But I think Bill has. Shall I check with him now?"

"Soon's you can. I have another assignment for Leon."

"What? Where? When, Joe? Another sea voyage?" I'm all ears; my turn to listen. But it's apparent he's not in the mood to talk. Not now.

Merry comes back into Joe's office. "They'll be here at 0900 tomorrow. Two O.N.I. and two G-2 officers. They'll do the debriefing right here. I suggest Bill Brady's office."

"Okay, Leon. See you here in the morning. One suggestion. Cut the crap when you give these four guys your report. They may not have as much time as I did today. Eh? I'll give you your next assignment tomorrow afternoon. I have to take care of a few of the details while you're entertaining our visitors."

I leave The Office. I can use a long walk around Central Park.

Chapter Sixty-Four

Debriefing is finished. In answer to questions about the Officer of the Armed Guard, I admit only I observed he was not popular with the Navy crew or the Merchant Marine officers.

I go to the Chief's office, eager to learn my new assignment. Joe's office door is locked. Merry puts her index finger to her pursed lips. She makes spooning motions to let me know Joe's having lunch in his office and doesn't want to be disturbed. I go to Merry's desk.

I whisper, "How long?"

Looking at her wrist watch she silently mouths, "Fifteen, twenty minutes."

Duplicating the spooning motions, I indicate I'm going to lunch. In a whisper, "Back in half an hour." I leave The Office.

Thirty minutes later, I knock on the Chief's door and listen for the familiar signal, "Come." I come in and shut the door behind me.

The Chief points to a chair. I sit down. Our eyes meet in a favorite game, "Who'll blink first?" I'm eager to get to the meat so I blink first.

Satisfied he won the game this time, the Chief speaks. "Details of your new assignment." He removes a file from his locked desk-drawer and continues. "You've been gone for a while, so you may not realize how much we've grown."

"Chief. I used to know everybody here. Now, I hardly know anyone. They probably don't have the foggiest idea of who I am, except I seem to come and go frequently."

"That's right, Leon." Joe, my Chief, puts an arm around my shoulder, a new high for him in displaying feelings. Wearing a pleasant smile, he walks me into his office, shuts the door, points to a chair and invites me to join him in a cup of coffee while we chat. "Are you ready for more?"

I try not to reveal my suspicions. He's buttering me, leading up to something. "I'm ready."

"Let me give you as much background as I can." He hesitates. "There are a lot of mixed feelings in Washington and other high and low places about the Russians."

My ears perk up. I have my own mixed feelings about Russia as one of our allies against the Nazis. Russian and Ukrainian lore played an important part in my formative years.

"Are you listening to me, Leon?"

The Chief caught my mind wandering, triggered by the mention of the Russians. I apologize. "Sorry, Chief. We've never talked about the Russians before. You have my undivided attention."

"We don't know very much about certain aspects of the Russians and we do have to refine our knowledge."

"I'm not sure I follow you, Chief."

"Among the things we are not sure of is how do the people and lesser officials really feel about us and about the other allied countries? We don't have any doubt they're fighting on our side right now. But what are their plans and intentions toward us after the war's over?"

I lean forward. "Chief, I get the feeling you're deliberately trying to be vague, not very specific. I don't have any idea about where you're heading. Can you be more direct?"

"You're right, Leon. You see we get lots of reports from our Ambassador in Moscow. We even have one of our own men in Moscow."

"Oh?"

"Yes. He's been pestering us to bring him home. He feels he's not very effective. Maybe he isn't, but we have no way of knowing whether it's because of some deficiency in his own skills or the Russians' intense appetites for secrecy and harassment.

"Our man's movements are very restricted. He isn't allowed to travel outside Moscow. And, because of the stringent Russian laws regarding public behavior, he can't even get the civilians to talk to him. The penalty for talking to foreigners, which they call 'fraternizing' and includes all military allies, can be as much as six months imprisonment for their own people, mind you. So, the plan to use our man as a source of information is not working at all.

"He's fluent in the Russian language but it's not helpful. He can't have a conversation. He's tried everything, including giving away American cigarettes on a large scale. They are a very valuable commodity in Russia. However, they accept our man's cigarettes and quickly dash away before he can become friendly."

This is fascinating. I haven't twitched, coughed or moved a muscle. But, I still don't know how this involves me. Is he thinking of replacing our man in Moscow with me? I don't think I'd like to fill his shoes in Moscow. My fluency in the Russian language is questionable. I understand conversation much better than can speak the language. I don't think my fluency is as good as it has to be for me to pose successfully as a Russian.

Joe tells me more. "The Russian Government is tight-mouthed about their dealings with German prisoners. We must know something specific about what happens to German pilots who get shot down over North Russia." He hesitates. "Also, and very confidential, our military and political strategists are looking ahead to the post-war period. With so many variables and options to consider, there's a sharp division of thinking among the military and the politicians." He hesitates as though he is wondering how much to tell me about Washington's thinking. "After we win the war against the Nazis, some of our generals want to take on Russia. What d'you think of that?"

"I don't know, Chief. A military strategist, I am not! People strategy? Okay. I'm comfortable there."

"Yes, I know. We—I mean Washington—have a new strategy. It requires someone like you, a person who's a risk taker, is willing to stick his neck out. We need several field agents in North Russia and in other places we can enter with reasonably unbreakable covers. Maybe there's no such thing as an unbreakable cover. But I proposed an unusual one to Bill Donovan. He gave me the go-ahead. And you fit the description perfectly!"

If I lean any further forward I'll fall off my chair. "I'm not with you, Chief. Maybe, if you keep on talking, I'll catch up to you—maybe."

"Okay, Leon. Let's try it this way. As a double and triple check on dispatches that come through the Embassy in Moscow, Washington needs first-hand reports on the mood of the Russian people and officials in other parts of Russia, especially the prevalent attitudes toward Americans. Why not rely totally on the Embassy reports? The Americans in the Embassy can't move outside of Moscow. They're shadowed 24 hours a day by the OGPU. Maybe all of the internal security police sections we know of, and some we may not even know about, tail us wherever we go in Moscow. Leningrad and Stalingrad are a shambles from heavy bombardments and blockades. We can't get our people in or out of those two cities."

"Chief. I'm not with you yet."

The Chief is being more patient than usual. "It's a complex situation. We're supposed to be allies. But the alliance only means we're fighting the same enemy. We're not buddies. Ideologically, we can never get together."

"Strange, isn't it Chief? I understand Russia depends on the allies, meaning the United States, for supplies; food stuff, medical and military equipment. On the way to Scotland, everybody on board the *Collis P. Huntington* talked about the rough convoys into North Russia. They say losses from U-Boats, mines, torpedo planes and dive bombers make the North Atlantic run past Norway and into the Arctic Circle, around the North Cape into North Russian ports the most dangerous sea corridor in the world. They call it the 'Murmansk Run' or 'The North Cape Run' and tremble at the thought of making these runs. I've heard many horror stories.".

The Chief is quiet now. Immobile. He looks directly into my eyes. Slowly at first, it comes to me. "Chief! I think I've caught up to you. You want me to go to North Russia. Right?"

He nods in the affirmative.

I sit back in my chair, fold my arms and hold my chin in my right hand in a deep-thinking posture. "You...they...want me to sign on a ship going to North Russia? Is that the unusual proposal you made—and they accepted?"

"Exactly, Leon. You can sign on as Chief Radio Officer. You would have no duties while the ship's in port. You'd be free to roam and, with discretion of course, see all sorts of conditions for yourself—and you'll be able to see how far you can go."

"What means 'see how far you can go'? Come again, please?"

"We'll see you have all the rubles you need to buy your way in or out of any situation. We'll supply you with cases of cigarettes. Boxes of chocolates. Scotch by the case. And, should you run into any special women, we'll make sure the ship store is well-stocked with perfume and soap. I hear there's a severe shortage of those items. Propaganda pictures make the women look tougher and rougher than the men, but we know the Russian women like to keep themselves clean and smelling pretty—if they can get the necessaries."

"When do you want me to go on this one?"

"Soon." His slight smile betrays what hasn't yet been said.

"You've already worked out all the details, haven't you, Chief?"

"We have, Leon. But we want you to want to go on this one. You have to 'volunteer', as someone wiser than I once said."

"Give me the details and let me sleep on them overnight. I'll give you my answer in the morning."

"Sorry, Leon. This job has to be kept as tightly wrapped as Operation Torch, the invasion of North Africa, was. Give me your answer in the morning. If you volunteer to go, you'll get all the details quickly, probably tomorrow afternoon, in a joint meeting with O.N.I. and G-2. They're very enthusiastic about this one."

I stand up and extend my hand to the Chief. "Suppose I say no. What happens?"

The Chief is prepared for this one. His benevolent smile is gone. "Leon. I think we've been though this before. You'll be drafted in a week and immediately assigned to me. See you in the morning, Leon. Sleep tight."

"Yeah. Sleep tight, colonel."

Actually, I do not sleep tight. There are no viable options available to me on this assignment. One thing's certain, I am definitely going to Russia. I toss and turn most of the night. My mother's favorite Russian proverb serves me well: *The morning is brighter than the night.*

Chapter Sixty-Five

A hot shower, shave and leisurely breakfast make this morning much brighter than last night. Wish I had listened more closely when, in a reminiscent mood, Mom used to tell me stories about her and my father's experiences growing up in the Ukraine. I could visit and ask her to retell those tales, but my mother is a pretty sharp lady. It would certainly reveal to her the truth about my job—and possibly jeopardize the safety of her family still in the Ukraine. An inadvertent comment made by Mom could unintentionally expose my cover. No. Better not even hint at a possible trip to Russia.

"Hi Bill. Good morning...everyone."

Bill Brady points and nods. "The Chief's waiting for you."

"Good morning, Chief!" I feel more cheerful than I did when I left him yesterday.

"How'd you sleep?"

"Lousy."

The Chief motions me to sit. "Did you consider the Russia assignment?"

"Yes. That's why I slept lousy!"

He looks concerned, not about my sleeping but what he'd have to do if I say *nyet*, no to Russia.

I force a smile and some humor. "Chief. Can I go to Russia, please? Please say yes!"

He can try to be humorous, too. "Well...I don't know. But, if that's the way you want it, I'll see what I can do for you." He breaks into a big smile, gets up, comes over to me and shakes my hand so hard I'm concerned about possible bone fractures.

"Yes, I 'want it' but this doesn't mean I want to spend the rest of the war in North Russia. I'm really a warm weather person. But, now we've decided, tell me more about the assignment, please."

"Where'd we leave off yesterday?"

He's testing me, again. I know he has a remarkable memory for conversations. I test him right back. "We were talking about how sexy Russian women are."

"We've exhausted that subject. Let's move right along to the next. You remember Captain Hudnall and your trip to Scotland?"

"I do. Great leader, Captain Hudnall. It was a pleasure to work with him. As a matter of fact, the whole bunch was great. Marvelous camaraderie. I don't think I'll ever find a finer group. Except for the 3rd Mate."

"You mean the guy who fell asleep in the fog?"

"The very same."

"Well, I've some good news for you. Captain Hudnall and the *Collis P. Huntington* are in port right now."

My eyes light up. I'd enjoy a friendly, social visit to Captain Hudnall on board the ship. I miss completely what the Chief is implying. I'm not making the right connections between Captain Hudnall and the trip to Russia...until I notice the Chief looks like the proverbial fat cat licking the canary's feathers off his front.

Realization dawns. "Chief. D' you mean the *Collis P. Huntington*'s headed for North Russia?"

"Yep!"

"And you want me to be on it?"

"Yep!"

"Does the *Collis P. Huntington* need a Chief Radio Officer?"

"Yep!"

"This puts a new light on the whole assignment." *The horror stories of the miseries of sailing under a hard-nosed skipper make me seriously hesitant about the long journey to North Russia. No combination could be worse. But, Captain Hudnall! This makes a big, big difference. He's the best of the best!* "Chief, I wonder if Captain Hudnall would have me on his ship again?"

"Why not, Leon?"

"I did pull out after one trip to Scotland. I wonder who's shipping out with him?"

The Chief moves toward his office's door and puts his hand on the doorknob. "Why don't you go to the ship and find out for yourself? Merry will give you directions." He edges me toward the door which is now open. "Come back here tomorrow morning and we'll continue our discussion in the briefing with O.N.I. and G-2."

He closes his door, probably to call Donovan to announce, "New York's part in the Russian adventure is all set! You-know-who is going. Right. No. He volunteered!"

An hour later, dressed in my Merchant Marine uniform, I board the *Collis P. Huntington.* Captain Hudnall doesn't seem surprised to see me. *Is there any significance in his calm and very friendly attitude toward me*?

I remove my cap and, at the Captain's invitation, I follow him to his office and relax on the settee against the outside bulkhead of his office.

He's as pleasant as I've ever seen him. "Sparks, glad to see you. We worked well together on the Scotland trip. Do you have a ship?"

We chat about the war and a few other cabbages and kings. I'm curious about who are the ship's officers for the next trip. And where has the ship been since we made the voyage to Scotland.

I'm more than surprised when he tells me the ship just returned from Casablanca. I don't mention my own voyage to Casablanca with Operation

Torch. It would take a lot of explaining, and even the explanation is more than I want to or can get involved in. Captain Hudnall is feeling talkative. Unusual for him. A rare treat for me.

"Mr. Bach retired again when we came back to New York. The 2nd, you know Mister Thompson, he is now Chief Mate. You and he got along nicely. I have new 2nd and 3rd mates. Hand-picked them myself. The Chief Engineer is new. In fact the entire complement of engine room officers is new. They all look good to me. Lots of seagoing experience on Liberty Ships. The Purser? Same one. George Leitner. You've a lot of friends on board. You might want to make the rounds, Sparks. They'll be glad to see you."

I'm sincere when I say, "Sounds to me, Captain Hudnall, you've assembled a fine group of officers and crew. What about Mr. Wells, the Armed Guard officer? Is he still on board?"

"No, Sparks. He was reassigned to a shore desk. No idea who we're going to get next."

"Do you have your radio operator yet?"

The Captain looks at me and smiles. "Not yet. The job is open."

I innocently ask, "Do you know the destination for the next voyage, Captain?"

"Not exactly. I'll find out in a couple of days at the convoy conference."

He's holding something back. The cargo's markings and the ship's manifest should tell him what part of the world the ship is headed. If it is Murmansk, he knows it. The deck cargo is covered and doesn't provide a clue. Airplanes can be delivered anywhere there's a U.S. Ally. But, he must have seen the cargo as it was being stored in the ship's holds.

Captain Hudnall speaks directly. "Well, Sparks, Mr. Wortman. Are you coming aboard as my Chief Radio, or did you just happen to be drifting by and decided to stop in and have a chat?"

"If I'm welcome, Captain, all I need is time to collect my things, check out of the hotel, say good-byes and I can move back into my cabin on the *Collis P. Huntington.*

We're both standing. "Be on board tonight. We're moving out into the Hudson River tomorrow morning. Remember, there's going to be a convoy conference the day before we sail and I want you to go to it with me. The Navy will supply the ship with two assistant radio operators before we sail. The Armed Guard comes aboard any minute, today."

"Captain. If I'm not on board tonight, please don't worry about whether or not I'll show up. I will be here before the conference. I promise."

I'm thinking of O.N.I. and G-2. If there's going to be a briefing, it will have to be completed tomorrow. The briefing is for my benefit. I have many more questions, lots of them. What, if any, are my specific tasks? Objectives? People to be wary of and aware of? Who are my contacts in North Russia? Any special warnings about such items as unwritten Russian rules and regulations? How do I get my reports back to the Chief? How do he and I communicate? I must have answers before the *Collis P. Huntington* sails.

Chapter Sixty-Six

The briefing session in the Chief's office goes well and all the questions I could think of are answered. No note taking is permitted. Several warnings impress me. "*Beware of the tendency of Russian sentries to shoot on sight. Beware of the dangers of drinking Vodka, especially on an empty stomach.*"

We don't know the specific port the ship will put into. There are only three possibilities: Murmansk, Archangyelsk or Molotovsk. Most likely? *Nye' znayoo*—I don't know. Port assignments are made when the convoy gets close to the most northern sector of Russia. The intelligence map shows Murmansk inside the Kola inlet is the most westerly port. Continue east and enter the White Sea. Archangyelsk is the first usable port on the coast of the White Sea.

Approximately 15 miles to the southwest is the smaller village of Molotovsk. Deeper inside the White Sea, south of Molotovsk is Lake Onega and the town of Onega with forests which can provide pulp as ship's ballast for the return voyage. The pulp is usually discharged in the United Kingdom. Replacement ballast? Whatever they can find. Rocks, sand, dirt, anything that can be loaded into a ship's hold.

They key information for me concerns my contacts in Archangel, pronounced Ar-khan-gyelsk. My primary contacts are two U.S. Navy lieutenants who act as the Office of the American Consul. They will advise me about any others I can rely on. Their names? Warschel and Horschel! I can't resist a vaudeville line, "Snappy songs and happy chatter with Warschel and Horschel." Either my humor is greatly appreciated, or O.N.I. and G-2 are just being nice to me. Warschel and Horschel, my contacts, cover Murmansk to Molotovsk.

What are my specific tasks? Principally, I must learn first hand from my own investigations and experiences what the attitudes of the Russian officials and the people are toward the Allies, especially Americans? What happens to German prisoners of war who are sent to North Russia? The Russians are highly accurate, deadly with their anti-aircraft gunnery. So, what happens to the Luftwaffe pilots who are shot down and captured? This occurs quite often. They, the Luftwaffe pilots, disappear quickly. Russia refuses to discuss the subject. Why?

Sounds too simple to me. "Is that all you're shipping me off to Russia for?"

"We selected you for this task because it is extremely important you do come back."

The reaction is a noiseless nodding of heads. And silence.

I look at each of the five men in turn, trying to extract more information. This causes no reactions. Doesn't produce any more clues. So, I delve more directly. "How do you suggest I go about accomplishing these tasks?"

The Chief challenges me. "Based on nothing more than we've told you, how would you go about doing them? What does your instinct tell you?"

I give the Chief's question long and careful thought before answering. "I'd try to make contact with Russian officials and establish good relations with them. Then I'd press the Russian rules and regulations to their limits. Even if I get myself into trouble, learn precisely what does go on with German prisoners. Test the attitudes of the people and the officals. Try to get myself in-and-out of trouble. See what happens. Get to Archangyelsk, somehow, and make my report to Warschel and Horschel." I direct this question to no one in particular. "What do you think?"

The intelligence guys look at one another for reaction. After a long interval of quiet, the senior officer, the O.N.I. lieutenant-commander, approves.

The Chief offers a disconcerting reminder. "Leon, remember there's no telephone number I can give you. You are completely on your own. But, I, we are confident you can handle this one."

"Thanks, Chief. Now, I'd better locate the *Collis P. Huntington* and make myself to home." Turning to the lieutenant-commander, "Say, Commander. Can you find out if the ship's still at the dock? Or, if she's moved out into the Hudson, can you help me get to her?"

Without hesitation, the lieutenant-commander picks up the Chief's telephone, dials a number, asks a few questions of whomever is at the other end, moves off to a corner of the room and has a quiet, inaudible, private phone conversation. The rest of us make small talk just to assure the lieutenant-commander we're not trying to eavesdrop.

He finishes his telephone call. "Okay, Leon. You're all set. Go right now to the 79th Street Pier, the marina, on the Hudson River. An ensign name of Reilly and two SPs will be waiting for you. Identify yourself as Radio Officer Wortman of the Collis P. Huntington and they'll take you to your ship immediately."

The Chief pumps my arm, smiles and advises me, "If it's a liberty boat, remember to sit down. Hah! Hah! I'll be eager for your reports, through Warschel and Horschel, of course."

"You're assuming I can get to Archangyelsk. The map doesn't show any way to get there from Murmansk. If the ship docks at Molotovsk? This map indicates a railroad track between Archangyelsk and Molotovsk. Looks like it runs non-stop through the middle of nowhere. Assuming it's running. Well, so long everyone. I've a liberty boat to catch to take me to a Liberty Ship. See you in a year or so. *Da svidánya*, you all!" Just showing off my Russian.

Surprise! The G-2 officers respond, "*Shchislívava putí*! Have a good trip!"

One of the O.N.I. men adds, "*Da skórava paká*! See you later!"

The Chief looks a bit sad. "So long, Leon."

I hurry out the door, buss Merry on the cheek, shake hands with Bill and almost say "*Nazdaróvye*!" But, it's not wise for me to say the equivalent of "Cheers" in Russian! Let them hear about my new assignment directly from the Chief, not indirectly from me! I head for the 79th Street Pier.

"Ensign Reilly?"

"Yes, sir. You are...?"

"Radio Officer Wortman of the *Collis P. Huntington.*" I produce my coast guard papers and passport.

"Fine, sir. Let's go down this ladder to the liberty boat."

The boat's coxs'n and two sailors are waiting. As soon as the ensign and I are on board, the sailors push the boat away from the pier and we head out into the river at a fast speed. The ensign is navigating. He searches for landmarks on shore to help locate the ship's anchorage. He shouts headings to the coxs'n and, a short time later, we approach the *Collis P. Huntington*'s starboard side. She's riding low in the water. Her holds must be full and it seems every foot of space on the decks is laden with all sorts of war machines in unmarked, dark, weather resistant wrappings.

I go directly to Captain Hudnall's cabin. "Keeping my promise, Captain."

"Never doubted it for a moment, Sparks."

"Thank you, Captain. Is the armed guard on board?"

"Yes, indeed. And, your two Navy radio assistants are in the cadet cabin between yours and the radio room. They're eager to meet you."

"Two!" The magic number for a Murmansk run. "I'll meet with them in the radio room, check out the equipment together and set the radio watches. Then I want to take them to the chart room and familiarize them with the direction finder gear."

"Right, Sparks. I suggest you clear that with the Chief Mate. He's been busy organizing his charts and papers. You know how he is, neat as a freshly laundered dress shirt!"

"Thanks for the suggestion, Captain."

"And, Sparks, a boat will hail us about 0800 tomorrow to take you, me and the Armed Guard officer to the convoy conference ashore. We should be back here about 1300. The Steward will delay lunch for us. Right after lunch, in the officer's mess, I'll distribute the confidential papers we'll most likely be given at the convoy conference."

"Any idea of the size of the convoy?"

"No. But we'll be given the information at the conference."

"Thank you and please excuse me, Captain. Gotta get with my Navy radiomen."

First, I stop off at my room, I change from my blue uniform into khakis. Leaving all insignia of rank behind, I knock on the cabin adjacent to mine. The door is opened wide by a young man in light blue Navy fatigues. Putting my hand out, I greet him. "I'm Sparks."

He salutes. "Yes, sir. I'm Jacovski, Radioman 2nd Class, sir."

The second man, even younger than Jacovski, stands up and salutes. "Sir. Blanstock, Radioman 3rd Class, sir."

Neither one of them can be more than 18 years old. So what! I'm 22. "Glad to meet you fellas. We're going to be closely cooped up together in the tiny radio room for...well...it could be for a long time. So can we be less formal when we're together, eh? Call me Sparks. Everyone does. What names do you use, when your being informal, friendly like?"

The two radiomen look at each other and beam. Jacovski says he likes to be called "Jac." For himself, Blanstock prefers "Stock."

"Sounds good to me. We all have one-syllable names." Let's go to the radio room, take the equipment apart and see if we can put it together again." We'll have plenty of time, hours, days and months to swap life stories. I do learn Jac and Stock had just graduated from high school when they were drafted. No, they had no experience with radio equipment or the Morse code until they got to the Navy camp where they were tested and assigned to communications school.

Do they like copying and sending Morse code? They love it! Speed? They both admit to about 15 words-per-minute, error free. I wonder, are BAMS transmissions sent at 15 words-per-minute because it's the speed the Navy radio operators learn in school? Or do they teach the operators to copy at 15 words-per-minute because it's the BAMS speed? Either logic is plausible.

Or, as they say where we're going, "*Kharashoh*! Good."

Chapter Sixty-Seven

The Captain and I are formally dressed in our Navy blue uniforms, white shirts and black ties. The convoy conference is not held ashore, but on a large freighter at anchor in the Hudson River not far from the *Collis P. Huntington.* With respect to instructions, nothing unusual happens. Orders to ships' masters and radio operators are the same as I've heard at previous conferences. The Armed Guards, represented here by their officers, receive no verbal instructions but are handed envelopes by the U.S. Navy captain who attends this conference. We are told which radio operators and specific ships are assigned to monitor the low-frequency Direction Finder, the DF Watch.

The purpose of the DF watch is again made very clear. When a U-Boat sights a convoy, it briefly but repeatedly transmits a radio signal, a series of the German letter ü, *dit-dit-dah-dah.* Their objective is to enable other U-Boats to home in on the transmissions and form a "wolf pack" for a concentrated, simultaneous attack on the convoy. As each U-Boat sights the convoy it, too, sends the *dit-dit-dah-dah* homing signal. When an operator on DF watch intercepts the homing signals, he must race to his ship's signaling light and instantly send the information to the commodore of the convoy. The message must briefly include compass bearings of the U-Boats' transmissions with respect to the convoy, and the radio frequency of the homing signals.

As we come closer to the United Kingdom and head toward the Arctic, the DF watches must also be on the alert for a repeated series of A's, *dit-dah dit-dah.* These are transmitted by Nazi airplanes to provide homing signals for both U-Boats and other Nazi aircraft. Personally, I am relieved to know my ship is not ordered to stand DF Watch. It would necessitate standing on one's feet for the entire DF Watch in the ship's small chart room where the direction finder is located. I can just see the stress as the Captain, 1st Mate, 2nd Mate, 3rd Mate and one of the radio operators constantly bump into one another.

We return to our ship. The Chief Steward and the messman serve lunch to the assembled ship's officers. Nobody's chatting. We're waiting for the Captain to open the topic of the convoy conference. Captain Hudnall places his napkin on the table and stands up. All eyes are on him. He briefly describes the conference and hands the confidential documents in their labeled, sealed envelopes to the Chief Mate, Chief Engineer and me.

"Gentlemen. The convoy begins to form at 0500. Our pilot comes on board at 0600. We immediately up-anchor and move into the lower bay under our own power. The pilot will disembark and, under the guidance of the convoy's escort, we get into our position within the convoy." The Captain also tells us the number of our ship's position in the convoy, wishes us "fair sailing" and, as he leaves the salon, stops halfway out the door and adds, "We are going to the U.K. and then around the North Cape."

Before going to our respective stations to inform our assistants, we have a brief conversation. "Glad we aren't in a coffin corner." This could mean we're not heavily loaded with explosives; we're not an ammunition ship. Some surprise is expressed that the convoy isn't going directly to Russia but is bound for the U.K. Probably a separate, smaller convoy will be formed there for the Murmansk run. Small convoys could mean a higher ratio of escort ships to merchant ships. None of us argues with the benefits of being small, in that case.

Aside from the expected, intermittent depth charges pinging loudly through our ship, the voyage is uneventful. Despite fair weather all the way across the Atlantic, as far as we can tell no direct contact is made with either U-Boats or the Luftwaffe.

Put 60 men on a ship and, before the trip is halfway over, there will be anywhere from 60 to 120 rumors floating above, between and below decks. By the time we put into Gourock, Scotland. Yes. Gourock again. Gossip, scuttlebut has us putting into at least 60 different ports between Saudi Arabia in the miserably hot Persian Gulf to the freezing cold of Murmansk. One rumor had us going the long way 'round Cape Horn to the Pacific. Well, such tales add spice to the suspense. Outlets and releases from tension and boredom often take interesting forms. No harm in them. Provided you use the appropriate filters for such seamen's tales.

The 2nd Mate calls to me, "Can you come to the flying bridge? I think the shore is trying to signal us, Sparks!"

I grab a pencil and pad and race up the ladder to the flying bridge. Sure enough! The signaling light is pointing directly at us repeatedly blinking the initials of our ship, CPH. I respond with our signaling light, *R GA* Roger. Go ahead.

The next signal from shore is, *QRX*. The international Morse code for "*Stand by*." The Captain, 1st and 3rd Mates and the Chief Engineer have all come up to the flying bridge. After I fill them in on what's transpired, all eyes focus on the shoreline. Several minutes later the shore signals *dit-dah-dit-dah-dit-dah*, a series of three A's without spacing, international Morse for "*Attention. I am about to send a message*." I respond, *Roger. GA. Go Ahead.*

The signaling-light asks, "Is Captain there?"

"*Roger.*"

"*Advise Captain to stand by for dock instructions.*"

"*Roger.*"

The instructions are unambiguous. "*Tug boats to come alongside within two hours. Move the ship to an unloading dock in Greenock. Further instructions when Captain comes ashore. SK*"

"*R SK*"

No need for a meeting of the ship's officers. They all heard the letters of the message as I called them out and the 2nd Mate wrote them down. The bos'n's deck-gang prepares the winches to raise the anchor and the water hoses to wash down the anchor's chains. The 1st Mate and the Captain take their positions at the wheel of the flying bridge on the top deck. This affords a panoramic view to aid navigation. I go down to the Navy radio operators' cabin, advise them we're being moved to a dock. I ask them to stand by the radio receiver for communications from the shore radio station. Then I return to the flying bridge to keep my eyes open for messages from the signaling light on shore.

Several hours later our ship is secured alongside the dock with its huge cranes, numerous large vehicles, trucks and many flatbeds. They'll haul the cargo away just as soon as it is lifted out of the ship's holds and off the ship's decks and set on the flatbeds.

This evening, the Captain and I are called ashore to a conference. We are told by an admiral of the British Navy, "Sorry about the rather sudden change in plans, gentlemen. Too much air and U-Boat activity on the Murmansk run. A convoy on the way up is catching hell right now. We've not enough escorts to take another convoy through right now. Maybe next time. Sorry."

In a jeep, on the way back to our ship, the Captain Hudnall and I stare straight ahead. Perhaps we have the same mixed feelings. Glad we're not going to Murmansk. We'll probably head back home for another cargo and start all over again. Just postpones the inevitable.

My feelings are, perhaps, a bit more complex. The Chief, O.N.I. and G-2 are going to get me to Russia eventually. I'd just as soon not postpone the event. But, I have to "go with the tide," as they say. I'll go ashore long enough to find some new books to read on the way home. I remember once Captain Hudnall mentioned he was a fanatic for the game of checkers. Played it for months on end, long time ago, when he was shipping out as 3rd or 2nd Mate. I'll try to find a good quality checker set to present to him as a gift from his ship's officers. It's popular, I'm told, among the Brits and Scots.

Ah! There's an American Red Cross Servicemen's Center in Greenock. The things our ship needs should be available there. I'm shocked when the young American lady at the reception desk adamantly insists, "Our supplies are for the Army and Navy, not for the Merchant Marine!" She isn't listening when I explain, "There are 29 men of the Armed Guard on board my ship. They're all U.S. Navy."

Apparently, no one has ever told her that American merchant ships carry U.S. Navy Armed Guard crews on every voyage. Probably she's never noticed American freighters are also heavily armed for battle with the enemy. Merchant Marine crews, too, are assigned gun stations during enemy attacks. I'm perplexed and frustrated by such ignorance. I give up on her and resolve never to ask the American Red Cross for anything.

For a change of mood, I visit a crowded pub not far from the docks and ask where I might find a good quality checker set? I luck out! The generous Scots toss questions and statements at me in rapid fire. "What d' ye want wi' a checker set, lad? Dart's 'r our game. Requires a sharp eye, sense o' balance, good judgment and smooth control o'er the muscles in yer arm!"

How can I argue the point? In the interest of upholding and even improving international relations between the United States and our Scottish allies, I compromise. "Great suggestion. I'll try to buy boards and sets of darts for the ship."

One mellow old Scot comes over to me. "We've a better suggestion. Go to the British Merchant Navy Club in Greenock and tell them what it is ye want. They'll supply ye with all ye need fer the officers and the crew...at no charge to ye, lad! It's the least we can do to thank ye for riskin' yer arses bringin' shiploads to us. Ye say yer ship can use some readin' material? Magazines and books? They've been collecting 'em just fer the very purpose of supplyin' the men and ships of the merchant fleets."

He gives me directions and, midst slaps on the back, repeated warm-beer toasts for everything from an early victory to my personal health and long life, I manage to work my way out of the pub and head in the direction of Greenock and the British Merchant Navy Club.

When I return to the ship, I need help to bring the heavy boxes of goodies up the gangway. I spread the merchandise on the bunk, desk and floor of the Chief Mate's cabin. He's agog at my bounty. We pick out the nicest looking set of checkers for the Captain and one for the Chief Mate himself. He feels he'd better practice in case the Captain challenges him to a match. One dart board is for the wall of the officers' salon. One for the crew's mess and one for the Armed Guard's mess. The books and magazines? We must find a place to set up a circulating library for everyone to access; maybe the slop chest, the ship's store. It's neutral territory.

In an appropriate ceremony in the officers' salon, we present the checker set to Captain Hudnall. He's as delighted as a kid with a new toy. Perhaps, in this setting, he is a kid and we have given him a new plaything. He immediately challenges the 1st Mate to a game. The 1st glances at me with an "I told you so!" grin.

The Chief Steward attends to the distribution of the dart boards and checkers to the crew. The Armed Guard officer delivers the goodies to his crew. I reserve one dart board for Jac and Stock to hang in their quarters. Jac ask if it's "okay for us to have some of the Navy guys in our room once in a while for a round-robin series of dart matches on the way home?"

"Technically, you should ask your officer for permission. I have no authority except in the radio room."

Although Jac and Stock live in the midship housing next door to me, they can't roam around the four decks as I am privileged to do. They have little to look forward to for the next month to break the monotony of radio watches. The Armed Guard crew's quarters are not spacious. In fact, Jac's and Stock's cabin on the bridge deck is even larger than the one assigned to the officer in command of the Armed Guard.

After giving the matter some thought...well, a few minutes thought, anyway...I suggest, "If your buddies have to visit your cabin—on ship's business, of course—they'd better use the outside ladders to reach the bridge deck. And advise them to be especially quiet when they get to the second deck. Their officer's cabin is there, just below mine. Also, we never had this conversation. Right?"

"Right, sir! I mean, Sparks."

Once in a while I do have to remind them to keep the noise level down. The Armed Guard officer never catches on. He just wonders why the Navy radio operators are happier than the other Navy personnel. They have such a high morale. I claim my good management techniques are responsible. He doesn't believe me, and continues to wonder why. He visits me often while I'm on watch, which makes me somewhat anxious about possible noises from the Navy radio operators' cabin next door. I ease the situation by suggesting Jac and Stock move the dart board across their cabin to the bulkhead adjoining the radio room's.

Chapter Sixty-Eight

The weather is fine for the first two days of the return voyage. The sky is blue and clear. Perfect...for enemy activities. The convoy is placed on continuous General Quarters. Full alert. Guns manned. Armed Guard and merchant crews at their gun stations. Everyone scans the ocean, the horizon and the sky in anticipation of just about anything the persistent Nazi enemy might offer.

Suddenly, our food is less plentiful. Portions are diminishing. On the fourth morning, we have no cereals, no canned milk or sugar for our coffee. Fortunately we do have coffee. Our supply of eggs and fruit gave out long ago and expectedly on the way to the U.K. We do have bread baked in the ship's galley, but butter is severely rationed to one pat per person for the each meal. An Army travels on its stomach? Well, so does a ship's complement. When we left the states we had loaded enough foodstuffs for at least a nine-month voyage. What happened? We don't have to wait long to find out.

Later in the day after the fifth miserable breakfast, I'm on the bridge talking with an obviously angry Captain Hudnall and a disturbed Chief Mate. We're reviewing our planned responses to enemy attack and, in case the convoy scatters and we must travel alone, how we should stand watches. Suddenly the 2nd Mate, followed by the Chief Steward, handcuffed, enter the bridge. The Armed Guard officer holds a revolver pointed at the Chief Steward. The Captain must have been expecting this scene. It could explain why he's been so angry. He speaks with slow and deliberate restraint. "Remove the handcuffs, please."

He directs his controlled anger at the Chief Steward. "We'll have the entire story right now! Don't try to lie. We have several eye witnesses in the galley. If I think you're trying to lie to me, I'll turn you over to the crew."

At the mention of "turn you over to the crew," the Steward nervously shifts his weight, rolls his tongue around his dry mouth, looks imploringly back and forth at each of us witnessing this bizarre scene. None of us offers friendly expressions. I'm mystified. This must have something to do with our food supplies. In a few dramatic seconds, it all comes out.

The Captain accuses the Steward of black marketing the ship's stores for his own profit. Seems when the Steward learned we were not going to North Russia but were returning to New York for a new load, he had the surplus food supplies unloaded and delivered to a black market operator. He might have gotten away with it. Two things betrayed him: 1) he grossly miscalculated the size of the inventory for which he was accountable and, 2) his own galley-crew recognized what he was doing but, afraid of reprisals, waited until we were two days out to sea before passing word of the Steward's mischief to the Captain through the officers' messman. When the Captain learned of this, he ordered the 2nd Mate and the Armed Guard officer to arrest the Steward and bring him to the bridge immediately.

It's a painful scene for all of us. Everybody loses in this one. The Steward has committed a very serious crime against the ship's officers and crew. He has broken maritime customs and laws. The Navy could have something to say about this, too. The Armed Guard has also been victimized by the greedy Steward.

The Captain wants the Steward out of his sight. He doesn't cite all the rules, regulations and laws the Steward has broken. In his strongest tones and with fists clenched in a visible attempt to control his anger, he shouts orders to the Steward. "For your own protection—the crew would love to get hold of you and deliver justice their way—for your own protection, I repeat, you will stay in your cabin for the rest of this voyage. You will share our food rations. You may leave your cabin only to go to the head—nothing more. One of us will escort you for your protection. As soon as we reach port, I will personally hand you over to the authority of the War Shipping Administration." He turns away and waves his arms in disgust. "Get this man below. Out of my sight!"

The Chief Mate estimates at the present convoy speed we'll be in New York—if that's where we're going—in about 12 or 13 days. Our diet becomes black coffee, bread and rationed butter, and a green vegetable I'd never even heard of, "Kurley Kale." It's boiled and tastes awful! The galley crew finds some canned tomato sauce to pour onto the Kale. It helps a little. None of us complains very loudly about the food and the invariability of our meals. Although eager for a hot meal to satisfy the hunger created by the tiring hours of standing watches, nobody hurries at the end of his watch to the officers' salon. Like children eager to end a trip, the men ask over and over again, "How much further?"

The Captain tells us the convoy's course should take us directly to New York. I'm standing in the bright sunshine on the flying bridge with the Chief Mate. He's slowly scouring the dead-ahead horizon with his binoculars. He mumbles, "I think...I think...Yes!" He shouts, "There she is!"

Several us run to him. "What? What do you see?"

He's all smiles. "Sparks, would you ask Captain Hudnall to join us on the flying bridge, please?"

The Captain looks through the binoculars for an interminable length of time, lowers the binoculars and hands them to the Chief Mate. They're both smiling from ear to ear.

The Captain, still smiling, is very calm. "We can see the top of the Coney Island Parachute Jump! We can expect to be at anchor in the Hudson River...probably tomorrow afternoon!"

Well. How can you keep such wonderful news to yourself. The Captain tells the Chief Engineer who tells his assistants who tell the engine gang. The Chief Mate tells the 2nd who repeats it to the 3rd Mate. He lets the bos'n know. And the bos'n spreads the word among the deck gang. I tell it to Jac and Stock who tell it to the Armed Guard and, somehow, word reaches the Armed Guard's officer. George, the Purser comes running to the radio room where I have the watch. "Is it true?"

So, the whole ship knows we're coming home to ice cold milk, soups, meats, fresh oranges and vegetables. The whole ship? Nobody's thinking about the steward in his cabin on the first deck. If any of us does think about him, it's not with sympathy. He's specifically the ship's enemy, accused of doing more harm to us than the Nazis on this trip.

The *Collis P. Huntington*, under the control of a port pilot who boards the ship in lower New York Bay, drops anchor, by wonderful coincidence, opposite the 79th Street Pier. The ship's engine-room telegraph signals "Stop Engines." The *thump-atta-thump* slows down and quits.

Unfortunately our arrival time is several hours after customs and immigration offices have closed for the day. Officially, port activity has stopped. All Merchant Marine officers and men must pass through those offices when reentering the country. The Captain, Chief Mate, Chief Engineer and I, have finished another hot dinner of that revolting Kurley Kale with tomato sauce and black coffee. We are on the lonely flying bridge staring at the darkened city's silhouette outlined against the evening's blue sky. It's so quiet.

Breaking the silence, I say, "Captain Hudnall. I have an idea. I don't mind risking trouble with customs and immigration. If I can hail a small boat cruising on the river, probably out of the 79th Street Marina, could I ask them if they'd take me ashore with them? That way I can get to our Port Captain at the American Range Liberty Lines, explain the situation and ask him urgently to send milk, eggs, fresh fruit, vegetables and meats to the *Collis P. Huntington.*"

With mock authority, he advises me. "Sparks. You know I can't witness you breaking the laws of entry. So, if you don't mind, I'll just go below for a while. However, in any conversation you might happen to have with the Port Captain, tell him if he can't get food to us tonight, he's invited to come aboard for hot Kurley Kale!"

Within 20 or so minutes, a 28-foot cabin cruiser comes close enough for me to shout my request. They respond, "Sure, sailor! Come on down the Jacobs Ladder!"

"Please wait a minute for me to get my passport and papers!"

Wearing a borrowed trench coat over my Merchant Marine khakis to ward off the chill night air, I hastily climb down and jump onto the cruiser. A short while later I'm on the phone with the Port Captain. He had been informed we were at anchor off 79th Street but he had no idea about the critical situation with the food. "Absolutely! I'll have stores on board the ship in an hour! I'll personally bring the civilian and military police in the morning. Good work, Sparks! Where're you going now?"

"Me? I'm going to Brooklyn for some of my mother's home cooking."

Chapter Sixty-Nine

The subways to Brooklyn don't run frequently at night. I'm the only passenger in my car. I take a seat in a corner that affords a view of all the car's doors and seats. A basic safety precaution. The click-clack sounds and rocking motions of the train quickly put me to sleep. A loud screech as the train strains to negotiate the sharp turn toward the Brooklyn Bridge awakens me. Without moving my head, I scan the train to see if anyone else has boarded it. For amusement, I hum to myself a paraphrase of the song that's become so popular here and in the U.K. "*There'll be blue birds over the white sands of Rockaway.*" Lousy rhyme. But it's mindless and, at this moment, relaxing. Better think of a believable story to tell Mom. Hard to fool her. I won't try. I'll just omit most of the truth. Why make her worry?

The tight hugs and warm kisses feel good. Didn't realize I missed them. Well, after the war is over, won and done, maybe we can all play catch up with the missing years.

Mom draws away from me and declares, "You look terrible! You even smell terrible. What is this...these clothes you're wearing? Some kind of uniform? Go take a hot shower. Then we'll have something to nosh with our tea."

I'm forced into a small lie. "No mom, this clothing I'm wearing is just something I picked up at an Army & Navy store. My good clothes are at the hotel."

"How come you look so thin? Haven't you been eating? Have some more milk."

"I've been eating well, Mom. I feel great! Isn't that what counts? I'll shower and then we'll talk. Do you have any steak? Any of your spaghetti? Haven't had anything like it in weeks!"

Wow! A hot shower with fresh, city water...and the tub I stand in isn't rolling from side to side. I allow the shower water to pelt me hard until I empty the hot water heater.

"You never change. You still use up all the hot water! But I'm glad you keep yourself clean. A shower a day keeps something away. I don't know what. Darling Leo, I'm so glad to see you. I wish I could hear from you regularly."

How can I tell her she won't hear from me for the next six months or even for a year? I can't. I remember Mom telling my older sister Rose, "You think it's easy to be a parent? You'll find out some day."

After the absolutely delicious steak and spaghetti, Mom pours me another glass of ice cold milk. Oh, is it goo-ood! I accompany it with an oversized piece of her fantastic chocolate cake. Mom smiles at me, just like a mother watches over her child. I need a night's solid sleep. I can't return to the ship at this hour.

So, when Mom asks me to "spend the night at least," I don't argue, not one bit. Minutes later, I'm sound asleep in my old bed.

I sleep no more than six hours. *Who's on the radio watch now? Am I on next?* My head clears and I realize I'm not in my radio-officer bunk. I dress quickly, brush my teeth with my fingers, briskly wash my face and hands, push my hair back and go downstairs to the kitchen. Mom is already there making a monstrous portion of scrambled eggs with bacon, a large glass of orange juice, toast and coffee. No doubt absence and normal hunger do contribute to my hearty appetite. Don't know why her scrambled eggs always taste so good. Maybe it's because she always burns the butter. Unintentionally, her culinary secret.

After a third cup of coffee with her, I look at my watch. "It's really time for me to go Mom. Yes, I do have to."

I put on my coat and cap. We walk together to the front door. Hugs and kisses. And I uselessly tell her, "Try not to worry, Mom. My job keeps me from writing often."

"Often?" She exclaims, "Not even once in a while, is more like what doesn't happen. This I don't like, Leo!"

We say our emotional good-byes; I take the subway back to 79th Street and walk west to the Marina. Customs and immigration are there in force, doing their jobs. Frankly, I don't want to explain how I entered the United States at night. Funny, when you think of it. How I, citizen Wortman, "entered" the United States.

Wandering over to the berths used by the owners of private boats who tie up at the Marina, I see the nice people who took me ashore. "Certainly. No problem sailor. Take you right back to your ship in a jiffy. Happy to do it." So, I leave the United States.

The *Collis P. Huntington* is a very happy ship this morning. I had no idea seamen like milk. Stories, novels of the sea always have a returning ship's crew, officers too, heading for the nearest bar for beer and heavier beverages. I'm learning the truth is they miss milk more than alcoholic stuff.

Everyone on the ship greets me as a hero and salutes me with a glass of milk in one hand and fresh fruit in the other. Where's Captain Hudnall? The story, as I hear it from the Chief Engineer, is the Port Captain arrived last night on a tug boat with all these good eats. Said he'd send the authorities to bring the Steward ashore first thing in the morning. Sure enough, military police, a couple of armed U.S. Coast Guard sailors and a Coast Guard officer, came on board. They left ten minutes later with the Steward in handcuffs. Captain Hudnall and the 1st Mate went ashore with them to press charges.

About two, maybe three hours later, the Captain and the 1st Mate return to the ship. "Not much to tell. There'll be a hearing in a couple of days to decide if the Steward is to stand trial. Not a pleasant situation for anybody, Sparks. No doubt, he'll go to jail. I've no idea which jail."

I ask Captain Hudnall for permission to leave the ship for several days on personal business. The Captain gives his okay. He suggests I contact the Port Captain to find out where the ship's berth is, if and when I want to come back on board. I pack my bags and, again, hail a passing cabin cruiser, and this time I enter the United States legally.

Chapter Seventy

A quick taxi ride, and I'm back at The Office. Merry likes the way I look, clean shaved and in my Merchant Marine uniform and notices I've lost a lot of weight. "Haven't you been eating, dear?"

"Yes, honey. I've been eating." Details of the voyage home are best forgotten.

Merry nods toward the Chief's door. "He's been waiting to hear from you."

Knock. Knock.

"Come!"

"Hi, Chief! You heard about my trip to North Russia?"

"Yes. I received a message the day you arrived at Gourock. Too bad you had to waste so much time. Are you ready to try again?"

"Sure. It isn't every day I get several chances to go to North Russia."

"Good. Ask Merry to book you into a nearby hotel for a couple of days. Washington is locating another ship for you, one that's specifically equipped for Russia. Keep in touch several times a day. And be ready to move."

A week later, the Chief tells me to be ready to go any time now. "A new Liberty Ship, specially fitted for the North Atlantic run, is being launched in Baltimore, Maryland and...congratulations! You are her Chief Radio Officer."

"What's her name?"

"The *John La Farge*, Sparks."

Two days later, I'm on a commercial flight to Baltimore, Maryland. Who do I sit next to? Mr. Thompson, the 2nd Mate of the *Collis P. Huntington*!

"Hey, Sparks! Good to see you. What're you doing on this plane? Going to Baltimore?"

"Yeah. I'm picking up a new Liberty Ship, just launched."

"Hey. So am I! The *John La Farge*."

Shaking my head in disbelief, "Small world, isn't it? I'm to be her Chief Radio."

He breaks into laughter. "I'm her 1st Mate! Got my papers a couple of days ago."

This is good news. Mr. Thompson, whom I'd known as "2nd," is one heck of a nice guy. He's in his 50s. His hair is white and long at the back. Small, blue-gray eyes radiate a big smile. He stands about 6' tall, a bit overweight. Good checker player, too.

"Congratulations, 1st. What happened to the *Collis P. Huntington*? Did Captain Hudnall stay with her?"

"Sparks. This has to be one of the all-time big coincidences. Captain Hudnall's skipper of the *John La Farge*! George Leitner's her Purser. Hey, this is great!"

It's fantastic. But, something's strange here. How much does Joe, my Chief really know and doesn't tell me? Is Captain Hudnall more than a ship's Captain? I believe in luck, but I'm suspicious of coincidences of this magnitude. At any rate, I do feel my luck continues to be good. Coincidences are working in my favor.

On the pier, as we approach the *John La Farge*, Mr. Thompson gestures upward toward the main deck of the ship. "Look!" Around the ship's body, from stem to stern, is a thick, wide band of steel. "You know what that means? It's reinforcement, a steel band to keep the ship from breaking up in rough seas. And you know what that means. We're going to North Russia this time. Through the North Atlantic to the North Cape."

I feign surprise, shock and dismay.

Wearing half a smile now as we move to the gangway, Mr. Thompson observes, "Bet fully one-third of the new crew develops symptoms of appendicitis before we sail!"

We board the *John La Farge*. She's so new the paint still smells. Look! No rust! Clean as a whistle! None of the metal platings are tarnished or corroded!

The radio room has a new piece of equipment, an approved all-band short-wave radio receiver. This means we'll be able pick up broadcasts from all over the world. While we're at sea we won't feel cut off any more. We'll have news 'round the clock, news of what's happening overseas and back home, and we'll have it at sea and while we're in port in Russia.

Captain Hudnall and George Leitner boarded the ship yesterday. We have a great reunion over mugs of hot coffee, naturally. The ship's riggings and fittings have been finished. Weather permitting, the *John La Farge* will make her trial run tomorrow under the control of a port pilot. A variety of inspectors will be on the ship to evaluate her performance. A radio technician will come aboard to calibrate the new direction finder. The Navy's Armed Guard and its officer join us this afternoon. They'll fire all the guns several times, separately and simultaneously, during the trial run to test the ship's ability to withstand the concussions.

The next day out on the bay the only negative incident I'm aware of concerns the radio room's wooden, emergency-escape kick-out panel in the bulkhead to the right of the transmitter. The fierce, repeated impacts and recoils of our stern 5-inch-38 and the forward 3-inch-50 cannons blow the kick-out panel off the bulkhead. It will be fixed before we sail.

The Chief Engineer proudly reports the top speed of the *John La Farge* "calculates to be 12-knots. As fine a speed for any Liberty Ship I know of!" The Chief Mate reports "She responds well to the wheel!" Everybody is delighted with the ship's trial run. A very satisfying maiden voyage.

The Armed Guard officer, Lt.jg Bernard Bergstroff, is about my age. Taller than I am. He does seem friendly and talkative. The opposite of his predecessor, Jim Wells.

Bergstroff brings the two Navy radio operators to the radio room. As on the last voyage, these radiomen don't look more than 18 years old. However, they've both been on Liberty Ships before, on runs to the U.K. They probably have no idea of where we're bound. And I can't tell them. Loose lips sink ships, and all those other patriotic slogans. The lieutenant leaves us alone to get acquainted. As on the *Collis P. Huntington*, they'll be quartered in the two-bunk cabin between mine and the radio room.

Several days after the *John La Farge* is inspected for damages incurred during the trial run, Captain Hudnall, the Chief Mate, the Armed Guard officer and I are called ashore for a brief conference with several Navy officers. Instructions are to proceed from Baltimore, sailing close to the east coast, north to New York without Navy escort. We're not sure having a fast Liberty Ship is a good thing. So far it has only earned us the right to "proceed without Navy escort."

The solo voyage at top speed to New York goes well without incident, although several times we pass floating debris and empty lifeboats. We put into Hoboken, New Jersey where they have facilities for degaussing large ships. The procedure is supposed to remove the ship's residual magnetism and reduce it's attraction to magnetic mines.

Several days later the ship moves to a loading dock in Brooklyn and I take the subway to Manhattan for a final visit with the Chief.

"Do you have everything you need, Leon?"

"Can't think of anything else. Oh, yes. It's going to be cold in the Artic Circle. Can you get me one of those bulky, water proof half-coats like the Navy gunnery officer showed me? It's very dark in color, has a huge fur collar and the deepest pockets I've ever seen."

"I'll check it out. Give me a day or two. I'll have it delivered to your ship with anything else I find."

The coat, exactly the one I wanted, and a mysterious, unmarked heavy carton are hand carried to my cabin by Bill Brady. Bill and I chat for a few minutes. He shows me where 10,000 rubles are loosely sewn into several places in the coat's lining. The carton contains 24 bottles of hard-to-find Scotch. Bill points out, "For medicinal—or any other purposes inside Russia."

Finally the ship is loaded. The holds are filled with large, unmarked cases of cargo. Locomotives and what appear to be airplane fuselages are secured by huge link-chains to the ship's main deck. Word spreads quickly. "This ship is going to Murmansk!" And the Chief Mate's forecast of the crew's abdication comes true.

Nobody faults the quitters. Yet, those who stay with the ship are hard put to explain, even to themselves, why they do stay. I know why I stay. The Chief did give me an option: "Volunteer or go as a draftee!" I volunteered. None of the ship's officers quit the ship. The Captain, Chief Mate, Purser and I feel bonded by our previous voyage and experiences on the *Huntington*. None of us mentions it, but sticking closely together reinforces individual strength and courage for what is yet to come. We're a chorus of men whistling in the dark or walking through a cemetery at night—with arms tightly linked.

The bos'n and the 1st Assistant Engineer visit the union's hiring hall and quickly replace the crew members who'd developed symptoms of appendicitis. Fully loaded and manned, the ship is ready to join a convoy.

At the convoy conference ashore, some emphasis is put on U-Boat "Wolf Pack" attacks. Probably because our equipment is new and recently inspected and calibrated, I draw the DF watch for the merchant ships in the convoy. The escort also has the DF watch. It's routine. I'm reminded of the "A" and "Ü" signals transmitted by enemy aircraft and U-Boats and the importance of notifying the commodore of the convoy, by signaling light, as soon as I hear one of these signals or any other unusual transmissions. All ships in this small convoy of 16 are bound for North Russia. The conference ends with handshakes, brave smiles and expressions of "Good luck, gentlemen."

So far, I have not been seasick. In fact, they tell me "Seasickness is a rare disease among good seamen."

The next day the convoy is at sea headed for a rendezvous off Halifax with an escort of small, frisky Canadian Corvettes. Because of their diminutive size, they are referred to as "Baby destroyers." Because they are fast, they are sometimes referred to as "Greyhounds of the sea." The *John La Farge* has the starboard, stern position—coffin corner.

The sea, the weather and the entire ship seem uncommonly quiet.

Time for my turn at the radio watch. I have to relieve Stock, the younger Navy operator.

I enter the radio room and see Stock seated at the typewriter. He holds a bucket between his knees as he types. The odor in the room explains everything. The dreaded seasickness disease! Stock begs me not to tell the lieutenant. He'd be assigned to shore duty and he has always dreamed of going to sea on a big ship.

Well, I am not one to come between a man and his dreams.

Chapter Seventy-One

The weather is unusually clear and the North Atlantic, they say, is extraordinarily calm for this time of year. The signaling light of the commodore's ship is very active. Fortunately, the two Navy radio operators are able to operate our light, read the messages and send our replies. Our time is heavily occupied taking turns searching with the DF, copying and decoding BAMS traffic, monitoring the 500 Kilocycles distress frequency, and operating the signaling light. I concentrate on the DF.

The convoy's heading indicates we could be steering for the United Kingdom; however this is temporary. The heading changes frequently. The 2nd Mate charts our course. On paper it looks like zigs and zags, which lengthen our voyage. We hope the commodore of the convoy isn't just testing our steering mechanisms and remembers a straight line is the shortest distance between here and there. Of course he does. But it's uncomfortable for us not to know the reasons for these multiple changes. This procedure continues for several days.

Captain Hudnall and Mr. Thompson have been huddling over the charts, frequently checking the barometer. The Captain leaves the chart room. I ask Mr. Thompson, "Chief, what's happening? You and the Captain look concerned. Why?"

Mr. Thompson looks at his charts. Rubs his chin and, without looking up, answers my questions. "Captain Hudnall has a lot more experience than I do with these things; a lot more. He thinks we're in for some pretty rough weather as soon as we're north of Scotland." For emphasis, he repeats, "Pretty rough weather!"

There's no way for me to use the ship's radio to call for weather reports. Radio silence is mandatory for ships at sea and weather reports are not broadcast by shore stations. Such broadcasts would help us, sure, but they would also help the enemy. As far as weather forecasts go, we and the rest of the convoy are on our own.

The Captain is right! A very cold wind is blowing with increased velocity. The ocean is beginning to boil as though in torment. It's an awesome display of giant swells and fierce white caps. Our escorts, the corvettes are being tossed around violently. We watch them with feelings of compassion for the men they carry.

All of us have begun to add layers of clothing as protection against the increasing cold. The heat-radiators throughout the ship are not quite capable of keeping us warm. I wear a heavy, wool sweater all the time now. Our ship's three mates stand their watches inside the small wooden glass-windowed hut mounted on a platform on the flying bridge just forward of the smoke stack. This affords a wide-angle view of the sea around us. The ship's wheel and telegraph inside the hut are mechanically linked to those inside the main bridge on the deck directly beneath the hut. A speaking tube provides voice communications with the Captain's cabin, the main bridge and the engine room.

Tonight I come off watch and, as usual, go down to the officer's salon for coffee. The ship rolls so strongly it is impossible to move along a passageway without being bounced from bulkhead to bulkhead. I ask the messman for a thermos of hot coffee and three mugs. I want to take them to Mr. Thompson and the wheel man on watch on the flying bridge. A coffee-klatch in the North Atlantic. When I pour the hot coffee for the Mate, the wheel man and myself, you'd think I am Santa Claus. We sip and silently survey the enraged scene. There is no thought of prayer. No attempts at conversation. The loudest sound is still *Thump-atta-thump-atta-thump-atta-thump.* This time, I think it is my pulse that is *thump-atta-thumping.*

The ship directly forward of our position bobs violently up and down. The ocean's waves appear as giant hills and deep valleys. At one moment the forward ship appears to be higher than we are. We have to look up to see her. Then she's lower than we are and we look downward. We are all rising and dropping with the waves and rolling hard from beam to beam. In this kind of sea, the engineers keep their hands on the engine's giant throttle. They have to sense the ship's pitching and rolling. When the ship's screw is out of water they instantly slow the engines. When they sense the screw is back in the water, they move the throttle to bring the engines up to speed. The sound of the engine's *thump-atta-thump* is continually varying with the changes in the throttle's setting.

Mounted on the forward bulkheads of the main bridge and the flying bridge are simple mechanical devices, "clinometers." Each has an inverted half-moon scale calibrated in degrees. A pointer loosely dangles and scans the scale. Each time the ship starts a roll, I can't avoid watching the clinometer. The Mate and the wheel man are watching it, too At the maximum point of each roll, whether to starboard or port, the ship seems to hesitate and shiver mightily. With a fearsome snap, it slowly returns to its normal, upright position and, without hesitating even for a moment, continues its roll, right past the central zero-degree mark on the clinometer.

"Mr. Thompson," I ask in a half whisper, "has anyone calculated the maximum roll angle?"

"You mean before capsizing, Sparks?"

"I guess that's what I'm really asking."

"The Chief Engineer says he hasn't seen any written reports but it's estimated by some of his buddies at 55 degrees."

Mr. Thompson, the wheel man and I automatically look up again at the Clinometer and hold my breath as the pointer moves toward 55. I learn to hold on tightly at the peak of each roll to prevent myself from being violently tossed about. Staying in one's bunk is impossible. Sleep is hard to come by.

With the Captain's permission, I suspend the DF watch. In this incredible weather it's impossible for a U-Boat or any aircraft to shadow the convoy and launch an attack. Mr. Thompson wonders aloud about his personal preferences: "Bad weather in the North Atlantic prevents enemy action, right? Good weather invites the enemy. Lousy options."

Frankly, I much prefer enemy action to this terror-filled North Atlantic weather. At least our ship can fight, shoot back at the enemy. But in this kind of weather one feels totally helpless.

Off to the port side and forward of our position, where we estimate the commodore's ship is, I see a rapidly bouncing light blinking the attention call: *dit-dah-dit-dah-dit-dah.* It must be a message from the commodore of the convoy.

I leave the relative comfort of the flying bridge's enclosure and, holding on to any rigging I can, I reach our portside signaling light. I respond *dit-dah-dit dah-dah-dit dit-dah. Roger. Go ahead.*

Reading a signaling light that moves rapidly up and down and from side to side in this storm is extremely difficult. The signaling light sends a query. *dit-dit-dah-dah-dit-dit.* A question mark. It is requesting the identify our ship. Twice I transmit the initials of our ship's name, *JLF.* Mr. Thompson has joined me. I shout the message as loudly as I can. Our course is being changed. Certainly not to evade the enemy. Mr. Thompson uses the speaking tube to notify Captain Hudnall.

Mr. Thompson has been observing a change in the sea. He believes the course change is to keep the convoy "headed into the sea." This will keep the motion of the waves moving from bow to stern. It would be certain disaster, probably capsizing the heavily laden ships to have the waves "on our beam." The power of the sea is utterly awesome! Frankly, downright frightening.

Ice begins to form on the ship and its deck cargo. Several days later, ice and frost cover our ship and the ships of the convoy. All wear blankets of white shrouds. They are like ghosts floating, bouncing wildly on the sea. The sound of the ocean, the wind and the ship blend into a forceful, ominous monotone that rises and swells ever and ever louder. Never quiet.

Food service continues, even in rough weather. I can't imagine how the cooks operate the galley but, with few interruptions in the meal schedules, we have hot food and gallons of coffee. The white tablecloths in the officers' salon are deliberately wetted down to provide a non-slip surface. The tables are equipped with hinged edge-pieces. These fold upward and latch in place to create a barrier to prevent plates of food, tableware, water and coffee from sliding off the table.

Nothing to laugh at, but I can't help some amusement at the sight of a dozen men holding onto the tables with one hand, trying to feed themselves with the other hand as their chairs swivel rapidly left and right in unavoidable unison.

The intensity of the North Atlantic storm increases. None of us is able to sleep. One cannot sleep and hold tightly onto the side of his bunk-bed to keep from being thrown across the cabin. One just goes without sleep.

I am in the enclosed flying bridge with the 1st Mate and the wheelman. No conversation. Our minds are weary from the lack of adequate sleep. Our bodies and muscles ache from the continuous struggle to keep our balance as the ship rolls, pitches and bounces.

In a hoarse whisper, the Mate speaks with horror in his voice. "My God! Look to our port beam!"

A ship off our port beam is being lifted high above the ocean as the gigantic waves move from bow to stern. When a wave peaks at the midship point, we can actually see her bow and stern fully exposed at the same time. Two simultaneous peaks lift her high up at which time she is supported only by her bow and stern. Her keel and hull become exposed. Still the storm, wind and waves grow worse.

We are mesmerized by the terror of this sight. But we are unable to look away.

The worst of nightmares! Suddenly, the ship we have been helplessly watching—bow and stern supported on the peaks of two enormous waves—cracks open like a walnut and, within seconds, the two halves sink completely out of sight! Nobody could have survived that destructive power. No one could have gone to the aid of the poor unfortunate officers and crew. We have just witnessed the awesome, horrifying power of the sea!

The 1st Mate recovers from the shock and calls to Captain Hudnall through the speaking tube. He reports the incident. All the Captain says is, "Thank you." What more can he say?

The Mate turns to me. "Now we can see why they put a steel band around the *John La Farge.* Thank God."

The short daylight hours and the long, stormy nights continue until the convoy, according to the mates' reckoning, has gone past Norway, around the dreaded North Cape, past Kola Inlet and Murmansk. We're no more than a day's run from the mouth of the White Sea. As suddenly as it began, the storm stops and the ocean restores itself to a calm state.

Now, all we have to worry about is the enemy. I recall Captain Hudnall's comment on bad weather versus calm seas in enemy-infested waters. What can one do against the strength of nature when it is on the attack? Nothing.

On the flying bridge, Captain Hudnall and Mr. Thompson survey the convoy. "We've lost two ships somewhere along the way." We can only imagine their fate. The Corvettes have gone; perhaps into the relative safety of Kola Inlet. So, we are among the survivors! But, we're not home-free yet. The ship goes on full alert. Armed Guard and merchant crews are at their gun stations. At the start of the storm, the guns had been covered with tarpaulins to protect them against the frigid winds, ice and frost. Now our guns and cannons are uncovered, ready for action. We can only hope the firing mechanisms are okay.

A few hours out of the White Sea, the Armed Guard's bow-lookout telephones the bridge. "Objects on the horizon off the port bow. Possibly aircraft." All eyes strain to see. The forward cannon and the 50mm anti-aircraft guns sight on the objects. The attitude reflects our mood: "We have come through five days and nights of storms and no Nazi is going to get us now without a fight to the finish!"

The Captain, three mates and the gunnery officer are on the flying bridge with field glasses, watching the objects. Definitely aircraft. Three of them. Friends or foes? Too far away to tell. However, these planes are performing acrobatics. They're not circling. They're slowly moving closer and closer to the convoy while they continue this unusual routine. At last they're close enough for us to observe the planes' markings. The Red Star. Russian. However, we stay on the alert. Our gunners continue to track the planes' movements. At last the planes fly over and wig-wag a sort of greeting and fly off to our starboard. Our attention returns to the ocean as well as the sky. We're in the Barents Sea where U-Boats and the Luftwaffe often operate in packs.

The bridge lookout reports, "Small boat approaching 15-degrees off our starboard!" The bow and stern cannons rotate to confront this new intruder. The starboard 50mm anti-aircraft guns sight on whatever is approaching. The Captain focuses his binoculars and calls out, "It's a small cabin cruiser. Maybe a 28-footer!" Sure enough. It is exactly that, with a red star on its flag. The little boat turns in circles just ahead of the convoy. Like a playful puppy dog, it seems to tells us: "Follow me!" This can't be the Russian Navy's North Atlantic Fleet!

Several hours later, as we sail at reduced speed inside the White Sea, another cabin cruiser joins the first. It leads eight of the ships, designated by the convoy's commodore, eastward toward Archangyelsk. The *John La Farge* and the remaining five of the convoy are directed by signaling light to proceed to Molotovsk. According to our charts, Molotovsk is a small port deep inside the White Sea.

At last, we're tied up at a very primitive dock. Captain Hudnall uses the ship's telegraph to signal the engine room: "Stop engines." I close down the radio room.

The ship and its inhabitants are at rest, quiet for the first time in many days and nights. None of us wants conversation right now. We heave deep sighs of fatigue. The word "tired" is inadequate. We're exhausted. Worn out from the lack of sleep and the intense tension. The Casablanca assignment never left me feeling so drained of energy. My only solace is to sprawl on a bunk that isn't rolling and pitching me about. I want to burrow under a heavy pile of warm blankets.

Safer now—I think. So long everyone. Must get some shuteye. See you later!

Chapter Seveny-Two

A soft but persistent knocking on the door of my cabin disturbs my deep, dreamless sleep. Struggling to regain full consciousness, I untangle myself from my comforting pile of blankets and coats and open the door. Two strangers stand there. One is a very short man, about five feet six inches in height. The other is at least six feet tall. Mutt and Jeff are dressed in heavy, comically oversized coats, thick scarves and fur hats. A quick estimate puts their ages in the mid 40s to early 50s. They smile, extend their hands and introduce themselves.

"*Dabro pazhalavat*! Good welcome you to Molotovsk!" He's the short one, Mr. Shuracov, identified as the top-ranking civilian official, Port Captain of Molotovsk. Probably, his Russian is much better than his English.

"Yes, my friend. We welcome you!" The taller one appears to be the older of the two. His English is excellent, spoken with an American accent. He is Mr. Matusis, Assistant Port Captain. Salt and pepper hair. He sports an untrimmed black mustache and a handsome, long, carved-ivory cigarette holder...but it has no cigarette. He hintingly waves the empty holder. I offer him a pack of cigarettes. His eyes open wide with joy. Mr. Shuracov looks at the pack of cigarettes with apparent envy. I quickly offer him two packs of cigarettes for himself and hand a second pack to Mr. Matusis. They react by exchanging a few sentences with each other, too fast for me to follow. For an investment of 24-cents, four times the six-cents each pack costs at the ship's slop chest, I have made friends of two important local officials.

Still standing in the doorway, Mr. Matusis inserts one of his precious, new American cigarettes in his ivory holder, lights it, turns to me, stands erect, shoulders back, and makes a short speech. "We recognize the difficulties in reaching the Soviet Union. Therefore, I am authorized to award you a hero's bonus, 600 rubles to spend as you wish during your visit to Molotovsk."

"*Spasiba! Ochen kharasho*! Thank you! Very good! Sorry, I don't know more Russian words. But I do thank you very much for your kindness."

Mr. Matusis translates my gratitude for Mr. Shuracov. Once more they have a rapid-fire conversation in Russian. Mr. Matusis turns to me and smiles. "You are our American friend. *Nazh druk Amyerikanski*. Therefore, Mr. Shuracov and I invite you to attend a party we are having tonight in Molotovsk. Can you come? Please do!"

All I really want to do is sleep for the next 12 hours. However, this is a wonderful opportunity for me personally and, of course, my assignment. My Chief would be proud of me. So, I accept. "But, Mr. Shuracov, Mr. Matusis, I don't know how to reach Molotovsk from here." Truly, when we docked, all I could see from here to the horizon was a flat expanse of blinding, white, snow covered landscape.

"Of course, my friend. May we come into your cabin, please?" I invite them to use the settee. Mr. Matusis withdraws a large, black leather folder from the inner folds of his coat. He opens it, hands me 600 Rubles, my reward. He takes out a sheet of heavy paper, strips off a post-card size piece. He asks to borrow my pen. Using the folder as a writing desk, he wants me to spell my full name. He writes on the paper, signs it and hands it to me. He pockets the pen.

"This, Mr. Wortman, is a permission pass, a port pass. With it you may travel without escort as far away as Archangyelsk." He exchanges a few more words with Mr. Shuracov. "The party begins at six o'clock this evening, in approximately three hours. In two and a half hours, a jeep and a driver will call for you at this dock. Molotovsk is approximately two miles from here. You will be taken to the party and returned later. Mr. Wortman, you are our guest of honor." They rise from the settee and bow slightly.

"My friends. I am greatly honored by your invitation." *Amazing what one can accomplish with a few packages of cigarettes!*

"Very good, Mr. Wortman. Would you introduce us to your Captain, please?"

They may be the top ranking officials in this part of the world, but they don't know much about protocol. They should have called on the Captain first. I suppose, when they climbed the ladder, mine was the first door they came upon. So they knocked and a new friendship was established. I do have enough cigarettes to help me establish many more friendships.

Second thoughts occur to me about proprieties. Perhaps Russian protocol for high-ranking officials, such as Shuracov and Matusis, requires introductions to another high-ranking individual, such as the Captain of a ship, be made by a third party. Inadvertently, I am the "third party." The Captain is probably sound asleep, as are all the officers and crew. I suggest Mr. Shuracov and Mr. Matusis return tomorrow at the same time for introductions to all the ship's officers. They are pleased by the suggestion of an official ceremony and, with reminders of tonight's party, they depart. "*Da svedaniya Mr. Shuracov*! *Da svedaniya Mr. Matusis*!" So long!

With a polite bow, they bid me farewell again. "*Da svedaniya Mr. Wortman*!"

I feel like the ship's social director, a very tired and sleepy social director. I'll tell the Captain later, before I leave for the party. Winding and setting my alarm clock, I've time enough for one hour's sleep. I need it!

By 1730 hours, I am dressed in my finest party-going uniform. I go to the officers' salon for something to eat in case food is not included at tonight's party. Mr. Thompson is there for the same purpose. I tell him of my meeting with the Port Captains, Shuracov and Matusis, and the party invitation I've accepted and their desire to meet the Captain. I also tell him about the suggestion I made for them to meet all the officers. Mr. Thompson says he'll tell the Captain and he's sure Captain Hudnall, a very sociable man, will be delighted. He advises me the outside temperature is about 50 below and I must dress accordingly. At 1745, Mr. Thompson and I step out on deck. A jeep and a Russian soldier are at the gangway. The soldier salutes me and I climb into the jeep for the two mile ride to Molotovsk.

And what a strange night-ride it is! Because of air raids, we drive without headlights on a snow covered, narrow road which, according to the high mounds at its edges, has only recently been plowed. The soldier drives as though he is either in full attack or retreat—tearing ahead and skidding wildly! I am not amused. The North Atlantic didn't get me. The Nazis didn't. The thought of being killed or injured by a maniacal Russian driver bothers me. Mercifully, in a short amount of time we skid to a stop at a large building, a very big log cabin. The soldier steps out of the jeep, salutes and escorts me to the door of the structure.

Mr. Shuracov and Mr. Matusis take charge. Mr. Matusis takes my heavy, great coat and hangs it on a wall just inside the entrance. The two men escort me into a long and wide room. A big fireplace provides wonderful warmth to my chilled body. Twenty or 30 others are there, most of them in uniform. It appears I am the only foreigner. Immediately on our entry into the room, a line forms, a reception line. Mr. Shuracov is smiling but silent. Mr. Matusis makes all the introductions. The group includes a captain of the Russian Navy. Several women in Russian-military uniforms; all Navy officers. A few of the people are in civilian clothes made of heavy fabrics.

After introductions, I am escorted to a small table laden with dark, coarse-grain Russian bread—*chohrniyee khlyehbuh*—which I grew up with. And, best of all, caviar to eat with the bread. I love the stuff! This caviar is new to me. It is compacted into flat slabs. Not an oily spread. One simply lays a slab of caviar on a slice of bread and bites off mouth-filling chunks. The *chahee*, hot tea, goes perfectly with the bread and caviar. Heaven, at last I've found you!

The entertainment begins. Several young men dressed in traditional blouses, wide trousers with their bottoms tucked into black leather boots perform Russian folk dances that display amazing acrobatic feats. Scratchy music accompanies their marvelous performances. Eventually, we all join in the dancing, Fox Trot style.

Mr. Matusis asks, "You would like to see our Mickeyphone?"

"*Pazhalstah.*" Please. Of course I would. What's a Mickeyphone? We follow the source of the music to a far wall in the room. There on a small table is a windup gramophone liberally covered with decals of Walt Disney's Mickey Mouse; hence the "Mickeyphone" name.

Close to midnight now. Despite the fascinations of this group of people, some of whom I would like to get to know much better, I have to struggle to keep my eyes open. Mr. Matusis is aware of the reasons for my fatigue. He summons the soldier driver of the jeep. A reception line forms again. I shake hands and salute as I move toward the door. "*Spasibo! Spasibo! Dobro vyecher!*" Thank you and good night! And back to the ship I go, risking my neck in another wild, jeep ride.

After a solid night's sleep, I go directly to Captain Hudnall's cabin and describe the hospitality of the previous evening. Yes, he's delighted to host the two Port Captains. "We'll meet in the officers' salon, Sparks. I've already asked the Steward to prepare some cakes and coffee for all of us. I'll seat Mr. Whatsisname and the other Mr. Whatsisname at my table. You'll sit with us, Sparks. Please write their names down for me. I'm not very good at foreign names, you know. Much better at southern American names."

I meet Mr. Shuracov and Mr. Matusis at the top of the gangway, take their heavy coats and hats and escort them to the salon. The ship's officers are in their uniforms, in a formal reception line. I introduce Captain Hudnall who makes the introductions to the ship's officers. We take our seats. And, just as the Captain is about to signal for the cakes and coffee, Mr. Matusis produces two bottles of clear liquid. Vodka no doubt. He goes from table to table filling our water tumblers. That's a lot, a whole lot of vodka for Americans who are more used to bourbon or scotch. *Beware of the dangers of vodka—especially on an empty stomach.*

Mr. Matusis remains standing. Mr. Shuracov stands up. We all follow suit. Mr. Matusis raises his vodka glass and elaborately toasts the ship, the ship's officers, the United States of America and the Soviet Union. He then gulps down half the glass of vodka.

Now, Captain Hudnall may not be a teetotaler, but he's certainly not a vodka drinker. He takes one sip, realizes the potency of the liquid, stops and addresses the 1st Mate. "Mr. Thompson. Please break out the medicinal supplies." He hands a set of keys to Mr. Thompson. Mr. Thompson is back in a jiffy with two bottles of scotch. I'm sure Captain Hudnall's intent is to protect his ship's officers, not to stage a drinking contest. Then we do have our coffee and cakes. We discover our Russian visitors prefer scotch to vodka.

Captain Hudnall invites the two Russian visitors to tour the ship's bridge, cabins and quarters. Mr. Shuracov and Mr. Matusis announce they must leave to attend to matters at their offices. We are advised winter is quickly taking charge of the White Sea. Soon the ships will be frozen in and unable to leave until the spring or summer thaws or a powerful ice breaker can reach us. We are not greatly concerned about supplies. The *John La Farge* is provisioned for a nine month voyage.

What's more, we do not look forward to another stormy, winter voyage.

Chapter Seventy-Three

My next move is to go to Archangyelsk and meet my two primary contacts, Lieutenants Warschel and Horschel. They make it easy. They come to the ship in Molotovsk. Both are Navy career officers, in their late 30s. Warschel and Horschel could pass for brothers. After a break for a warming mug of hot coffee, the three of us take a walk around the dock where the likelihood of being overheard is remote. The U.S. Consulate in Archangyelsk consists entirely of Warschel and Horschel and Ames, a Marine sergeant who drove them to Molotovsk in their jeep.

Warschel advises, "Believe us, Leon. It's easier and more comfortable to make the trip by train. It leaves Molotovsk every morning about 0500 and goes straight through to Archangyelsk. It leaves Archangyelsk at 1700 and returns to Molotovsk. It's slow. Takes almost a half hour to cover the 15 miles between the two towns."

Horschel echoes Warschel's advice and adds, "Every once in a while the train is attacked by Nazi airplanes. They rarely hit the train itself, but they do mess up the tracks. If the train is overdue, a search party goes out from either Archangyelsk or Molotovsk, depending on who's expecting the train. They make repairs overnight and maintain the schedule."

"Astonishing people! I think I'm going to enjoy this assignment." I brief the two lieutenants on my own knowledge of my assignment and how I learned just yesterday how to accomplish it: Cigarettes!

Warschel and Horschel agree. A simple approach. The hunger for real cigarettes among the heavy-smoking Russian people and the military should loosen things up for me. We agree on a security procedure I'm to follow whenever I come to Archangyelsk. As soon as I arrive in Archangyelsk, I'm to walk directly to the American Consulate, the house in which the three men live and work. I'll drop off an article, anything will do, at the Consulate. If I do not reclaim the article in person within 24 hours, they will assume I am being detained by the Russian authorities and will search for me. They tell me where their headquarters, which are also living quarters, are located in Archangyelsk.

They advise me not to carry any kind of a weapon, knife or gun, when I leave the ship, either to go to Molotovsk or Archangyelsk. The Russian police might use the weapon as a reason for shooting or arresting and detaining me. Be careful not to be seen openly holding a sustained conversation with a Russian civilian. This is fraternization; very illegal for the civilian. In Archangyelsk, stay at the *Intourist*, the foreign travelers' hotel. Mostly it's occupied by Russian officers, state police and national security agents. They'll be very much interested in your reasons for being in Archangyelsk.

"Do we have any contacts with Russians, military or civilian?"

Warschel answers, "Only one, unfortunately. Nadazha Petrovnaya. She's the director of the *Intourist* Hotel. Her English grammar is perfect, spoken with a charming Russian accent."

Horschel adds, "We're not sure why she plays our game. Maybe it's because we keep her in cosmetics, perfumes and other lady's things she can't otherwise find here. Be cautious."

Puzzled, I ask, "How does she get away with it? Aren't the police suspicious?"

"That's why we're not too sure of her. She's attractive and sociable. You might borrow a few soap bars from the ship and give them to her when you can do it without being seen. Soap is almost impossible to get here."

After a few minutes of reflection and walking together without speaking, I suggest, "I'll cultivate and strengthen my friendship with Shuracov and Matusis. Expect me in Archangyelsk in about a week...with soap for Nadazha. Okay with you two? I'll bring chocolates for the kids in town? How about staying on the ship for lunch?"

"Great idea! As long as you're not serving caviar!" exclaims Horschel.

Warschel interrupts. "However...we'd better visit your Armed Guard officer first. We really should be his guests."

"Understood. His cabin's just below mine. If he doesn't think to ask you, tell him you've been invited to stay for lunch. See you in the salon. I'll tell the Chief Steward."

Bergstoff, the gunnery officer does extend the invitation. Captain Hudnall is pleased to meet Warshel and Horschel. And an enjoyable time is had by all.

Shuracov rarely visits the ship during the next week. Matusis comes aboard every day. You'd think we were the only ship at the docks. Each time he shows up I make certain he has a shot or two of Scotch from my personal hoard, and a fresh pack of cigarettes. He's hooked on both. This guarantees I will become his best American buddy.

Several days later, while Matusis and I are sitting and he is chug-a-lugging Scotch in my cabin, I reach into one of the pullout drawers under my bunk, remove a whole carton of cigarettes, open it and offer him a single pack. I do not return the carton to the drawer, but place it on the settee next to him. He obviously has trouble keeping his eyes off it.

"Where, Mr. Matusis, did you learn to speak such excellent English, and with an American accent?"

"I lived in Chicago until 1925 when my parents returned to the Soviet Union."

"Marvelous. You do speak so well." I avoid telling him my parents are Ukrainian-born. I shift the conversation's direction to a discussion of the Nazi prisoners of war. "Tell me Mr. Matusis, I'm very curious. What happens to the

Nazis prisoners, especially the pilots your excellent anti-aircraft gunners shoot down?"

He's obviously disturbed by this question and hesitates to answer. I give him all the time he needs to think it over. I'm in no hurry. He lights up another cigarette, inhales deeply and, as he begins to speak, I hand him another motivational pack of cigarettes.

"What happens to them? We put them in a prison camp...which is more than they do for Russians who are taken prisoner."

"Is there such a prison camp near Molotovsk?"

He's reluctant to talk about it but, after a long pause, he continues. "Yes, there's one south of Molotvsk, between here and Onega."

In an obvious maneuver, I suggest he accept the remaining eight packs of cigarettes. "Please, my friend, Mr. Matusis. Take these for yourself. I have many more any time I want them. Please."

He quickly takes them out of the carton and distributes them among the deep pockets of his overcoat. "*Spasibo! Spasibo*! You are a very generous man."

Seizing this moment of devoted friendship, I boldly ask, "Do you think we might be able to visit one of the camps? I would find it very interesting. Do you think so?"

He looks away and takes a long time to think about my request. "Yes, it can be done. I will arrange to borrow a jeep from the Navy Captain you met at the party in Molotovsk. You and I shall drive there together. I suggest you bring many packages of cigarettes for the prison guards. And...please...please don't tell anybody about this."

I sense he especially means do not tell Shuracov. Of course I won't tell anyone.

"Can you get away tomorrow morning, Mr. Wortman?"

"Yes, I can."

"Follow the road toward Molotovsk on foot. I'll be waiting about half way with the jeep. We shall meet at 0600."

The next morning, wearing my bulky windproof coat with its deep pockets filled with dozens of packages of cigarettes, I start walking on the road to Molotovsk. My heavy coat with its cigarette-padding makes my walk feel and look more like a duck's waddle. I meet Mr. Matusis as planned. He knows the way. It's about an hour's drive over a roughly plowed, snow-covered road.

We pass through several small forests. Fortunately, he's much more cautious than the soldier who drove me to and from the party. On the outskirts of a forest ahead, I see a wooden structure very much like those one sees in the movies. It resembles the early western Army forts built as stockades with pointed-tip logs to house the U.S. Cavalry troops in their wars against the Indians. There's an armed sentry at the wood-gate entrance. As we approach, Mr. Matusis slows down to a crawl, reaches into an inside pocket and withdraws a sheet of paper. He asks me to be ready to display the port pass he'd given me.

The sentry recognizes Mr. Matusis, but asks me "*Ktoh vui*?" Who are you? I show him my pass and, without saying anything, at the same time thrust a package of cigarettes into his hand. Magic! The sentry salutes and says, "*Kharashoh*," steps back, salutes again, opens the stockade's huge, wood door and waves us through. Well, I'm in now. Hope I can get out.

Only one large building close to the entrance to the stockade has glass windows. A half dozen small cabins are spread out in an open area. They have windows, wide open windows without glass. I see now what happens to the prisoners, as reluctantly confirmed by Mr. Matusis with a sardonic smile. "You see, Mr. Wortman, we remove their flight clothing and, within a short while, they lose all interest in living. Mr. Wortman, we have no problem with Luftwaffe prisoners. They kill our people. But we do not kill them. They just don't care to go on living!"

When the wind is not blowing, the temperature is at least 50 degrees below zero. He means they freeze to death. I've seen enough.

Some Russian soldiers carrying rifles with fixed bayonets come out of the building with windows and approach us. They recognize Mr. Matusis. He introduces me as his friend. I hand each of them two packs of cigarettes which produces much excitement and chattering. They put their guns down on their wooden stocks, barrels upward, and takes turns shaking my hand and declaring their gratitude to all Americans.

I reward the sentry at the gate with two more packs of cigarettes. Mr. Matusis and I silently drive back on the road to Molotovsk from which point we started this morning's adventure.

The first person I meet when I get back on the ship is Captain Hudnall. "Sparks. You okay? You look like you've seen a ghost."

"Yes, Captain. I think I saw lots of ghosts today."

Chapter Seventy-Four

My breath freezes as soon as it leaves my nostrils. My moustache quickly freezes and hurts. I cannot do anything about the cold, but I can do something about my lip-adornment. I will shave it all off as soon as I can find a basin of hot water.

The two-mile walk from my ship to the train station goes quickly. The train to Archangyelsk is on time. Mr. Matusis boasted it usually is on time. I board one of the two cars and find a space on a wooden, unpadded bench. Most of the passengers are soldiers. No special accommodations for officers. Everybody ignores me. There are wooden shelves, one above the other. Each is occupied by a passenger lying on his back. In a few minutes, many of the passengers start tearing newspapers into narrow strips. They take something shredded, resembling light brown tobacco, from their pockets and use these ingredients to roll their own cigarettes. The air is stifling. Thick with smoke that doesn't smell at all like tobacco. The stench of unwashed bodies combined with the hand-rolled smokes is indescribable.

I feel guilty about the many packs of American cigarettes I carry jammed into my pockets and in my duffel bag. But, I can't afford to share them indiscriminately. Our ship's whole slop chest itself is inadequate for such a task. I refrain from smoking until we reach Archangyelsk.

The train moves slowly across flat fields of snow. We arrive at Archangyelsk in about 30 minutes. The train station provides shelter for some kids. Several, about seven to twelve years old, immediately spot and surround me, stretch their arms and hands toward me and call out "*Shocoladh*! *Shocoladh*! *Amerikanski shocoladh*!" I suppose as far as chocolate candy is concerned, Russian, Moroccan, American children are all alike. I distribute a meager share. One enterprising boy grabs the larger of my two duffel bags and unambiguously signals he can carry it for me. Of course he expects compensation, and well he should.

"*Gdyeh nakhodyitsah Amerikansky Consul*?" He understands I'm asking for directions to the American Consul. He shouts "*Da! Da!*" and points. I let go of the larger duffel and he leads me to the destination. I reward him with a pack of cigarettes and another piece of chocolate. He's happy. I'm happy.

Lieutenants Warschel and Horschel and the Marine sergeant are just finishing breakfast. I join them. Frankly, we eat better on our ship. Maybe our Steward, with the Captain's permission, can improve their inventory of provisions.

I park the small duffel with Warschel and Horschel...our security scheme. They direct me to the *Intourist*. "Easy to find. It's the largest building and made of gigantic logs and wooden planks, just like almost every structure in Archangyelsk."

I head for the *Intourist*, enter the extraordinarily wide lobby and scan for Nadazha Petrovnaya. She's described as a short woman, about 35 years old, long blonde hair always pinned in a bun at the back, neatly dressed, seated at an ancient desk to the right of and 25 feet beyond the entrance to the *Intourist*. I have no difficulty identifying her and I approach.

I display my port pass signed by Matusis. "I am Leon Wortman. Chief Radio Officer of the *John La Farge* docked in Molotovsk."

She's almost pretty, even in her bulky woolen sweater with the collar turned up. She smiles, stands and offers me her hand. "I am Nadazha Petrovnaya. Pleased to meet you Leon Wortman. How may I help you?"

"You speak English very well, Nadazha Petrovnaya. We must talk later. At this moment I need a sleeping room for several nights. Do you have one available?"

She looks down at a large book lying flat and open on her desk. Turns a few pages. Scans them with her fingers. Looks up at me. "*Da. Da.* Yes. We have a comfortable room, not very large, on the second floor. Please go to the woman at the desk at the top of the stairs. Give her this card and she will show you to your room, please."

"May I come back later and chat with you?"

"I am here every day until 6 p.m.." A non-committal response.

The woman at the top of the stairs is neither smiling nor conversational. I assume she speaks no English. She looks at the card, enters the time and some other information in the book lying flat and open on her desk. I can't read her Cyrillic scrawl. As Nadazha said, "The room is not very large." In fact it's very small. It has only a short bed with head and foot boards resembling an old fashioned brass bed, but painted white. There's no closet. No chair or towel. No heat. No lock on the door. "*Gdyeh tooahlyet*?" She motions—the toilet is to the right.

Time now to get to work. I intend to engage as many civilians as I can in a sort of broken-English fractured-Russian dialog. If they won't talk to me at all, I'll assume they're afraid of being accused of fraternization. We'll see how much their fear is reduced by the sight of a pack of American cigarettes.

First, I try to do my job without the power and influence of cigarettes. No success at all. I try all morning until hunger exerts its overpowering influence. I head back to the *Intourist* for food. I drop my heavy coat on my bed and add a warm sweater under my uniform's jacket. The lady at the top of the stairs directs me to the dining room on the first floor. The doorway to the dining room is extremely wide. The ceiling is at least two stories high. Elegance in North Russia. I stand there and survey the scene. Many empty wooden tables and chairs are spread throughout the room. Only uniformed officers are seated and eating. No civilians or peasants.

Three elderly musicians are seated on a platform against the wall opposite where I am standing. One, a lady in a black dress with a round white collar is seated at a piano at the right of the stage. An older man in a black suit is seated to her left. He holds a violin. The third person, also dressed in black, has what appears to be a balalaika. The man with the violin sees me, gets to his feet, says something to his associates and they launch into a song. They're obviously paying a tribute to me, a visiting American officer. So, out of respect for their intentions, standing very erect in the entrance to the room, I remove my cap, place it between my left arm and my chest, and stand at attention as they play with patriotic fervor three choruses of "*Don't Sit Under The Apple Tree With Anyone Else But Me*." When they finish the song, the three musicians bow deeply in my direction. I bow, too. Then I put on my cap and salute them. They bow again. None of the Russians in the room takes overt notice of this tender ceremony.

I move to an unoccupied table. Soon, an elderly man wearing a dark apron comes to my table and hands me a paper menu. Ah! *Caviar*! And *chohrniyee khlyehbuh*! And *chaeeh*! All the genuine caviar, black bread and tea I can fit into my stomach! Fantastic! I shall spend the duration of the war at this very table! However, time and war can't be kept waiting.

I return to the street and continue my search for a Russian willing to engage in a dialog. This time I display a loosely concealed pack of cigarettes in my hand. The results are better but I soon realize most of those who stop at the sight of the cigarettes assume I'm looking for a woman's companionship. Some signal me to follow them to a more private location hidden from public view where we might talk without being seen. Police and armed sentries are everywhere.

However, my communication skills with the local citizens are not too effective. One person's Russian is quite different from the other. I'd heard there are 129 different, very different dialects spoken in Russia. Few of the people in Archangyelsk are natives. Most have been ordered there to work in the miserable winter climate—and they may not leave until the government says so. I conclude I'll have to concentrate on Russian officials, military or otherwise, who have been exposed to international travelers—military or otherwise.

After four days of effort, which is not very fruitful, I say good-bye to Nadazha, promise we shall talk next time, check out of the *Intourist*, go to the American Consulate, make an oral report to Warschel and Horschel, pick up my security bag and offer chocolates to a lad eager to carry my bags to the 5PM Molotovsk train. I think I will have lots of time to return to Archangyelsk to improve communications with Nadazha Petrovnaya and the people.

Chapter Seventy-Five

Time is meaningless. The Russian days extend to weeks and then become months. All of us have difficulty adjusting to the tempo. All that seems to matter to anyone is unloading the ships' cargoes and hauling them away. However, despite Russia's vital need for supplies, military and civilian, I am bewildered by the slow speed of their progress at this dock. Rush—but not too quickly. Stop—very suddenly. Wait—for no apparent reason.

Warschel and Horschel visit me regularly to exchange oral reports. Wonder what they did to deserve this kind of duty. They confess to being bored stiff with the routine. Their Marine sergeant has become a heavy drinker out of sheer boredom. All three men are married. Russian women, in their layers of clothing to ward off the extreme cold, are shapeless, sexless creatures. Men can resist anything but temptation. Here, there is no temptation. Faithfulness to their wives is easy to maintain. Captain Hudnall and the officers are involved in a round-robin checkers and darts tournament. For me, checkers, darts and card games go just so far, not very far, as a diversion from boredom or as a major medium of entertainment. I am frustrated.

Mr. Matusis continues his regular visits to the ship for his rations of cigarettes and scotch. Even he has become boring to me. I tell Warschel and Horschel I intend to press him harder for information. I am urged to use caution, not to push Matusis too hard. But I'm not sure what is meant by "not too hard." My instincts have to be my guide.

A few weeks later, I feel bold, perhaps reckless. Mr. Matusis is on board and, as has become our custom, I invite him to my cabin, bring out a full bottle of Scotch and pour him a major size drink in a water glass. I refrain from drinking. An upset stomach is my alibi. Mr. Matusis feels depressed. A full carton of cigarettes cheers him up. He smokes, drinks and becomes more talkative.

"Mr. Wortman, my friend, do you ever get lonely for your family?" Without waiting for an answer, he continues. "I do. Very lonely."

"I understand, Mr. Matusis. Where is your family?" I'm truly sympathetic.

"My wonderful wife is in Moscow. And my lovely daughter is in Georgia, South Russia."

"Why aren't you together?"

Another pause for a big swallow from his glass, "We cannot be together. They have deliberately separated us."

"Why is that?"

Pausing frequently for more sips, "I am an official, second highest civilian in Molotovsk. I go freely on and off the ships while they are here at the dock. They know I could easily stow away on one of the ships and leave Russia." The alcohol is becoming effective.

I press harder. "You must be very lonely, Mr. Matusis."

"Yes, I am very, very lonely for my wife and daughter. But they don't care."

"Who are 'they'?"

"Moscow. The OGPU. The NKVD. The security agencies. Others. And Shuracov."

"You lived in Chicago until 1925 when your parents moved back to Russia. Would you go back to the United States?"

"Not necessarily."

"Where would you like to go?"

"Someplace, anyplace in South America."

"How would you get there?"

"After the war I will ask for a diplomatic assignment overseas so I can take my family with me and...when I get it...I will never return."

Mr. Matusis is very disturbed. A tear rolls down his cheek. He buries his head in his hands. Obviously he is sobbing. I wait for him to regain his composure before I press him again.

"Tell me, Mr. Matusis. With your knowledge of the English language, why aren't you number one in Molotovsk instead of Shuracov who speaks very little English?"

There is anger in his voice. "Because I am a Jew! A Jew cannot be the Port Captain!"

Anyone who has ever gotten drunk knows there are lucid moments when one is aware of one's drunkenness and tries to struggle out of the pit of embarrassment; usually unsuccessfully. Mr. Matusis suddenly becomes aware he has spoken too freely, said things one does not dare to say to anyone, anywhere in Russia. He struggles to his feet. Empties his glass. Carefully puts the glass down and shouts loudly as though concerned his statements have been overheard or the room is bugged. He delivers to the walls a dramatic, patriotic, dogmatic Russian speech.

"We are a pioneering nation! We will not see the fruits of our labor for 75 years! We are struggling now! But soon our struggles will be ended and we will live happily and forever in a utopian society the whole world will envy!" He grabs his heavy coat and, with dramatically heroic strides, leaves my cabin and slams the door.

He'll be back soon, I am sure. How do I know? He forgot his carton of cigarettes.

I restrict my activities to the area of the dock. I succeed in engaging some of the sentries in conversation. None of them speaks English. I struggle with my own combination of Russian, Ukrainian and Polish dialects. We have one common language that binds us together. A large supply of American cigarettes. The sentries know me as a prime supplier.

All the sentries are here on leave from the front lines. On leave? Yes. They don't go home when "on leave." They're ordered to take their leave unloading and guarding the cargoes. Some have come from the Stalingrad and Leningrad battlefields, scenes of some of the most furious fighting in military history. These are battle-toughened soldiers whose orders are to shoot on sight anyone who looks or acts suspiciously when near the Soviet Union's property. They look quite menacing in their heavy brown coats with fur collars pulled up around their ears and large woolen hats with earflaps and handsome black boots. Each hat has a bright red star on its front. They happily accept my offers of cigarettes...provided we can do it secretively behind a high mound of cargo.

Suddenly, there's a horrendous crash from the direction of the dock! The sentry I am talking with quickly pockets the pack of cigarettes, unslings his rifle and races toward the source of the sound. I follow but, prudently, not at a run. A group of sentries is at the base of one of the large cranes. They look down and then up. While unloading a locomotive from a ship's deck, something slipped and the locomotive crashed through the dock into the water below.

An officer runs over with revolver drawn, surveys the scene and comes to an instant conclusion: it's the fault of the crane's operator. He orders the operator to come down at once! A woman, the operator, comes out of the small enclosure at the top of the crane and very slowly climbs down the stairs to the ground. She's sobbing, shaking and crying, weakly repeating: "It's not my fault. It's not my fault." However, this is a war zone where the military rules. The officer is her judge and jury and executioner.

He orders three sentries to take her behind one of the sheds about 200 feet from the dock. A few minutes later I hear a fusillade of gun shots from the direction of the shed. The sentries return alone and resume their "leave."

Hot water has been pumped continuously through our radiators in an effort to bring some heat into our cabins. Despite this, the inside bulkheads of our rooms are covered with ice.

Chapter Seventy-Six

The long wait is coming to an end. Warschel and Horschel have come aboard to tell the Captain the *Joseph Stalin*, the largest ice breaker in the North Russian fleet, will arrive tomorrow morning to open a path out of the White Sea and into the Barents Sea. Our destination is Murmansk where we will receive further instructions. This is all Warschel and Horschel know. I invite them to share a warming farewell drink of Scotch with me. They come to my cabin and shut the door. We review my accomplishments in Molotovsk and Archangyelsk. They will make good use of the information I gave them about Matusis. It's just as well I didn't spend any time with Nadazha Petrovnaya. They now seriously doubt she has anything but total dedication to her government, the USSR. I give Warschel and Horschel ten cartons of cigarettes and the remainder of my case of Scotch to augment their dwindling official supply.

Later the same day, Mr. Matusis comes on board in his official capacity as Assistant Port Captain. He's working in the salon collecting all the port passes he's given out, recording the receipt of each of them in a book. The ship's officers are waiting their turn. When my turn comes, Mr. Matusis looks up at me. He hesitates to speak. He frowns, forces a smile as though he's thinking, "I'm glad you are leaving here. You know too much and I am afraid of you." Well he should be. And I, too, am glad to be leaving here. I offer my hand. We shake briefly and wish each other good health. *Zahvahshuh zdahrohvyuh*!

The deck crew readies our ship. The Chief Engineer is building a head of steam in the ship's engines. With a great roaring sound as it breaks a channel in the ice pack, the *Joseph Stalin* moves forward, stops, reverses engines and then moves forward again. In four hours the *Joseph Stalin's* brute force clears the area around the six departing ships to allow us to move under our own power away from the dock.

The Chief Mate, Mr. Thompson, estimates the ice is at least six feet thick. Our ship is last in line and follows the narrow channel through the broken ice. The North Russian weather is clear and calm, but still extremely cold. We move at a speed of about four knots toward the mouth of the White Sea.

Suddenly, with an exceptionally loud cacophony of grinding sounds, the ship shudders violently. It continues to shake viciously as we try to move forward! The General Alarm bell sounds! Possibly a mine! Not a torpedo! No U-Boat could have broken through the ice.

The Ship's Officers and the deck gang race around the ship, looking down over the sides, at the ship's bow, starboard and port sides and the stern. The Chief Engineer is at the stern. He rings the bridge and, using the lookout's telephone, tells the Captain, "We've hit a huge, submerged log stuck in a giant block of ice!"

"What damage, chief?"

"I think one of the screw's blade's been badly bent, Captain! It's what's making the ship shake."

"Can we continue in the convoy?"

"Depends on the convoy's speed. We daren't do more than five or six knots, Captain!"

"Okay, chief. Come to my cabin, please. You, too, Mr. Thompson."

I tell the two radio operators and the gunnery officer what we think happened. At normal speed, we would have a full day's run in the perilous Barents Sea west to Murmansk. A half hour later, the Captain comes to the radio room and asks me use the signaling light to report to the commodore of the convoy, a British freighter, "Struck log. Bent screw. Max speed 6 knots."

The commodore signals, "Stand by." Fifteen minutes later he signals, "Convoy speed is 10 knots." End of message.

This means we must straggle behind the unescorted convoy, proceed alone as a lame ship. Perfect weather for U-Boats and Luftwaffe. The commodore has doomed us. Captain Hudnall issues orders for everyone to wear life jackets all the time. I stand by the Captain. Both radio operators are on watch. At our speed, it's going to be a long day and a half, almost two days between here and Murmansk.

Freighters traveling unescorted usually bring U-Boats to the surface. They take the crew prisoner or set them adrift in lifeboats to freeze. When everyone is clear, the U-Boat shells the ship, a procedure less costly than launching a torpedo. On the other hand, dive bombers, torpedo planes attack to kill all! Floating mines are in a destructive class by themselves. The Armed Guard is at the gun stations. All eyes scan the sky and the ocean, nervously alert for an attack.

The Chief Engineer comes to the bridge to discuss a repair plan with the Captain. The empty ship rides high in the water. He proposes to slowly pump water into the empty #1 hold while we are en route to Murmansk. This will begin to raise the ship's stern and screw out of the water. As soon as we drop anchor at Murmansk, he'll speed up the pumping until the screw's bent blade is completely out of the water. Then, they'll put one of the large life-rafts over the side as a work-platform, tie it to the ship's stern and the entire engine gang will work full time cutting off the bent edge of the blade. How long will it take? Depends on how their tools, chisels and drill bits hold up. No one has a better plan to propose, so the Captain approves.

Impossible to explain, despite clear, blue skies and calm seas, we neither see nor hear the slightest indicators of the enemy. We sail as though on a pleasure cruise—but with our ship's bow gradually going lower into the water and our stern beginning to rise. At last, we enter the Kola Inlet and head for a group of ships anchored in midstream.

Word has apparently been spread among the ships in Kola Inlet about the probable demise of the *John La Farge*. The moment the other American freighters recognize us, they blow their whistles for minutes on end and raise a heck of a joyous noise! We blow our whistle repeatedly in happy response. We find a clear spot and drop anchor off Murmansk.

A Russian Navy officer, captain's rank, boards the ship as soon as we have dropped anchor. He takes a report from Captain Hudnall and advises us not to fire at any aircraft that fly over, regardless of their identification. The surrounding snow-covered hills conceal Russian anti-aircraft guns. They have lost Russian planes to trigger-happy Allies. So, please. *Nyet*!

All hands are eager to help launch the life raft and tie it to the ship's stern. In a few hours the bent screw is clear of the water. All day and night, under floodlights and ignoring frequent bombing runs by enemy aircraft, the engine gang works without rest. Twenty-four hours of heroic hard, manual labor pay off. The bent part of the blade silently drops into the sea and the water is pumped out of hold #1.

Our ship is ordered to move below Murmansk to Kola for a load of ballast materials. Our holds are filled with pulp wood. Excellent. It floats! After taking on all the ballast we can hold, our ship moves back to Murmansk. Our maximum speed is estimated at 10 knots.

June 1, 1944. Once again, our ship anchors off Gourock. But we do not move to a dock. We are directed to steer to Loch Ewe, one of the numerous and exquisitely lovely inlets and lakes on Scotland's west coast. It's a short run. We arrive and find an enormous assembly of ships at anchor—freighters and warships of many types. British Commandos and American Rangers are training and practicing beach landings. Live ammunition is being used by the "defenders." Two-men submarines, amazingly tiny craft, are moving about the Loch under an overcast sky.

We've been listening closely to the short-wave news broadcasts. Certainly, the invasion of Europe is to take place any day now. Exactly where and when? A well kept secret, of course. We expect the *John La Farge* will be in the invasion fleet. With a cargo of pulp wood? Strange. Perhaps we are going to be a troop transport. We're all guessing. None of us really knows.

On June 3, 1944, a British officer comes aboard the *John La Farge*, hands Captain Hudnall a large envelope to be opened today at 1300 hours and then he leaves. The envelope contains the usual convoy documents for the Captain, Chief Mate, gunnery officer and radio officer. The destination is not given, only our position in a convoy and a compass heading, which takes us essentially due west of Loch Ewe. Two hundred miles out we will receive, by signaling light, a new heading and our next rendezvous position. Departure time is 0600 hours, June 4,

1944. The ship's unbalanced propeller continues to make us vibrate and shake. Nothing can be done about it now. Convoy speed is to be 10 knots. We can barely handle it. Our damaged and missing screw-blade restrains our capabilities.

There's the commodore's signaling light! We're now 200 miles west of Scotland. I call out the heading and rendezvous information to the 1st Mate, Captain Hudnall and the gunnery officer. We rush to the chart room to enter the data on the map and estimate our probable destination. If we continue sailing in a straight line and the weather holds up, we will be in New York City in approximately 15 days.

Our radio is tuned to the BBC. "*Today, June 6, 1944, the invasion of Europe has begun!*" It appears we are not part of the invasion fleet. All of us have mixed feelings. We are glad the long-expected battles have begun. We feel a sense of having deserted our soldiers by heading back to the United States at this time. However, we are somewhat relieved. After long months in the Arctic, we'll be home and warm again.

U-Boat activity on the return trip is non-existent now. Hard to believe. The German Navy hasn't surrendered. Better keep our eyes open. Our escort is small. Most battle-capable ships are taking part in the invasion of Normandy. Perhaps all Nazi units are concentrating on Europe.

After an uneventful crosssing, we see our landfall. The top of the parachute jump at Coney Island, Brooklyn. When we reach land again, first thing everybody's going to do is drink gallons and gallons of milk. Then go home to see their families. They haven't heard from us, nor we from them, in the longest time. Me? I'm going to The Office to be debriefed by the Chief and O.N.I. and G-2.

Brooklyn will have to wait.

Chapter Seventy-Seven

"Welcome back!" The Chief greets me with a friendly handshake and a smile. He had been notified by O.N.I. of my departure from Scotland. Merry is out of The Office on an errand. Bill? Transferred to London. Bob? Still with The Office as an administrator. The Office has been expanded—taken over the entire floor.

O.N.I. and, possibly, G-2 are expected to arrive soon. In the meantime, the Chief is eager to hear me describe the geography and climate of Russia, the ports I'd been to. I suggest he and I go for a stroll in the warm sunshine and greenery of Central Park. "I haven't seen green grass in almost a year, Chief."

"You bet. But let's not take too long." The Chief hasn't changed. Pleasure must not be allowed to interfere with business. I enjoy the 20-minute stroll around the lower end of Central Park. It is a glorious day. The canyons of New York's streets look great. No snow.

The Chief comments "You seem a lot more settled, quieter, older."

"I am, Chief. There's nothing like a couple of rides through a North Atlantic storm to age a man. Follow up with a sub-freezing climate and months of sheer boredom. You'd age rapidly, too."

Two O.N.I. officers are waiting for us at The Office. G-2 considers North Russia the Navy's exclusive domain. I urgently need a large glass of milk to drink while I'm being debriefed. Merry produces a bottle of milk from the refrigerator. Three hours later, O.N.I. and the Chief have wrung everything out of my memory of people, events and places. As soon as they leave, the Chief suggests we go out and have a bite to eat. Okay with me, provided we can have the "bite" at the Stage Delicatessen.

Over a corned beef sandwich heavily loaded with cole slaw and a dish of half sour pickles, we have light conversation about how the war is progressing in Europe. The Chief suggests I enjoy a little holiday. Relax. Just hang out at The Office. Take things easy for a while.

"Joe. You're getting at something. What do you really have in mind for me?"

"Nothing, Leon, at the moment. Just some rough ideas Washington's kicking around. No point in talking about them until they've something solid. Where will you be for the next week?"

"I think I'll stay at my sister's place in the Rockaways. Swim a bit. Maybe I'll even try fishing."

"Swell. Give Merry your sister's phone number, in case you and I have to get together?"

I return to the *John La Farge* which is already being loaded with military goods. Most of the crew has already left the ship. The Armed Guard's been transferred. They all need a holiday, too. I say good-bye to Captain Hudnall, Mr.

Thompson and the other two deck officers, the Chief Engineer and his assistants, George Leitner and several of the crew members who are staying with the ship. I don't think I will ever again find a group so compatible. Captain Hudnall, Mr. Thompson and George have decided to stay on the *John La Farge* for one more trip. With her new propeller, the *John La Farge* will again be among the fastest Liberty Ships. No doubt.

After a few days of doing nothing more than lie in the sun on the small, quiet, private beach at my sister's, the Chief telephones. He tells me to come to The Office for a day or two. Frankly, I'm glad he called. I feel guilty about my inaction. That day, I take the Long Island Railroad to Pennsylvania Station and a taxi to The Office. I eagerly listen to what Washington and the Chief have planned for me.

"This is what we have in mind, Leon. We know all about your experiences in Archangyelsk and Molotovsk. Washington feels you did a fine, very valuable job while you were there."

This I find hard to believe. But who am I to argue with Washington.

"The two Navy officers in Archangyelsk...what're their names?"

"Warschel and Horschel."

"Right. Warschel and Horschel have learned from that woman in Archangyelsk...what's her name?"

"Nadazha."

"Yes. Nadazha Petrovnaya. She told them Mr. Matusis is very angry with you. It seems he talked too much and is afraid you might turn him in. She doesn't have any idea what he told you but he, Matusis is very concerned."

"Sorry. Just doing my job."

"So, here's the general idea."

I strain so far forward, eager to hear the details, I almost fall off the chair. I'm growing impatient. "All right, Chief. Get to the point, please!"

"O.S.S. believes your close contact with Matusis should be exploited further. The *John La Farge* is going back to North Russia in about a week. She still needs a Chief Radio Officer."

"You want me to be on her when she leaves. That's what you're getting at, right?"

"Only if you volunteer, Leon. I want to be fair about it."

"Before I 'volunteer' as you put it, give me a day to think it over. I suppose the same conditions prevail. If I don't 'volunteer', I'll be drafted and assigned back to you."

The Chief's smiles. "You say it more nicely than I do, Leon. Much more nicely."

The same afternoon I board the *John La Farge* as an interested visitor. Captain Hudnall invites me to stay for dinner. It's great to sit in the salon again with my good friends, Mr. Thompson and George Leitner. The new Chief

Engineer has gone ashore for the evening. His 1st Assistant is new. The 2nd and 3rd have not been selected yet. Same for the 2nd and 3rd Mates. The Captain's being very selective. Wants to be sure all of his officers have sea experience and have compatible personalities.

"Yes, this ship's going back to North Russia. She needs a Chief Radio Officer."

George turns to me. "How about it, Sparks? We proved we work well together."

"Let me think it over. If I come back tomorrow morning in uniform and with my luggage, you'll have your answer."

Captain Hudnall smiles. Mr. Thompson and George smile.

The next morning I show up at The Office in my Merchant Marine uniform. The Chief thinks I made the right decision. I head for the *John La Farge* with my luggage. Captain Hudnall, Mr. Thompson and George have my answer and they're pleased.

One week later, the convoy forms in lower New York Bay and I'm on board, assigned once again to the DF watch. We have the starboard coffin corner. Too bad. It means once again we're an ammunition ship.

The new Armed Guard officer, Lt.jg H. Unterman is a very congenial guy. A distinct change from his predecessors. Unterman and I are about the same age and immediately become good friends. Because of our destination, two experienced Navy radio operators are on board to assist me. Usual accommodations. Four hours on watch and eight off. The new Chief Engineer, Mr. MacDonough is a jolly, short, gregarious, white-haired "ole sea animal," as he calls himself. His self confidence and faith in the *John La Farge* reinforce us. His assistants are all experienced seamen, but they're loners. The 2nd and 3rd Mates are cheerful, experienced and knowledgeable. Yes, indeed. Captain Hudnall has again hand picked a fine group of officers.

As before, the convoy heads toward Halifax to pick up more ships and escort vessels. It's strange to be voluntarily repeating the last trip. Maybe this time we'll have favorable weather as well as no U-Boats, floating mines or air attacks. Maybe North Russia will be warm. Dream on!

Chapter Seventy-Eight

As soon as the Canadian contingent joins us, the convoy is instructed to change its heading to a more northerly bearing. This brings us to the southern coast of Greenland. The next maneuver has us sailing north by east, skirting the ice-covered white coast of Greenland. We receive a signal to head southeast, in the direction of the United Kingdom.

I take the early morning DF watch and begin the routine of sweeping the radio spectrum while rotating the DF's direction-sensing loop antenna. The 1st and 2nd Mates, using their beloved sextants, take the ship's bearings quite often during the daylight hours. Both of them are beside me in the chart room plotting the convoy's course, and updating our position on the charts.

A cold chill races down my spine. In my DF's earphones, I hear a repeated: *dit-dit-dah-dah...dit-dit-dah-dah...dit-dit-dah-dah.* The U-Boat homing signal! Quickly, I rotate the loop antenna to determine the direction from which the signal is coming. I call out the bearing with respect to our ship to the Mates and race to the flying bridge and the signaling light. Captain Hudnall's there. "We've picked up a weak U-Boat signal, Captain. Approximately 50 degrees!" A few seconds later the commodore's signaling light responds to my "attention" call. I send the short message, "*Weak dit-dit-dah-dah, 50 degrees.*" I wait for acknowledgment, switch off the signaling light and race back to the DF.

Within minutes, I hear a weak U-signal at 90 degrees. And another at 120 degrees. Still another at 180 degrees, directly astern of the convoy. The Captain and the 1st Mate stand next to me as I call out the bearings. The 1st Mate charts the U-signals' bearings. The 3rd Mate comes in to the chart room. I ask him to get one of the Navy operators to join me. At this critical moment I don't want to give up the DF watch. Continuing to call out the U-signal bearings, my assistant writes them on a slip of paper. He knows exactly what to do. We'd rehearsed it, just in case. He races to the flying bridge and sends the information to the commodore's ship and then returns to me at the DF.

A few minutes later, maybe five minutes later, an urgent call comes from the flying bridge. "The commodore is signaling us!" My assistant races to the bridge. The commodore's message gives us a new heading to be executed in the next five minutes. The Captain and the 1st Mate huddle over the charts. "This heads us for the west and north coasts of Iceland."

Night time now. The Ü-signals haven't stopped. I'm unable to determine their distance from the convoy. I can only estimate by the relative signal strengths whether they are closing on us or losing us. Signals are getting stronger. A wolf-pack is closing on us. New *dit-dit-dah-dah* signals put a U-Boat directly ahead of us.

The convoy hugs the west coast of Iceland, changing headings frequently. We're sailing between the coasts of Greenland and Iceland. When we reach the most northerly point of Iceland, we receive new headings. East toward Norway to the North Cape. We're not turning back. The convoy's going to try to run for it!

The convoy's speed is increased to 11 knots. Fair weather continues and the ocean remains calm. Excellent. Unfortunately, conditions are just as exceptional for the U-Boats! Their homing signals are becoming stronger. They're moving closer to the convoy!

By the time we are well past Iceland, I've reported 15 different Ü-signals. It's daylight now. By word of mouth rather than by sounding the General Alarm bell, the Armed Guard and merchant crews are instructed to take their stations and be ready for action. Everyone on deck wears a life jacket and tests the small, battery-operated red-beacon lights clipped to their life jackets' collars. The tiny corvettes are no match for a U-Boat wolf pack. How'd they ever decide to send a convoy on the Murmansk run with so small an escort?

We see a group of ships astern closing on the convoy at a rapid speed. Our 5-inch-38 cannon aims carefully but holds its fire. Lt. Unterman is at the stern cannon studying the approaching vessel with his large binoculars. The stranger is signaling now. Good news! It's a U.S. Coast Guard Cutter and several corvettes. Coast Guard Cutters, the Captain tells us, though not heavily armed are often faster and larger than destroyers. We sound the ship's horn in salute to the cutter as she comes close to our beam and passes us. Perhaps with all the U-Boat radio activity, those who make such decisions have carefully reconsidered the chances for survival of our poorly defended convoy. Another change in heading. We're not trying a run for the North Cape; not now. We're steering for Scotland.

Once again, the ship is anchored off Gourock. The same day a British Navy officer comes aboard and delivers sealed orders for the Captain. He advises me to expect a technician at any moment who will come on board to install a special receiver in the radio room. Special? What is its purpose? It turns out to be an ancient, battery-operated Marconi radio to enable us to monitor the escort's voice communications. I don't need it, but I am advised I may not refuse it. The antique equipment and a loudspeaker are installed on the radio room bulkhead above the typewriter. An extension speaker is mounted on the forward bulkhead of the bridge.

The Captain opens his sealed orders. From Gourock we are to move north to Loch Ewe, Scotland. The convoy will sail from Loch Ewe to North Russian ports. Because of renewed U-Boat and Luftwaffe activities in the North Atlantic, the escort is being significantly increased for this specific run.

Finally, we depart Loch Ewe and form the convoy to Russia. More ships are approaching. The commodore signals these are additional escort vessels. Our positions are changed to make room in the starboard column for a baby aircraft carrier, a converted freighter with slow-flying British Swordfish biplanes on board for spotting U-Boats. Several British destroyers also join us. The U.S. Coast Guard Cutter leaves, probably to escort a west bound convoy. As the convoy heads north into the open ocean west of the Hebrides Islands, the ratio of escorts to merchant ships now appears to be one-for-one.

The corvettes race back and forth at a distance from the convoy. They suddenly slow down—probably to use their sonar equipment which theoretically can detect the sounds of U-Boat engines—then quickly resume their race. Sonar isn't very effective, but it may be the best we have.

The four antique destroyers on our starboard are holding their positions, which means they're not actually part of the escort. They must be a protective screen, torpedo interceptors on our starboard flank. Through the binoculars we can see the destroyers are lightly manned. Probably just enough crewmen on board to operate these ships. No doubt they are being transferred to the Russian Navy.

Half a day out of Scotland, the convoy's speed is increased to 11.5 knots. We're heading straight for the North Cape, the northern tip of Norway, in the Barents Sea. The temperature is dropping rapidly. The days are going to be short, the nights very long. The Luftwaffe is well within striking range. I continue the DF search, listening especially for "A"-signals.

Suddenly the escort's voice communications radio, which has been quiet up to now, breaks into a series of rapid, short messages. The General Alarm bells ring! They seem louder than ever. I run to the starboard wing of the bridge. The commodore and the escort are flying the black flag: *enemy in the vicinity*! I race to the flying bridge for any new instructions from the Captain. He points toward the stern of our ship. I see six aircraft, low on the horizon, slowly flying back and forth in some sort of formation, too far away to enable positive identification. Lt. Unterman, the Armed Guard officer is on the flying bridge with a telephone connected to all the gun turrets and the fore and aft cannons. He has been told this is a typical tactic of the Luftwaffe, intended to jangle everyone's nerves. At some point in time, not a very long time, the aircraft can be expected to turn and race in to attack the convoy's stern. And that's exactly what happens! The aircraft are JU88 dive bombers and each is also equipped with a single torpedo!

The corvettes are running close to the convoy. The destroyers are further out. Our gunners track the airplanes' movements through the cross-hair sights of their turret-mounted guns.

I race to the radio room where the two Navy operators are on duty. With a deafening roar and formidable concussions, the 5-inch-38 stern cannon begins to fire. It fires again and again, shaking the ship severely each time. Within seconds, the anti-aircraft guns on the flying bridge and at the ship's stern start firing, which means the JU88s are close in and flying low. Our 3-inch-50 cannon at the ship's bow and the 50mm anti-aircraft guns add their sharp, raucous voices to the discordant concerto. The combination of ear-splitting *ack-ack-ack* and booming blasts make it impossible to monitor the radio.

I step out onto the small deck aft of the radio room and look to our starboard. An airplane skimming the tops of the waves is making a torpedo run directly toward our ship! Just a speck at first, it slowly grows larger as it closes the distance. All the starboard 50mm guns and the fore and aft cannons concentrate their fire on the torpedo plane. I am transfixed by the sight. My ears shut down. My brain shuts down. Everything seems to be happening in silent, slow motion.

With no more than seconds to go before the plane is close enough to loose it's torpedo, a shell from our 5-inch-38 explodes under the plane's right wing. It is tossed up into the air, cartwheels and crashes into the ocean with the torpedo still attached to its underside! Our guns swing around and prepare for the next attack.

The JU88 dive bombers fly over the convoy and, at a safe distance, circle the convoy for another run. Several more torpedo planes make runs but are driven off by the combined fire from the destroyers, corvettes and armed merchant ships. No torpedoes have yet been fired by U-Boats. Unterman's guess is they'll wait for darkness, come in close to the convoy and launch their attacks.

The two Navy radio operators join me on the afterdeck. All we can do is observe the action. Another pass is made by the JU88s. One starts a low-level run on our column. Our stern gun, the 5-inch-38 is firing as fast as the men can feed it shells. Several other ships in the convoy are throwing all the fire they can at the plane. The noise is deafening. I hold my hands tightly over my ears and watch the speeding dive bomber, now in a descending angle, as it closes on its target—our ship! The shells from our stern cannon explode in the air creating huge puffs of smoke and deep-throated roars. Suddenly, the attacking dive bomber goes out of control and plunges into the ocean, downed by one of our shells!

The remaining JU88s fly over the convoy. Unable to come in at a low altitude, they climb out of the range of the convoy's guns, turn to starboard and fly off in formation. The torpedo planes are probably over the horizon and out of sight.

The attack ends as suddenly as it began. Several minutes later the black flags come down. All clear—for the present. I ask my radio operators the name of the gunner's Mate in charge of the 5-inch-38. "Comerford. Jim Comerford."

"I'd sure like to shake his hand. Gad, what shooting!"

I'm alone on the midnight to four watch. A knock on the door.

"Sparks? I'm Jim Comerford. May I come in?"

May he come in? You bet! He's the hero-of-the-hour on the *John La Farge*. I don't know how the generic hero is supposed to look, but I estimate Jim is about 25 years of age, a husky redhead, almost handsome, 6'2" Irishman. He's frowning, definitely depressed. I shut the door and point to the chair at the typewriter.

"Sit down, Jim. Can I get you anything?" I pause to study his expression. "Why do you look so downhearted, Jim? You should be proud. You knocked down a dive bomber *and* a torpedo plane in the first attack on the convoy! You saved the ship and probably our lives!"

He hesitates. "I'm not sure how to say this. But..." He pauses. Begins again. "But, technically, I missed the dive bomber."

I'm surprised, baffled and amused. "Missed? I saw it drop into the ocean. What do you mean 'technically I missed,' Jim?"

He looks up at the ceiling. "Well...you see. I set the range and timing for the proximity fuses in the shells. That particular shell was supposed to explode directly under the plane and disable it. Instead, the shell went through the plane!"

Is he kidding? "But you did shoot it down, Jim."

"In gunnery school that would be a technical miss."

"No, Jim. Technically the JU88 was destroyed and we're okay. You saved the ship and a lot of lives."

Jim sees the humor in the situation. He sits upright, breathes deeply and slowly begins to smile until he breaks into a full tension-releasing laugh. "Whew! Glad I came here to talk with you. The word around the Armed Guard is you're okay. Thanks. Thanks a lot, sir!"

"Jim. As far as the officers of this ship are concerned, you made a direct hit, not once but twice today. Enjoy the glory, pal! You can bet, as soon as the *John La Farge* docks, the bos'n will paint two large silhouettes of airplanes high up on the smoke stack. The ship's victory emblems! Our score card!"

All we have to do is make it around the North Cape to a friendly port. Right? Right!

Chapter Seventy-Nine

The sea is calm. We're floating in a semi-dark, suspenseful world. Suddenly a voice on the escort radio calls out, "Aircraft overhead! Flares! Flares!" The message is heard on our bridge. The General Alarm bells sound again. Parachute flares are being dropped from aircraft! They generate an astonishing amount of light. The bow watch is alerted to look for floating mines.

The Wolf-Pack attacks. "Torpedo tracks! Torpedo tracks!" Torpedo tracks criss-cross the convoy! Huge explosions! Ships have been hit! Our ship's hull pings and rings repeatedly as the escort unloads depth charges in rapid succession. The escort radio calls out, "Hearse! Hearse! One-two-fife! One-two-fife!" An abbreviation for "U-Boat sunk at 125 degrees with respect to the center of the convoy." "Floater" is a U-Boat on the surface. The depth charges continue to ping and ring throughout the night—too many to count. Two of the four old-destroyers on our beam are gone.

At full light, despite a moderately choppy sea, two of the British Swordfish biplanes take off from the carrier to search for U-Boats. We hear the pilots talking to one another, to the escort and the carrier as they fly easterly in the direction of Norway. One of the pilots calls out, "Floater! Floater! Seven Fife! Seven Fife!" He circles the U-Boat to guide the escort to his location. Ominous silence for a few moments. Then one of the two pilots calls out, "Nasty's firing on us! Firing on us!" The escort calls out, "Roger! Return to base! Return to base!"

Then, as though play acting a drawing-room scene in a British movie, one of the Swordfish pilots calmly says to the other, "I say old boy. You've been hit." We listen for the other pilot's reply. None comes. The escort engages the surfaced U-Boat in a gun battle. We listen closely to the escort radio for a victory call. It comes in loud and clear. "Hearse one! Hearse one! Eight-zero! Eight-zero!" Then all is quiet. Only one Swordfish returns to the carrier.

Captain Hudnall asks me to come to his cabin. "The chatter of the escort radio is extremely disturbing to everyone on the bridge. It's about time, I think, the thing should have a breakdown. It just can't hold up under these conditions, Sparks."

"I understand, Captain." Within the next five minutes the loudspeaker on the bridge goes dead. I do not disconnect the one in the radio room. The escort's dialog fascinates me.

Captain Hudnall comes to the radio room. "Tsk. Tsk. Our loudspeaker seems to have gone dead, Sparks. Anything you can do about it?"

"Not 'til we get to port, Captain. Sorry!"

The Captain heaves an artificial sigh of despair and returns to the bridge.

The attacks begin again and continue without letup. All four World War I destroyers have been sunk. Two more freighters are lost in JU88 dive-bombing attacks. The escort ships move so rapidly we are unable to keep count of their number. We believe at least two more destroyers and two corvettes, maybe more, are missing. Probably, more of the convoy's freighters are lost. It's impossible to accurately follow the escort's voice-radio communications. The rapid chatter contains many words whose jargon I cannot translate.

The U-Boats and JU88s pursue us relentlessly for four days and nights. No one is able to sleep. General Alarm conditions are active around the clock. Because of the continuous noise of depth charges, anti-aircraft and cannon fire, neither my two Navy radio operators nor I are able to copy most of the BAMS. The few we can copy and decode continue to describe "unidentified orange object sighted." None of the sightings have been within a thousand miles of this convoy's location. The BAMS have been useless to us.

Our ammunition supplies are almost exhausted. The escort's losses must be greater than we realize. On the morning of the fifth day, the weather becomes variable, ranging from absolute calm to moderately rough seas. But no fog, no gales. During a lull in the enemy attacks, I copy a blinker signal message from the commodore. "Proceed north to ice fields without escort. Best wishes." The escort is pulling out.

Mr. Thompson, who's been tracking our position by sextant every day, calculates we are approximately 500 miles west of the North Cape, where the worst usually happens. Possibly both the enemy and our escort are regrouping for an all-out attack near North Cape. Just a guess. Captain Hudnall calls an emergency conference in the chart room with Mr. Thompson, the Chief Engineer, the gunnery officer and myself. We feel angry, betrayed.

Captain Hudnall instructs me to signal the ships directly forward and on our port beam. Tell them, "Head due north deep into the Arctic Ocean. Enemy cannot follow." Then ask, "Are you with us?" The three Liberty Ships agree to follow us in single file. In answer to our questions they can all hold a speed of 11.5 knots. The remainder of the ships decide to stay together and steer directly for the North Cape and Murmansk. They're heading right into suicide alley. Who knows? Maybe we are, too.

We fall back and out of the convoy and steer due north at 11.5 knots. The three other ships fall in closely behind us. Those of us who participated in making the decision to proceed due north do not put on life jackets. The engine room gang, too, goes without lifejackets. All others are wearing theirs. Perhaps it's a childish display of braggadocio. We're tempting the fates. "*Come on! Try to get us if you dare!*" We've heard, if one must take to the water, the shock of the water's icy temperature can kill within 30 seconds. If one succeeds in getting into a lifeboat, the frigid air kills—less quickly but just as fatally. So, what the hell!

Something unusual, no doubt orders from the homeland, has discontinued the attacks. We proceed without incident. This weather is absolutely incredible. The Arctic Ocean is perfectly calm. No wind. No turbulence. The sun is powerful. The climate is almost warm. In the interest of safety, Captain Hudnall reduces our speed to six knots and changes the heading to due east.

I signal the ship astern of us and ask it to relay the speed and course changes to the next ship in line. The sky is cloudless. North of Spitsbergen, we spot icebergs. Absolutely beautiful, tall, motionless. The icebergs reflect the light of the sun and the sky, iridescent blue-white. Their mirror images are exquisitely reflected in the absolute calm of the Arctic Ocean. Picture card stuff. But I'm not thinking about taking pictures. This image is engraved in my mind. But, how long can we continue to stay among the icebergs?

Captain Hudnall and the mates make the decision. When the convoy is due North of the White Sea, we'll execute a change in course. Our convoy will make a 90-degree turn to starboard and steer due south for the White Sea. We'll have to run between Spitsbergen, owned by Norway and reported to be occupied by the Nazis, and a group of islands identified only as Aleksandra. Our charts do not show details about Aleksandra's ownership or inhabitation. Our signaling light relays the information to our small convoy.

Despite our extreme shortage of ammunition, the Armed Guard and the merchant crew continue to man the guns, maintaining their courageous spirits. Slowly and continuously they sweep the horizon and the sky. The Navy radio operators and I continue to monitor the distress frequency and the DF. We hear *SOS* calls, ships in distress for reasons other then enemy action and many strong *SSS* calls from ships in distress as a result of enemy submarine action. Possibly they are from ships that went the other way when the convoy split up.

Our DF does not pick up any U-Boat or Luftwaffe homing signals. The four-ship convoy turns due south and increases speed to 11.5 knots. The distance between the Spitsbergen and Aleksandra Islands is great enough to keep us over their horizons, well out of the line of sight from either one of the two.

I'm on watch alone at night in the radio room when Lt. Unterman enters. He looks awful. His eyes are filled with terror. He's actually shivering. I help him into the chair at the typewriter table. A grown man crying is a pitiful sight. And he's crying, close to hysterically. I'm concerned he'll be heard by his radiomen on the other side of the bulkhead. I talk to him, without effect. He stands up, eyes wide and darting to the left and right as though looking for a place to hide. For his own good, I slap his face as hard as I can. No effect. I slap him again. His eyes close. I help him to the chair.

I softly and slowly call him by first name. "Harold. Harold. We're going to be all right. We're going to make it all the way to the White Sea. Nobody's going to hurt us." He stops crying. In another five minutes he recovers his self control. I share coffee from my thermos with him. He apologizes for breaking down. I assure him no one will learn about it.

He tells me the ship he was on prior to this one was torpedoed in the warm waters off the Azores. It happened at night. He, the ship's officers and crew had to abandon ship. Jump into the water. The survivors turned on the lights clipped onto the collars of their lifejackets. The U-Boat surfaced and machine-gunned the lights. He can still hear the screams. He wasn't hit. He thinks he survived because he instinctively switched off his light as soon as the U-Boat started firing. The U-Boat submerged. He and a few other survivors floated among the dead and wounded for almost 24 hours before a group of destroyers from a convoy returning to the United States picked them up.

Unterman spent a week recuperating in a hospital. Some well-meaning but terribly misguided "desk-sailor" believed he should go right back to Armed Guard duty to prove to himself he's okay. He had no choice. He was assigned to the *John La Farge*. No. He didn't know it was going on the dreaded Murmansk run.

He doesn't want to be alone. Not just yet. I suggest he stay here with me in the quiet of the radio room for the remainder of my watch. We're both silent. I turn the radio down. We can't do anything to help a ship in distress anyway.

The loudest sound we hear is the repetitive voice of the ship's engines. "*Thump-atta-thump*! *Thump-atta-thump*! *Thump-atta-thump*!"

Chapter Eighty

Our small convoy passes between the two groups of islands and heads into the Barents Sea. We have approximately five or six hundred miles of open water ahead of us. Assuming no breakdowns, attacks or bad weather, Mr. Thompson estimates it will take the convoy two, maybe three days to reach the mouth of the White Sea.

We're in the unusually calm Barents Sea—U-Boat and Luftwaffe territory. We haven't had the slightest hint of detection or action. Our luck is holding. Incredible!

On the morning of the third day, a few hours ahead lies the White Sea. Mr. Unterman calls out, "Aircraft on the horizon. Dead ahead. Off the bow!" Well, if these are Nazi planes, they're in for a very tough fight with our hardened Armed Guard and merchant gun crews just itching for a fight—despite the shortage of ammunition!

Captain Hudnall, Mr. Thompson, Lt. Unterman and I watch the aircraft through binoculars and wait for them to turn in toward us for the attack. The aircraft begin to perform acrobatics. Captain Hudnall continues to observe the planes. "Bet they're Russians. Skittish about getting into shooting range of trigger-happy North Atlantic convoys. Let's see what happens."

Unterman adds, "The gunners are ready, sir."

The airplanes do a sky-dance and move closer to us. Dance again and move still closer. Captain Hudnall shouts to Mr. Unterman, "Have your men hold their fire."

Mr. Unterman relays the order over the gunners' telephones. These may very well be Russian planes. But, after what we've been through, it sure is hard on the nerves. On Captain Hudnall's orders, I signal the ships behind us. "Possibly Russian aircraft. Hold fire." The message is relayed down the line.

The Captain shouts, "Ahhh...hah! They're coming over us, high up in some kind of formation. Wiggling their wings. Looks familiar, doesn't it?"

Lt. Unterman adds, "Yes sir, they're out of shooting range. I can see Red Stars on their wings. They're Russians! Russians!" He telephones the gunners with the same message." There's joy in the gun turrets! Everyone's cheering, shouting and slapping the nearest person hard on the back!

The planes circle us and fly off ahead wiggling their wings as they pass over. "Follow us! Follow us!" We adjust our heading to the direction we assume they want us to go. I signal the ship astern of us, and the message is relayed to the next ship and the next.

Within a few hours, we are met by a small cabin cruiser which leads us directly into Molotovsk. A few more hours and all four ships are secured. We are at the very same dock as last time.

The three Captains and 1st Mates of the other ships in our small convoy rush along the dock to our ship. "Congratulations, Captain Hudnall! Great seamanship, Captain Hudnall!" Lots of handshaking and back slapping. A real happy day!

Captain Hudnall is very gracious and enjoys the compliments, but suggests, "We better all return to our ships and get some well-deserved and much-needed sleep."

Fortunately, Mr. Shuracov and Mr. Matusis do not come aboard knocking on doors. We are too bushed to be sociable or even polite. Try us tomorrow, please.

The next morning, they do come aboard. Mr. Matusis is not too friendly toward me. He's almost hostile, but not enough to refuse a carton of cigarettes. Much to my surprise, he invites me to a party tonight in Molotovsk. Again, I am the only Ally invited. As before, a jeep will pick me up and return me to the ship.

This party differs considerably from the first time I came to Molotovsk. Mr. Matusis ushers me into a small log-cabin theater equipped with a 16mm movie projector and a powerful sound system. Without an introduction to the subject, I sit alone through two very lengthy combat films, complete with sound-added, continuous ear-breaking rifles shooting, tanks rolling, cannons blasting and soldiers falling. Vicariously, I participate in "The Battle of Leningrad" immediately followed by the "Battle of Stalingrad." The message comes through to me. "If you think you're having a difficult time, look what the Russian people are going through!" The films have a fatiguing, depressing effect on me.

After the contrived show, I am served black bread, caviar and unsweetened tea. I accept and hold in my hand, but do not drink, the vodka. Two young women in their early 30s and in unbecoming civilian clothes are introduced to me. Neither one is physically attractive; not in the slightest. Their excellent use of English comes with a strong Russian accent.

"I am *Lyuda Chontin*. Happy to meet you, Mr. Wortman."

Her female companion joins in. "And I am...not yesterday...not today...but Tamara! *Tamara Lontovnaya*." We all laugh politely at this humor. Tamara's smile is exceptionally big and displays a full set of steel teeth. This is considered by some Russians to be an especially attractive addendum to a woman's personal beautification. I've heard of this custom but have never seen it before. Now I see it close up. I hide my revulsion and succeed in keeping the caviar down in my stomach.

Mr. Matusis looks at the two women, then at me. "Lyuda and Tamara will be your guides during your stay in Molotovsk. If you travel outside Molotovsk, perhaps to Archangyelsk, they will accompany you to assure you are well taken care of." He smiles. He's one up on me. How can I make contact with Nadazha

Petrovnaya in Archangyelsk now? I may have to forget that part of my job. The jeep returns me to the ship. Captain Hudnall is waiting up for me, eager to hear the details of the evening. Finally, I go to my cabin and fall into a sound sleep.

The next morning, Lieutenants Warschel and Horschel and their Marine sergeant arrive from Archangyelsk. After they have their official meetings with Captain Hudnall and Lt. Unterman, Warschel and Horschel come to my cabin and shut the door. Based on information from Nadazha Petrovnaya, they give important cautions. "Two women have been assigned to accompany you, wherever you go. They are probably agents for one of the Russian security agencies. Could be the OGPU, NKVD or any other one of their internal security police. Mr. Matusis is very much afraid of you. Probably because of the incident when he drank and talked too much. Be extremely careful, Leon."

"I appreciate the advice. I've already met the two women, Lyuda and Tamara. Do you think Matusis will try to stop me while I'm in Molotovsk?"

"We're not sure. Matusis might wait for you to go to Archangyelsk. He thinks you're likely to be alone there. He's afraid to do anything serious to you. He wants you kept away from the authorities, especially away from talking to the security police. He used the words 'disable Wortman' when he spoke with Nadazha."

"Suppose I test his intentions right here in Molotovsk first. If nothing happens, I'll go to Archangyelsk. I'll go nuts hanging around the ship, these docks and Molotovsk for the next few months."

Horschel and Warschel look at each other, then back at me. "We know what it's like. Believe us, pal. Our world is still restricted to Archangyelsk to Molotovsk and back again! It's our 15-mile universe."

Warschel looks at me for a moment and becomes very serious. "Do what you think you have to, Leon. But..." He pauses for emphasis. "...do not go beyond Molotovsk alone. No prison camps this time. Always take someone with you. Do you still have the small duffel bag you used to drop off at our house? Good. Let's do the same thing. Come by for it every 24 hours."

"Sounds like the thing to do. I'll carry lots of cigarettes and chocolates with me. Highly valuable assets!"

Warschel asks, "If and when you do go to Archangyelsk, who can you take along with you?"

"Lt. Unterman. Maybe George Leitner, the ship's Purser."

"Unterman is Navy. He won't realize it but he'd provide better protection without endangering himself. The Russians don't want to mess around with the U.S. Navy. But you are Merchant Marine, a civilian. Less complicated."

Chapter Eighty-One

Next morning after breakfast I decide to leave the ship to stretch my legs in a walk along the dock. I put on a heavy jacket and leave the officers' salon. About 50 feet back from the docks is a string of storage sheds, crude huts with wide doors. My two escorts, Lyuda and Tamara are standing at the shed opposite the *John La Farge*. I walk over and greet them as politely as I can.

"*Lyuda. Tamara. Dobree dyehn. Kahk vui puzhivahyihtyih?*" Nothing wrong with a simple good day. How are you? My unexpected use of Russian surprises them.

Tamara inquires if I speak Russian. "*Ah, gospodyin Leon Wortman. Gahvaritye pahrooskyee?*"

I want them to think I don't understand Russian at all. "You've just heard almost my entire Russian vocabulary. Oh! I do know two more words, '*nyet*' and '*dah*'."

Polite laughter.

Lyuda asks, "My we walk with you?"

"Please do. I need the exercise. I hope the sentries won't be disturbed."

Tamara responds, "Not at all, I am sure."

Perhaps she means the sentries won't be disturbed as long as I walk with her. With long, slow strides we walk along the dock between the ships and the sheds. We return by walking in back of the sheds. They're doing their jobs. I'm just doing my job, too.

Almost casually, Tamara inquires, "Do you have any plans for today or this evening?"

"No. I have no plans at all for my stay here in the White Sea."

"Good. May Lyuda and I help you spend the time pleasantly?"

Is she flirting or working? "It will be very much appreciated. I didn't have anyone to help me when I was here earlier this year. It was a lonesome time for me."

"No need for anybody to be lonely in Russia."

We've completed the loop. We're walking toward my ship's gangway. I stop and turn toward them. "You can do me a big favor." They look at me expectantly. "Please call me Leon. In America, among friends, we do not say both the first and last names."

"And, Leon, you will please call us by our first names, too?"

"*Da Lyuda. Da Tamara.*" Right there on the dock the three of us hug and exchange kisses on both cheeks. The Russians are emotional people. My two new buddies are not aware my mother and father were born in the Ukraine, which makes me almost Russian. My father's name was actually *Vertmanov* from *Ovrutch, Ukrainia*. It became Wortman at Ellis Island, New York. My mother's maiden name was *Turovskaya*. Her family's background is the village of *Turov, Ukrania*. Washington suggested I should not reveal I still have family in Russia.

I invite Lyuda and Tamara to come on board the ship for hot coffee, or tea if they prefer.

They look at one another for approval. Tamara smiles and speaks for both of them. "You are very kind, Leon. We'd very much like to visit your fine ship and enjoy your hospitality. But I don't think the sentries—they're watching us—would approve of such fraternization."

Lyuda and Tamara have a brief side-conversation. Tamara turns to me and invites me to visit their small office in Molotovsk. Only doing their job, I suppose. No reason to fight it.

"I'd like that. Perhaps tomorrow. *Spasibah*."

"Very nice. We'll meet you here at the gangway at 8 a.m., tomorrow."

"*Da sveedahnyuh, Lyuda. Da sveedahnyuh, Tamara*." So long for now.

I'm alone, sipping coffee in the officers' salon and reviewing in my mind what has just happened. It appears the two women intend to monopolize my time ashore. How do I handle this?

George Leitner comes into the salon and sits down next to me. "Tradition of the sea. Sparks gets the girls every time! Can I have one of them?"

I look at him quizzically. "What do you mean, George?"

"I saw you walking with the two Russian ladies. Do you really need both of them? Can I have one?"

"George! Were you close enough to get a good look at them? Tell you what George. I have a date with them at 0800 tomorrow. They're going to show me their office in Molotovsk. Come along?"

"You're on! By the way, Sparks. What do they do? Who are they? How'd you meet them?"

I affect a wicked smile. "Who are they? A couple of security agents. How'd I meet them? Tradition. Can you come with me tomorrow morning?"

The next morning, I introduce George to Lyuda and Tamara. I can see he's not thrilled. The four of us trudge along the snow-covered two-mile road to Molotovsk. We pass two bodies lying at the side of the road, arms and hands pointing up to the sky. Sentries or vodka? Lyuda and Tamara ignore the sight. George and I have no interest in doing a visual autopsy.

The office actually has two rooms, one for official business, the other for sleeping. A small wood-burning stove is provided for cooking. We enjoy hot tea, served Russian style, in a glass. I produce some chocolates. Lyuda and Tamara are overjoyed. They break off small pieces and dump them into their tea as substitutes for sugar. George and I imitate them. I must remember to bring some real sugar next time. The office is relatively bare. One ancient desk, several chairs, a telephone and a few, short stacks of communist literature printed in English. Not very exciting reading for us. Lyuda and Tamara spend the time reciting communist logic and dogma to us. I know George is as confirmed a believer in our brand of democracy as I am. We listen attentively, politely—but do not argue politics.

George and I are on the road again, returning to the ship. The two bodies we'd seen earlier are not there now. We are about 200 feet from the dock. A man is running clumsily across the snow, away from us, the road and the docks. A sentry is pursuing the man. The sentry stops, raises his rifle to his shoulder and shouts, "*Stoy*! *Stoy*! Stop! Stop!" Either the man doesn't hear the sentry or he's in a panic.

Lest there be confusion—or this is a trick—I grab George by the shoulder and force both of us to halt immediately. The sentry fires once. The running man topples forward and lies still. The sentry races over to the prostrate man and, using his booted foot, rolls him over onto his back. Satisfied with his kill, the sentry slings his rifle onto his shoulder, waves at us and walks casually back toward the docks. George's horrified eyes follow the sentry. *Beware of the tendency of Russian sentries to shoot on sight.*

I take George firmly by the arm. "Let's not run. Walk normally. George, stop shaking."

Such scenes are repeated frequently during the next few months. Battle-hardened soldiers sent from the front lines to "spend their leave" as sentries, are a good choice as protectors of war materials. Perhaps they're not the wisest choice as guardians of their own civilians. I like to think our own battle-tough American soldiers are better able to keep their perspectives.

It's September 1944 and I am so bored I'm a bit concerned about my own stability. One's self-control and judgment capabilities do become unpredictable when one is inactive. Warschel and Horschel visit the ship often. I admit my restlessness to them. They understand and urge me not to do anything foolish. For a change of scene, I want to spend more time in Archangyelsk. I feel I have not performed as capably as I might on this assignment.

Warschel reluctantly admits, "Try it, Leon. But I do caution you again not to go alone. And be very careful. Take Unterman with you. What about Lyuda and Tamara? Will you ask them to accompany you?"

After a moment's thought, I tell them, "I know Unterman wants to see Archangyelsk. He's getting bored, too. I'll ask him to come with me. We'll pay a courtesy call on the American Consulate and I'll leave my small duffel behind. As for Lyuda and Tamara, my preachers of communism—I've got to think about how to lose them."

Warschel approves with the admonition, "Careful, Leon. There's just so much we can do here if you get into trouble with one of the security agencies."

"What about Nadazha? Can I count on her for help?"

"We're no longer sure of whether she's more loyal to Russia or to the American goodies we've been giving her."

Warschel says, “To Russia.”

And Horschel adds, “We think she’s getting nervous. If she’s discovered to have been playing both sides, she’s gone from here—for good!”

“Okay. See you in Archangyelsk in a day or two.”

Chapter Eighty-Two

Two days later, Unterman and I walk the two miles to Molotovsk and catch the 0500 train to Archangyelsk. Unterman observes, "Your lady friends are going to miss you."

Everybody has the wrong idea about our relationship.

"Tell me, Sparks. Is there anything between you and them?"

I'm not sure Unterman really understands my answer. "Yes, about six thousand miles and two cultures!" Let him draw whatever conclusions he wants.

With a couple of *shokahlahd-hungry* kids as luggage porters, we arrive at the American Consulate, Warschel's and Horschel's headquarters. They share their breakfast with us. Unterman produces a bag of sugar and a few pounds of coffee. As usual, I produce cigarettes. Unterman excuses himself for a moment. Warschel looks a bit concerned when I tell him the two ladies are not with us and I didn't tell them I was going to Archangyelsk. "You realize they'll find out quickly. Careful! Very careful, Leon, while you're in Archangyelsk. We will not be able to get you out of a jam."

I drop my small duffel bag when we leave to get rooms at the *Intourist*.

Nadazha Petrovnaya greets me with minor enthusiasm. Because I've been here before, Unterman thinks I'm an experienced guide to the sights of Archangyelsk. The major part of my expertise is with the *Intourist* dining room. If Unterman doesn't like a diet of coarse black bread, caviar and tea, he has a problem. We are given two rooms distant from one another.

The rest of the day is uneventful. We just stroll around the snow-covered city. The roads are very wide. The few vehicles we see are military. One sight fascinates us. It is a colorfully robed Laplander riding in a sleigh drawn by a reindeer. A rare spectacle.

I don't alert Unterman, but I'm aware we are being tailed. Our "tail" is a tall man dressed in an old cloth coat and fur hat. He's definitely neither a peasant nor a civilian. His very straight, stand-tall bearing and highly polished officer's boots are contrasts that give him away. Most likely he's tailing me. No doubt, Lyuda and Tamara have sounded the alarm.

Unterman and I turn in early. We're really not used to all the walking we've done today and we did get up very early to catch the train. It's so cold in my room, I go to sleep with all my clothes on.

Some time during the night, I am aware of activity in my room. My eyes are accustomed to the darkness. Without moving any more muscles than I have to, I look to my right and see two men going through my large duffel bag. I know there's nothing incriminating or enticing in the bag other than a dozen cartons of cigarettes and chocolate bars. The two men quietly repack my bag and leave the room.

In the morning, I suggest to Unterman we drop in on Warschel and Horschel and sponge a free breakfast. My real reason is to inform them about being tailed and my luggage searched. Warschel urges me to get back to Molotovsk on the next train tonight. I agree. However, we still have several hours to do our sightseeing before the train leaves.

"Hey, Unterman! There's what I've been hoping we'd find." I point to the structure about 200 feet ahead.

"You mean that old cavalry fort?"

"Looks like an American early-western movie prop, doesn't it? Vertical logs. Points at the tops. Wide front entrance. It's a peoples' bazaar; a sort of open marketplace where people bring personal items to trade or sell to each other." I look behind us to see if our tail is still with us. He is.

The moment Unterman and I pass through the wide gateway into the bazaar, we are pestered for *Amerikanskeeh shokahlahd* and *Amerikanskeeh syeegahryetas!* When I hand out some cigarettes, I darn near start a riot. The man who'd been tailing us is among those with outstretched hands. He insists on buying a pack from me. He waves 50 rubles in my face. My coat lining is already stuffed with rubles. To quiet him, I accept the money and he takes the pack of cigarettes. At last the commotion stops. I would like to buy a small souvenir to bring home with me. I spot a pair of small, stemmed silver liqueur-cups for which I negotiate two packs of cigarettes. *Spasibah! Spasibah!* Unterman precedes me as we leave this imitation of a wild west fort.

As I pass through the wide doorway, two Russian soldiers with rifles and fixed bayonets appear on either side of me. The man who'd been tailing us steps up, opens his coat to display a blue uniform. He draws and points a revolver at me and shouts in his best English, "You are arrest, please!" Despite his poor grammar, the point is well made.

Unterman panics and starts to run. The soldiers turn and raise their rifles. I shout as loudly as I can, "Stop, Unterman! Stop! Stop!" I don't know whether the soldiers would have shot him, but one doesn't run when two rifles are pointed at one's back! Unterman, hands raised above his head, comes back to my side. He has the same terrified expression I saw when he broke down in the radio room.

Keeping my calm, I tell him, "Harold. They don't want you. Believe me, they do not want you. You're okay. Find your way back to Warschel and Horschel. Tell them I've been arrested. Don't worry, Harold. Don't worry. I'll be okay. See you soon on board the ship."

The arresting officer waves his gun at me and says, "Come, please."

We must be an unusual parade, even in Archangyelsk. The officer leads the way. I follow him. The two soldiers, rifles and bayonets leveled at my back, are behind me. We march through the snow-covered roads, I estimate a distance of two miles, until we reach a small building with barred windows. Inside, I am turned over to another officer. This one wears a brown uniform. He leads me to another room and closes the door. I haven't been searched. I reach into my oversized coat and offer him a package of cigarettes, *Amerikanskeeh syeegahryetas!* It takes all his will power, but he refuses them. After waiting about half an hour, another uniformed man enters the room and, in Russian, tells the other, "We are ready. Bring the American."

During this sequence of events I haven't been searched or shackled. I am led into another room. Three blue-uniformed officers are seated at desks, barred windows at their backs. I am given a chair and a polite invitation, "*Sahdeetyihs, pazhahlistuh.* Please have a seat." Another empty chair is at the right of the three officers. The officers look friendly enough. Nothing for me to do but wait for their next move. An interpreter is needed. The door opens and in comes Nadazha. She blushes and nervously tells me she is the interpreter to which I say, "*Ohchihn khuhrahshoh.* Very good, Nadazha."

I am charged with black marketeering. Selling cigarettes. Is there a witness? Yes. They bring in the witness. He's the arresting officer, still wearing the old overcoat over his blue uniform.

Nervously translating, Nadazha asks, "How do you plead?"

Nadazha and the tribune of officers are totally surprised when I plead "Guilty. I did, in fact, sell a pack of cigarettes to the witness." No use denying it.

Still translating, Nadazha asks, "Didn't you know it is against the law for an American to sell cigarettes to a Russian? That is black marketeering."

"I know it now."

"Why did you do it?"

I rise and expound dramatically. "I have so much and your people have so little. I was giving cigarettes away, sharing them with your very nice people, my allies in this terrible war. This man insisted he wanted more and waved 50 rubles at my face. He wouldn't stop, so I gave him a pack of cigarettes and he insisted I keep the 50 rubles. Then I was arrested and, with great loss of dignity, I was paraded at gun point through the streets of Archangyelsk. That is not the proper way to treat a good friend and ally!"

Nadazha translates as I speak. Each of the three officers of the tribunal writes rapidly on sheets of paper. They stand and have a hushed conference. My eyes and Nadazha's meet. We smile. She shakes her head at me as if to say, "You are crazy!" Maybe I am.

Nadazha reads my sentence from a sheet of paper one of the officers hands her. "You plead guilty to black marketeering. You are ordered to leave Russia. There is a five o'clock train returning to Molotovsk. You will be on that train."

No problem with the train but, I inform the three Russians, my ship has to wait for a convoy to be formed. I cannot leave Russia before then. There is no other way out. The officers huddle again and advise me unambiguously to be on my ship before midnight. I may not leave the ship again while it is in Molotovsk. What will be done with the three reports the officers have been writing? One will stay in Archangyelsk. One will be delivered to the American Consulate, Warschel and Horschel. The other will be sent to headquarters, which they don't name, in Moscow.

I thank the three officers and hand each one of them two packs of cigarettes. Their eyes open wide at the sight of such bounty. They're somewhat embarrassed and make weak expressions of *nyet, nyet*. I press the packs into their hands and reluctantly, but with smiles, they accept. Nadazha whispers, "You are quite crazy" and hurriedly leaves the courtroom.

I go to my room at the *Intourist* to pick up my bags and say a last good-bye to Nadazha. She implores me not to miss the train to Molotovsk. I assure her I intend to be on it. I hurry to Warschel and Horschel's place. Unterman is there, eager to leave Archangyelsk. The poor guy hasn't the slightest idea of what's going on. I pick up my small security-duffel and invite Warschel and Horschel to walk with us to the train. Unterman hurries on board. I linger outside to talk with Warschel and Horschel. They'll visit the *John La Farge* in the next day or two.

The next morning I go on deck to see if Lyuda and Tamara are on the dock. No, they're not. However, a Russian soldier is standing at the foot of the gangway. I start down the gangway. The soldier turns to meet me. He asks for "*Duhkoomyenti*! *Pahspoort*!" I hand him my port pass issued by Matusis. The soldier reads it, steps quickly back, unslings his rifle, blocks my way and shakes his head meaningfully. *Nyet! Nyet!* I turn around and return to the ship.

Mr. Matusis has successfully disabled me.

It's now the first of November 1944. Warschel and Horschel have come aboard to say good-bye. They advise Captain Hudnall a small convoy to Murmansk will be formed as soon as the icebreaker *Joseph Stalin* can clear a path out of the frozen White Sea. We're repeating our last departure. However, this time we clear the White Sea and make Murmansk without incident.

An unusually large number of ships, including British destroyers, are assembled in the Kola Inlet. We move to Kola for a load of pulp-wood ballast and then return to anchor just off Murmansk.

A boat, resembling the American PT-Boats races to our ship's starboard side. The Captain, Unterman and I are ordered to attend a convoy conference now. We are given time to put on our uniforms before we climb down and onto the boat. With Nazi bombers flying overhead and Russian anti-aircraft guns spitting fire, the PT speeds further into Kola Inlet, turns hard to port and enters a large cove. There, at anchor are a cruiser and her large escort of destroyers and corvettes. All fly the British Flag. The cruiser is identified by our Russian guide as the famous battle-scarred, *H.M.S. Black Prince*. At the gangplank, we are piped on board. Another new experience for me. I imitate the series of salutes executed by the other officers in our small group. We are conducted to a large conference room filled with standing-room-only uniformed British Navy and Merchant Marine officers.

Each officer of captain's rank or higher is introduced by name. Captain Hudnall recognizes the name of one British officer. He was the commodore of the convoy that abandoned us on our previous voyage because our ship could not run at 10 knots. Captain Hudnall rises to his feet, points an accusing finger at the man and, in a strong voice for all to hear, gives him a tongue lashing such as I have never heard before. The victim of this lecture sits shocked, mystified, immobile and speechless. Captain Hudnall finishes the verbal blast and sits down. No one comments.

A British officer of admiral's rank is seated at the head of the conference table. He tells us the one remaining Nazi battleship of the dreaded "Pocket Battleship" class, the 35,000-ton *Tirpitz*, has been located at anchor in Norway's *Trondheim Fjord.* Intelligence reports she is making ready to go to sea. The combined British and American Navy units are determined to engage the *Tirpitz* in a final battle.

To tempt her to come out and fight, our convoy will run approximately 25-miles off the coast of Norway. The battle cruiser, *H.M.S. Black Prince* and the British Home Fleet's battleship, *H.M.S. Rodney*, will sail inside our convoy. On the horizon, an armada of battle units of both the British and American Navies will race in to attack the *Tirpitz*. What if she doesn't come out and fight? In this eventuality, aircraft from the combined-fleets' carriers will fly into *Trondheim Fjord* and blast her permanently out of action.

We receive our convoy-orders. More DF watch for me. U-Boats are still active; always in small wolf packs. The Luftwaffe is less active. No explanation offered. Within two days our convoy forms a single line to leave through the narrow mouth of the Kola Inlet. The first ship out carries the commodore of the convoy, the same commodore who decided to leave our lame ship to run on its own in the Barents Sea.

Captain Hudnall and I are on the flying bridge watching the convoy's single-file startup. The opening of the Kola Inlet into the Arctic Ocean is narrow. Only one ship ship at a time can exit. Silently, we stare and glare at the commodore's ship. She is the first ship to expose her bow into the open ocean. Suddenly, a torpedo strikes her below the water line, midship at the engine room! Captain Hudnall is unruffled. He turns to me and, without emotion, says, "That's ironical justice, Sparks. Ironical justice."

The escort lays down an aggressive pattern of depth charges. Other small craft speed to rescue the crew. The rest of the ships are delayed about an hour. Then we make a new start. You can hear a pin drop aboard ship as we leave the relative safety of the Kola Inlet. Fortunately, no other ships are hit as they leave Kola Inlet.

On November 12, 1944 we are opposite Trondheim. Our guns are manned and we are all wearing lifejackets. The *Tirpitz* does not come out. The British Navy and aircraft from the carriers go on the offensive. In the evening I tune to a Russian short-wave radio station broadcasting news in English. Captain Hudnall, the 1st Mate and the gunnery officer are all crowded into the radio room. None of us will ever forget the announcement: *"Today the German underseas fleet has been increased by 35,000 tons. The Tirpitz has been sunk!"* We do not cheer. But we are very much relieved we are no longer "bait."

The *Rodney*, *Black Prince* and their escort units leave the convoy. We reach the United Kingdom without incident of any kind, weather or enemy action. Both are benevolent.

The *John La Farge* puts into Belfast, Ireland where our pulpwood ballast is quickly discharged and replaced with other materials.

Chapter Eighty-Three

Soon we are back in New York City. As is expected of me, I go to The Office to report to the Chief. He seems genuinely happy to see me, alive and assignment completed. "Good job, Leon. I have to call O.N.I. and G-2. The usual, you know. You have to be debriefed while your mind is still back in Russia."

"How soon can we do it?"

He glances at the wall clock. "I doubt it can be done in one session. Hang around The Office for a while. I'll try to get the debriefing started this afternoon."

"Fair enough, Joe. There's one aspect of the assignment I want to get off my chest."

"Oh?"

"You once told me, briefly, about some of the generals wanting to continue the war into Russia—after we beat the Nazis. Remember?"

"I remember. Go on."

"Let me tell you a little bit of action, or call it reaction, I observed about the Russians."

The Chief holds his chin and strokes his upper lip with his right hand. I have his undivided attention.

"The Luftwaffe ran air raids one after the other during daylight hours. This you already know. One of my tasks had been to find out what the Russians did with those pilots who'd been taken prisoner. I found out. I'll describe what they did in the debriefing. It's important, also, to recognize the reactions of the people to the air raids."

"I'm listening closely, Leon."

"Well, Joe. To me, they're an incredibly strong people. Each time the Luftwaffe came over, the Russian *ack-acks* forced the planes to fly high, out of range of the guns. The Luftwaffe usually flew beyond the docks and dropped their bombs in the forests. The Nazis must have known the Russians had built log cabins for civilian families inside those forests."

Joe is absolutely silent as he keeps eye contact with me.

I continue verbalizing my thoughts and memory. "Just imagine how we *Americanskis* would react to such an attack. Our first thoughts would be of our families. We'd run home to protect them. I'm not saying this is wrong. It's the American way and I wouldn't change it for anything or anybody. But let me tell you how the Russians react to these attacks."

Joe releases his chin, clasps his hands together and leans forward. I am giving him first hand observations which, I know, he'll take back to Washington.

"Chief, when the planes came over and dumped their bombs in the forests, I didn't see one person—nobody—run to their families and homes. Nobody ran to hide. They'd stop working only long enough to violently shake their fists and shout and swear at the planes. Then they'd go back to work with greater detemination than before the air raids!"

Joe exclaims, "Some kind of people, eh?"

"So, Joe. That's what we'd have to deal with—if we tried to tackle the Russkies—after we beat the Germans. Even Napoleon couldn't beat the Russians. The Nazi armies are stalled. And their supply lines to the Russian borders are shorter than ours would be. What makes any of our generals, including Patton, think they can beat the Russkies—and the Russian winter?"

Joe sits back in his chair, swivels around and heaves a long, deep sigh. "Thanks, Leon. You present an eyewitness view. I'm sure Washington will listen closely to my report."

I also tell him about the unburied bodies in the forest. *"We are too busy taking care of the living."* I take a long pause before I continue. "Joe. I'm wrung out. It's been rough sitting out the war, aboard ship, like a prisoner. I can use a vacation."

Joe rubs his chin in thought. "Kermit Roosevelt is with the O.S.S. For the duration of the war, he's turned over his large home and estate at Oyster Bay, Long Island, to the government for use as a rest and recreation hostel. They can only take a dozen men at a time. Let me see if we can schedule you for a week or two of rest and recreation.

Chapter Eighty-Four

After two weeks of so-called "R & R"—which means sharing quarters with battle fatigued field officers who've seen and been through rough times—entertained at frequent dances and tea parties sponsored by the young ladies of Oyster Bay's high society—art lessons from volunteer teachers—I decide I've had enough. I'm ready to go back to work. An unmarked station wagon takes me back to New York City.

Merry is not her usual light-hearted cheerful self. "Joe's been transferred overseas. Let me introduce you to his replacement, Colonel Sanford Streifer." She whispers, "He's a full Colonel. Always wears his uniform. I think he actually hates field agents and the whole bit about spying."

"Hello, Mister Wortman. I heard you were taking some R & R at Kermit's place. Are you ready to go back to work...or do you need more play time?"

I bristle. "Have you read my record and related reports, sir?"

"No. But I'll get around to it. More important stuff to deal with now."

I do not like this man. Merry's right. Joe Franken was no ball of warmth. But this Colonel Streifer is pure ice. "Now that you mention it, Colonel, I think I'll take another week off. Catch up on the movies. Maybe have a date or two with an American girl."

"Okay, if you have to. Keep in touch." Sounds as though he couldn't care less.

Three days later I return to The Office. I tell Colonel Streifer—he does not allow anyone to become familiar enough to use his first name or the nickname Chief—"I've decided to temporarily leave the O.S.S. and return to my civilian job." He reacts with loosely controlled anger. You'd think I'd personally insulted the man. His behavior convinces me I made the right decision. But, there's some unfinished business.

"Pardon me, colonel. I have been told I would be recommended for the Distinguished Service Medal and a military honorable discharge would be arranged."

"Oh? I can't find anything in your record stating such a recommendation exists."

"Pardon me again, colonel. I'll be glad to name the source of the recommendation."

He's very much annoyed by my persistence. "When and if I see Colonel Franken, we'll talk about it." He stands up. Obviously, this conversation is over. "Good luck—as a civilian or whatever. I'll hold onto your O.S.S. IDs until you return."

Within less than two weeks I receive a new draft card reclassifying me "1A."

My former employer, WHN, from whom I'd taken military leave, is delighted I'm back for a while. The radio station is short handed.

On one of my visits to my mother in civilian clothes, I learn Emil, a high school buddy is home on leave. He's been stationed at Fort Dix, New Jersey since he was drafted into the Army. Never went overseas. It'll be great to get caught up on everbody's whereabouts. His parents' home is the fourth house down the street from my mother's.

I ring the doorbell. Emil comes to the door in a buck private uniform. He opens the door, glares at me and shouts, "*You f—g draft dodger*!" He spits on me and slams the door shut!

This one hurt. I realize I am probably unwelcome in the old neighborhood.

Except for a few brief late-night visits to my family, I vow I shall never again return to the scenes of my childhood, never again see the many guys with whom I'd grown up. Frankly, I don't really care if they never learn the truth.

For me, I feel, the war really is over.

Epilogue

After the death of President Franklin Delano Roosevelt in April 1945, Vice President Harry S. Truman became president. Four months later, World War II ended. Bill Donovan couldn't convince President Truman to make the O.S.S. a permanent agency for centralizing intelligence gathering-and-analysis operations. The O.S.S. was formally dissolved. In September 1946, President Truman created the Central Intelligence Agency, the C.I.A. Whether or not he was aware of it, the C.I.A. recruited many former O.S.S. people. Bill Donovan retired with the rank of Brigadier General and returned to private law practice.

For many years after the end of World War II, pairs of strangers frequently approached me and quietly said, "Come back in, Leon."

Without exception, I asked, "Where's my medal? My honorable discharge?"

"Come back in and you'll get your medal and the discharge."

"First, the medal and the discharge."

"First, come back in."

Although I did not want to "come back in" on their terms, I did frequently take on special assignments for the C.I.A. Yes, I was angry and bitter. Why beg for things I had earned and been promised? But I remained as I had always been, a highly patriotic, a totally loyal citizen.

At one point in this manuscript, I refer to an encrypted Morse Code message. It ended with the plain English words: *"Get me the hell out of here! Get me the hell out of here!"* I had no idea who the sender was or from what part of the world he'd sent it. No one would explain it to me—confidential information. Over the years, I often thought about that extraordinary message. Who? Where? Why? In 1951, I found the answers. Let me tell you about it.

I had gone to work in New York City for Audio-Video Products, Inc., the eastern sales agency for professional magnetic tape recorders manufactured by AMPEX Corporation of Redwood City, California. Ken, A-V's sales manager and I had become good friends. Our workdays were always too busy for small talk. So, our social hours took place at the end of every day over one vodka martini at 5:30 p.m. at the Blair House Restaurant on 56th Street. During one of those relaxed and comfortable hours, as we exchanged light conversation about our experiences during World War II, we realized both of us had worked for the same organization. He'd already been stationed in Moscow by the time I joined the group.

As details emerged, I discovered he'd been the sender of the unusual "Get me the hell out of here!" message. Ken explained: He worked out of the American Embassy building in Moscow from which he routinely made his transmissions to the Chief. He wanted out. His cover had been blown. Closely tailed everywhere, he'd been rendered ineffective as a field agent and was extremely frustrated Eventually, by the time I went overseas, he had been brought out of Russia through Cairo, Egypt, returned to the United States and civilian life.

Did I ever see any of my various Chiefs again? During one of our end-of-the-day martinis at the empty bar of the Blair House, a man quietly slipped onto the stool at my right. Of course there were many empty bar-stools at that time of the evening, but he deliberately chose the one next to me. Engrossed in my conversation with Ken at my left, I hadn't particularly noticed the newcomer. Ken, open-mouthed, stared over my shoulder at the man on my right. Cookie, the bartender came over and asked the newcomer, "What'll you have, sir?" He replied, "Same as they're having."

I spun around at the sound of the voice. Colonel Joe Franken in civilian clothes! No greetings. All three of us sipped our drinks in silence. Then, without looking at either Ken or me, the colonel spoke just loudly enough for us to hear. "I need a man in Bombay right away."

As though we'd rehearsed it, Ken and I stood up, faced the colonel and quietly said, *"Go to hell, Joe!"* and sauntered out of the Blair House.

Ken and I realized our former colonel or one of his agents must have been tailing us over a period of time and knew of our 5:30 p.m. Blair-House ritual. We had to either discontinue our pleasant end-of-the-day custom or change the location of our rendezvous each night. We chose the latter and were never again bothered by the colonel. Where is he now? He may be operating high up in the C.I.A., or retired, or gone to C.I.A. heaven. I haven't heard.

Eventually Ken's career and mine took different paths. He and his wife divorced. Ken moved from New York City and left no forwarding address. In 1978 on a business trip to Washington, D.C. while walking through the lobby of my hotel, I saw Ken walking toward me. Now, when a field agent is on assignment, one of the things the agent dreads most is being recognized by anyone, a friend or former associate. As we approached one another, our eyes met briefly. It was obvious he'd seen me. When he abruptly changed his direction away from me, I realized Ken had gone "back in." We never again met in public or private.

What about Bud Corval? In 1960, I was traveling on business from New York City to Batavia, New York. I detoured to visit Syracuse, New York where I had once lived for a short, pleasant time. I didn't have time to visit any former friends. I just wanted to be part of the old environment for an hour or so. One of my favorite watering holes in Syracuse had been The Chimes Bar & Grill. It was still there.

I hopped onto an empty stool at the bar and ordered a beer. Looking into the large mirror on the bar's back wall, who should I see sitting next to me? Bud! I never forgot good old Bud, to whom I owed so much for his help in Casablanca. I'd often wondered if he'd gone back to Virginia to resume his civilian career as a trainer of racing horses. Our eyes met in the mirror. He gave no sign of recognition. Talking into my beer glass, without mentioning a name, I asked, "What're you doing now?" He quietly replied, "Same thing." and immediately left the place.

After the war, Bill Brady married an English lady, retired and stayed in England. He did visit me one time in New York City with his wife and daughter. We had a grand reunion.

I never had the good fortune of meeting my friends, officers who sailed on the *Collis P. Huntington* or the *John La Farge.* I would have especially liked to see Captain Alfred W. Hudnall again. I like to think he lived a long, happy life after the war in Virginia. Mr. Thompson, 1st Mate, had often talked about buying a chicken farm in New Jersey after the war. I like to think he fulfilled the dream. George Leitner never talked about futures, what he'd do or where he'd go after the war. We never again crossed paths.

And what about Leon Wortman/Vertmanov/Jacques Brevier/Léon Dejacques—me? He/they/I all remained as stubborn as the C.I.A. We would not "come back in"—at least not officially.

A strange thing happened. When he held the office of president of the Federation of Russian States and just before he resigned the position, Mikhail Gorbachev mailed a medal to me with a certificate for my "work against the Nazis in the Great Patriotic War." (I had been unable to accept an invitation to travel to Washington, D.C. for an award ceremony at the Russian Embassy.)

In late December 1991, I received a second invitation to a Russian medal-award ceremony this time to be held in January 1992 on board the *S.S. Jeremiah S. O'Brien*, a fully-restored World War II Liberty Ship almost identical to both the *S.S. Collis P. Huntington* and the *S.S. John La Farge.* The *O'Brien* is docked at the Port of San Francisco. In a brief ceremony, a representative of Boris Yeltsin who had replaced Gorbachev as President of the Federation of Russian States, handed me a second medal and a certificate of commendation and authenticity.

The local radio, television and newspaper media gave the ceremony generous coverage. Not many men had twice made the Murmansk run and lived. The per capita losses on the "run" were second only to the U.S. Marine casualties in the invasion of Guadalcanal. I never mentioned my real work inside Russia.

So, 48 years after the end of World War II, I received a medal, two of them. Ironically, they came from the country that a long time ago had arrested, tried and expelled me. Although neither is the medal for which I had yearned, they provided some balm to soothe the pain.

And in 1992, by an Act of Congress, I received an honorable discharge. However, this is for my duty as a member of the Merchant Marine during World

War II. The discharge document is issued by the U.S. Coast Guard. I also received a Merchant Marine Combat Bar, an Atlantic Theatre of Operations ribbon and a Mediterranean Theatre ribbon.

Stated reason for the discharge: “End of hostilities.”

-30-

About the Author

At the start of World War II, I worked as a radio station engineer. Shortly after my 21st birthday I was hired by the Outpost Division of the U.S. State Department as a Field Representative/radio-foto expert. After several transfers through various government agencies, I found myself in an intelligence division of the U.S. Military. I declined a captain's commission but continued as a civilian employee of that division where I received training in survival and hand-to-hand combat. When the division became part of the new Organization for Special Services (OSS) I was sent on several deep-cover assignments from Africa to North Russia for a series of adventures I can never forget. My earlier experience and fluency in foreign languages combined with the courage of youth and an intense patriotic spirit were very much on my side.

Printed in the United States
719300001B